JOSIE

Also by Lynda Page

Evie
Annie

JOSIE

Lynda Page

HEADLINE

First published in 1994
by HEADLINE BOOK PUBLISHING

10 9 8 7 6 5 4 3 2 1

British Library Cataloguing in Publication Data

Page, Lynda
Josie
I. Title
823.914 [F]

ISBN 0–7472–1027–6

Phototypeset by Intype, London
Printed and bound in Great Britain by
Mackays of Chatham PLC, Chatham, Kent

HEADLINE BOOK PUBLISHING PLC
A division of Hodder Headline PLC
338 Euston Road
London NW1 3BH

For
Our Chris

Sisters are an accident of birth, forced together without choice. Sisters fight, borrow, take for granted and blackmail; sisters give comfort, support, advice and love.

We've done these things and grown up to become friends. I am proud to call you my sister.

With love from
your big sister, Lynda

ACKNOWLEDGEMENTS

John – thank you for your support; I could not have managed without it.

Tina – if all the pain, tears and anguish of writing achieved only the result of our friendship then, for me, it was all worth it.

Chapter One

'Marilyn, I'm warning you. If you leave me on me own again, I'll . . . I'll . . .'

'What? Sack me? Don't make me laugh!'

'I will, Marilyn. I'm sick to death of running this stall by meself. You're always using some excuse for clearing off. If you go I'll sack yer and that's that.'

Marilyn Rawlings swung round on her heels, glowering fiercely at the large frumpy figure of her nineteen-year-old cousin Josephine Rawlings. For a moment she wanted to laugh at the comical vision Josie created as they stood facing each other behind the family-owned vegetable stall on a freezing cold November afternoon in 1966.

Josie's thick dark brown hair was pushed untidily beneath a knitted, tea-cosy style, brightly striped woollen hat, the shapeless black coat she wore doing little to hide her ample figure, and the brown suede, side-zipped calf-length boots, covering a pair of black thick-knitted tights wouldn't have seemed out of place on their ageing grandmother. Lost inside her fat cheeks was a rather attractive face, its large brown eyes framed with thick lashes that curled gently at the ends. Usually kindly, those eyes were now flashing with anger as she tried her utmost to bring Marilyn to heel, failing miserably.

Marilyn narrowed her eyes in exasperation. How dare her cousin speak to her like this? Josie should be grateful she had bothered to turn up at all instead of whining on because she wanted to leave early. She wanted to grab hold of Josie's shoulders, shake her hard, and tell her exactly what she thought of her. But she couldn't be bothered to make the effort. She stamped her foot in irritation. Standing here arguing the point was a waste of time and she had things to do. More important things than serving rotten vegetables to rotten customers.

She tilted back her pretty blonde head. 'You wouldn't get any other fool to work on this tuppenny ha'penny stall for a fiver a week, so just be grateful you've got me. Now you stay if yer want to, but I ain't standing round in this cold no longer. Sod the

1

customers, they can go elsewhere for all I care.'

Josie inhaled sharply and placed her hands on her generous hips. 'Marilyn, I mean it this time. If you leave me again . . .'

'Josie Rawlings, I've as much right to be on this stall as you have. You ain't got no authority to sack me and you know it. Now we ain't seen one customer in the last couple of hours and I'm freezing to death, so I'm off and I don't care what you say.' She tossed her head defiantly. 'I'll be round for me wages later.'

'Wages!' Josie spluttered. 'You've got to be joking! You've hardly worked all week, I'm damned if I'm gonna let Gran pay yer wages.'

'You'd better,' Marilyn hissed. 'Else I'll get me dad to come round and you know what'll happen then. All hell'll break loose.'

Josie shuddered. The prospect of her overbearing oaf of an uncle coming round and kicking up a stink didn't bear thinking about. The man frightened her to death and Marilyn knew it. It wouldn't have been so bad if Josie's mother, Maisie, had still been alive. She would have sacked Marilyn and stood up to her brother. But her beloved mother wasn't here to deal with this matter. This was her responsibility.

As she fought desperately for the right words to say, Marilyn interrupted, smiling sweetly into Josie's round face. 'You don't really mind, Josie. After all, you've n'ote else to do, have yer?'

Josie stood rigid. Marilyn was right. She hadn't. So under the circumstances what right had she to keep her cousin here? She slowly nodded her head. She might as well give in now. She could stand here all day and try and reason but it would be pointless. As always, her pretty, long-legged, vivacious cousin had got the better of her.

'Good old Josie,' Marilyn said, slapping her on the shoulder. 'You know I'd do the same for you. I've got a heavy date tonight and you know how long it takes us girls to get dolled up.' She frowned. 'No, 'course, you wouldn't, would yer?' She bent down and rummaged between the wooden boxes of vegetables and sacks of potatoes for her brown leather bag, grabbed it, straightened up and slung it across her shoulder. 'Now if you've got any sense, you'll pack up and get off home. Tarra.'

Josie sighed deeply. 'Tarra.'

She stared after her cousin as she made her way through the maze of empty market stalls. Normally at this time of night the place would be teeming with customers clamouring to get last-minute bargains. But the bitterly cold weather had kept all but a handful away. She sighed again and dug her hands deep inside her pockets. Marilyn was right. If she had any sense she would pack up the nearly frozen vegetables and head for home. But her grandma wouldn't be pleased.

'Oh, hell,' she uttered under her breath. For once she would do what she wanted and at this moment that was to pack up and get home as quickly as possible.

'No, please, not tonight. Please don't do this to me tonight.' Tears of frustration and anger stung Josie's large brown eyes as she pounded her fists together in exasperation. 'I promise, honest, I promise to take better care of yer, only please don't let me down tonight,' she pleaded.

She took a deep breath, said a silent prayer and tried the ignition of the old Ford Commer van once more. But her prayers and promises went unanswered. Nothing happened. She rubbed her hand over the misted windscreen and stared out into the murky darkness. Her only companions now were the corporation dustbin men clearing away the debris of the day. The snow was thickening fast and she wished with all her heart that she had taken Marilyn's advice and packed up hours before. If she had done, she would now be sitting in front of a blazing fire, eating a hot meal whilst watching one of her favourite programmes, Crossroads, and not in the middle of the deserted market square, cold, tired and raven- ously hungry, desperately trying to coax life into an unyielding vehicle.

With a heavy heart, she slid herself awkwardly off the seat, gathered her two full carrier bags of shopping, made sure the vehicle was securely locked and inched her way down the empty streets towards the bus station, slipping and sliding over the icy pavements. She arrived at her destination and settled herself in a corner of one of the many concrete shelters, shivering uncontrol- lably as she waited patiently for the cream and brown vehicle to arrive.

'Spare a few coppers, lady?'

'Pardon?' Josie jerked up her head in astonishment. An extremely tall, gaunt, unshaven man swayed before her, his hands thrust deep inside the pockets of his grubby macintosh, the top of a bottle of gin clearly visible.

'I said, spare a few coppers for a cuppa tea,' he slurred, belching loudly. 'I ain't eaten fer days.'

'Yer maybe ain't eaten, but you've found the money for yer booze!' she retorted.

She shifted uncomfortably on the bench. She wanted the man to leave, he unnerved her. As she moved, a shaft of light from the street lamp illuminated her. The man stared and then a smile flickered over his thin, blue-edged lips.

'Oh, I'm sorry, me duck. I didn't realise you were one of us.' He shuffled forward and plonked himself down beside her, wrenching

3

the gin bottle from his pocket. "Ere, 'ave a swig of this, then yer can come wi' me.' He hiccuped loudly, then belched again. 'I've got a place under the railway arches on Central Street. It ain't The Grand Hotel, but yer welcome to share it wi' me and the others.'

'What?' she exclaimed indignantly as it dawned upon her that this horrible creature was associating her with a bag lady. 'I ain't one of you, I happen to be waiting for a bus. Now clear off!' she shouted, wrinkling her nose at the terrible stench that emanated from him.

'Eh!' The man leant over and peered at her through his blood-shot eyes. 'Waiting for a bus, eh! I could 'ave sworn you were one of us.' He held out his trembling hand. 'Giz a couple a' bob fer a cuppa tea . . .'

Josie dived into one of the carrier bags and pulled out the first thing she laid her hand on. 'If yer don't clear off, I'll . . . I'll hit you with this,' she cried, waving a jam swiss roll in the air.

'Okay, okay,' the man said nonchalantly. 'No need to take that attitude, we all mek mistakes.' Sniggering loudly, he eased himself up and made to stumble away. He stopped abruptly and turned back. 'If yer waitin' for a bus, you'll wait a bloody long time, Missus. They stopped running 'alf 'our ago.'

Josie's shoulders sagged and she groaned. This news was the last thing she wanted to hear.

She watched blankly as the man shuffled from the shelter. Suddenly compassion for this poor creature rose up in her.

'Just a minute,' she shouted as she delved into her coat pocket. 'Have this,' she said, thrusting her bus fare into his gnarled palm.

He gazed down at it, then raised his head. 'Bless you, me duck,' he said gratefully. He turned and was soon lost in the swirling snow.

Josie sank down wearily on to the bench. She had been up since four-thirty that morning in order to be at the front of the queue at the wholesalers, had run the stall practically single-handed for their handful of customers, been mistaken for a down and out, and now faced the prospect of a three-mile walk home with the inevitable lashing from her grandmother's tongue for being late.

Home for all of Josie's nineteen years had been a three-bedroomed, run-down, terraced house in Newfoundpool, or 'the pool' as the locals referred to it; a crowded district of back-to-backs built during the middle of the last century to house many of the workers on the Great Central Railway that was then slowly forging its way north.

The variety of local shops, all mainly family concerns, catered for the community's needs as did the several public houses which were usually packed to bulging on a weekend. At the bottom of Beatrice Road, the main thoroughfare, was a small hosiery factory, working men's club and a fish and chip shop expertly managed by a middle-aged Greek couple and their six children who had settled in Leicester after the war.

Josie's grandfather had wisely, with the help of the local building society, bought their property in the late 1930s for the princely sum of £200, and if still alive would have seen a good return on his money as the houses were now fetching, in the more prosperous years of the sixties, at least £1,500 – more if you had a bath or modernised kitchen which unfortunately their house had not.

Josie had grown up in these streets, gone to the local Ingle Street Junior School, played with gangs of children in the maze of alleyways connecting the backs of the houses and gazed longingly at the groups of teenagers draped on walls or street corners, playing their transistor radios as loudly as possible, much to the annoyance of local residents. It was a community where everybody knew your business, where gossip ran rife, but where there was always a willing hand and a sympathetic ear should you need one. But for all this, the thought of the long arduous journey home through the endless streets of thickening snow filled Josie with dread.

Oh, life was a bitch sometimes, she thought, deflated, as she picked up her bags. Surely there was only so much a body could stand in twenty-four hours? Still, there was nothing for it unless she wanted to spend the night in the freezing bus shelter. She might have known though – the slightest hint of snow and Leicester came to a standstill. In these modern times, with all the new gadgets and inventions, the transport department still couldn't get its act together, and she strongly suspected that she wasn't the only person stranded in town even though it felt like it.

Her trudge through the deserted Leicester back streets seemed to go on forever. So exhausted was she that she didn't hear the suppressed giggles of the three young lads hiding in an entry between a row of terraced houses until she was upon them. The three boys shot out, shouting abuse and waving their arms in the air.

'Fatty Rawlings, Fatty Rawlings,' they chanted.

Josie let out a shriek of shock and anguish as she let go of the two carrier bags. They fell with a thud, contents scattering across the pavement. As she desperately tried to gather her wits, she slipped on a patch of ice and fell all her length, her backside hitting the hard sodden ground with a thud. The three boys jeered and laughed as they danced around the prostrate figure, kicking their feet against the battered groceries, sending a dented tin of baked beans rolling into the gutter.

Suddenly a loud shout split the air.

'Ged out of it, yer buggers! And you, Vincent Bagley, I'll tell yer dad, then we'll see you laugh the other side of yer smug ugly mug.'

The three boys froze as they saw the broad figure of Jim Brown, a neighbour, striding towards them through the darkness. Vincent jerked two fingers at Jim before he bent down, grabbed a packet of Garibaldi biscuits and ran after his mates, still laughing and taunting, to disappear through a jitty connecting the maze of alleyways.

Jim reached Josie and shook his head at the sad figure sprawled beneath him. He held out his hand to help her up, straining with all his might as she eased herself awkwardly off the wet ground.

'All right, Josie lass? I don't think they meant no 'arm. Just larking about.'

Josie took a deep breath and looked down at her wet coat and laddered stockings. She ran her hand tentatively over her bruised backside. 'I'm fine, thanks,' she said lightly.

'Good.' Jim smiled as he bent down and began to gather the shopping together. 'Them lads want a good hiding, if you ask me. No discipline. I blame the parents. They shouldn't be allowed to roam the streets at this time o' night, 'specially in this filthy weather. It's a pity National Service 'as bin stopped. It'd have done some of these young 'uns some good. Might have taught 'em some respect.' He paused and looked up at her. 'A' yer sure yer all right, gel?'

Josie managed a smile. 'Yeah. Just me bum hurts a bit.'

Jim laughed. 'Well, could have bin worse. You've enough padding on your backside to cover a settee.' He stopped abruptly. 'Ah, sorry Josie, I didn't mean . . .'

'It's all right, Mr Brown,' she said quickly, used to taunts about her size. 'I did bounce twice before I hit the pavement.'

Jim laughed. 'That's the spirit, gel. No harm done, eh? Just yer pride.' He straightened up and handed her back the two battered bags. 'Now if I were you, I'd get indoors as quick as yer can and get yer wet things off. It's a bloody awful night to be out in.'

Josie accepted the bags. 'I will, and thanks.'

'My pleasure, and give my regards to yer granny.'

'I will.'

Josie turned and slowly continued her journey up the steep hill. She turned into Hawthorne Street and unlocked the front door, sighing with relief. In all her nineteen years, she had never been so glad to reach home.

Winter had arrived with a vengeance in the year 1966 and the end of November found the country in the grip of an arctic freeze. The public services were ill equipped for such weather, each passing year saw little improvement, and the residents of the city resigned themselves to several months of frozen pipes, shortages of coal and fuel, power cuts and very irregular services from the public transport system. But whatever the weather, the army of market traders would set up their stalls in the ancient market place and serve their customers in their usual jovial manner. On arriving home that bitterly cold night, for the first time in her life, Josie wished her occupation was anything but the only one she had ever known and loved.

She placed her bulky body against the faded painted brown door and shoved hard, harder than she'd intended, grimacing as the door sprang open and banged loudly against the wall of the room. The back room of the terraced house was in total darkness, the only light coming from the dying embers of the fire. Instead of the warmth that should have greeted her on such a night, the room felt chilly and unlived in. Josie frowned hard as she inched her way over to the old oak table in the centre of the room and unburdened herself of the overflowing carrier bags. Where was her grandmother? The absence of the old lady brought a sudden fear rushing over her which settled like a lead weight in her stomach.

Walking back towards the door, she switched on the light and blinked as it flooded the room. She clutched her hand to her throat. Slumped in the armchair was the shrunken figure of her grandmother. Her head had flopped over to one side, her ill-fitting false teeth had slipped and were on the verge of falling out, and her bony arm hung limply over the side of the chair. The grey blanket that had covered her knees lay on the floor.

She was dead. Josie knew even before she rushed over and knelt before her, grasping the thin hands between hers, tears of desolation and love for the old woman cascading down her cheeks.

This old lady, who had taken over her upbringing since her mother's death six years previously, and whom she loved dearly, despite her cantankerous ways, was practically all she'd had in the world. Now she was gone and it was all Josie's fault for leaving her so long on her own in such foul weather.

'Oh, Grandma, Grandma,' she wailed. 'What am I gonna do without yer?' She raised herself and crushed the limp body to her.

'Ahh . . .' A wail of protest hit the air. 'I can't breathe. I can't breathe. Yer crushing me.'

Josie let go of the old lady and stared with shocked astonishment into the gnarled face.

'You ain't dead! Oh, Grandma, you ain't dead,' she gasped in relief.

'Dead! Do I look as though I'm dead? What the hell's got into yer, gal? I ain't ready to meet me maker just yet.'

'Oh, Gran, Gran . . .'

'Ged off, yer daft ha'porth,' she cried, wriggling free from Josie's grasp. 'My God, gel, what a bloody shock yer gave me. I could have had a heart attack.' She put her fingers in her mouth and pulled out her teeth, inspected them, pushed them back and smacked her lips together. A trickle of saliva rolled down her chin which she wiped away with the back of her hand. She looked up at Josie disdainfully. 'Christ knows, I never gerra good sleep and when I do, you, yer fat lump, have to go and wake me!'

Josie leant back on her haunches and looked with relief and fondness at the old lady. 'I'm sorry, Gran. It's just . . . well, you looked like you were dead, and it's so cold in here.'

'Well, that's your fault! You never left enough coal,' Lily Rawlings snapped as she eased herself up in the armchair and pulled the blanket around her.

Josie looked towards the empty bucket. 'I did. I filled the bucket before I left this morning.'

She rose and picked up the chipped enamel container from the hearth. Braving the elements once more, she made her way down the icy yard to the coal shed. Back inside she placed several small lumps on the dying embers, held up a piece of newspaper and waited while it drew.

Lily sat in silence, closely watching her granddaughter as she busied herself with the fire. She wished she hadn't shouted at her. The poor girl had a hard enough time as it was without her grandmother's sharpness added to her burdens. But she couldn't help herself. Besides, she thought, I'm old, I'm entitled to be cantankerous.

She sighed softly, half closing her heavily lidded eyes as the fire crackled and spurted with renewed life, and welcome warmth began to seep through her tired bones. Life hadn't treated her fairly in her latter years. The business with Stanley had fair knocked the stuffing out of her; then to lose her husband, and not long after that her beloved daughter Maisie – well, it didn't seem justified somehow. The only comfort she had now was young Josie. The girl was a blessing and Lily knew she should try to show more gratitude towards her. Not many young girls these days stayed at home to look after their ailing grandmother.

She sniffed loudly. 'Yer were late tonight. I was worried about yer,' she said softly.

Josie managed a weary smile. 'Yeah, I know. Sorry, Gran, but it's bin one of those days . . .'

'I can see it has,' Lily interrupted. She raised her eyebrows, her resolve to be nicer forgotten. 'By the state yer in, I'd say yer fell through the 'edge back'ards. So what did 'appen to yer?'

Josie peered down at her dishevelled appearance. 'I slipped on the ice.'

'Yer a clumsy bugger, so you are, our Josie. Anyway, I'm starvin'. You said you'd come home at lunchtime and get me something to eat.'

'I couldn't get home. The weather turned bad and our Marilyn went off again and left me on me own. I couldn't get anyone to watch the stall.'

Lily frowned deeply. 'I put *you* in charge of the stall, Josie. You'll have to learn to be more firm with her. She runs rings round you, she does, and I ain't paying her five pound a week for gallivanting off every time she feels like it.'

'I know, I know. But she's always got some good excuse. Anyway, she's your granddaughter, same as me, so why don't you have a word with her?'

Lily muttered something inaudible under her breath. She eyed Josie for a moment. 'Yer too soft, that's your trouble, Josie. If I were younger . . .'

'Yes, Gran. You'd be on the stall, ruling us with a rod of iron. Well, for all your age and bad legs, you still do.'

'Cheeky bugger!' Lily suppressed a smile. 'Well, what did keep yer? It's nearly seven o'clock, you should have bin home hours ago. It's no fun being on yer own all day. I can't fend for meself like I used to.'

'The van broke down again.'

'Broke down! What yer done to it this time?'

'I ain't done nothing,' Josie said defensively. 'I think it must be the starter motor.'

'Starter motor indeed! I'm sure it's the way you drive it.' The old woman folded her bony arms under her thin chest. 'Where is it now?' she demanded.

'At the back of the Corn Exchange. It's quite safe, all the stuff is locked up inside. Anyway, let's face it, Gran, nobody's gonna pinch it 'cos the bloody thing won't start and they wouldn't get very far, there's hardly any petrol. I had to walk all the way home 'cos all the buses'd stopped running. You know what Leicester's like. One flake of snow and the whole town comes to a standstill.' She flopped down in the armchair opposite. 'Good job I shut the stall a little earlier than normal, else I wouldn't be home now,' she said before she could stop herself.

'Shut the stall early!' Lily's mouth dropped open in shock. 'In all my born days, Josephine Rawlings, I've never heard the likes. Shut the stall early, indeed. What d'you think you were playing at?'

'Gran, I shut the stall 'cos there were no customers. There wasn't any call for frozen cabbage and Brussels sprouts today.'

Lily tightened her lips. 'No need to be sarky. When me and yer grandad ran that stall, we never shut early. Stayed 'til the last, and we never let a bit of snow bother us. Out in all weathers we were and never had the luxury of a van. A handcart for us . . .'

'You did have a van. I've seen photos of you, Grandad and me mother standing beside one.'

'Oh, that weren't ours,' Lily lied.

'Weren't it?' Josie replied tersely. She knew her grandmother was lying in order to make her feel guilty for the brokendown van and for the fact that she had shut the stall early. Josie eyed her for a moment and then her face softened. She did not enjoy arguing with her grandmother, and somehow always managed to come off the loser. 'Okay, you've made yer point.'

'I should think so. I never want to hear you've shut up early again. Is that clear?'

'Look, Gran. I run the stall now and I do me best,' Josie erupted. 'If I ain't good enough, then you'll have to get someone else.'

Lily tightened her lips. 'Don't you take that attitude with me, gel. I'm an old woman. You shouldn't bully old women. You don't have to live with my aches and pains.' She grimaced and let out a shrill cry. 'Oh, me back. Oh, the pain's terrible, it's shooting down me legs.' She leant back in the chair and closed her eyes, her face contorted with pain.

Josie leant over, full of concern. 'Gran, I'll get your pills. I'm sorry. I didn't mean to shout.'

The old lady's eyes opened. 'I don't want me pills, I want me dinner!'

Josie froze in frustration. She made to speak, then changed her mind. Sighing deeply, she rose and stood before the table. Oh, to come home to a warm house and a meal waiting for me. What bliss, she thought wearily. She picked up the bags and turned to her grandmother. 'I'm rather tired, Gran. I thought I'd open a tin of soup.'

'Tin a' soup! I want a decent dinner. I ain't 'aving no tin a' soup. What you thinkin' of, gel? An old body like mine wants feedin' proper and I ain't gonna settle for no tin a' soup. I've had nothin' all day.'

'Gran, there's plenty of food in the larder, you could easily have helped yerself.'

'Could I!' Lily snapped. 'I've had a bad attack of rheumatics today. I've bin crippled up. But no one was caring about that, was they?' She struggled up and shuffled over to the back door, grabbing her coat.

'Where a' yer going?' Josie asked.

'For a stout, and I've a couple of people to see. I'll be back for me dinner later.'

'But it's snowing, Gran. You can't go out in this. You'd fall all yer length. Besides, you said you weren't well.'

'Well, maybe I ain't. The doctor sez stout's good for me, full a' iron. Which is more than I can say for a bloody tin a' soup!'

10

Grabbing her walking stick, Lily hobbled out of the door, leaving Josie staring after her.

She sank down on the chair by the table, rummaged through one of the brown carrier bags and pulled out a packet of ginger nuts and a jam swiss roll. Biting a piece off a biscuit, she gazed around. It was a large room and, with a fresh coat of paint and new wallpaper, could have been made quite cosy. The parlour at the front of the house was never used now; its main use was when visitors called, but they had dwindled drastically over the last few years and now the room was only opened once a month for a quick dust and sweep. Josie couldn't remember the last time the house had been decorated. With no man on hand to do it, her grandmother had quashed the idea of employing someone. 'I can't afford that, I ain't made a' money,' she had moaned. So the house had been left, year after year, to deteriorate slowly, and the once highly varnished doors and cream-painted walls were now peeling and dingy from age and lack of care.

The furniture was old but comfortable. The worn moquette suite and the old oak corkscrew-legged wind-out table and matching chairs had been bought by her grandfather from a second hand dealer many years before as had the odd assortment of other pieces dotted around the edges of the room. The extension panel of the table had been lost; rumour had it that it went on the fire many years before when money had been tight.

Josie's eyes alighted on the television set that sat to the left of the tiled fireplace and she smiled as she remembered how she had badgered her grandmother to buy one. 'What d'yer want one of those things for? We never had things like that in my day,' she had grumbled. In the end Josie had given up and saved from her own small wages for a second hand set purchased from a dusty radio and television shop on the Hinckley Road. From the moment it arrived her grandmother became hooked and would argue ferociously over the programmes; she had her favourites and was going to watch them regardless of what anyone else wanted.

To Josie this magical wooden box with its tubes and valves was a lifeline. It enabled her to see a world alien to her. She would sit for hours gazing at the flickering black and white screen, losing herself in the serials and films that unfolded before her.

Josie's room was at the back of the house and was the smallest of the three bedrooms. She had covered her faded pink rose-patterned wallpaper with pictures of her favourite pop stars and would fall asleep at night gazing into their unblinking eyes. Her dreams were always the same. She had somehow been transformed into a Twiggy or Jean Shrimpton lookalike, and one day she would be

11

spotted and rescued from her dull life, to be whisked off to a life of glamour and excitement.

But dreams were not reality and Josie was no fool. She knew it would take more than a miracle for her to look like Twiggy. And as for men – well, Josie had never had a wolf whistle let alone a proper date, and at nineteen, going on twenty, wondered if she ever would.

She rose and stood before the oval mirror that hung over the fireplace to study her reflection – something she rarely did. She was a big girl admittedly, but surely not as enormous as people made her out to be? She was at the most only a couple of stone overweight and with the right help could make much more of herself. A few years ago, people of her size were fashionable, but not now that fashion dictated you must be as thin as a rake. Fashionable clothes for people of her size were hard, if not impossible, to come by, and to get on in this era and be accepted you had to have 'the look'. So how did you make yourself attractive when all you had to choose from were the frumpy designs the shops stocked in larger sizes?

The loose-fitting dresses and elasticated-waist skirts she had painstakingly run up on the old treadle sewing machine did little to hide her ample frame. Josie was no dressmaker. If ever she was to make her fortune, that was one area she could forget.

She scrutinised her face. She wasn't ugly. Far from it in fact. Her oval-shaped face had creamy-olive skin and large brown eyes fringed around with thick dark brown lashes, and with a little more attention than she gave it, would be the envy of any woman. Her long thick brown hair, put into the hands of the right hairdresser, could be her crowning glory. But what was the point? Her body was the problem, and until she could get that into shape the rest of her hardly counted. Josie didn't know how, and had no one interested enough in her to ask.

She returned to the table again and sat down. Good old Josie. That was what she was known as, and unbeknown to everyone she hated it. She wasn't good old Josie, she did mind being put upon, used and treated like a door mat. She was a woman with feelings and a brain, one who wanted to escape and better herself. But what did she do about it? And if she did find the answer, what would happen to her grandmother?

One day, maybe one day, she thought longingly, something will happen to change all this. She gazed down at the empty biscuit and swiss roll wrappers and grimaced. Whilst she had been sitting thinking, she had unwittingly demolished the lot.

She stood up, picked up the bags and headed for the kitchen.

The stone stink was still full of the breakfast dishes and the plates and cutlery her grandmother had used for the lunch she said she hadn't had. As Josie turned on the tap, she heard the front door slam shut. Seconds later Marilyn put her head round the kitchen door.

'Hi. Where's Gran?'

Josie turned her head abruptly and looked hard at her cousin. Marilyn was a year older than Josie, and to look at the pair were exact opposites. Framed in the doorway stood her ideal: a Twiggy lookalike, with her short black skirt and white frilly blouse, legs that went up to her armpits and natural blonde hair that cascaded down to her shoulders. Marilyn never had any trouble saying no. If she didn't want to do something, she didn't and that was that.

Marilyn flicked back her hair and addressed Josie again.

'You all right?' she asked casually. Without waiting for an answer she turned, walked back into the room and tossed her white and grey fun fur coat over the back of a chair. She flung herself down in the armchair her grandmother had not long vacated and started to peel off her shiny black plastic boots.

'You've got a nerve, coming round here tonight. Because you swanned off early, I didn't get home 'til gone seven,' Josie complained as she picked up the tea towel, dried her hands and followed Marilyn through. She sat down in the chair opposite and frowned. 'Anyway, how did you get here? The buses ain't running.'

'I walked.'

'Walked?' Josie scoffed. 'Surprising what lengths you'll go to when you're pushed, Marilyn Rawlings. You wouldn't have walked if you'd have been going to work.'

'Don't be sarky,' Marilyn said crossly. 'I just hope this bloody snow stops soon or my friend won't manage to pick me up and I'll be stranded here.'

'What friend?'

'Just a friend. Anyway, where's Gran?'

'She's gone down the pub for a stout. So there's no chance of getting yer wages if that's what you've come for.'

'There'd better be! I've booked to have me hair done tomorrow afternoon.' She patted her blonde tresses. 'I'm gonna have it cut like Cilla Black's. What d'you think?'

'Marilyn! Not tomorrow. Saturday's our busiest day. Couldn't you change your appointment for Monday or something?'

'No, I couldn't. I fancy a change of hair do and I want it done as soon as possible. Anyway, you can cope, you always do.'

'It's a matter of having to, ain't it, Marilyn?'

She smiled sweetly. 'Look, don't let's fight, Josie. I've come to ask a favour.'

'Favour! What kinda favour?'

She took a deep breath. 'I need to borrow some money.'

'Some money. What for?'

'I can't tell yer. But I need a lot.'

'How much is a lot?' Josie frowned. 'Marilyn, a' you in some sort a' trouble?'

'No, I ain't,' she snapped. 'I just need some money, and quick.'

Josie scratched the back of her neck. 'Well, I've got twenty quid saved. Yer can borrow that, but I want it back.'

'That's not enough.'

'Ain't it? Oh.' Josie shrugged her shoulders. 'Well, I can't help yer then.'

'Yes, yer can.' Marilyn lowered her head and looked at her cousin through her lashes. 'Gran's got loads stashed under her bed.'

Josie blew out her cheeks and stared at Marilyn in astonishment. 'That's Gran's money, yer can't have that.'

'Why not? She must have thousands, and she'd never know.'

''Course she would, yer daft bugger, she counts it every night. Anyway, she ain't got thousands and you know it. The stall don't bring in that much and betime we pay everything out, there ain't that much left for saving.'

Marilyn jumped out of the chair. 'Don't you believe it, Josie. She's got loads, I tell yer, and she wouldn't miss what I need.'

'Well, if yer that sure, why don't you ask her yourself?'

''Cos she won't give it to me. Gran's a tight old skinflint and you know it. She could spend some of the money doing this house up. Instead you live in a freezing hovel just 'cos she's too mean to spend anything.' Marilyn wrung her hands together. 'Look, Josie, I wouldn't ask if I weren't desperate, and I don't know anyone else with that kinda money that'd help.'

'You are in trouble, ain't yer, our Marilyn? What yer done? What's happened?' Josie cried as she stood up to face her cousin. 'Yer not pregnant or anything, are yer?'

'No,' Marilyn snapped. 'I told yer, I ain't in trouble. I just need the money. Now are yer gonna help me or not?'

'No,' Josie said with conviction. 'I'm not stealing from Gran for another of your hare-brained schemes. You're asking too much of me this time. Whatever she's managed to put by over the years is her business and we ain't got no right to take it. If yer want it that bad, you'll have to ask her yourself, 'cos I don't want no part of it.'

'Okay, Josie, you've made yer point. I'll get it some other way.'

'How?'

'That's none of your business.'

'Suit yourself,' Josie said nonchalantly. She eyed Marilyn thoughtfully. Just what was her cousin up to? Marilyn had always had a selfish streak and would tell any amount of lies to get what she wanted. So what lie, if any, was she telling now?

Marilyn was the product of an ill-matched alliance between

Stanley Rawlings and Hilda Godley, whose marriage had caused bewilderment throughout the community. Why had such a handsome man married such a timid plain creature? the residents had asked for months afterwards. He could have had the pick of any of the good-looking women for miles around. But more to the point, just before his marriage, why had Stanley so abruptly left the family business? That was the question that niggled them the most and to this day it remained a mystery. No one had been able to find out what had happened to cause such an irretrievable rift. Not even his sister Maisie's tearful pleas. Only Lily knew the full truth and she was staying tight lipped. Their only contact, if it could be that, was the fact that every Friday night Lily would place several five-pound notes inside an envelope and despatch it to her estranged son. That practice had continued ever since the rift.

Stanley had lived and worked alongside his mother and sister, delivering fruit and vegetables around the surrounding housing estates, until one day his mother had arrived home unexpectedly early and an almighty row had erupted between them. He had hurriedly departed with all his belongings and had never been seen near the vicinity again.

Shortly after that he married Hilda in the dismal Register Office on Pocklingtons Walk, with none of his family present, and moved into a small semi-detached house on Braunstone Lane. To an onlooker the marriage would have appeared happy, but from the moment of Marilyn's conception, and much to the dismay and confusion of his wife, Stanley showed not the slightest interest in their existence. He moved into the spare room and stayed there with no reason or explanation, seeming perfectly content with the situation.

Hilda, resigned to rejection and unwilling to divorce her husband because of the stigma, poured all her love on to her daughter, going without things for herself in order to try to make up for her husband's bewildering behaviour. The result was a spoiled, selfish child who would throw a tantrum and wail and scream until she got her own way.

On Marilyn's fifteenth birthday, Stanley, much to Hilda's dismay, suddenly acknowledged his daughter's existence and tried to become the heavy-handed father. Marilyn's carefree life was challenged as he strove belatedly to protect her from the harsh realities she already knew about. Marilyn found this hard to accept and spent her time plotting ways to do what she wanted without his knowledge, often using Josie as a scapegoat. She'd lost count of the times she had suffered her uncle's wrath as he stormed down to confront her on the market stall, blaming her for something his daughter had done.

Marilyn had always been a rebellious child, getting into all sorts of scrapes at school, like playing truant to listen to pop music round at a friend's house or the time she had got hold of a pile of glossy photographs of Adam Faith, forged his signature and sold them to unsuspecting school girls as the genuine article. And there was more, much more that Josie could remember. So what had she done now? It must be bad for her to be so desperate for so much money.

Josie struggled with her conscience. The few pounds she had saved were towards having an indoor toilet fitted for her grandmother. The old lady risked life and limb every time she ventured over the broken paving slabs in the yard, not to mention the possibility of catching pneumonia from the icy wind that whipped through the rotting wooden door and gaps in the ancient brickwork. That money had taken ages to save and she was still far short of her target. But, she supposed, lending what she had to Marilyn wouldn't hinder her plans, not in the short term.

Marilyn was her cousin, she was her family, and it was her duty to help the girl. Besides, she thought ruefully, if she didn't give over the money freely, she knew Marilyn would quickly wheedle it out of her now she knew about it. She should have kept her mouth shut. But it was too late.

She raised her eyes. 'Look, Marilyn. You can have that twenty quid if it'll help, and I can give yer another two out of this weeks' wages. But I'll give it yer on two conditions.'

'Oh, what's them, then?'

'That you pay me back as soon as you can, and that you start to pull yer weight on the stall. 'Cos I'm fed up, Marilyn. Fed up with covering for yer and doing all the work by meself. That stall's bad enough to run with two . . .'

'Okay, okay. I promise yer'll have the money back in a couple of weeks. Now stop going on, Josie, yer sound like me dad. Always nagging.'

Josie eyed her suspiciously before she went to collect the hard-earned coins from her piggy bank. She slid them into a big brown envelope and hesitantly handed them over.

Marilyn stared disdainfully at the envelope. 'Ain't yer got n'ote smaller, Josie? I can't very well lug that lot about with me.'

Her hackles rose. 'Take it or leave it, Marilyn, and don't be so bloody ungrateful.'

Marilyn tutted loudly. 'Okay, no need to be so touchy. I said I'll pay yer back. Now, a' you got summat to eat? I'm starving.'

'I ain't started the dinner yet.'

'A biscuit or piece a' cake'll do.'

'Er . . . I forgot to get some. Why are yer hungry anyway? Didn't you have dinner at yer own house?'

'I ain't bin home. I told Mam this morning I was coming round here straight from work and wouldn't be home 'til late. Said we were having a girls' night.'

'Oh! Are we?' Josie asked hopefully.

'No, I'm going out. That was just an excuse to save me getting the third degree. I've got me stuff in the passage to change into. You don't mind, do yer?' Marilyn said, pulling a chair out from the table and sitting down.

Josie sighed. 'Would it make any difference if I did?'

Marilyn smiled.

'What time's Stephen picking you up?'

'Who said anything about Stephen?'

'Oh, sorry. I just automatically thought you were seeing him,' Josie said, joining her cousin at the table.

'So does he. It's about time Stephen Kingsman realised I've got other friends. He ain't got the monopoly on me,' said Marilyn haughtily.

Josie inhaled sharply. 'You and Stephen have been seeing each other on and off for years. That bloke loves you.'

'That's his hard luck. And I prefer it meself when it's off.'

Josie scowled fiercely at the callous way in which her cousin spoke and turned her head to stare into the fire, worried that she might betray her own feelings. She couldn't recollect a time when she hadn't been in love with Stephen; even the mention of his name sent shivers down her spine. Right from their introduction as toddlers she could remember feeling a warm glow of pleasure when in his company, and that pleasure had grown to love as the years had gone by. Unrequited love, but love nevertheless in Josie's eyes.

A picture of him rose to mind. She saw him with his hands thrust deep inside his pockets, long legs astride, his laughing pale blue eyes sparkling with life. His well-shaped head was topped by a mass of long thick fair hair, which as fashion dictated waved naturally down to rest past his collar. He was tall, well over six foot, and very handsome, very intelligent, and very much in love with Marilyn. And there was nothing Josie could do about it.

Stephen's father owned the cafe that supplied the market traders with their mounds of food and endless mugs of tea and coffee. Stephen, having successfully studied for a catering degree, had big ideas for his own future, and as far as Josie was aware, these plans included marriage to Marilyn. It hurt her dreadfully to see the way her cousin treated him. If only his feelings could miraculously be transferred to her! That was a laugh. Stephen had only ever looked at her as a friend, and that was probably only because she was Marilyn's cousin.

She turned her gaze back to Marilyn, folded her arms and leant

17

on the table. 'You should tell Stephen how yer feel, put him out of his misery before it's too late.'

Marilyn laughed. 'Not just yet. I might need him. 'Sides, he's good for a giggle when I'm at a loose end.'

Josie gawped. 'That's wicked, Marilyn. 'Specially when you know fine well how the bloke feels about yer. What's wrong with him anyway? He's got everything someone like you could wish for.'

'Don't make me laugh, Josie! If you think I'm gonna marry Stephen and spend the rest of me life serving greasy chips to fat, loud-mouthed market folk, you're not on. I want something better for myself.'

'Oh, such as?'

'Well . . . I might just have a few irons in the fire,' she said slowly.

A frown appeared on Josie's face. 'You stuck-up bitch, our Marilyn! That family make a damned good living outta that cafe, and those so-called loud-mouthed market folk . . . well, I hate to remind you of this, but that's us. We belong to that lot.'

Marilyn stood up and walked over to the fire. 'You might, Josie, but I don't. I hate the market and always have done. I only work on the stall 'cos I dread the thought of an office or a factory. And anyway,' she said sulkily, 'me dad insisted.'

'Yeah, well, if you had gone in an office, you wouldn't be able to keep nipping off, would yer? You'd soon have been sacked.'

Marilyn sniffed loudly.

'You live in a dream world, Marilyn,' Josie continued. 'It's about time you came back down to earth and realised that *this* is reality. Getting up in a morning and doing a good day's graft. If you pulled yer weight we could expand the stall and start making some real money. And if you'd got any sense, you'd grab Stephen, 'cos he's the best offer you're gonna get. He's got lots of ideas, Marilyn. He's gonna make something of himself . . .'

'Oh, is he?' she cried. 'Well, if he's that much of a catch, why don't *you* make a play for him?' She narrowed her eyes spitefully. 'I know you fancy him. You'd make a good pair, you two. Him cooking the chips and you eating 'em!'

'There's no need to be nasty, Marilyn. That was uncalled for.'

She took a breath. 'Yeah, I'm sorry. But *you're* one to talk about *me* having me head in the clouds! You're the one that spends all the time watching the telly and reading those stupid romance books. They give you ideas, Josie. They fill your head with things that will never happen. Well, not for you anyway.' Her eyes suddenly darted to the clock. 'Oh, bugger, is that the time? I'd better hurry. We're going to a new club that's opened near the Palais. 'Sposed to be really good. All the "in" crowd goes there.' She smiled warmly at Josie. 'Get us something to eat, there's a love. A tin a' soup'll do.'

18

She noticed Josie's smile. 'What's so funny?'

'Nothing, just something Gran said. You go and get ready. I'll do the soup for yer.'

'Good on yer, Josie. I won't be a tick.'

Josie watched as Marilyn glided out of the room. She made her way to the kitchen, peeled some potatoes for her grandmother's dinner and threw the peelings on the back of the fire. She watched for a moment as it spluttered and hissed. Then she went back to the kitchen, put the potatoes and the soup on the old gas cooker, threw several sausages under the grill and finished washing the dishes.

Twenty minutes later, Josie placed the bowl of soup and plate of bread on the table just as Marilyn came through the door, dressed in a tight, short red skirt, matching tights and halterneck white top, her blonde hair brushed and cascading over her shoulders. She plonked a vanity case holding her vast assortment of makeup on the table, and sat down.

'Oh, great,' she said in appreciation. 'I need this. It's freezing up those stairs.'

Josie laughed as she sat down. 'You should have lit my fire.'

'I did. But the heat it throws out wouldn't cook a slice of toast in a month of Sundays.' Her eyes darted to the clock on the mantel. 'I'd better hurry. My date'll be here soon and he ain't the kinda bloke to be kept waiting. That reminds me . . .' She eyed Josie warily. 'If Stephen does call, tell him you ain't seen me.'

'Marilyn . . .'

'Please, Josie?'

'Okay,' she said reluctantly. 'But this is the last time.'

Marilyn raised her head and sniffed deeply. 'I smell burning.'

'Oh, God. The spuds.' Josie jumped up and raced through to the kitchen. She yanked the saucepan off the stove and threw it into the sink. 'Blast!' she groaned loudly as she looked at the blackened mess. 'Oh, sod it. I'll go to the chippy. If Gran don't like it, that's tough.'

Chapter Two

'Oh, no,' Josie groaned as she closed the book and stared at the cover in dismay. Someone had ripped the last couple of pages out. Now she would never know what happened to Angelique. Would the beautiful, courageous woman stay and marry the rich, besotted Sultan or go off on another adventure? That was a question that would remain unanswered and she wouldn't be able to sleep for wondering.

She yawned loudly and glanced at the clock. It was just gone ten-thirty and time for her to go to bed. She had an early start in the morning, and if Marilyn was going to play truant again whilst she had her hair done, most of the work, as usual, would fall upon Josie.

After Marilyn had departed for the discotheque with her mysterious escort, Lily had returned and grumbled vigorously at the lack of a meal, but had smacked her lips in pleasure after Josie had trudged down the street and fetched them both a portion of cod and chips. Full of food and stout she had retired to bed, leaving Josie free for once to watch her programmes on the television without exasperating interruptions. Tonight's offering had been Ready, Steady, Go, Double Your Money and Bonanza, after which she had settled down to finish her novel. After her disastrous day, her pleasant evening had abruptly ended with the missing pages. She would now have to scour the bookshops for another copy and hope nobody noticed whilst she stood and read the ending. She would have to find out what happened to the heroine. She wouldn't rest peacefully until she did.

She rose from the comfort of her armchair and made her way over to the window which overlooked the small back yard. The light escaping through the sash window cast deep eerie shadows. The snow had stopped and thankfully was thawing; the guttering on the coal shed had broken and a steady stream of water gushed down, causing a huge puddle outside the back toilet. If the temperature plummeted further again during the night, the yard would be like a skating rink come morning. She would have to remember to sprinkle plenty of salt over the area before her grandmother got up or the old lady could do herself serious damage, especially if she ventured out in her holey slippers as she usually did.

Her thoughts turned to Marilyn. Just what did she need all that money for? Knowing her cousin as she did, she felt sure it wouldn't be for anything legitimate.

She sighed loudly, let the heavy floral curtain fall back into place and walked towards the fireplace, her eyes alighting on a photograph of her mother on the mantelpiece. She smiled and picked it up, gazing fondly at the black and white photograph, her mother's laughing eyes staring back into hers.

'Okay, Mam,' she said aloud. 'What d'you think our Marilyn's up to this time, eh?'

Still holding the photograph, she sat down again. An image of her mother rose before her. She was standing at the table kneading pastry for one of the delicious meat pies. Her shapely body was clothed in a pretty candy-striped cotton shirtwaister, her natural blonde hair expertly styled by a Twink Home Perm. Josie leaned back and rested her head on the back of the chair. Her mother had been beautiful, full of vigour and energy, and had been admired and respected by everyone who knew her. When Maisie Rawlings had walked into a room, the atmosphere livened. She had possessed a quick tongue, a wicked sense of humour, and strong loyalty to her family and friends.

Her father's death had brutally ended her dreams of one day owning a fashion shop. She had worked long and hard, putting her flair for fashion to good use by raising herself from store room run-about to first assistant in the ladies' department of Lewis's Department Store, learning all she could on the way. But her father's ill health, followed by his death and her mother's estrangement from her brother, meant there was no one to help run the family fruit and vegetable stall. Reluctantly, she shelved her dreams and joined her mother, standing in all weathers on the market stall, battling against the other traders for business. Her good-humoured nature stopped her from dwelling on what might have been and she threw herself whole-heartedly into her work.

At twenty-four years old, Maisie fell pregnant. Lily had been beside herself. Her daughter should have known better than to commit such a crime, and to cover her embarrassment and hurt Lily spent many hours shouting at her either to marry the father or go away for a while, give birth and have the baby adopted. But Maisie had stood firm. She could not marry Frank Mitchell when she didn't love him. It was too much of a sacrifice to make for the sake of giving her child a name. She was not ashamed of her condition. She was proud and wanted the baby desperately. She would raise the child herself, give it all the love and care it needed, and woe betide anyone who tried to make her do otherwise.

21

Lily had had to relent or lose her beloved daughter. To her great surprise friends and neighbours rallied round and wished Maisie luck. Knitted garments, gifts and offers of baby-minders had flooded in, and eventually Lily had to admit that it was all due to her daughter's popularity. When Josephine Lillian Rawlings had screamed her way into the world Lily had proudly welcomed the visitors into her home to view her new grandchild.

Josie, as she was soon to be called, grew into a pretty, dark-haired child, cocooned and surrounded by the love of her mother. They went everywhere together. If Maisie was baking, Josie had a little bowl with her own mixture at the side; on the stall, Josie sat in her pushchair and delighted the customers with her baby chatter; when Maisie was persuaded to go on a date, either her daughter went too or no date.

Josie's first day at school had seen Maisie with tears in her eyes as she had stood at the gates of the Ingle Street School with the rest of the mothers. She watched her beloved daughter, dressed smartly in her new gaberdine coat and grey school pinafore, her satchel filled with pens, crayons and writing books in a satchel strapped firmly to her back, as she stood hesitantly, surrounded by all the other little girls and boys, waiting for the bell to sound and herald the start of their school life. Maisie had felt proud. Her daughter might have no father but she was the best presented of all of them. She had stood by the gates long after the other women had departed. Her little girl was growing up and Maisie's pride was suddenly tinged with sadness.

That night, for the first time, five-and-a-half-year-old Josie questioned the absence of her father.

'Everyone else has a dad. Why ain't I?' she asked in bewilderment, her little face puckered. 'Mary Pratt, in the older gels' class, says I'm a little bastard. What's a little bastard, Mam?'

Maisie's breath left her body and she gasped for air, dropping the plate of corned beef and tomato sandwiches she had made in readiness for her daughter's return. She had never intended that Josie would not know of her origins, but had wanted to tell her when she felt her daughter was ready to understand. How did you explain to a child of such tender years that she hadn't a father simply because her mother had chosen it that way? That she had been attracted to the man but not enough to wake up every morning next to him and spend her days catering to his very need just because of one mistake. The pregnancy had come as a dreadful shock at first but after a short while had become most welcome. This baby had come about through no fault of its own and Maisie had vowed to make sure it never suffered.

Ignoring the mess, she went over to her daughter, hugged her

22

fiercely then placed her gently on her knee. Carefully, she told the young child of her beginnings.

On finishing, Maisie raised her head proudly. 'You ignore her, my darling. You're not a bastard,' she said harshly. 'You're a love child – my love child. I cared for your father very much, but not enough to marry and spend the rest of me life with him. I chose to look after you meself and I don't regret my decision for one minute. That Mary Pratt's a silly little girl. If you want my opinion, her surname suits her perfectly.'

Josie stared at her mother in awe. 'Was me father handsome, Mam?' she asked, visualising the princes in the fairy stories her mother read to her every night.

Maisie smiled. 'Oh, yes. The handsomest man you ever saw. You take after him. You have his dark colouring and his beautiful big brown eyes.'

She hugged her daughter tightly, remembering the night she had sent Frank Mitchell away. He had been hurt, bewildered, full of hope that their relationship would eventually become permanent despite the knowledge it would take a special kind of man to place a wedding ring on Maisie Rawlings' finger. She never told him of her condition and the last she had heard he was happily married with three children and had emigrated to Australia. She had been relieved. That episode in her life was firmly over, but more importantly, the future held no surprises. Frank would never darken her door and she could tell Josie truthfully that she knew nothing of his whereabouts. But she would always think of him with affection. He had given her Josie and for that she would be forever grateful.

The years melted away and Josie grew into a delightful, inquisitive young girl. Maisie spared nothing to give her everything she required to make her future secure. If she needed special books or money for a school excursion then it was readily given. Maisie worked long and hard on the stall and she expected and demanded ample remuneration. Her hopes for Josie were high, she wanted her daughter to achieve all that she had been denied, and Josie readily fed off her mother's desires.

Just after Josie reached her fourteenth birthday, her mother died. A massive heart attack struck her one bitterly cold February morning as she made her way towards the market place to start work. The whole community went into mourning. How could a woman, so alive, so vibrant, die so suddenly, having lived only half her life? The shock had hit the small family badly. The bond and the driving force that had kept them together was gone.

Lily Rawlings aged drastically overnight and for several weeks took no interest in anything. Josie quickly agreed that if they were to survive, then she would temporarily have to give up her schooling and take over the stall. It didn't take her long to realise that her grandmother had no intention of returning. Her days on the stall were over as far as Lily was concerned. Gradually the household returned to normal, but instead of Maisie, it was Josie who kept things running. As was expected of her, she had taken the place of her mother, running the stall, the house, and taking care of her grandmother.

Josie's distress ran deep. She performed her tasks in an endless daze, her dreams of university and a career gone forever. But that was nothing compared to the loss of her mother. In her grief she turned to food. Eating gave her comfort. For a few blissful minutes she could concentrate on preparing enormous meals, and would hide her expanding body under thick knitted jumpers and shapeless skirts.

Eventually she learned to live with her grief and resign herself to her new life. To her pleasure, she found she grew to love her job. The market became her haven. Most of the market traders had known her since she had been born and welcomed the fact that the Rawlings stall would continue as it had done for generations before. The constant banter from her comrades and customers alike amused and delighted her, and before many weeks had passed Josie knew where her future lay.

Just after her mother's death, her uncle had come down to the market and demanded his daughter take her rightful place by Josie's side. On tackling her grandmother, to Josie's dismay the old lady had shrugged her shoulders and agreed. Until this time, Josie had had little to do with her uncle or his family. As a child she had overheard the arguments between her mother and grandmother. Her childish mind not grasping the situation she had come to her own conclusions. She did not care much for Stanley. Whatever he had done had caused his mother and sister so much pain. Having his wilful daughter unexpectedly thrust upon them did not please Josie in the least, but her uncle's threats and her grandmother's seeming indifference forced her to comply.

Thus was the pattern of Josie's life decided. The care and protection of the grandmother and the stall. The escapism she found in her books and in television. And as time passed, a reluctant affection for Marilyn despite her behaviour and Josie's endless worrying over her escapades. She had little expectations of a romance of her own but contented herself with finding pleasure in her day to day business and the achievements of others.

She hugged her mother's photograph's to her chest before putting it back on the mantelpiece. Oh, Mam, she thought sadly, I wish you were still here. I do miss you. She took a deep breath, bent down and picked up the poker ready to rake the fire down for the night. She jumped as she heard the loud hammering on the front door, and frowned deeply. Who on earth could it be at this time of night? Still carrying the poker, she made her way down the long dark passage towards the door and hesitantly opened it. Her face lit up in pleasure.

'Stephen!' she exclaimed.

The usually handsome young man was leaning precariously on the door frame, his face a picture of utter misery as he stared at her through a drunken haze. The navy woollen winter coat he wore was sopping wet; his thick fair hair, usually so well groomed, was tousled and covered in snow. In his hand he held a half-empty bottle of vodka. Josie's heart sank to see him in such a sad state and she knew only too well the reason why. She became conscious of her own appearance. Her bright pink candlewick dressing gown and winceyette nightdress enhanced her bulk and self-consciously she tightened the belt, hoping it might pull her in a little.

Inhaling deeply, she raised her eyes to meet his.

'She's not here,' she said slowly.

Stephen hiccuped loudly and leaned closer. 'I know,' he slurred. 'I saw her in a car with some bloke, heading towards town.' He raised the bottle to his lips and took a drink. 'I've come to see you. Thought you might like some company.'

Josie tightened her lips. 'Some company you'll be! You're sozzled,' she said sharply, but stood aside. 'You'd better come in. We'll freeze to death standing here. I'll make some coffee.'

'Don't want coffee, Josie. This'll do me fine,' he said, taking another gulp.

'I said, I'll make some coffee, and you'll do as you're told and drink it.' She raised the poker and waved it in the air. 'If you go home in that state, your dad'll kill yer.'

'If you don't first,' Stephen laughed, seeing several pokers flash before his eyes.

Josie lowered her arm. Her shoulders sagged and she managed a smile. 'Come on. At least have a warm by the fire.'

'Ta, Josie.'

She stood with her back to the door and watched as he stumbled down the passage. She felt a warmth rise up in her at his presence, which was quickly dispelled. He was only here and in this state because of Marilyn. She entered the room to find him slumped in the armchair, his wet coat in a heap on the floor, his shoes discarded by the hearth. He held out the bottle, a silly grin on his face. 'Have a drink with me, Josie?'

She shook her head as she picked up his coat, placed it on the back of a chair, rested the poker on the hearth and sat down in the chair opposite. 'No, thanks. I ain't never had vodka. I don't think I'd like it.'

'Oh, come on. You don't know 'til you try it. It's good for making you forget. Come on, take a swig.'

Josie relented and took hold of the bottle. Why not? she thought. Must be the only drink I'll ever get offered from a good-looking man. She took a large mouthful and spluttered as the clear harmless-looking liquid hit the back of her throat.

'Jesus Christ!' she choked as she handed back the bottle.

Stephen took another gulp. 'Who's the bloke, Josie?'

She slipped off her chair and knelt before the fire.

'Oh, nobody important. Just someone who was giving her a lift.' She said hesitantly, 'She's . . . er . . . gone dancing. It's one of her friends' birthday.'

'Dancing! She hasn't gone dancing, Josie, I'm not that stupid. Why do you cover up for her? I know she's with another fella. Why can't she just tell me, that's what I want to know? Why does she keep me hanging on?'

Josie shrugged her shoulders. 'She doesn't mean it, Stephen. I'm sure she loves you. It's just she can't stick to one man at the moment. She likes to have fun.'

'Fun! Marilyn wouldn't know the meaning of the word unless it involved spending lots of money. Anyway, what's this new bloke got that I haven't?'

Josie bit her bottom lip and raised her eyes. 'I don't know, Stephen, I haven't met him,' she said softly. 'Anyway, as far as I know she's only gone out with him tonight. She must have thought you were busy or something.'

'Busy or not, if she cared about me, she wouldn't be with another man. Well, this is it, Josie. I've finished with her.'

She sadly shook her head. 'You'll feel differently in the morning.'

'I won't.'

'I bet you will. This isn't the first time something like this has happened between you both, and I'm sure it won't be the last.'

'It is this time, Josie. At one time I'd have done anything for her. But not now. As far as I'm concerned, it's finished.' He flopped back and stared up at the ceiling. The room fell into silence.

'I should fall in love with someone like you, Josie,' he said unexpectedly, his voice low and husky. 'You wouldn't lead me a merry dance, would you?' He leaned forward and stared at her fondly. He hiccupped loudly and his elbow slipped. Josie automatically reached out to stop him falling out of the chair. He stared at her for a moment, then leaned over and ran his hand down the side of her face. 'Good old Josie. You'll make someone a lovely wife.' His handsome face creased into a drunken grin. 'How about it? Shall we get married, eh?'

Josie gawped as she stared at him. It was the drink that had spoken, not him. Once he'd sobered up everything would be back to normal. He would still be in love with Marilyn and she would be treating him like dirt. Josie turned her head abruptly towards the fire and stared into the dying embers. If only he could fall in love with her, she'd be the happiest woman alive. The silence was broken by a loud thud. She raised her eyes to the ceiling.

'Oh, God,' she groaned. 'We've woken Gran.' She stood up. 'I'd better go and see to her. I won't be a moment.'

Stephen watched her blurred outline disappear through the door and slumped further down into the chair as he took several more sips from the bottle. His head swam and he fought to keep his eyes in focus. Deep down he knew that drinking himself senseless would solve nothing; all it would do was give him a raging hangover in the morning.

His gaze fixed upon the red embers in the grate and he asked himself a question. What was he trying to solve? He tried to sieve through his muddled thoughts. If he was honest with himself, and getting blind drunk was as good a time as any to be honest with oneself, it was rather a relief that someone had taken Marilyn off his hands. Theirs was a relationship that had gone on for far too long. It had become a habit on both sides. He just pitied the poor bloke who was now lumbered with her and wondered whether he should warn him. But what the heck. Let him go through the traumas of not knowing from one day to the next where he stood. He slouched further down into the chair and half closed his eyes.

Suddenly he realised that it was his pride that was hurting, nothing else, and a tremendous weight lifted from his shoulders. He knew then that it was not any romantic feeling for Marilyn that was making him so miserable, it was only the fact that she was using him for her own ends; and if getting drunk had made him acknowledge these home truths, then the aftermath he must face in the morning would be well worth it.

Yes, Marilyn had been something pretty to hang on his arm and they had had some good times together. But the rest of the time had been spent wondering what the hell she was up to as she had failed yet again to appear and when she finally did, she never volunteered any explanation.

Granted, she had been entertaining – depending, of course, what kind of mood she had happened to be in; she was a good dancer, and she was a good . . . His mind blanked. A good what? She certainly didn't have much conversation – not like Josie.

He leaned forward and peered around. Where was Josie? Where had she disappeared to? He remembered her being here a while ago. He settled back in the chair. Now you could talk to Josie about anything. That girl had a sprinkling of knowledge on all sorts of

27

subjects. She was humorous too and was always laughing. Marilyn never laughed, unless it was at someone else's expense, and she took people for granted. Josie never took anything for granted, and you always knew where you stood with her. She had a knack of making people feel comfortable in her presence, just as she was doing to him now. He could sit here all night without feeling the need to rush off. Good old Josie, he thought warmly. The girl just needed taking in hand. She needed someone to care for and look after her. It would certainly be one lucky man who landed her.

Stephen raised the bottle to his lips again and drank. Where was she? Wherever it was, she'd been gone a long time. He was missing her. He wanted her to come back. The effects of the bottle finally took their toll. He sagged against the back of the chair and his eyelids drooped.

After she had left the room, Josie hurriedly climbed the stairs and entered her grandmother's bedroom. The large room was dominated by an enormous dark oak bed, under which supposedly was hidden a hoard of money. The headboard rose halfway up the wall and the shrunken body of her grandmother looked lost beside its vastness.

By the window sat a dressing table, its four huge drawers crammed with an assortment of odds and ends that had built up over Lily's eighty-four years. In the massive double wardrobe hung two long black skirts, one black and one white blouse, three hand-knitted cardigans, three pairs of knee-length woollen bloomers and two Aertex vests; the rest of the space was again filled with useless paraphernalia which her grandmother refused to part with. The grey-speckled lino covering the floor was holey in parts and the floorboards showed through. No amount of coaxing would persuade Lily to replace it.

'Your grandad put that down and it'll see me out,' had been her words.

As Josie entered the icy room her grandmother's small grey eyes stared piercingly at her.

'Who's down there?' she snapped. 'Every time I get to sleep someone wakes me. That hammering on the door was enough to give me a heart attack. Who is it?'

'Stephen,' Josie answered casually. 'He's come looking for our Marilyn.'

'Huh. 'Bout time that lad learnt his lesson. That gel leads him a right song and dance.' She pulled the assortment of blankets covering her higher under her chin. 'Pass me that bottle of stout,' she demanded.

'I'll make you a cuppa, Gran . . .'

'I don't want a cuppa, I want me stout. It's the only thing that

28

gets me to sleep. It's full of iron. Now pass me the bottle or I'll get it meself.'

Josie walked over to the small table at the side of the bed and picked up the half-empty bottle. She handed it to her grandmother, who snatched it out of her hand and took a large gulp.

'That's better.' She narrowed her heavily wrinkled eyes. 'Now leave me in peace and stop making so much racket. Bloody calling at this time a' night. Some people ain't got no sense.'

'He'll be off soon. I'm just gonna make him a cuppa coffee.'

'Well, you make sure he is. You've an early start in the morning.'

Josie opened her mouth to speak then thought better of it and, despite the protests, tucked the old lady firmly in and gently closed the bedroom door. She made her way down the stairs and into the back room. She found Stephen fast asleep, his long, muscular legs stretched out across the hearth. The practically empty bottle of vodka was still clutched in his hand.

She looked at him tenderly for a moment before switching off the overhead light, leaving just the glow from the fire, and stepped softly over. She carefully prised the bottle away and held it to her. Marilyn had a lot to answer for. Her callous attitude had driven the man who loved her so desperately to drink. Josie could see her now, cavorting on the dance floor with her new man, not giving Stephen a second thought. Poor Stephen. He was going to have a terrible hangover in the morning and all because of that little madam. Well, when she saw Marilyn next she would give her a piece of her mind. She shook her head sadly, placed the bottle on the table and went to rummage through the cupboard under the stairs. Finding an old blanket, she tugged it out and covered Stephen up.

Her movements roused him and he opened his eyes and stared up at her.

'Oh, you've come back,' he slurred, blinking rapidly. 'I thought you'd left me.' With a great effort he stood up awkwardly and supported himself on the back of the chair. 'I'd better go,' he said. His hands slipped and he stumbled, falling heavily against her. His weight made Josie lose her balance, and before she could regain it they both toppled over. She hit the floor with a thud, Stephen landing on top of her, his weight pinning her to the ground.

Josie felt her face redden at the predicament she found herself in.

'Oh, Stephen,' she said, forcing a chuckle as she tried to hide her embarrassment, 'yer more sozzled than I thought.' She made to push him off.

Stephen raised his head and studied the face beneath him, bathed in the soft glow from the fire. Through his fuddled thoughts it struck him with surprise that he had never really looked properly at this woman before. In all the years he had known her, how come

29

he had never noticed how attractive she was? Despite her size, there was something about Josie that was definitely appealing. He sighed softly as he studied her. A surge of desire raced through him. He wanted her. At this moment he wanted her more than anything.

Her large brown heavily lashed eyes stared back in bewilderment, searching his face, wondering what was going through his mind, and how she could get herself out of this predicament.

'Oh, Josie,' he said huskily. His eyes softened as he scanned her face again. Slowly, and much to Josie's confusion, he bent forward and kissed her long and hard. Josie's jumbled thoughts blanked as she found herself willingly responding. His lips left hers and sought her neck. His hands ran gently over her body and loosened the belt of her dressing-gown. Josie shuddered.

'Stephen . . .' she protested softly.

'No, no. Don't say anything,' he whispered hoarsely. With an awkward jerk, he pulled open her dressing-gown.

Josie's breath exploded from her body. Years of pent up feeling mounted as she gave herself to him, her body tingling with excitement as his touch electrified her whole being. Their love-making reached a climax, then was over. She lay motionless, her clothes disarrayed around her.

She exhaled a deep sigh of contentment. So this was it. This was love, and it was wonderful. All the stories she had read didn't do it justice. She lay for several moments, afraid to break the spell. Finally she dared to look at him, and smiled. He had fallen asleep. The bottle of vodka had done its worst. He was so peaceful. His rugged, handsome features had softened and he looked like a little boy. She eased herself up and straightened her nightclothes. Grabbing the blanket, she covered him up, put a cushion under his head, settled the fire and went slowly up the stairs.

She lay unable to sleep, a warm glow enveloping her. She felt so alive, so fulfilled, like a butterfly emerging from its chrysalis. Hope and excitement filled her, and it was all down to Stephen. At long last he had come to his senses and realised it was with her that his happiness lay. Now she would do her damnedest to make sure he never regretted his change of affections.

She began to make plans. They would court for a while before deciding their future. She saw the house they would buy, the children they would have, the wedding . . . Oh, the wedding would be wonderful. Lots of long flowing dresses and top hats. She momentarily frowned. How would Marilyn take this turn of events? Would she be hurt? No. Marilyn didn't care for Stephen, not in the way that Josie did, and her cousin would most probably be glad that she had taken him off her hands. Anyway, nothing was going to dampen her newfound happiness. Not even her spoilt cousin.

She clasped her hands together under the covers as realisation shot through her. She was no longer a virgin. At long last she was a woman, someone who had experienced love and had given the one thing she had held precious to the only man she had ever wanted. No longer would she lie awake at night worrying about becoming a dried-up old spinster. Finally exhaustion overtook her and she fell into a dream-filled sleep.

She awoke and lay still in the inky blackness of the early winter morning as her thoughts dwelled on the happenings of the previous night. It took her several moments to convince herself that it really had taken place. Stephen had made love to her. For the first time ever a man had wanted her and she was filled with excitement. She dived out of bed and rummaged through her wardrobe. She selected her best brown skirt and cream lacy-patterned jumper. She hurriedly washed, and brushed her hair until it shone. Poised at the top of the stairs, she took a deep breath and headed tentatively down. Stephen was still huddled on the floor, the blanket wrapped tightly around him.

She stood watching him for several moments, drinking in the contours of his sleeping face. Dragging herself away, she began her preparations. She wanted everything to be perfect before he awoke. As quietly as possible she got the fire going, set the table with a freshly laundered tablecloth and her grandmother's best china service, and prepared breakfast. He would need a hearty meal before he braved the day.

She placed the bacon, eggs, tomatoes and fried bread in the oven and tiptoed softly towards him. He was still sound asleep. She hesitated for a moment and looked at the clock. If she didn't wake him now her grandmother would be down and that was the last thing she wanted. She was already late for the wholesaler but that did not concern her. She still had all the produce left from yesterday and the cold of the night would have preserved it well enough to be sold today.

She quickly made her decision. Leaning over, she gently shook his arm. 'Stephen,' she said softly. There was no response so she shook his arm again. He roused and moaned loudly. Rolling over, he opened his eyes and his face creased in pain.

'Oh God, my head.' He groaned again, trying to focus. 'Josie!' he grimaced as she swam into view. 'What are you doing here?' He tried to sit up and fell back. 'Where the hell am I?'

'It's all right, darling,' she said softly. 'You're at my house.'

'What!' he exclaimed. 'How on earth did I get here?'

Josie gasped and stepped back in alarm. 'Don't you remember?' she asked, her happiness cruelly disintegrating.

'Remember . . .' Stephen raised himself up and placed his head in his hands. 'The last thing I remember is going into the off licence to buy a bottle of vodka. Oh, Josie, have I been here all night?'

Nausea swept over her. Her legs trembled and a shamed embarrassment flooded through her. 'Er . . . yes. You were rather drunk and fell asleep.'

'Did I! I'm so sorry,' he said apologetically. 'I hope I wasn't any trouble?'

She swallowed hard. 'Oh, it was no bother,' she said lightly. She turned away from him so he could not see the tears in her eyes. 'I've . . . er . . . I've made you some breakfast.'

'No, no. Thanks, Josie, but I couldn't eat anything.' He slowly raised himself up and ran his hands through his hair, grimacing as another pain shot through his temple. 'I hope you didn't put yourself out just for me?'

The inviting smell of the freshly cooked breakfast reached her nostrils, and the sight of the neatly laid table caught her eye. 'No, I had to cook for my grandmother anyway.'

'I could murder a cup of tea,' he said hopefully.

Without answering she made her way to the kitchen and poured him a mug of tea. When she returned he was leaning against the side of the fireplace, the blanket folded neatly across the chair. She handed the mug to him. She stood in silence as he drank and handed the empty mug back to her.

'Look, I'd better be off,' he said, eyeing her sheepishly. 'My mother has probably got the whole of the Leicester Police Force out looking for me.' He put his hand on her arm. 'Thanks for letting me stop, Josie,' he said sincerely. 'It was really good of you.' He made his way towards the door, then stopped and turned to face her. 'I don't think I'll manage the cafe today somehow, I feel dreadful. It'll be a long time before I touch a drink again.' He managed a brief smile. 'I'll see you soon, Josie.' He paused and eyed her warily. 'Er . . . you won't mention this to Marilyn, will you? Only she'll make a fool of me.'

Josie shook her head. 'No. No, I won't tell Marilyn,' she said distantly.

'Thanks,' he said in relief as he turned and left the house.

Josie stumbled towards the table and sank down. She rested her arms on the top as tears of despair flowed unashamedly down her cheeks. What a stupid fool she had been. He couldn't even remember what had taken place between them, and she had been daft enough to plan their future. 'Oh, God, what am I going to do?' she cried. She laid her head on her arms and sobbed.

Chapter Three

The wind whipped mercilessly through the stalls and Josie shivered uncontrollably as she twisted the corners of a brown paper bag and handed it to the old lady.

'Two shillings, me duck,' she said, trying her hardest to smile.

'Bloody daylight robbery if you ask me,' the old lady grumbled. 'One and three for two pounds a' Brussels, and 'alf of 'em look rotten to me.'

'Well, they're out of season . . .'

'Out of season! Yer daft lump! It's winter. Yer don't get Brussels in summer, do yer?'

Josie smiled meekly. 'No. Sorry. Look, just give us a shilling then.'

'Oh, right.' The old lady chuckled as she handed over the shilling piece, grabbed the bag and scuttled away.

'Josie, what's wrong with yer?' Marilyn asked, rubbing her gloved hands together. 'You've had a face like a bucket since I arrived and you've hardly said two words to me. It's bad enough having to work on the stall at all, without you having a mardy.'

Josie looked at her cousin and shook her head. 'It's nothing,' she said lightly. 'I just got out of bed the wrong side, that's all. She paused for a moment and took a deep breath. 'Look, Marilyn, Stephen came round last night and he was really upset . . .'

'Stephen!' Marilyn cut in sharply. 'Oh, I can't be bothered about him at the moment, I've other things on me mind.' She kicked at a potato that had fallen on the ground. 'Anyway, you ain't answered me question. What's wrong with yer?'

'I said nothing,' Josie snapped back. 'I'm just feeling a bit under the weather. I didn't get much sleep last night.'

'All right. There's no need to get shirty,' Marilyn fumed. 'Anyway, who wouldn't be feeling grotty on a day like this? It's cold enough to freeze a boiled kettle in two seconds flat.' She wrapped her arms round her body and did a little jig. 'I'll never understand what you see in all this, Josie. This job's pure purgatory to me.'

She smiled wistfully as she weighed out three pounds of King Edwards, accepted one shilling and sixpence and put it in the money pouch strapped around her waist.

'I can't explain it, Marilyn. It's everything. The people, the humour, even the smell of rotting veggies.' She paused for a moment and gazed out over the crowded market place, her eyes taking in the hordes of shoppers, all tightly wrapped in their thick winter woollies, pushing and shoving their way through the maze of stalls. She smiled at the cries of the other stall holders, trying to entice the shoppers to buy their wares. 'Don't you feel the excitement? Every day's different. There's always something going on, always something happening. I just love it. I can't imagine doing anything else.' She bent and picked up a sprout and examined it. 'That woman was right,' she said, ashamed. 'These Brussels are rotten. But I don't think it's because they were left in the van overnight, I think it's because we're being palmed off at the wholesalers. Since Old Wilson died and his son took over, the standards have gone down. I wonder what the other traders think?'

Marilyn looked casually at the vegetables. 'Look all right to me. People are buying 'em anyway, so does it matter?'

'Matter? Of course it matters. Maybe people are buying, but they won't come back to us when they get home and realise half the stuff'll be rotten by tomorrow.' She threw the sprout into the rubbish box on the ground, and sighed. 'We've got to find another wholesaler. Wilson's can't have the monopoly in Leicester.' She looked at Marilyn who was by now gazing across the stalls towards a dark-haired man examining some socks. She nudged her sharply in the ribs. 'A' you listening to me?'

Marilyn jumped. 'Yeah, course. We need to get a new wholesaler,' she repeated nonchalantly. 'Well, you deal with it, Josie, you're much better than me at things like that.'

'Marilyn, this is our livelihood we're talking about. We don't make half as much money as we should. We should have put in for the stall next to ours when we had the chance. We'd have doubled our output and profit. We could have diversified even.'

'What's that mean?'

'You went to school,' Josie said sharply. 'Oh, I forgot, you weren't there half the time,' she said sarcastically. 'Too busy larking about to learn anything. It means we could have tried to sell something besides vegetables and fruit.' She noticed her cousin had lost interest again. 'Marilyn!'

'Yeah, I'm listening. Look, Josie, I ain't really all that bothered. As long as I get me wages, I couldn't care less what we sell or what happens to the stall.'

Josie's temper rose. 'Well, in that case, why don't you do us all a favour and pack it in, then I could employ someone who is interested?'

34

Marilyn folded her arms and stared at Josie in defiance. 'When I'm good and ready.'

'Well, the sooner the better. It'll be heaven having someone full-time.'

Marilyn frowned fiercely. 'I promised to be here this morning and I am, ain't I?'

'Yes, I suppose. But that's only 'cos you've got a hairdresser's appointment this afternoon.'

Marilyn sniffed loudly. She looked through the stalls towards the clock on top of the Corn Exchange. 'I'll take me tea break now. I need to get some stockings from Jim's stall. He's got some Pretty Polly imperfects on sale for one and elevenpence ha'penny. I thought I'd get a few pairs.'

Josie nodded, glad to get rid of Marilyn for a few moments. They were only halfway through the morning and the strain was telling on her. She could only pray that she managed to get through the remainder of the day without breaking down. Beneath the surface she felt desolate and wanted nothing more than to crawl into bed and hide under the covers and be alone. But that would be impossible. It wouldn't take long for her grandmother to notice and demand to know what the matter was.

'Well, I'm off then,' Marilyn said, breaking in on her thoughts.

'Okay,' Josie muttered wearily. 'Don't be long, eh? I'm desperate for a cuppa meself.'

'I said I'd be back and I will.' Marilyn paused and looked with concern at her cousin. 'You don't look well, you know.'

'I told yer,' Josie snapped, 'it's nothing.

'Suit yerself,' said Marilyn as she grabbed her bag and headed off.

For once, Marilyn kept her promise. Half an hour later Josie poked her head round the door of the cafe, her eyes darting around the crowded tables. She sighed with relief. Stephen was nowhere in sight. He was hopefully still in bed, nursing an almighty hangover. She joined the queue at the counter.

'Usual is it, love?' Before Josie could answer Rene Kingsman turned and bellowed through the hatch that led into the kitchen: 'Two bacon and egg cobs, Alfie.' She turned back to face Josie, grabbed a mug and began to fill it with strong brewed tea. 'I believe I have you to thank for looking after my son last night? I didn't know he was still out 'til I saw him creeping in this morning. He'd had a right skinful, I could smell it on him. He's suffering for it, I can tell you. I can honestly say I've never seen him in such a state. I just hope his dad don't find out or there'll be trouble. He don't mind the lads having a drink, but he don't hold with them getting

35

so drunk they can't find their way home.' She smiled warmly at Josie. 'I hope he wasn't any bother?'

'No, no. He wasn't, honestly,' she answered lightly.

Rene waved away the proffered money as she turned and collected the plate of food and placed it on the counter. 'Have this on me, me duck. It's the least I can do.' She lifted the lid on a glass container, selected a Chelsea bun and put it alongside the cobs. 'I just thank God he never spent the night slumped in some shop doorway.'

Josie nodded a thank you, picked up the plate and a mug of tea. Noticing an empty table in the far corner, she quickly made her way over and sat down. She pushed the plate of food away. It would stick in her throat so there was no point in trying to eat. Besides she wasn't hungry and doubted whether she ever would be again. She stirred in two heaped spoons of sugar from the container on the table and supped gratefully at the hot liquid. The smell of greasy food and the hum of conversation were soon lost upon her as she sat alone with her thoughts.

'Hiya, Josie. Marilyn said I'd find yer here.'

Josie's head jerked up and she turned to see Judith Manship, a friend of Marilyn's, standing beside her, a mug of coffee in her hand. She inched around the table and sat down.

'How's things then?' she asked, putting down the mug and loosening her sheepskin coat.

Josie stared at the girl, bemused. Marilyn and Judy had been friends for years, and as far as she could remember this girl had never spoken more than two words to her. She was what Josie would describe as a 'hard nut', living for the moment and not allowing anything to interfere with her pleasures. Like Marilyn she dressed in the latest fashions and today she looked as though she had stepped from the pages of *FAB*. Beneath her coat she wore maroon hipster trousers held up by a thick black leather belt, her black ribbed polo neck jumper accentuated her fashionable flat bosom, her jet black hair was cut in a Mary Quant geometrical style, and from her ears hung large black and white plastic earrings. She was a very pretty girl and much sought after by the boys at the Leicester College of Art and Technology where, according to rumour, she was fairly free with her favours.

Judy was eyeing the plate Josie had pushed away. 'You gonna eat those, Josie?' She shook her head. 'Well, waste not, want not.' Judy grinned as she pulled the plate forward and took a large bite out of a cob. She wiped several crumbs and a sliver of egg yolk from the corner of her mouth. 'So, what's new then?' she asked again.

Josie shrugged her shoulders. 'Nothing,' she replied. The last thing she felt like was making conversation with this girl. They had nothing in common and she couldn't for the life of her think why

36

Judy was here and acting as though they had been friends for years.

Judy took another bite of the cob and a sip of coffee. 'Ah, come on, Josie, there must be something,' she mumbled. 'Read any good books lately?'

'One or two,' she replied offhandedly.

Silence prevailed whilst Judy finished the cob. She smacked her lips and pushed away the plate. 'I enjoyed that, I was starving. Ain't you gonna eat anything?'

Josie shook her head. 'No, I ain't hungry.'

Judy pulled a face. 'Unusual for you, ain't it? Marilyn says yer always stuffing yer face. Anyway, fancy coming out tonight?'

Josie's mouth dropped open. 'Pardon?'

'I said, d'yer fancy coming out tonight?'

'Me go out with you?'

'Yeah, why not? Might make a change for yer. Marilyn said you weren't doing anything tonight.'

'Marilyn! What's she got to do with this?'

'Nothing,' Judy said quickly. 'She just said you were down in the dumps and could do with some cheering up. So I thought you might like to go for a drink, that's all.'

'Oh.' Josie thought for a moment. 'No thanks. I've a few things to do tonight. But it was nice of you to ask.'

Was it her imagination or did she see a look of relief cross Judy's face? The girl stood up and fastened her coat.

'I'll be off then. See yer around, Josie.'

She inclined her head and stared down into her mug. The tea was practically cold but nevertheless she took a long drink. Ten minutes later Judy returned. She plonked a fresh mug of tea in front of Josie and sat down again.

'Er . . . how about one night next week?'

'Next week?'

'Yeah, to go out.' She leant her arms on the table. 'Come on, Josie. It'll do you good. You can't spend all yer time in front of the telly. Before you know it you'll be old and grey, and by then it's too late to have any fun. We could go dancing or summat. You'd like that.'

Josie scratched her chin thoughtfully. 'Do you really want me to come?'

'Yeah, 'course I do or I wouldn't be asking,' Judy said, pushing the mug of tea further forward. 'Drink that up whilst it's hot.'

'Oh . . . thanks,' she said absent-mindedly. Adding two spoons of sugar, she took a sip and raised her eyes. 'I would like to go dancing. I've never bin before.'

'Well, that's settled then. We'll make arrangements for next week.'

Judy looked at her thoughtfully. 'Have you always worked on the

37

stall? Ain't yer ever wanted to do anything else? Seems a bit of a boring life to me, and yer have to get up early.'

Josie smiled. 'Yes, it can get you down, the early starts. But I love the work. You meet lots of interesting people.'

'Do yer? I wouldn't have thought so.'

Josie laughed. 'Everyone has to eat, Judy, and it's surprising the number of people who buy a pound a' carrots and, while fiddling in their purses, proceed to tell their life stories, especially the old 'uns. Some of them are right characters.' She stared wistfully into space. 'I had plans to go to university at one time, but my mother's death meant there was no one to run the family business. I was quite upset once but now I'm glad. I love the work and can't imagine doing anything else.' She leaned on the table, her eyes shining. 'The market goes back hundreds of years, you know. It was originally sited on the Humberstone Gate until the council moved it to its present site here in Cheapside, and it has been said that you can buy anything on the market if you know the right people.' She suddenly stopped, blushed and lowered her head. 'Sorry, Judy, I was getting carried away. I didn't mean to bore yer.'

She shrugged her shoulders. 'Oh, that's all right. I could talk about men 'til the cows come home.' She picked up her mug and drained the dregs. 'Well, I'd better be going. I'm off round the shops.' She paused for a moment. 'What a' you doing this afternoon? D'yer fancy a browse round the shops?'

Josie's face lit up then dropped. 'Oh, I can't. I've left Marilyn on her own. If I don't get back she'll have a fit.'

Judy laughed. 'Oh, sod Marilyn. I know for a fact she leaves you high and dry all the time. So turn the tables for once. Leave her on her own and see how she likes it.'

'Oh, I can't. Anyway, I thought you were her friend?'

'I am. But it wouldn't be the first time Marilyn has done it across me. She's left me standing more than once outside Timothy White's whilst she was somewhere else with some bloke. Come on, Josie. It'll be fun.'

Josie's face lit up in pleasure. It would make a change. She hadn't been round the shops for ages, and since her mother had died never with company. She quickly made her decision.

'Okay,' she breathed. 'I'd love to but I haven't any money.'

'Neither have I. But who cares?'

Josie followed Judy out of the door. As they turned the corner, she bumped straight into Stephen. She gulped hard and her legs trembled as he caught hold of her arm, his handsome face close to hers. The effects of last night's escapades were still visible. As he looked down at her, a concerned expression appeared on his face.

'There you are, Josie. I've been looking everywhere.' He pulled her to one side. 'I need to talk to you.' He took a deep breath. 'Look, about last night . . .' He paused.

She reddened and lowered her face, staring intently at the cracks in the pavement. 'Oh, it's all right, Stephen,' she cut in. 'You were drunk and stayed the night. No big deal,' she lied. Her heart thumped loudly and she hoped he could not hear it.

'A' you coming?' Judy shouted tartly.

Stephen glowered angrily across at her. He turned his attention back to Josie. 'Look, we can't talk here. Can we go somewhere? I do need to talk. Please, Josie?'

She froze. In other circumstances she would have followed Stephen anywhere but after last night all she wanted was to get as far away as possible from him. Besides he would only want to talk about Marilyn and she couldn't face that.

'I have an appointment and if I don't hurry I'll be late,' she said firmly.

'Well, tonight,' he insisted. 'I'll meet you somewhere or come around to your house.'

'No, don't!' she shouted, much louder than she'd intended. In her confusion she missed the hurt expression that appeared on his face. 'I'm busy. I'm going out.' She pulled her arm free and moved across to join Judy. 'Are we ready then?' she said without a backward glance. 'We'd better go before the shops shut.'

Josie hadn't had so much fun for years. The pair visited every shop and store in the town centre. They tried on hats and coats, laughed themselves silly in Marshall & Snelgrove's wig department, and tested lipsticks and perfumes until there was none left to try. They arrived back in the market square as the clock in the town hall square struck four.

Josie rested her back against the window of the Pork Farms Pie Shop and exhaled loudly.

'Oh, Judy, I ain't enjoyed myself so much for ages.'

Judy giggled. 'Neither have I. I don't know about you but I smell like a Persian prostitute.' She paused. 'I never realised you were so much fun.'

Josie blushed. 'I thought I'd die when you made that snobby assistant in Lea's take out all those fur coats. You should have been an actress, Judy. I think she honestly thought you had money.'

'Served her right. Did you see her face when we walked in? She looked down her nose at us. Well, I don't like that so I put on me act. I do it quite often. I love to see their faces when I eventually tell them that I can't afford their rotten stuff anyway.' Judy delved into her pocket and pulled out a lipstick. 'Here, I got you this, thought you might like it.'

Josie stared at the lipstick in astonishment. 'For me?' She looked at Judy searchingly. 'But I never saw you buying anything. You said you had no money.'

Judy shrugged her shoulders. 'Must have bought it when you weren't looking,' she said cagily. She thrust it once more in Josie's direction. 'A' you gonna take it or what? You can wear it when we go out.'

Josie's face lit up in pleasure. 'Ta, Judy. That was a nice thought.' She put the lipstick in her pocket and smiled at her warmly. 'Well, thanks for a lovely afternoon. All I have to do now is face Marilyn.'

'I've told yer before, don't worry about her. I'll call by in the week to make some arrangements for our night out. Okay?'

'Okay,' Josie agreed. She turned and headed off towards the stall. Lightheartedness came over her. She'd had a wonderful afternoon and now that she knew Judy better was looking forward to her night out. Maybe things are looking up for me at last, she thought with pleasure. All she had to do was put the events of last night behind her.

She was greeted by Marilyn's stony face.

'Where the bloody hell have you bin? D'you know how long you've been away? Nearly four hours. Four bloody hours! You've got a nerve, our Josie.' Marilyn stamped her foot in temper. 'Not only have I had to run this stall by meself but I've missed me hairdressing appointment as well, and you knew how much I wanted me hair done. How could you be so thoughtless, Josie?'

She lowered her eyes in shame. 'I'm sorry, Marilyn, I completely forgot about your appointment. I thought you wouldn't mind. It's not often I get the chance of an afternoon off.'

'Huh!' Marilyn fumed. 'Well, where did you go?'

Josie's face lit up. 'Round the shops with your friend Judy.' She delved into her pocket. 'Look, she bought me a lipstick. Wasn't that nice of her?'

Marilyn eyed the lipstick with disdain. 'Bought? More like thieved. Judy's the best shoplifter I know,' she muttered under her breath.

'What did yer say? I didn't catch that.'

'Oh, nothing.' Marilyn paced backwards and forwards as she tried to calm her temper. She succeeded and smiled sweetly at Josie. 'A' yer . . . er . . . doing anything else with her?' she asked casually.

Josie turned to serve a customer. 'Oh, yes. We're going for a night out.'

'When?'

Josie frowned as she handed over the bag of leeks and parsnips and accepted the money. 'Sometime next week. Why?'

40

'Nothing. Just interested.' She breathed deeply. 'Friday would be a good night. Everyone goes out on a Friday.'

'I don't care what night it is,' Josie said excitedly. 'A' you gonna come with us?' she asked as she thought would be expected of her.

'Oh, no. I'll probably be busy anyway.' Marilyn bent down and gathered up her bag. 'I'm off.'

'What!'

'I said I'm off. You've been gallivanting all afternoon so now it's my turn. With a bit of luck, the hairdressers might still manage to fit me in.'

Before Josie could retaliate Marilyn had scooted off, leaving her for the second time in two days to clear up by herself. Still that was no problem, she was used to it by now. It was then that she remembered she had done nothing about the van. It was still at the back of the Corn Exchange with a broken starter motor.

'Damn!' she fumed. Still, at least the snow had kept off which meant the buses were running.

Two old dears and a mother with four young children thought that the woman on the stall must be mad as she filled their baskets and shopping bags with the last of the produce and charged them two shillings for the lot. This action gave Josie much pleasure as she saw the look of confusion on their faces change to happiness. After all, it was no loss to her or her grandmother. As this was Saturday night the goods would not keep until the following Monday.

An hour after Marilyn's departure, an exhausted Josie finally made her way towards the bus station and home.

'Thanks, Big Jack,' Josie said sincerely. 'How much do I owe yer?'

Big Jack Bates straightened his back and rubbed his oily hands on an old cloth. 'Nothing, Josie lass. I'd do anything for you and yer gran.'

'But it's a Sunday . . .'

'I know that. You just tell your granny we're quits for the time being.'

'Eh! I don't follow yer?'

Big Jack smiled warmly and patted Josie on the shoulder. 'You might not, but yer granny will.'

'Oh.' Josie breathed deeply and dug her hands down into her pockets. 'Well, I must say, it'll be good to have the van back on the road. I've been lost without it.'

'I bet you have. It's a pity you don't know much about engines. You could have fixed the battery cable yerself.'

Josie blushed.

Big Jack pulled on his coat. 'Right, I'll be off. I've another car to look at before I get to go for me Sunday lunchtime pint, and if I'm late for me dinner Gwen will batter me senseless.'

'Thanks again, Jack,' said Josie before she climbed behind the wheel and turned the ignition key. The engine purred into life and she smiled gratefully.

Later Josie sat facing her grandmother across the table as they ate their Sunday dinner.

'What did Big Jack mean about being quits, Gran?'

Lily tightened her lips. 'Nothing.'

'What d'yer mean, nothing? A man like him doesn't waive the bill for nothing, Gran, and especially not on a Sunday. So what did he mean?'

Lily raised her head and banged down her fork. 'I said nothing. Just mind yer business, and finish yer dinner before it gets cold.'

Chapter Four

'Hiya, Josie. All set for tonight?'

She hurriedly finished serving a customer and looked at Judy in astonishment. 'Tonight! That's a bit short notice. To be honest I thought you'd forgotten, being's you hadn't been around.'

Judy sidled around the stall, picked up an apple and casually bit into it. 'Sorry about that, I've been busy. Marilyn not around?'

'Ain't seen her all day. She went off yesterday lunchtime and I ain't seen her since. To be honest, I'm a bit worried. It wouldn't be the first time she's gone off, but it's not usually for this length of time.'

Judy shrugged her shoulders nonchalantly. 'Shouldn't worry if I was you. She'll turn up, she always does.'

'Yeah. But it's what she's got up to in the meantime that worries me. I don't know whether to go round and see me auntie and uncle, just to check she ain't ill or 'ote.' Josie frowned and bit her bottom lip. 'Only I ain't keen on doing that. Me and me uncle don't get on very well.'

'I told yer, she'll turn up,' Judy said quickly. She took a casual look round. 'If you want a hand, I'll help.'

Josie eyed the girl keenly. 'Would yer? Only I'm desperate for the loo and I've some shopping to do.'

'Well, go then. I'll watch the stall for yer.'

'Would yer! Oh, thanks, Judy.' Josie's face lit up. 'I'm ever so grateful. I was just about to ask Ma Simpson but she's done it for me twice today already. It's a bugger managing two stalls at once, 'specially on a busy day like this.' She grabbed her bag. 'The prices are all marked so you won't have any trouble. I shan't be more than half an hour.' She made to walk away, paused then turned back. 'You will be careful to weigh things properly and give the right change? Only I'm a bit particular on things like that, and the old folks, well, they'll watch yer like a hawk . . .'

'Josie, just go. And take your time. I'll be fine.'

Judy watched as Josie weaved her way through the stalls towards the public toilets on Horsefair Street. She was wearing a muddy brown pair of crimplene elasticated trousers, a thick fisherman's knit jersey and a bright blue anorak, with her striped woollen hat pulled down over her ears. What a sight! Judy thought wickedly. I hope to God she's got something decent to wear tonight or I'll be embarrassed. She turned to serve her first customer.

'Three pounds of spuds, Brussels, carrots, pound a' cookers, and onions. That'll be seven and six. Seven bob to you.' Judy eyed the young woman and waited, her hand outstretched.

'Seven shillings! That's a bit steep. I think you'd better add that up again,' she demanded as she delved into her purse and sorted through her change.

'I added correctly,' Judy said haughtily. 'If you want the best, you've got to pay for it.'

The woman begrudgingly handed over the money. 'There's one thing for certain, I shan't be shopping here again,' she grumbled as she walked away.

Judy smirked as she slipped the two half crowns and two shilling pieces into her coat pocket.

A breathless Josie arrived back half an hour later. 'Oh, that's better. Everything all right?' she said, placing her shopping underneath the stall and pulling her woolly hat further down over her ears.

'No problem.' Judy beamed jubilantly. 'Piece of cake, this market lark.'

Josie smiled gratefully as she opened the cash box and took out a half crown coin. She handed it to Judy. 'Here's for yer trouble. I did appreciate it.'

Judy accepted the money. 'No need for that, Josie, but ta anyway.' She put the half crown in her pocket with the rest of the money she had stolen. 'So are we on for tonight? Thought we'd go to the Il Rondo.'

'Il Rondo?' Josie repeated, wiping her hand across her forehead. 'I haven't got anything good enough to wear for a place like that.'

Judy inwardly groaned. 'But you must have something? Haven't you got a dress?'

'Well . . . yeah.'

'That's it then. I'll call for yer about eight. Okay?'

'Er . . . yes, all right then.'

Judy laughed. 'Don't look so worried. You'll enjoy yerself, take my word for it. They play some fabulous music. Searchers, Yardbirds, Stones and Tamla Motown.'

'Tamla Motown. Oh, I like that.'

'Good. About eight then, and if you're a bit short, I've plenty of money for the drinks.'

Josie felt a thrill rush up in her. She was going dancing. Good old Josie Rawlings was going dancing, and after a week like she'd had, it was just the tonic she needed.

Avoiding Stephen had been a nightmare. Her twice-daily visits to the cafe had ceased and on the several occasions she had spotted him making his way over to the stall, she had fled on some meagre pretext, leaving either Marilyn or Ma Simpson to cope in her absence. She couldn't face him, not after that night, not for anything. As far as she was aware he still had no memory of what had taken place. But she had. She relived the memories every night as she lay in her bed, hot shame filling her very soul as she remembered how she had willingly given herself to him. At least he had the excuse of being drunk. She didn't.

Well, tonight she wouldn't have time to think. She was going out and looking forward to it.

At four-thirty sharp, Josie started to pack up the stall. She had had a good day, selling most of the produce, and her grandmother would be pleased.

All the empty wooden crates and rubbish dealt with, she started the van and headed home.

'Out! What d'you wanna go out for? Ain't my company good enough?'

'Yes, 'course it is, Gran. It's only for one night and I won't be late home. Anyway, for as long as I can remember you've gone down the pub on a Friday. I'll more than likely be home before you are.'

'Huh, well,' Lily grumbled, 'I probably won't bother tonight, it's icy out there. I might fall all me length and freeze to death. And what if someone breaks in?' Her thin voice rose hysterically. 'I could be strangled in me own house, with no one to stop 'em.'

'Gran, stop it!' Josie snapped. 'It's only one night out. Anyone would think I was leaving home for good.'

Lily's small grey eyes widened in alarm. 'Oh, our Josie, you wouldn't do that. This is your home. You wouldn't leave me would yer?'

Josie sighed deeply. 'No, 'course I wouldn't. I'm just going out, that's all. You should be glad that I ain't like Marilyn. She goes out every night.' She walked over and hugged her grandmother tenderly. 'If you don't go down the pub, there is lots to see on the telly. You can watch Bonanza and tell me what happens to Little Joe and Hoss.'

'Oh, that tripe. Don't know why you watch it, our Josie. It's just drivel to me.'

'You love it, Gran, so don't tell fibs.'

'Huh, but I'll still be on me own.' Lily sighed forlornly. 'You just go out and enjoy yourself. Don't you give me another thought. I'll be all right.'

45

'Good, then I'll go and make yer dinner,' Josie said, smiling happily.

Josie quickly made her grandmother a large fry up of sausage, liver, egg, fried bread and tomatoes, and placed it before her.

'I'm not hungry,' she snapped.

Josie picked up the plate. 'Okay, I'll throw it away.'

Lily gaped. 'Leave it! I might as well eat it now. No point in throwing good food away.'

The corners of Josie's mouth twitched as she suppressed a smile. She placed the plate back on the table. 'Right, I'm off to get ready.'

Before Lily could say another word, she turned and walked from the room. In her bedroom she switched on her gas fire and waited for a moment for the heat to penetrate the room before she undressed. She knew she should have switched it on earlier, the little warmth it threw out would barely take the chill off the icy room. Over the past few days the temperature had fallen even lower and although it was only the end of November, people were beginning to talk of a white Christmas.

She placed her Tamla Motown Hits on the record player and took the only decent item of clothing she possessed out of her wardrobe and held it up. The lime green A-line dress with its V neck had been purchased from a colleague off the market several months previously. It was a generous size 16 and Josie, on finding the dress fitted with a squeeze, had spent some of her hard-earned savings, glad that she had for once managed to buy something that was halfway decent and fashionable. Its hem finished just above her knees, not quite short enough to show off her fat legs but short enough to be classed 'with it'. She rummaged in her drawer and pulled out a bright orange scarf. She nodded. Tied around her neck, cowboy-style, and tucked down into the V it would finish off the outfit.

She finished brushing her hair and carefully applied white eyeshadow and black eyeliner, remnants that Marilyn had left behind, and a touch of the pale pink lipstick that Judy had given her. She stood back and admired herself in the long wardrobe mirror. She felt nice. She'd never had the occasion really to dress up before and it was a change to get out of her shabby market clothing. She ran her hands over her body and turned sideways, breathing in as deep as she could to pull in her stomach. It had little effect.

Undeterred, she turned towards the wall and glanced at the many posters and pictures of favourite pop stars which she had stuck up with flour and water paste.

'Well, what d'you think?' she said aloud, giving a twirl.

The front door knocker startled her and she frowned. It was a little too early for Judy and she would have to answer the door. Her grandmother wouldn't, not while Josie was there to do it.

Cursing mildly, she ran down the stairs and yanked the door open.

'Stephen!' she gasped.

He smiled and ran his hand nervously through his thick hair. 'Hello, Josie. I'm glad I've caught you at last.' He noticed her clothes. 'You look nice,' he said admiringly.

Josie lowered her eyes shyly. 'Thank you,' she whispered. She took a deep breath and raised her head. It was then she noticed the box of chocolates he was trying to hide behind his back. 'Marilyn's not here. I ain't seen her for a couple of days . . .'

'It's not Marilyn I've come to see, Josie. It's you.'

'Oh!' she exclaimed. She shifted uncomfortably. 'I've already told you, Stephen. About the other night . . .' She lowered her face. 'It's okay, you staying . . . it was no bother, honest.' Her legs began to tremble. Oh, why did he have to come around tonight of all nights? 'Look, I've got to go. I'm going out.'

'Are you?' he said, dismayed. 'Oh! Anywhere nice?'

'Yes, dancing.' She raised her head, still managing to avoid his eyes. 'I'm going dancing at the Il Rondo.'

Just then Judy appeared. She looked nonchalantly at Stephen.

'Hi,' she said, addressing Josie as she pushed past him. She gave Josie the once over. 'Aren't you ready yet? You'd better hurry and change else we'll be late.'

Josie stared at her blankly. 'I am ready,' she said.

'Oh. Oh, well, I suppose you'll do.' She turned to Stephen. 'You waiting for a bus or summat?' she said sarcastically.

Josie blushed with embarrassment.

Stephen raised his eyebrows, his face set firmly. 'I need to speak to you, Josie. I'll call some other time.' He looked in Judy's direction. 'When it's more convenient.' He turned back to face Josie and leaned closer. 'I'd watch her if I was you. Marilyn and her make a good pair. But you,' his eyes softened, 'you're a different kettle of fish.'

Josie watched silently as Stephen turned abruptly, stuffed the box of chocolates down into his pocket, pulled up the collar on his coat and headed down the icy path. She wished with all her heart he hadn't come. But, regardless, nothing was going to spoil her night out.

'I'm off then, Gran,' she said lightly as she bent over and kissed the old woman on the cheek. 'The fire's banked up and I've made a sandwich in case you feel peckish later on.'

Lily prised her eyes off Take Your Pick and sniffed loudly. She pressed her hand into Josie's. 'Enjoy yerself,' she said gruffly.

Josie opened her hand and stared agog at the ten shilling note.

'Ah, Gran,' she said as tears of gratitude stung the back of her eyes.

'I want it back if yer don't spend it,' Lily said sharply. 'And mind you watch yerself with those lads. An innocent gel like you is easy prey . . .'

Josie smiled warmly as she bent over and kissed her grandmother again.

'I promise I won't do anything you wouldn't, Gran, and thanks for the money.'

Chapter Five

Josie lost count of the number of public houses they visited before they finally made their way along Silver Street towards the Il Rondo. Her heart quickened as they neared their destination. She was glad now that she had succumbed to Judy's chiding and accepted the rum and blacks that had been thrust upon her. They had quickly taken effect and she felt light-headed and carefree as she handed over her entrance fee and left her coat.

Patting her hair and smoothing her hands over her dress, she placed herself behind Judy as they pushed their way up the stairs towards the main dance area. The place was packed to bursting with teenagers milling around or dancing on the large dance floor. The music of Jimmy James and the Vagabonds blasted out from the discotheque housed at the side of a small stage set at the far end of the room, and the disc jockey, dressed in a shocking pink shirt, canary yellow hipster trousers and dark sunglasses, was gyrating to the music as he expertly cued the next record.

Judy looked stunning. Her minuscule pale blue dress with matching earrings and thigh-length black synthetic leather boots suited her figure perfectly. Josie couldn't help but notice the number of admiring stares the girl received as she glided across the floor, Josie's own large expanse of lime green and orange in close pursuit.

The bar was three deep in people and whilst they waited their turn, Josie looked around her in awe. She could never remember feeling so excited. Her feet tapped rhythmically to Little Eva's 'Locomotion' and her eyes sparkled as she watched the dancers moving to the pounding beat.

Judy soon joined her, and after downing their drinks they shoved their way to the middle of the floor, threw down their handbags and began to dance.

'Loosen up, Josie,' Judy shouted over the music. 'You're dancing like a stuffed dummy. Let yourself go.' She swung her arms in the air and did a twirl expertly in time to the beat.

Josie tried to follow suit and nearly lost her balance, closely avoiding a collision with a group of girls dancing next to them. Judy roughly grabbed her arm.

'Come on, let's have a breather,' she said, trying to hide her disgust as she guided Josie to the side of the dance floor. 'You've got to relax, Josie. You'll do yourself damage dancing like that.'

She bit her lip, ashamed. 'I'm sorry, Judy. I can't dance, it's no good . . .'

'Oh, everyone can dance,' Judy erupted, 'Just watch them on the floor. It's easy.'

'Yeah, it does look like it,' Josie agreed. 'But me legs won't do what me brain's telling 'em,' she laughed.

Judy exhaled loudly. 'Well, let's get another couple of drinks down you and then they might, with a bit of luck.'

'Judy.'

She turned abruptly to face two men and smiled in recognition. 'Hello, Damien, Trevor.'

'Fancy a drink?' Damien said, eyeing her openly.

'Yeah. I'll have a gin and orange.' She grabbed hold of Damien's arm and made to walk off with him. She suddenly stopped and turned back. 'Oh, by the way, this is Josie, Marilyn Rawlings' cousin.' She turned to Josie. 'Damien and Trevor are from the College. We're all on the same course.' She let go of Damien's arm and pulled Josie aside. 'For God's sake, Josie, look a bit more interested. We could have a good time with these two.'

Josie gulped hard and tried to place an inviting smile on her face. The two, tall skinny men were dressed identically in maroon mohair tight-trousered suits and white frilly shirts. Their dark brown hair was cut short in a 'mod' style and their Cuban-heeled black leather Chelsea boots enhanced stick-like legs. They both resembled dolly clothes pegs, she thought. She stiffened as the two men gave her the once over. Her face reddened and her palms felt sticky as their mocking eyes quickly left her and returned to Judy.

'She'll have a rum and black,' Judy said, pulling Josie forward.

'You get them in, Trevor, while we find a seat,' said Damien, grabbing hold of Judy and guiding her over to an empty table.

Josie stood for a moment, unsure whether to stay or follow. She decided on the latter and sat down, hesitantly clutching her handbag in her lap. Damien had his arm draped around Judy's neck and was whispering into her ear. She gave little giggles and playfully slapped his other hand away as it stroked her thigh. The pair totally ignored Josie's presence.

Trevor returned with a tray of drinks. He gave Damien a scornful look as he sat down and took a large gulp of his drink. Taking a deep breath, he turned to Josie.

'You at College?' he asked matter-of-factly.

'Er . . . no,' she answered, pulling nervously on her earlobe. 'I work on the market.'

'Oh?' Trevor turned further round, his face full of interest. 'Get things cheap, do yer?'

Josie nodded. 'Yes.'

He rubbed his hands together. 'Me and you might be able to do business. I've got lots of contacts at the College and elsewhere. What can you get?'

'Whatever you like. I can do yer a good deal on spuds and carrots at the moment.'

'Spuds and carrots?' he said disgustedly. He turned away, giving the girls on the dance floor his full attention.

Damien jumped up and grabbed Judy. 'Come on, let's have a dance.'

Josie watched as Judy and Damien disappeared amongst the throng of dancers.

Trevor took another large gulp of his drink and stood up. 'I'm off to the loo.' Without a backward glance he hurried away.

Josie squirmed in her seat. She prayed that Judy did not intend to stay with these two all night. Her high hopes for the evening were rapidly fading. Suddenly a hand gripped her arm and she cried out in pain. She jerked round to see a middle-aged balding man swaying before her. Several long strands of greasy hair that had been used to cover his thinning pate were hanging down over his ear. The light brown suit he wore was crumpled, the bottom of his olive green shirt hanging out. He banged down his pint glass on the table, slopping some of the contents over her dress. He pushed the strands of hair back over his head and grinned leeringly at her.

'Dance?' he slurred, thrusting his hips in her direction.

'No, thank you,' she mouthed, pulling her arm free.

'No! Wadda you mean, no? You stupid fat cow! I said, dance.' He grabbed her arm again and pulled her up.

'I said, no!' Josie screeched. She pulled herself free again and ran from him to hide behind a pillar. Clutching her bag to her chest, she took several deep breaths and tried to calm herself. Trust me to get the old drunk, she thought ruefully. After several moments she peered around the pillar to make sure the man had gone. He was still there, idling against the table, slopping beer all down his suit. Out of the corner of her eye she saw Damien and Trevor approaching, deep in conversation. She darted back behind the pillar and held her breath as they stopped just short of her.

'Trevor, I ain't asking you to marry the girl, just keep her occupied for a bit. I'd do the same for you.' Damien spoke aggressively. 'Just keep her outta the way, that's all I'm asking. You can dump her as soon as the coast is clear.'

Josie froze in horror as she realised they were talking about her.

'What if someone sees me with her?' Trevor asked harshly. 'It ain't your reputation that's at stake, it's mine.'

Damien placed his arm around Trevor and gripped his shoulder. 'Find a dark corner somewhere.'

'And what?'

Damien shrugged his shoulders. 'I don't know. Use yer imagination. I'm sure you can think of something to do for half an hour. Me and Judy will be gone by then.'

Josie heard Trevor sigh deeply. 'Okay. But I'm warning you, Damien, if anyone sees me . . .'

'That's my man,' he said, a huge grin on his face. 'Here, take the keys to the Vespa, I won't be needing that tonight. We're going to her house.' He gave Trevor a knowing wink. 'Her parents are out and I'm in.'

'Oi? What about the stuff?'

Damien's face darkened. 'Keep your voice down, man. We don't want everyone to know, they'll all be after some.' He paused for a moment, deep in thought. 'That pot was expensive, I'm not wasting it on Judy. She's a greedy pig, that one. If she knows we've got some, she'll want the lot.' He paused. 'Tell you what, I'll come to your pad tomorrow night and we'll have a session. Will your old folks be out?'

'Yes.'

'Good. We can play your records at full blast and get stoned. What d'you say?'

'Great idea.'

Laughing loudly, the two men moved out of earshot.

Josie's stomach lurched and nausea caught the back of her throat. She closed her eyes tightly to stem the flood of tears that threatened. How she wished the ground would open and swallow her. She was an embarrassment. The realisation hit her full force and all she could think of was to get away from this place as quickly as possible. It took all her will-power to regain the use of her legs, and with her head hanging low she dodged through the crowds of people, knocking several flying on the way. She ran down the wooden stairs and thrust her coat ticket at the attendant. Grabbing her coat, she headed for the door and gasped as the ice cold air hit her.

How could people be so cruel? And after Judy had begged her company. Why? Why did she do it? Josie raised her head and took several deep breaths. The rum and blacks she had downed were now giving her a pounding headache. Pulling on her coat, she thrust her hands in her pockets and headed up Silver Street towards St Nicholas Circle. She slipped and slid her way down the icy pavements, and by the time she arrived at her own gate was frozen with cold, her heart heavy and her face streaked with dried tears.

Chapter Six

Josie hesitantly inserted her front door key in the lock and gently turned it, praying her grandmother was either in bed or still down the pub. She could not face a cross-examination. Lily would want to know all the details and especially why she was home so early. Josie could not lie, she would have to tell the truth.

She frowned deeply as the door half opened and then jammed. Something was blocking the way and she had no idea what it could be. She reached for the light switch as she squeezed through the gap and peered around. Behind the door sat two unfamiliar large brown battered suitcases.

She stared blankly at them. Who on earth could they belong to? A loud thud sounded from above and she jumped in fright. Burglars! Someone was ransacking the house.

Instinctively she turned to run, then she remembered her grandmother. Where was she? Had they harmed her? Was she lying in a pool of blood somewhere? Oh, God. What should she do? If anything had happened to Lily, it would be all her fault. She shook with fear.

Pull yourself together, Josie Rawlings, she scolded. Whoever's in this house has no right to be, and you have to do something.

Gingerly she tiptoed down the passage towards the back room. The light from the fire cast long shadows and Josie's shoulders sagged in relief at the absence of any of her grandmother's outdoor clothing and her handbag. This mean she was still out. At least the old lady hadn't been murdered, which was one thing to be thankful for. But whoever was up the stairs had still to be dealt with. She stole over to the fireplace and picked up the heavy brass poker, then turned back and retraced her steps to the bottom of the stairs.

Holding the poker aloft, she took a deep breath and with a tremendous effort raised one leg and placed it carefully on the first step. When she reached the landing she exhaled softly in relief. So far, so good.

Her eyes were fixed upon her grandmother's bedroom door. A sliver of light shone from beneath and she could hear movement coming from inside. Again her instinct was to run, but she knew

53

she could not. Whatever or whoever was in the room had to be faced and she was the only one to do it. By the time she summoned the police the intruders would be long gone and the Rawlingses' belongings with them.

She stood before the door and with a shaking hand grabbed the handle and turned it. She shoved the door hard and charged through.

'Gotcha, yer thieving buggers!' she yelled at the top of her voice, waving the poker menacingly in the air.

The figure kneeling beside the bed swung round in horror and toppled over, landing heavily upon the cold linoleum.

Josie lowered her arm and gaped in disbelief at the person sprawled upon the floor.

'Marilyn!' she cried, bewildered. 'What on earth are you doing? You didn't half give me a fright.'

Marilyn eased herself up into a sitting position and rubbed her head where she had knocked it on the floor. 'I gave *you* a fright? What about me? I thought World War Three had started.'

Josie's eyes darted around the room. All the drawers in the dressing table had been pulled out and the contents tipped over the floor; the same with the wardrobe. Her grandmother's bed had been pushed across the room, a large expanse of missing lino revealed where several floorboards had been pulled up and several empty cardboard shoe boxes lay scattered about. Marilyn was clutching a plastic holdall. She eyed Josie warily as she quickly closed the zipper. Josie's anger rose. She stared at Marilyn with narrowed eyes.

'What are you doing, Marilyn?' she said coldly. She advanced further into the room and stared down at the gaping hole where the floorboards had been lifted and at the empty shoe boxes to the side. She gasped. 'You're stealing Gran's money?' she cried in disbelief. 'Marilyn, you are, aren't you? You're stealing Gran's money!'

Marilyn raised her head and sneered. 'Yeah, I am. I asked you to help me, but you refused. Anyway, it's only a loan, I'll pay it back.'

'Pay it back?' Josie shook her head. 'There'll be no need to pay it back.'

Marilyn looked at her hopefully. 'Won't there?'

'No. 'Cos you're gonna put it all back and get this room sorted out before Gran returns.'

Marilyn clutched the bag tightly. 'I'm not putting it back,' she said defiantly. 'I need this money, Josie. Anyway, it's not stealing, not when it's family.'

''Course it is, you silly bugger. You could be put in prison for what you're doing. Gran'll have a fit when she finds out about this. This'll kill her, yer know.'

'No, it won't. Gran's as tough as old boots. Besides, she don't use the money. Wh.. .ood is it, sitting under the bed?'

'It don't matter ..re it is, Marilyn. It's Gran's money, and what she does with it is no concern of yours. Now put it back.'

'No, I won't,' she spat, clutching the bag even tighter. 'I need this money and I'm having it. You shouldn't have come back so early, then you wouldn't have been involved. Judy promised . . .'

'Judy?' Josie closed her eyes tightly. 'Now I see it. You arranged all this. You needed me out of the house.' She opened her eyes which were now ablaze with anger. 'You bitch, our Marilyn! How could you?'

'Well, I had to do something. You weren't about to let me waltz in here and just take it while you watched the telly, now was yer? Besides, I thought it'd do you good to have a night out.'

'Like hell you did! All you think of is yourself. You never give anyone else a second thought.'

'Oh, shut up, Josie.' Marilyn strode across and pushed her hard on her shoulder. 'Now get outta my way.'

Josie took several steps back and raised the poker. 'You put it back now, Marilyn, or I'll . . . I'll . . .'

Marilyn laughed. 'What? Hit me. No, you won't, Josie Rawlings. You ain't got it in yer. Besides, to make me part with this money you'd have to commit murder.' She tilted her head. 'Are you really a murderess, Josie?' she said mockingly.

The women stared at each other. Finally, Josie lowered her arm. Marilyn gave a little gasp of relief.

'What do yer need the money for?'

'That's my business,' she said haughtily.

Josie raised the poker again. 'You ain't going nowhere 'til yer tell me.'

Marilyn exhaled loudly. 'Oh, all right.' She walked over and perched on the edge of the bed, still clutching the bag tightly. 'I've got the chance to be a top model. This is my tuition money . . .'

'Tuition?'

'Yeah,' Marilyn interrupted. 'I've got to learn, ain't I, and live in the meantime 'til the big money starts rolling in. And there's me clothes. I've got to have decent clothes when I go around the agents.' She pulled at her coat. 'Can't traipse round London expecting to get noticed in these shabby things.'

'London?' Josie gasped.

'Yes, London. I'm off to London to earn me fortune. Only you have to have money to get started and that's why I need Gran's. It would be no good asking me parents. You know what their reaction would be, 'specially me dad's. So this way is the only answer.' She paused. Her shoulders sagged and her voice softened. 'Look,

Josie. You didn't seriously think I was gonna work on the stall for the rest of me life, not with my looks and figure? I've always been destined for better things. I've told you that often enough. But like everyone else, you just thought it pie in the sky. Well, I'm proving you all wrong. I've got a great opportunity and I'm gonna grab it. Hundreds of gels would give their right arm to be getting the opportunity I'm being given. Flavell says . . .'

'Flavell! Who's he when he's at home?'

'Flavell Farnsworth. He's a top producer. He's the one that spotted me. He's gonna guide me, Josie, and introduce me to some important people.' Her eyes lit up in excitement. 'He says I've got great potential.'

Josie ran her fingers through her hair and frowned deeply. 'I don't doubt that, Marilyn. But how did you meet this bloke?'

Marilyn grimaced. 'You're as bad as me dad for questions.' She sighed loudly. 'I met him in the cafe . . .'

'Cafe! Kingsman's Cafe?'

'Yes. And before you start, he was having a cup of tea like everyone else. He had business in Leicester and he sat at my table. We got chatting and it went from there.'

Josie walked slowly over and sat next to her cousin. 'How d'you know he's on the level? Have you checked him out?' she asked more calmly than she felt.

Marilyn jumped up. 'Oh, shut up, Josie. I know he's what he says he is.' She glared angrily. 'You're just jealous. You know you'll never get the opportunity that I have 'cos you're too fat so you want to put doubts in me mind. Well, you won't. I'm off to London to make me fortune, and neither you nor anyone else is gonna stop me.'

Josie jumped up to join her. 'You can't just go off to London like this. You don't know what you're getting yourself into. And what about Gran? What d'you think she's gonna say about all this? It's okay you going off to make your fortune, but it's Gran's money you've stolen to do it with.'

'Oh, spare me the lectures, Josie. I knew this would happen. That's why I wanted you outta the way.' She stamped her foot on the floor. 'Gran's old. She ain't got long to live. But I have.' She stabbed the bag with her finger. 'This money's no use to her. It's only gathering dust under the bed and she can't tek it with her. So I'm having it.' She pushed Josie forcefully out of the way and before she could regain her composure had reached the door. 'Wish me luck,' she said laughingly, then she was gone.

Josie stared after her. The poker fell from her hand and landed with a thud on the floor. She slowly sank down on the bed and placed her head in her hands. What was she going to do? How would she explain all this to her grandmother?'

Automatically she stood up and began to straighten the room. Marilyn had certainly done a thorough job. Her intention had obviously been to take everything she could lay her hands on. After replacing the floorboards it took all Josie's strength to push the bed back. How on earth her slight cousin had managed to move this monstrosity defied belief. But she supposed you found the strength for anything if your need was strong enough.

She had just straightened the blue eiderdown across the bed and was going to make a start on the drawers and wardrobe when she sensed a presence. She looked across the room to see her grandmother framed in the doorway, leaning heavily on her walking stick. The old woman stared around the room, her eyes coming to rest on Josie. She slowly advanced towards her.

'Gran . . .' Josie uttered guiltily as she straightened up. 'I . . . I . . . don't know what to say.'

'Well, you'd better say summat quick, and it'd better be good. What's gone off?' she demanded. 'Have we had burglars, is that it? I'll kill the bastards, I will. Where are they?' Her eyes darted round the room and she waved her handbag in the air.

Josie rushed towards her grandmother and placed her arm around her. 'I think you'd better sit down . . .'

Lily shook herself free. 'I'll stand, thank you. Just out with it. I wanna know what's gone off?'

Josie walked over to the bed and sat down. She raised her eyes to meet her grandmother's. Very slowly, she opened her mouth, the words tumbling out as she did her best to explain. When she had finished Lily raised her walking stick and brought it down heavily upon Josie's legs.

She cried out in pain and rubbed her leg where a red weal had begun to form.

'What!' Lily shrieked. 'You let that little madam steal my money?' She dropped her walking stick and awkwardly lowered herself to the floor. She groped under the bed, pulling up the floor boards, and removed the empty boxes that Josie had just replaced. Her breath came in rapid bursts as she threw the empty boxes across the room. 'She's took the lot,' she gasped. She pressed her hand to her chest. 'It's all gone, Josie. Me life's work, all gone.'

Josie threw herself down and cradled her grandmother in her arms. The old lady was in great distress and Josie didn't know what to do.

'Shall I get me Uncle Stanley, Gran?' she ventured softly.

Lily shook her head fiercely. 'I'll not have that man in my house. Never! Do you hear?' With Josie's help she eased herself up and sat on the bed. 'Leave me, Josie.'

'Gran . . .'

'Do as I say.'

Josie opened her mouth then snapped it shut. She picked up her handbag and as she turned to leave noticed an object lying on the floor by the door. She bent to pick it up. It was a long black notebook. She turned towards her grandmother, her hand outstretched. Lily was staring unblinkingly across the room and Josie thought it better not to disturb her. She turned back and absentmindedly placed the book inside her own handbag.

Tea with a drop of whisky was what the old lady needed. That was good for shock, wasn't it? Then Josie could get her into bed and ask what she proposed to do.

As she busied herself in the kitchen her mind whirled. The police would have to be informed and also, surely, her Uncle Stanley? Just why was her grandmother so against him? For the first time she really wished she knew the story of their estrangement. A picture of Marilyn rose before her. How could her cousin be so callous and cruel as to steal money from an old lady? Was her modelling career so important? Had she not realised what repercussions her actions would cause? Josie shook her head. No. Marilyn would be on her way to London with not a second thought for anyone but herself.

She found an old bottle of whisky in the cupboard under the stairs, poured a generous measure into a cup of strong sweet tea and ascended the stairs. She found her grandmother already in bed, her clothes discarded untidily on the chair, her eyes tightly closed. Was it her imagination or had Lily aged considerably in the last twenty minutes? Her heavily lined face was grey and taut and she looked almost lifeless. Josie leant over and it was with relief that she heard shallow breathing. She carefully placed the cup on the table by the bed and stole from the room, closing the door gently behind her.

Sleep did not come easily and Josie woke with a sudden start. The room was in pitch blackness and she lay for several moments as she accustomed her eyes to the darkness. The events of the last few hours flooded back to her. She reached over and stared at her clock. The luminous hands on the dial read three-fifteen. She eased her legs over the side of the bed and put on her dressing gown. Padding softly, she made her way into her grandmother's bedroom and stared fondly at the old lady.

Love and compassion flooded over her as she stared at the sleeping figure. Lily Rawlings might be difficult and at times tiresome but she didn't deserve Marilyn's treatment of her. Josie sat down on the chair by the bed and gently took her grandmother's gnarled hand in hers to stroke it.

Lily opened her eyes.

'That you, Maisie?'

'No. It's me, Grandma. Josie.'

'Josie. Ah, Josie.' She exhaled deeply and turned her head towards her granddaughter.

'You should be in bed, you've got to get up early. The stall . . .'

'Never mind that, Gran. How yer feeling?'

Lily thought for a moment. 'Tired.' She reached over and patted Josie's hand. 'I'm sorry I hit yer with me stick, me duck. It were the shock.' She sighed deeply. 'She took the lot, you know, and she'd no right to that money.'

'I know, Gran,' Josie said soothingly. 'But don't worry about that now. We'll get it back . . .'

'No. I won't see that money again, not now Marilyn's got her hands on it.' She lapsed into silence. 'That money was for you, Josie,' she said softly.

'Me?'

'Yes.' Lily tried to lift herself but the exertion was too much and she fell back against the pillows. 'I wanted to make sure you were well provided for when I've gone.'

'Oh, Gran . . .'

'You would have bin. I had over a thousand pounds saved. It would have given you a good start.'

'Oh, Gran,' Josie whispered again, her eyes filling with tears.

'My Maisie would be turning in her grave if she knew what had gone on. But what Marilyn's done is only to be expected in the circumstances. After all, she's her father's daughter.' Lily slowly shook her head. 'Maisie thought the world of Stanley. But then she didn't know the whole truth. I couldn't tell her. It would have killed her.'

'What would have, Gran?'

Lily smiled weakly and patted her hand again. 'Best you don't know, me duck.' She raised her eyes to the ceiling. 'She wa' a good gel, was your mam. You were the light of her life and she had great plans for you.' A tear trickled down her cheek. 'She had to give up everything when yer grandad died. Bless her. She ran that stall and looked after us both and never complained. That money was in part to make up for what she'd had to suffer.'

'Gran, me mam didn't suffer. She was happy. She was always singing and laughing.'

'Yes, she was. But I feel she suffered because she had to look after me. I know she turned down many a good proposal of marriage. You weren't the problem, Josie. But nobody in their right mind could be expected to take on a cantankerous old lady.' She smiled wanly. 'I blame meself for her death. Maybe if she'd had an easier life she wouldn't have had the heart attack. Running a stall in all weathers and caring for us two weren't a bed of roses and I didn't exactly make life easy for her.' She sniffed loudly and gripped Josie's hand tightly. 'I'll make it up to you. You're a good gel, our Josie. I've bin a lucky woman to have you as well as yer mam. Not many women are that fortunate.' A note of urgency came into her voice. 'Josie, if anything should happen to me, I don't want Stanley to be told. Promise me?'

'I promise, Gran,' she answered, bewildered.

'Good, good. This house and everything in it is yours. He's not to receive one penny. One penny, is that clear?'

'Yes, Gran. Yes.'

Lily relaxed against the pillow and breathed deeply. 'I want you to make an appointment with the solicitors. I've never made a will. I should have, I know, but I kept putting it off. But in the light of what's gone off tonight, I think I'd better.'

'Gran, don't talk like this. You've got lots of years left in yer yet.' She leant over and gave her grandmother a hug. 'Don't you think about dying, I couldn't bear to lose yer, and don't worry about this business with the money, we'll get it sorted.' She swallowed hard to rid herself of the lump that was forming in her throat. 'And when we get it back, the first thing we're gonna do is have an indoor lavvy installed, 'cos one of these days either you or me is gonna break our necks on those paving slabs in the back yard, or catch pneumonia, and that wouldn't do. Not when Meg Richardson is having so many problems at the Crossroads Motel. We've both got to find out what happens.'

Lily gave a watery smile. 'You're a good gel, Josie.' She closed her eyes and her grip on Josie's hand loosened.

Josie leaned over and kissed her grandmother on the cheek, realising that the old woman was exhausted.

'Get some sleep,' she said, adding softly, 'I do love you.'

She stood for a moment and stared down at Lily before she turned and stepped quickly out of the room.

She rose several hours later and prepared her grandmother a lightly boiled egg, a plate of toast and a pot of tea, making sure there was plenty of sugar in the bowl. Her grandmother needed all the energy she could get. She ran her fingers through her dishevelled hair. She had made a decision and her grandmother would have to go along with it. For once in its long history the market stall would remain closed. Gran should not be left on her own today and they also had to decide what they were going to do about Marilyn. In the cold light of day Josie wished with all her heart that the events of the previous night had not taken place. Stealing from anyone was a crime. Stealing from your own family defied belief. She sighed. The thought of reporting her own cousin to the police filled her with dread. But what else could so do?

Arranging the tray as prettily as possible, she climbed the stairs, careful not to spill anything, and entered her grandmother's bedroom. The old lady was still sound asleep. her head had fallen to one side and her mouth gaped open.

Josie hesitated. Should she wake her or leave her for a while longer? She put down the tray and smiled fondly. Suddenly the smile vanished. She dropped to her knees.

'Oh, Grandma,' she wailed. 'Oh, no, NO!'

Her grandmother was oblivious to her cries of anguish. She had died peacefully two hours previously.

Chapter Seven

'You did a grand job, gel. Your grandmother would have been proud of yer. Best send off I've ever been to.' Dora Patterson patted Josie's arm and smiled. 'Now if there's 'ote else I can do, me duck, just give us a shout. Okay?'

Josie smiled meekly. 'Thanks, Dora. I did appreciate all your help. I couldn't have managed without yer.'

'Least I could do. Your granny were a good woman, Josie. One of the best. She did me and my mother many a good turn when we were in dire need, and things like that are never forgotten. Now I must be off. The kids will be home from school soon and yelling for their tea, and I've nothing ready.'

'I'll have to be going too, Josie,' Big Jack Bates said, placing his empty plate and sherry glass on the table. 'Like Dora, if there's anything me and Gwen can do, you've only to ask.' He placed his large hands on her shoulders and stared into her ashen face. 'She'll be a great loss to us all, Josie.' He bent over and kissed her lightly on the cheek, then stood back and looked at her for a moment. 'I don't suppose this is the right time to ask, but will you be carrying on the business?'

'The business? Oh, the market stall.' She ran her fingers through her hair. 'Yes, of course. I have to earn a living . . .'

'No. Not the market, that's not what I meant . . . Look,' he hesitated, ashamed, 'now's not the time, Josie. I shouldn't have mentioned it.' She stared at him perplexed as he patted her arm. 'A good night's rest is what you need, gel. You're all in. I'll see meself out.'

Josie gazed slowly around the empty room. It was the first time she had been on her own since her grandmother's death. Friends and neighbours had been wonderful, helping her to arrange the funeral and the food for afterwards. She had been both amazed and comforted by the number of people who had attended. Representations from nearly all the market stalls and the neighbourhood had been made, and cards of sympathy and floral tributes had flooded in. She hadn't realised or appreciated before just how respected her grandmother had been. She knew the old lady had many acquaintances but had never grasped how much regard they had held her in.

The one big problem that worried her was that she had not informed her Uncle Stanley of his mother's demise. She had followed her grandmother's wishes, but had she been right in doing so?

She picked up the last of the dirty crockery and took it through to the kitchen where she placed it in the sink. She had no other clearing up to do. The neighbours had seen to that before they left to attend to their own families. This warmed her. She could not have faced clearing up after the terrible day she had had. She returned to the back room and placed several more lumps of coal on the fire. The emptiness of her grandmother's chair leapt out at her and she shut her eyes tightly. She had suffered badly when her own mother died. She thought the distress and anguish she had gone through then could never be equalled. But this loss seemed worse somehow. At least then she'd had her grandmother's love and needs to keep her mind occupied. They had helped her greatly towards recovering from her bereavement. But now there was nothing urgent to do, she had only her own needs to think of and cater to. At this moment she would even have welcomed Marilyn's presence.

The gnawing ache in her stomach heightened now that she was alone and she couldn't remember the last time she had eaten. But food was the last thing she wanted. It was funny how she had sought the solace of it when her mother had died. Now the thought of anything passing her lips nauseated her. What she longed for most was for someone to put their arms around her and tell her everything was going to be all right. Someone – someone like Stephen.

Accompanied by his parents he had attended the funeral, and it had warmed her to see him there. He had sought her out as most of the mourners were leaving the graveside. He had stood to the side of her, nervously fingering his black tie; she was feeling dowdy and drawn in an unbecoming thick black coat, a scarf tied tightly under her chin, several strands of damp hair sprouting out of the sides.

'Josie, I'm so sorry about your grandmother.'

She had smiled up at him gratefully.

'And you, Josie? How are you?'

She had shrugged her shoulders. 'Fine. I'll be fine,' she had replied hoarsely, fighting back the tears.

He had placed his hand gently on her arm. 'Come on, I'll walk you to your car.'

She had gone with him, his arm around her for support. As they had crossed the wet grass he had stopped, his face full of concern and compassion.

'If there's anything you need – anything – you're just to ask, Josie. That goes for my parents as well. They told me to be sure and tell you.'

She smiled in gratitude. 'Thank you.'

They continued walking to the car. As they approached, the driver removed his cap and opened the car door in readiness for her.

She paused and looked up to him, clutching her handbag tightly between her fingers. 'There is one thing,' she had ventured. 'Me grandmother's things. I have to go through them. I'm dreading it, I can't face it on my own. Would you ... would you help me, please?'

'Of course. I'll come tomorrow afternoon as soon as the lunch-time rush is over. We'll do it together.'

As she had driven away in the car it struck her that not once had he mentioned Marilyn's absence. Maybe he would tomorrow. Still, his company would be nice. It would be something to look forward to even though she was dreading the job they were going to undertake together. Her feelings for him had not lessened but the events of recent days had put that night she had given herself to him right to the back of her mind. Maybe one day she would be able to close the door firmly on the memory and forget all about it.

She reached for the poker and chivvied the fire. The flames spurted and crackled and this reminded her that the coal in the shed was getting low. She would have to order some more, the winter had hardly begun despite the icy conditions of late. But to buy coal and pay the bills she would have to earn some money. Although the funeral expenses would be settled out of her grandmother's insurance money, that was all it would cover. The food and other incidentals had taken all she had left in her purse and the weekly takings.

Thank goodness she had found the takings bag under her grand-mother's chair. She would not have managed financially otherwise. She had never envisaged a funeral could be so expensive. Not that she begrudged a penny of the cost. Her grandmother had deserved and received the best. She frowned deeply. She had not put her Uncle Stanley's money aside. She hadn't a clue either how much it should be. She wished now that she had not given Marilyn her savings. That twenty-two pounds would make all the difference.

She sighed forlornly. What did she do about Marilyn now that her grandmother had gone? If she went to the police she had no proof about the stolen money. Would anyone believe her? She doubted it very much. She would either have to forget about it or take advice. But whose? She decided to sleep on it and make up her mind in the morning when she was more clear-headed.

She looked slowly around the room again. It looked more dingy than ever. Still, at least she had a roof over her head and a way to make her living. Things could have been worse.

The loud banging on the outside door interrupted her thoughts and she jumped. With heavy steps she made her way down the dark passage. Just another kindly soul paying their last respects, she thought wearily. I'll get rid of them quickly and go to bed.

She unlatched the door and pulled it open. Without a word or a glance in her direction, Stanley Rawlings strode past her. She slowly closed the door, her heart thumping loudly inside her chest. She hadn't the strength for a confrontation. She followed him down the passage and into the back room where she hovered by the table, unsure whether to ask him to sit down or offer him a cup of tea.

He was standing with his back to the fire, his long legs apart, hands clasped firmly behind his back as he waited for his presence to have the desired effect upon his niece. He unclasped his hands and ran long slender manicured fingers through his light brown, carefully groomed hair. The charcoal grey suit and white shirt he wore were hand-made, as were the black leather shoes that encased his feet. Stanley Rawlings was always smart. Not a hair was out of place on his handsome head, not a hanging thread or piece of fluff marred his immaculate attire. His unlined face, cleanshaven skin belied his forty-eight years though the pale blue-grey eyes, staring so coldly, were anything but attractive.

Josie trembled under his scrutiny.

'Fine state of affairs to hear of my own mother's death from the obituary column,' he said icily. 'Why wasn't I told?'

Josie's mouth dropped open as she grasped the back of a chair for support. 'Grandma didn't want you to know,' she said, stumbling over the words. 'She told me before she died.'

'You lie. My mother and I may have had our differences but she would have wished me at her funeral. Besides, as sole beneficiary I had a right in law to be here.' He turned towards the fire, ran his fingers along the tiled shelf and inspected them. 'You don't keep the place very clean,' he said slowly.

'I do my best.'

He turned to face her, the corner of his mouth twitching. 'But your best isn't very good, is it?' He held out his hand towards her, spreading his fingers wide. 'Judging by the amount of dust.'

Josie cringed. If he was trying to undermine her, he was succeeding.

He inhaled deeply and pulled himself up to his full six-foot height, his eyes slowly scanning the room. His gaze rested on her.

'She died rather suddenly. I wasn't aware she was ill?'

'She wasn't. No more than her usual aches and pains,' Josie replied nervously, twiddling with a button on her black blouse. 'Doctor says it was a heart attack.'

'Hmm. Well, she was old. Best way to go,' he said flatly. 'Where's her handbag?'

'Pardon?'

'I said, where's her handbag?'

Josie gasped. His cold attitude shocked her. He was showing not the slightest sign of grief for the loss of his mother.

'In her bedroom, with the rest of her things,' she said slowly.

He pulled at his earlobe and eyed her cautiously. 'I trust you've touched nothing?'

'What d'yer mean?'

He exhaled impatiently. 'You haven't gone through her personal stuff?'

'Oh, no. I was going to do that tomorrow.'

His face darkened. 'I hope you were not. That is for me to do. Anything of hers belongs to me now.'

Josie's face flushed. 'Oh, but you're wrong. Grandma wanted me to have everything. She told me so.'

'Have you got that in writing?'

'No . . .'

'Well, then, you haven't a leg to stand on,' he said smugly. 'No court in the land would take any such claim seriously. And personally, I don't care what my mother said or promised you before she died. All she had is now mine. And that, my dear, is the law.'

He stared at her blankly before he strode out of the door and up the stairs. Several moments later he was back, his cold blue-grey eyes ablaze with fury.

'Where's the book and the money?' he demanded savagely, grabbing her by the shoulders and shaking her hard. 'We all knew where she kept it. It's all gone. Where is it?'

Her teeth clattered together and she gulped hard. 'Marilyn took the money,' she spluttered.

'What!' he shouted in disbelief. 'You're saying my daughter stole from her grandmother? You're lying.'

'She did, honest she did! She came round last Friday night while we were all out and helped herself to Gran's savings. I came back early and caught her. She said she was going to London to be a model and needed the money for tuition and to live on. The shock of what she did helped bring on the heart attack, I'm sure it did.'

He thrust her away and strode across the room. He knew she wasn't lying. This was just the kind of stunt his daughter would

66

pull. Just wait until he got hold of her! He'd wring her neck. The little madam had told them she was going with a friend to Blackpool for the week. He felt his blood boil in his veins. That was *his* money. The inheritance he had waited patiently for, knowing it was piling up year after year, just waiting for the day when it would be his. He had stayed with Hilda, putting on a family front, comforted in the fact that one day he would be able to break free and live life his own way. Now that was in jeopardy because of his own daughter's greed.

He stared into the fire, his mind racing. He had to salvage something from this mess.

'The book. What about the book?' he said harshly.

Josie shook her head fiercely. 'I don't know what you're talking about,' she said quizzically. 'I don't know anything about a book.'

He knew from her manner that she was speaking the truth. Blast his mother! Where had she put that book? From past experience he knew she never went anywhere without it, so it must be around somewhere. When he found it he could begin to redeem the situation and recoup what Marilyn had taken. He turned to face her, his eyes full of distaste. This was his sister's child but he felt no love or compassion for her. He detested imperfection and this woman screamed it. She would have to go. She was in his way.

A way of being rid of her came quickly to mind. 'I don't believe a word you're saying.' He walked slowly around the table to face her. He leaned over, his face inches from hers. 'It's my guess you stole the money and are using my daughter as a scapegoat. I've no doubt Marilyn's gone, and the best of luck to her, but you've used that situation to your own ends. She isn't here to defend herself, is she?'

'But that's not true!' cried Josie.

'So you say, but will the police believe you?' He breathed deeply as he waited for the impact of his words to sink in. 'You'll go down a long time for robbery, and maybe even manslaughter. A charge of murder wouldn't stick. After all, I don't think you really intended my mother to die.'

She was gazing at him, her eyes wide in horror. She wasn't really hearing all this, she couldn't be. His accusations were so shocking she was unable to speak.

He straightened up and narrowed his eyes, choosing his words carefully. 'You're family, Josie. Unless I'm pushed to, I wouldn't shop my own family to the police. If you leave quietly, we'll let matters lie. I'm moving into this house – that's if I don't decide to sell it.' He wrinkled his nose in distaste. 'Though I doubt it's worth much. The same goes for the stall.'

'The stall! You're selling the stall?'

Stanley smirked. 'You don't think I'm going to let you have it, do you? After what you've done?' He breathed deeply. 'There's nothing here for you.'

'You can't . . . you can't do this! It's my house and my stall. Gran said . . .'

'Gran said, Gran said,' he mimicked. 'She's dead. And for all I know, you killed her. The best thing you can do is get out of here before I change my mind and call the police.'

'Call them!' she shouted. 'I don't care. I've nothing to hide. You can't throw me out, you can't! I've nowhere to go.'

His eyes glazed over and his face darkened. 'I'm not playing games. Get your things. I want you out of here, now.'

The look on his face and the tone of his voice left Josie in no doubt he meant business. She suddenly felt very afraid. He had the look of madness in his eyes. Any reasoning with him was out of the question, she could see. She turned and fled to her room. Finding several discarded brown carrier bags under her bed, she filled them as quickly as she could with whatever came to hand. This couldn't be happening. It just couldn't. It was all a nightmare, it must be.

He was waiting for her at the bottom of the stairs. She hesitated on the last step.

'I've no money,' she ventured.

'Haven't you?' he sneered. 'Put down the bags.'

Without hesitating she did as she was bid and watched in silence as he rummaged through them.

He raised himself. 'Just checking. Can't trust anyone these days.' He held out his hand. 'The keys to the van?' he demanded.

'No. Not the van. Please, Uncle Stanley, I need that.'

'So do I. The keys.'

She delved into her pocket and pulled out the van keys, reluctantly handing them over. He watched, a smile playing on his lips as she picked up her bags and let herself out of the front door.

The cold night air met her as she dragged her already weary body down the street, heading – where was she heading? She turned the corner into Beatrice Road and collided with someone. Apologising profusely, the woman took a step back and straightened her hat. She stared at Josie for a moment. In the collision she had stumbled back against a lamp post.

'Josie? It is you, Josie, isn't it?' she asked breathlessly.

She nodded and stared across at the woman, confused.

'You probably don't recognise me. I'm your Auntie Hilda.' She stared quizzically at the bags. 'What's happened. What's he done?'

'He's thrown me out.'

'Oh, no. Oh, Josie love, I'm so sorry,' she said sincerely. 'I never thought he'd stoop so low as to chuck his own family out on the streets.' She pulled nervously on her handbag strap. 'I knew he was angry. To be honest, I've never seen him in such a rage. It was reading of her death, you see. He must have thought you were trying to pull a fast one.'

'A fast one?'

'Yes. Trying to get what was due to him.' She screwed up her face. 'Though he don't deserve it. He deserves nothing of your grandmother's,' she said harshly.

Josie placed down her bags. 'Can't you talk to him, Auntie Hilda?' she pleaded. 'I've nowhere to go and no money. I don't know what I'm gonna do. I don't even have a job any more.'

'Oh, Josie. He wouldn't listen to me. I ain't existed for years in his eyes. To be honest, I don't know what I'm doing here now. But it was instinct. Instinct told me there was gonna be trouble and I might be needed. Though what I was gonna do, I'd no idea.'

Josie shivered violently, the icy cold damp air seeping through her clothes.

'I just knew I had to come,' continued Hilda. 'But I probably wouldn't even have gone into the house. Oh, I'm sorry, Josie love. I feel so useless. But I'm no match for him and never have been. If I'd have had more gumption, I'd have left him years ago.' She sniffed loudly and Josie sensed she was desperately trying to hold back the tears that threatened.

Despite her own grave position, she suddenly felt sorry for this tiny woman whose distressed state confirmed her genuine concern at the situation, although she was seemingly powerless or unwilling to do anything to rectify it.

'I understand, Auntie Hilda. Don't upset yourself,' she found herself saying. 'I'll manage somehow.'

Hilda unclipped her handbag and rummaged through it. 'Here, me duck. It's the least I can do,' she said, thrusting her hand into Josie's pocket. 'It's not much, but it's all I have. I wish I could do more but I can't. When Marilyn gets back from Blackpool, I'll have a word with her. See if she can come up with something.' She bent forward and pecked her niece on the cheek. 'Take care.'

With that she turned and scuttled back in the direction she had come.

Josie put her hand inside her pocket and pulled it out. She stared down. Her auntie had given her fifteen pounds. She shut her eyes tightly. The money was a godsend. She put it in her handbag and picked up her belongings.

Chapter Eight

Josie walked and walked along long silent icy streets, conscious that if she didn't find shelter soon she would surely freeze to death. As predicted by the forecasters the temperature was plummeting and a night under the stars was not recommended. At this late hour she knew she would not get lodgings; landladies would have closed their doors long since. Besides, the little money she had would not last five minutes if she spent it recklessly.

She stopped in her tracks and looked around, trying to get her bearings. She was on Groby Road. To the left lay the allotments, to the right the heart and chest hospital, and further long the cemetery. What on earth had possessed her to walk in this direction? A lone figure walking a dog on the opposite side of the road stopped and looked over at her. She pressed herself against the allotment railings in panic; in the darkness the figure looked quite menacing. The rusty metal gave way against her weight and she fell backwards. Stunned for several moments, she picked herself up, her eyes darting wildly around.

The allotments were deserted. Frozen stalks of dead produce that had been left to rot and bushes and trees rose eerily from the ground. Through the darkness several dilapidated wooden buildings loomed. An idea struck. Would one of these buildings provide her with shelter for the night? She decided to risk it. Anything was better than walking the streets.

After trying several doors, one gave way, the rusty lock disintegrating under her hands. She placed down her bags and peered round. The small building was cluttered with odds and ends of gardening equipment that had been left to lie over the winter months and the smell of must and damp rose strongly, but it would do, it would have to. In any case, she thought determinedly, it was only for one night and in the circumstances she felt sure the owner would not object.

Rummaging round, she unearthed an old paraffin stove and, wonders of wonders, it had fuel still in it. On the window ledge she found a half empty box of matches and after fumbling with the mechanics the stove burst into life. She said a silent prayer of thanks.

Clearing a small space, she unfolded an old striped deck chair, and with several pieces of dirty sacking to help ward off the cold, made herself as comfortable as possible. Against the odds she slept. The scratching of mice and the weaving of spiders did not distract her. The traumas she had faced and worry for the future over-rode her fears.

She woke with a start. The paraffin stove had long since given up and the early morning cold chilled her to the bone. She shivered and brushed a cobweb from the end of her nose, sending the spider flying, along with several of its victims. Clutching the sacking tightly to her chest, she realised with alarm that she could not feel her feet. She quickly looked down and relief flooded through her. They were still there. She stamped them heavily upon the rotting floor boards until a tingling sensation indicated life.

She sat for a moment and collected her thoughts. Was she really here? Had her uncle actually made all those untrue accusations and thrown her out of the only home she had ever known? And her job. The beloved market place was no longer open to her. He had even taken that away. What was she to do? How was she going to survive? She must get somewhere to live and then a job. But first she must get herself cleaned up and something hot inside her or she would die of pneumonia or something equally horrible.

Putting back the stuff she had used, she brushed down her coat, ran her fingers through her hair and collected her bags. As she busied herself she thought of the poor bag people and tramps. She now had an inkling of what their life was like and she shuddered. She did not like it.

It was still dark as she unobtrusively left the allotments and made her way to the public toilets at the bottom of Groby Road. Luckily it was too early for any other users and she quickly swilled her face in lukewarm water and brushed her hair without any questioning looks. The Pop In Cafe on Fosse Road provided welcome warmth and she ordered a slice of toast and a mug of tea from the slovenly, bleary-eyed waitress, hesitantly breaking into the money her auntie had so kindly thrust upon her.

The waitress arrived with blackened toast spread sparingly with bright yellow margarine, the mug of tea slopping its contents over the dingy red formica table. Josie eyed her.

'Do you know of any rooms going around here to rent?'

The waitress sniffed loudly, wiping her hands on her greasy apron, and thought for a moment. 'Might do,' she said cagily. 'For you, is it?'

'Well . . . yes.'

The waitress looked her over. 'Try up Wentworth Road, just past Fosse Park. There's several houses let out as bedsitters. You just might be lucky. People are always being chucked out for not paying the rent. Mostly students.'

'Oh, thanks,' Josie said warmly. It was a start. She'd go as soon as she had finished her food.

Wentworth Road was a dismal parade of three-storey Victorian dwellings, badly in need of a face lift. The first four houses, owned by landlords who grossly overcharged for dingy rooms with limited facilities, overlooked the park, trees blocking most of the light that tried in vain to shine through their grimy windows.

Josie knocked hesitantly at the door of number two and patiently waited; her bags placed strategically to the side of the green moss-covered stone step. The badly peeling brown-painted wooden door opened abruptly and a woman dressed in a pure wool cream coat edged around with fur, with matching hat and large gilt earrings poking from beneath, stood frowning down at her. She clicked shut her handbag and started to pull on cream leather gloves.

'Yes?' she asked sternly.

Josie quaked beneath her scrutiny. 'I . . . er . . . heard you might have a room to rent.'

'Did you. How?'

'From the waitress in the cafe down the road.'

'Huh!' she uttered. 'Doesn't take long for news to travel.' She eyed Josie up and down. 'Are you a student?'

'Er . . . no, no. I work.'

The woman's eyes brightened. 'Well, I suppose that's something. Getting the rent out of a student is the devil's own job. You'd better come in.'

The passage was dark and dreary. She marched ahead of Josie and opened a door to the right of her and entered, Josie following close behind.

'Well, this is it,' the woman said flatly as she looked at her gold wrist watch.

The room, like the passage, was cold and uninviting. It was a large room, its walls covered in cream brocade paper, greying with age; the woodwork and ceiling, once white, were now yellowing. The large bay sashed window had dirty net curtains covering the grimy glass. By one wall sat a divan bed, minus its legs. The long back wall housed an old gas cooker, a stained sink unit and a kitchenette painted bright green, its many surfaces needing a good scrub to be rid of the grease of successive users. Across the room by the boarded-up fireplace sat a two-bar electric fire, one element of which was broken.

As she stared around, Josie's heart sank. Her expectations hadn't been high, but she hadn't quite anticipated this. Her grandmother's house had become neglected over the years but it had been luxury compared to this.

'Well, do you want it or not? I can't stand round here all day. It's no skin off my nose if you don't. I'll be able to let it easily. Good accommodation is hard to come by. You're lucky to have caught me. The last tenant left rather abruptly and I was just checking the inventory before I advertised it again.' The landlady puffed out her chest and clasped her gloved hands together impatiently as she waited for Josie's answer.

'How much?' she asked.

'Two pounds ten shilling a week and I need a month in advance.'

Two pound ten a week. A small fortune. She'd have to get a job and quick to keep the payments up. This woman was asking for nearly all the money she possessed. The allotment shed came to mind. She couldn't spend another night like that, even though it had been most welcome at the time.

'I'll take it.'

'Good. What's your name?'

'Josephine Rawlings.'

She took out a notebook and wrote down some details. She raised her head. 'That's ten pounds in advance and the gas and electric meters take shilling coins. My husband will be round to empty them once every two months. You're not to have pets, play loud music or have any parties. And no boyfriends staying overnight. Break any of these rules and you'll be evicted.' She accepted the money Josie gave her and forced a smile. 'I hope you'll be happy. I'll be round to collect the next month's rent on the due date. I come during the day, so leave it on the table and I'll let myself in. I'll have a rent book for you by then and I can also check that you're keeping the place clean.' She held out a key to Josie. 'Don't lose this. If you do, it'll be half a crown to replace it. And I don't take kindly to tenants locking themselves out and calling on me in the middle of the night. So be warned.'

With that she turned on her heel and left the room, closing the door behind her.

Josie looked forlornly around her, walked over to the bed and sank down. It groaned under her weight and she could feel the lumpy mattress protrude uncomfortably beneath her.

So this was to be her home. She hoped not for long.

Collecting her bags from the doorstep, she switched on the electric fire, glad to find some units still remaining in the meter, took off her coat and put her few meagre possessions away. The recess between the fireplace and the window had been curtained off. A previous tenant had stuck up a makeshift pole and had left some wire coathangers. At least she could hang up her clothes. Opening the compartments in the kitchenette, she found two each of knives, forks and spoons, several pieces of chipped crockery and a couple of blue enamel saucepans, a tub of salt and an unopened packet of tea, a half full bag of sugar, a tin of mouldy evaporated milk, a block of rancid butter and a packet of Vesta beef curry.

The curry she decided to have for her tea and idly read the instructions on the packet as she leaned against the sink. She lifted her eyes. The room needed a good clean; traces of several past residents were still much in evidence. That would be her task for the rest of the day. It would help to ease the feeling of loneliness that was mounting, and while she worked plans could be formulated.

Early evening found her sitting at the gate-legged table by the window, eating the curry and scanning the *Leicester Mercury* job column. There was plenty of work on offer. The sixties was boom time according to politicians and the pages of every newspaper. Office, hosiery, shop, and other types of workers were being cajoled by high wages, more holiday entitlement and better conditions, but every position Josie spied wanted experience and she had none. She was beginning to despair when an advert caught her eye. 'Looking for a new career? Let us fix you up. Workers of all types required. We guarantee success. Empress Employment Agency.'

'Hmm,' Josie sighed thoughtfully as she ran her eyes over the advert again. A feeling of hope rose inside her. This was for her. She definitely needed a new direction and they did guarantee success. She quickly made up her mind. She would pay them a visit tomorrow.

Her eyes travelled down to the congealing mess on her plate and she grimaced. She had eaten some concoctions in her time but this beat the lot. It was awful, and where was the meat the packet had promised? Still, it didn't matter. She wasn't hungry. She pushed the plate away and yawned. She was exhausted. What she needed now was a good night's sleep. Clearing the table, she got undressed and pulled back the grey blanket on the divan bed. No sheets. She climbed on to the practically threadbare mattress and pulled the grey blanket plus her heavy coat over her, lay back on the moth-eaten pillow and stared up at the ceiling.

Five nights ago she had lain in her own bed, her grandmother snoring softly in the room across the landing. She had had a comfortable existence, her grandmother to care for, a job and a future. Albeit not very exciting, but a future nevertheless. Now she had only a room which if she couldn't keep up the rent would also be gone. What was to become of her? The question was quickly pushed to the back of her mind. A few nights ago, she would never have envisaged her estranged uncle accusing her of murder and making her homeless, so she dare not think what lay in store. She was just glad her grandmother was not alive to witness it all.

Loneliness and grief began to threaten again, so she quickly switched her thoughts. What were the other tenants like? Were they young people, elderly, or students as suggested by that slovenly waitress? She would find out in time. But first she had to see about a job. The agency had given the impression that this would be quite easy. She felt optimistic.

She turned over and pulled the cover further up as she tried to blank her mind. She needed sleep. She would face what she had to in the morning and it couldn't possibly be any worse than what she'd just been through.

Chapter Nine

Josie climbed the three flights of narrow stairs and paused on the landing. She smoothed her hands over her coat, hoping the black elasticated skirt and white blouse beneath were smart enough, and patted her hair, wondering if she should have tried to do something with it instead of leaving it to hang down on to her shoulders. The damp air had penetrated, clumping thick tendrils together, leaving no sign that she had spent over ten minutes brushing it to a high sheen. Her eyes lifted to the sign on the door. She forced herself to enter.

The attic rooms occupied by the Empress Agency were small. Three desks, cluttered with papers, and several filing cabinets filled the cramped space. A kettle sang merrily on the gas ring on a table in the corner, surrounded by a half empty bottle of milk, a bag of sugar and several dirty cups. A telephone rang and was answered by a middle-aged woman at the far side of the room. Josie stood on the threshold, unsure what to do. A young girl raised her head from her work, eyes quickly scanning her.

'Can I help yer?' she asked tonelessly.

'Er . . . please,' Josie replied, inching forward. 'Your advertisement in the *Mercury* said you had work. I've come to apply.'

The girl's heavily black-lined eyes opened wide and she smoothed her hand over her short bleached blonde hair. 'You want to register?' She sniffed loudly, picked up a form from her desk and held it towards Josie. 'Fill this in and someone will see you shortly.'

'Thank you.' She smiled, accepted the form and looked around her. Two wooden chairs and a coffee table were placed strategically behind the door. The rickety table held a couple of outdated magazines and an overflowing ashtray. Josie made her way over, sat down and studied the form.

As neatly as possible she filled in her name, address and schooling where indicated, then frowned deeply. The form requested to know what experience she had and what office machines she could use. Well, she didn't have any, did she? She chewed on the pen she was holding. Before she had time to think the middle-aged woman approached. She smiled kindly, her hand touching the single string

76

of pearls that hung round her sagging neck, her matronly chest protruding magnificently from beneath her pale yellow twin set.

'My name is Mrs Tweedle. Welcome to the Empress Agency. Come this way, my dear.'

Josie followed and sat down as indicated in a chair to the front of her desk. Marjory Tweedle frowned as she glanced over the form.

'You haven't finished filling it in, have you?' She smiled reassuringly. 'Never mind. I'll help you. These forms can be a little daunting.' She pressed her fingertips together and leant forward, pen poised. 'Now, what experience have you had?'

Josie gulped. 'Not much . . . well, none really. But your advert said . . .'

Marjory inhaled deeply. She had known that advert was worded wrongly. She had tried to tell the owner, Christobel Empress, but she wouldn't listen. Now they were getting all sorts of no hopers, as she had envisaged they would, all expecting placements. And here was another. She eyed Josie from beneath her sparse brown lashes. She did look a nice girl. If she lost some of that unbecoming weight and did something about her dress sense, she would be very presentable and much easier to deal with. Marjory sighed softly, put on her horn-rimmed glasses and glanced over the form again. She would try to help as she always did.

'What actually have you been doing?' she asked, raising her eyes.

'Markets,' Josie said hesitantly. 'I've been running my grandmother's market stall for the last five years.'

'Oh, well, that's a start.'

'Is it?' Josie asked hopefully.

'Oh, yes. I presume you handled the books and such like?'

'I did. I also handled the buying from the wholesaler.'

'Good. Well, maybe something along the accounts line would be suitable for you.'

Just then the outer door opened and another woman entered. She was expensively dressed and her high-heeled shoes clicked smartly over the floor as she walked across and placed her handbag and briefcase on to her desk. She looked across at Josie blankly. Slipping off her coat, she walked round to the back of Marjory's chair and glanced over her shoulder at the application form, raising her eyes now and again at Josie as she scanned it.

'Marjory,' she said sternly, 'can I have a word?'

She strode out of the office and stood on the landing, waiting impatiently for her employee to join her. Marjory arrived nervously clutching the bottom of her twin set.

'What are you doing?' Christobel Empress snapped. 'Get her out of here. We can't send her to any of our clients! Our reputation would go right down the drain. She has no experience and those clothes of hers are only fit for the rag bag.'

'Christobel, she isn't that bad, and her clothes – well, I've seen worse. She just needs taking in hand.'

'Oh, and you propose to do that, do you?'

'I can help, yes,' she said softly. 'She only came because of the advert. I kept trying to tell you, it's worded wrongly. But we have put our promise in black and white and we should at least try to honour it. We can't turn her away, Christobel. Let me try to find her something, please? I'm sure I can.'

Christobel sniffed haughtily. 'You're a do-gooder, Marjory Tweedle. You'd be better off as a missionary. Remember, this is my agency. You are just an employee. I have my reputation to think of. Now, I said, get rid of her.'

Resigned to defeat, Marjory made to return to the office. Christobel caught hold of her arm.

'Just a minute,' she said, the corner of her mouth twitching. 'I have an idea. Send her to Frizley's Finance.'

'Frizley's Finance! I can't do that.'

'You can and you will. That man is driving me crazy. Not one of the girls we've sent is suitable and I am fed up with threatening court action for settlement of his bills. Send her and we'll get rid of him for good. He won't use us again after that.'

'Oh, Christobel, we can't,' Marjory pleaded. 'It wouldn't be fair on the girl.'

'Do it. If you won't, I will.'

Christobel marched back into the office, smiling sweetly at Josie as she sat down behind her desk and picked up the telephone.

Marjory arrived back shortly afterwards and placed a cup of tea in front of Josie.

'We might be able to help you,' she said, trying to ignore the girl's expectant look. 'Do you think you can handle a switchboard and reception?'

Josie gulped. 'I've never . . .'

'That doesn't matter,' Marjory hurriedly cut in. 'They'll show you. Just say you're rusty. The woman there is very nice, she'll go over it with you. It's very easy. These new PBX boards are so simple compared to the old plug ones. You'll soon pick it up, I'm sure. And the reception part of the duties . . . well, that's a doddle. It'll come naturally to someone like you.' She smiled kindly. 'It's just a temporary position, it being a week to Christmas. Placing anyone in a permanent job is impossible just now. People don't like to recruit so near to the holidays.'

Only a week to Christmas, Josie thought. She'd forgotten the holiday was so near. Her problems had pushed that right out of her mind. She would have to succeed in this job, she needed the money to tide her over.

'We can discuss a more permanent position after the new year,' Marjory continued. 'We'll have more chance of success then. In the meantime this will be a good exercise for you. Give you the feel of things, so to speak.' She averted her eyes. Who was she trying to kid? The girl had no chance at Frizley's. Some of their best girls had been sent packing for one reason or another. There was no pleasing the man. She handed Josie a time sheet and showed her how to fill it in. What a shame, she thought. The girl looked so grateful. 'Here's the address. Report there at two o'clock.' She paused for a moment. 'Best of luck.'

Josie rose. 'Thank you. I'll do my best. Just say I'm rusty and they'll show me, is that right?'

Marjory nodded and watched as she left. She sighed deeply, gave Christobel a look out of the corner of her eye and returned to her work.

Josie pushed open the wooden door of 166 London Road and entered the dimly lit passage. She waited for her eyes to accustom themselves to the gloom and studied a board on the wall announcing the various companies that occupied the four-storey premises. Frizley's Finance was situated on the second floor and Josie hesitantly climbed the stairs and stood before a glass door. She could see movement inside and sudden panic welled up in her. Just what was she doing here? She had no experience of this kind of work. Her legs refused to budge an inch further.

A picture of her grandmother rose to mind and tears pricked the back of her eyes. Was it only several short days ago that the cantankerous but precious old lady was ruling her life? She'd had a home and a job that she loved then. Had she really lost all that? Now, after spending a night in an allotment shed, she was living in lodgings that were not much better. She shuddered and inhaled deeply as she tried to take stock.

Things could be worse, she tried to convince herself. At least she had a roof and the chance of making some money. Even though she would have to bluff her way through, it was either that or starve and become homeless. The thought of another night in that awful shed spurred her on. She forced a smile to her face and pushed open the glass door.

The room was similar to the one occupied by the Empress Agency and housed a comparable amount of office furniture and equipment, but whereas the agency's accommodation had been cluttered in the extreme, this room was tidy and therefore felt more spacious. The window filling most of the far wall had a deep sill on which a collection of house plants jostled for space. A figure bending over one of the desks straightened up as she entered and a pair of twinkling hazel eyes studied her.

79

'Can I help you?'

Josie, still with the smile fixed firmly on her face, quickly glanced over at the woman addressing her and her throat tightened. The dark grey box-pleated skirt and crisp white blouse buttoned high at the neck accentuated her plump homely figure, and Josie noticed that the fingers of her clasped hands were ringless. The fingers unclasped and plumped up the tightly permed mousy hair as the woman waited for a response to her question.

Josie cleared her throat and moved her gaze to the diamanté brooch fashioned in the shape of a butterfly that was pinned to the woman's bosom. 'I've come from the agency,' she said softly.

She smiled broadly as she advanced. 'Oh, good. I was beginning to think they weren't sending anyone and I'm desperate for help.' She held out her hand in welcome. 'Come on in, my dear. Put your coat on the back of the chair, I'll show you where to hang it in a moment.'

Josie did as she was bidden and sat down at the desk that was indicated. She stared in horror at the grey box upon it with its dozen or so switches, and swallowed hard.

'My name's Miss Grandmore,' the woman said, perching on the corner of the desk. 'But when Mr Frizley's not around you can call me Patricia. I know it's not the done thing to call your work colleagues by their first name but I think that practice is so stuffy and outdated. After all, working with people day in, day out, you get to know them better than your own family.' She gave a small laugh. 'Mr Frizley's a stickler for protocol, especially in front of our clients. I suppose it could be something to do with the fact that his Christian name is Bertram.' She flushed slightly, realising she was speaking out of turn to a relative stranger. 'And you are . . .?'

'Josephine Rawlings. But I prefer Josie.'

'Josephine. What a lovely name. It suits you perfectly, my dear.'

It was Josie's turn to blush.

'Right, down to business. As you are aware, we are a finance company and deal with all sorts of loans for shops, houses, cars, etcetera. Some clients can get a bit abusive, especially if Mr Frizley turns them down for whatever reason. But I'm sure you can handle that. Our last receptionist left to have a baby. Silly girl, if you ask me. Fancy getting married and pregnant before the age of seventeen! Still, it was her choice and I must admit, she seemed happy enough. Though God knows how she'll manage once that baby comes along. She left here still under the delusion it was all hearts and flowers. Her and that clot of a husband have a rented bedsitter in Highfields.'

She shook her head sadly and then smiled warmly at Josie. 'I'm sorry, dear, I was getting carried away. This is the switchboard,' she said, indicating the grey contraption on the desk. 'It's fairly quiet just now so you have plenty of time to familiarise yourself with it. We have three outside lines and just four working extensions, but it can get fairly busy, especially first thing in the morning. I'd like you to handle the post and do the preliminaries with the clients when they first arrive. I'll show you that part in a moment. Mr Frizley has uncharacteristically taken a few days' leave. I've worked for that man for ten years and never known him take a holiday before.'

She paused and stared across the room. 'I wonder why he's bothered to now? Christmas can be one of our busiest times.' She turned back to Josie.

'Still, it'll do him good. I told him I was perfectly capable of handling things. You don't work for someone for years without learning a thing or two. We'll manage between us, eh, Josie? You look a capable girl.'

Josie smiled weakly. She felt herself warming to this chatty woman. Marjory Tweedle had been wrong to instruct her to tell lies about her experience. This woman would soon cotton on to her and send her packing. To lie further, she knew, would just make matters worse. Oh, but she needed this job if she was to get over the Christmas period financially. Her heart sank as she wrestled with her predicament. But there was no other course of action, she would have to come clean even though it meant she would lose the work or she wouldn't be able to live with herself. She took a deep breath.'

'I'm sorry, Miss Grandmore, I can't do this job.'

'Why?' Patricia asked in bewilderment. 'Is it something I've said?'

'No, no.' Josie took a deep breath. 'I've no experience, you see. As much as I'd love to handle the switchboard and the clients, I've never done it before. The agency told me to tell you I was rusty, but I know you wouldn't be fooled by that for long.' She grabbed her bag and made to rise.

Patricia inhaled sharply and placed her hand on her shoulder to stop her. 'It's not your fault, my dear. That blasted agency would stoop to any level to make a placing, regardless of qualifications. You're not the worst we've had by a long chalk. I trust you won't be going back there, not after the way they have treated you? I shall be having words, believe me, and I'll make sure we never use them again. Their rates are astronomical anyway.' She rose from the desk and eyed Josie thoughtfully. 'Stay there,' she commanded.

She walked over to her own desk, picked up the telephone and dialled.

'Mrs Empress, please.' She waited, tapping her fingers

81

rhythmically upon the desk. 'Ah, Mrs Empress. I was not amused by the latest girl you sent to us. This is the last time we use your agency, and as for the money you say we owe, well, take us to court and see how far you get. I shall take great pains to tell the judge how you blatantly lie about the girls' qualifications, and how you fiddle the time sheets for your own ends.' She slammed down the telephone and stared over at the quaking girl opposite. 'That's told her. Now, how quick are you at learning?

Josie gulped. 'Very quick.'

'Good, that's what I was hoping you'd say. The work I want you to do is very easy, you'll soon pick it up. I'll pay you the same hourly rate as the agency out of the petty cash and square it with Mr Frizley once he returns. He won't mind, he'll be making a saving on their commission. Is that all right with you?'

Josie nodded.

'Good. Then let's not waste any more time, and if you work out I'll approach Mr Frizley about it becoming permanent. Now take that petrified look off your face, it's enough to frighten anyone to death!'

Josie turned thankfully into Wentworth Road. She had walked the three miles home in order to save the bus fare and the icy air now chilled her to the bone. How she longed to flop down in front of a blazing fire and watch her favourite programmes on the television, her grandmother's chiding remarks ringing in her ears. The electric fire with its broken element and the tin of beans and loaf of bread that she had bought on the way home did nothing to stir her enthusiasm but, regardless, what a wonderful afternoon she had spent under the helpful guidance of Patricia Grandmore.

The woman was a natural teacher and within no time Josie found herself mastering the switchboard and had taken in all she needed to regarding the handling of the clients. She found she was looking forward to the morning. It hadn't taken her long also to realise that Patricia Grandmore was hopelessly in love with the yet unseen Bertram Frizley and she wondered if he knew how his employee felt about him? She smiled as she let herself in through the dilapidated entrance door and stood before her own room, fumbling through her handbag for her key.

She sighed, annoyed. Where was that damned key?

Just then the front door burst open and a girl of about her own age breezed in, her arms full of books and papers, her long black hair falling over her face. One of the books caught the corner of the door and sent the lot flying out of her arms to land with a thud on the floor, the papers scattering over the threadbare lino.

'Shit!' the girl spat as she kicked the door shut. She raised her head, sensing Josie's presence, and smiled. 'Hello. You must be the new tenant.' Leaving the debris, she walked jauntily towards Josie, digging her hands firmly into the pockets of her black duffel coat. 'What's up? Lost your key?' Without waiting for an answer, she stood on tiptoe and ran her hand over the door lintel. 'Here,' she said, holding out something. 'The last tenant was always locking himself out so he had a spare one cut. Old Lady Muck knows nothing about it. Call her out and she plays merry hell, and charges into the bargain.'

Josie accepted the key. 'Thanks. The other one is in here somewhere,' she said, looking down at her bulging handbag.

The girl giggled. 'It's a wonder you can find anything in there.'

Josie giggled too. 'Yes, it is a bit full. 'Bout time I cleaned it out.'

The girl held out her hand. 'I'm Susan Shaw. Sue to my friends.'

Josie accepted the proffered hand. 'Josie Rawlings. Pleased to meet you.'

'I was just about to make a coffee. Fancy one?'

Josie smiled broadly. The invitation sounded wonderful. 'I'd love one. Thank you.'

'Give me a minute to get the fire on and that lot picked up, then come in. I'm through the back there. In the dungeon, as Peter and I call it. Peter lives in the very end room. You'll meet him later. He pops in every night for a coffee after work.'

'Right. I'll look forward to it. Can I help with the books?'

'No, I can manage. I've had enough practice. I'm always dropping the damn things. But thanks for the offer.' She turned and retraced her steps.

Josie opened her door and before closing it behind her, replaced the spare key on the lintel. She felt a warm glow envelop her. She had met two nice people today and a third was to come by the sound of Peter. She put down her meagre shopping and switched on the light. Nothing happened. It took several moments to realise the meter had run out. Fumbling in her bag, she found a shilling coin and put it in the meter, wondering how long it would last for. The electric fire gave out little heat and she made a mental note to tackle Old Lady Muck as Sue had referred to the landlady. If it wasn't fixed soon she would surely freeze to death.

After busying herself for a good ten minutes, she tentatively knocked on Sue's door and entered after hearing the girl's shout of welcome.

She hadn't envisaged a room could be worse than the one she occupied, but this one was. It was much smaller and being at the back of the house reeked of damp. Sue had made it as cheerful as possible with large black and white photographs of Bob Dylan and a colourful poster of the Beatles' *Sergeant Pepper* LP cover, CND paraphernalia, and a large psychedelic scarf, all of which were secured to the walls with drawing pins. Every available space was littered with pencil sketches on large sheets of white paper, drawing equipment, overflowing glass jars filled with paintbrushes in discoloured water, and dirty coffee cups and plates, several of the latter still encrusted with the remains of congealed food. The gas cooker had lost its door and its burners were on full blast. But at least this room was warm.

Sue smiled and beckoned her through. 'Come on in and make yourself comfy,' she said, indicating several large colourful cushions on the floor. She laughed at Josie's expression. 'These are more comfortable than chairs. Try one and see.'

Josie cleared a space and inched herself down, nodding in agreement. 'Yes, they are.'

'Milk and sugar?'

'Please.'

Sue poked her nose into a milk bottle and grimaced fiercely. 'Black, I'm afraid. Milk's off and I forgot to get some fresh.' She handed Josie a mug of steaming black liquid. 'So, Josie Rawlings, what brings you to this hell hole?'

Josie lowered her head and took a sip of the hot coffee. 'Oh, I needed somewhere to live,' she said slowly.

'Well, you must have been hard up. No one comes to live in this dump voluntarily. I'm only here myself 'cos I got chucked out of my last lodgings. Had a party that went on rather too long and was rather too loud.' She laughed loudly. 'The deaf old bat next-door said it was the first time she'd heard anything for years. Anyway, as I'd just about used up all my allowance, I had to settle for this. It isn't cheap and it isn't cheerful but it's better than nothing. My folks would have a fit if they could see it. It's going to take tactical planning on my part to keep them in the dark until my next cheque's due and I can move somewhere more suitable.' She flopped down on a cushion and drew her knees up under her chin, staring thoughtfully at her new neighbour. 'Well, what really brought you here?' she asked again.

Josie returned the stare. It would be heaven to open up and share her burdens but she had only just become acquainted with this girl and knew nothing about her, although she did seem really nice and just the kind of person to have as a friend. She gazed at the girl under her lashes. It would be lovely to have a true friend, someone to share secrets with. Would Sue fit the bill? Would she want to? Or was this tête-à-tête a one-off? Raising her eyes, she watched as Sue took a sip of her coffee and flicked a tendril of her long black hair behind her ear. Before Josie had time to make any response there was a knock at the door. Sue jumped up.

'Oh, that'll be Peter.' She rushed to the door and pulled it open.

A man of medium height with thick brown hair and startling blue eyes stood on the threshold. He eyed Josie cautiously.

'Oh, you have company . . .'

Sue grabbed his arm and pulled him forward. 'Come in and meet Josie. She's the new tenant from next-door.' She turned and smiled broadly at Josie. 'Meet Peter Parfit.'

The three settled down with fresh mugs of black coffee and chatted. Josie learned that Sue was a nineteen-year-old student at the College, studying Art and Design.

'Oh, do you know Judy Manship?' she asked.

'Her! Yes, I do. Little tart! I wouldn't trust her as far as I could throw her. And as for Marilyn, that friend of hers . . .' She blew out her cheeks. 'Right reputation they have, and they deserve it.'

Josie flinched. Luckily Peter sensed her unease and changed the subject. He told her he originally came from Manchester; was an apprentice accountant at H. Chawner & Son, and attended day release at College, studying for his articles. Josie watched him through her lashes, his thick Mancunian accent entrancing her as he explained the intricacies of his job. He was a good-looking man and reminded her momentarily of Stephen. She quickly blocked her thoughts and wondered instead if he had a girl friend? She presumed he had. A good-looking, intelligent man like him was bound to. Probably had a string of them, in fact.

When Peter paused for breath, Sue took over. Although she was the same age as Josie, there any similarity ended. Her beloved parents had a large house in an area on the north-western outskirts of the city known as Leicester Forest East and were fairly affluent, her father being high up in the insurance business. She had an elder brother with whom she didn't have much to do because he worked in London and didn't come home very often, and her mother filled her time entertaining on behalf of her husband and doing voluntary works.

The girl, whose turned up nose and overgenerous mouth downgraded her from being beautiful to just pretty, giggled a lot. She had no long-term plans for her future. She only did enough at College to pacify her tutors and parents. She hadn't wanted to study Art and Design but it had sounded the easiest option to follow and had made her parents happy that she was at least attempting something.

She loved life. She had plenty of friends and liked nothing more than to go to parties and dances. The Swinging Sixties could have been designed with her in mind and she revelled in the freedom and new experiences open to teenagers. In that respect she reminded Josie of Marilyn, but unlike her, Sue had an air of sincerity about her.

Then it was Josie's turn. Very cautiously she told them of her years on the market stall and was greatly surprised to see their eyes light up with interest. Pleasure spread through her as she answered their eager questions, and before she knew it the events that had led to her arrival at Wentworth Road had spilled out.

Both listened aghast.

When she had finished Sue blew out her cheeks. 'And I thought I had a hard life! Being forced through boarding school then College is nothing to what you've endured. I don't think I could have faced what you have and come out the other end intact.'

'Me neither,' Peter chipped in.

Sue leant over and patted Josie's knee. 'Well, Josie. Whatever's happened in the past, you have us now.' She turned to Peter. 'That right, Peter?'

'Yeah,' he nodded. 'But that uncle of yours sounds a right bastard. Tell me his name. I know a few people who'd sort him out for a small fee.'

Sue grunted. 'If you hold him down, I'll do it for nothing.'

They all collapsed into laughter and Sue rose to make some fresh coffee.

Peter finally looked at his watch.

'Well, I've brought some work home with me so I'd best get down to it, else I'll have one unhappy boss in the morning.'

Josie followed suit, afraid of outstaying her welcome. 'Yes, I must be off too.' She picked up her mug and placed it in the stained sink. She turned to face them. 'Why don't you both come to my room from work tomorrow and have coffee with me?' she invited.

To her delight they both accepted and voted from here on to take turns each night.

Josie returned to her dismal room with a more positive attitude than when she had left it. She had had a wonderful evening and felt much better for sharing her burdens with two such kind people. All in all, what an eventful day it had turned out to be.

It was Christmas Eve and Josie had been at Frizley's precisely five working days and enjoyed every moment of it. She quickly learned that appearances could be deceptive. Patricia Grandmore was a very humorous woman and had Josie at times squirming in her seat with her mimicry, though always out of earshot of any clients that were there. Josie wondered why this lovely woman had never married, she would have made a good wife, and sincerely hoped that the elusive Bertram Frizley came to his senses and grabbed her before it was too late.

She raised her eyes from the envelopes she was addressing and smiled at Patricia who was standing before her.

She handed Josie a brown envelope. 'Here's your wages, Josie, and I've added a little extra as it's Christmas.'

'Thank you,' she said gratefully.

'You've earned it. And I definitely want you back after the holidays.'

'Oh, I'd love to come back.'

'Good. I shall be speaking to Mr Frizley about you as soon as he puts in an appearance.'

Josie clasped her hands together. Things were working out far better than she had dared hope. In such a short space of time she had learned so much and was really beginning to think she was cut out for office life. Just then the door burst open and a short portly man, dressed in a loud checked suit, red shirt and abstract-patterned broad kipper tie, strode through, his balding pate shining under the fluorescent strip lights. Behind him hovered a bleached blonde no older than eighteen, encased in a full-length brown fur coat, her heavily made up eyes blinking rapidly.

Patricia swung round, her mouth dropping open. 'Mr Frizley! How . . . how good to see you back,' she uttered, her eyes fixed upon the blonde.

Josie gawped. This was Bertram Frizley? She would never have recognised him from any description Patricia had given her. The man would have been more at home on a car lot than in the world of finance and he certainly wasn't the type of person she would have envisaged a lady like Patricia falling for.

'It's good to be back.' His voice like his attire was loud. He turned and ushered the blonde forward. 'Meet the wife,' he said proudly.

'Wife!' Patricia gasped. 'But I don't understand . . .'

'You soon will, woman.' Bertram guffawed. 'This is Mandy,' he bellowed. 'We met a few weeks ago at the Financiers' Ball. Come on, Mandy, say hello. She won't bite you.'

Mandy smiled weakly and winced as her tight-fitting red patent stiletto shoes pinched her corn. 'Pleased ta meet yer, I'm sure,' she said in a high squeaky voice, giving a small curtsey.

Out of practice, Patricia offered her hand. 'You're in finance?' she asked.

Mandy shook her head. 'No. I was a waitress . . .'

'Was is the operative word,' Bertram boomed. 'Mandy's joining us here. I want you to take her under your wing,' he addressed Patricia. 'Teach her all you know.' He seemed to notice Josie for the first time.

'From the agency, I presume?'

'Yes,' Patricia began.

'Well, no need to have anybody else from them crooks. Now we've got Mandy.'

She looked petrified.

87

Bertram rubbed his fat hands together. 'We're not stopping long, just wanted to make introductions. But we'll have a coffee before we go.'

Josie rose. She'd make them coffee, anything to get away and collect her thoughts. Patricia had seemed to shrink before her eyes. The shock of Bertram's announcements had affected her badly and Josie's heart went out to the older woman. What an awful thing to happen and not just to Patricia, to Josie as well. She had lost her job. Absent-mindedly she piled spoon after spoon of sugar into the white porcelain cups, not caring whether they took it or not, and carried them through.

Not before time Bertram left, ushering his new wife along with him. His shouted a Merry Christmas as the door slammed shut behind them.

For several moments Patricia stared at the closed door. She slowly turned, her face filled with shock. 'I'm so sorry, Josie,' she uttered. 'I don't know what to say to you. It was wrong of me to build up your hopes like that.'

Josie sighed deeply. 'It's not your fault. Please don't apologise. Anyway, at this moment it's you I'm worried about, not me.'

'Me? You're worried about me. Why?' Patricia walked slowly back to her desk and sat down.

Josie clasped her hands together. 'Patricia, you've been so good to me, I've really enjoyed working with you. Not many people would have given me the chance. I can hopefully get another job, but you . . .' She lowered her eyes. 'You love him, don't you?'

Patricia gasped them laughed ruefully. 'Is it that obvious?' She sighed deeply. 'Yes . . . yes, I do, and have done for years. Stupid, isn't it?'

Josie remembered her own situation with Stephen. 'Not so stupid,' she said slowly. 'We can't help our feelings, however futile. But you'll meet someone else.'

'Will I? I'm forty-five, Josie. Time has run out for me, I'm afraid.'

'No, it hasn't. You're a lovely woman. There's bound to be someone out there for you. You just ain't been looking, that's all.'

'No, I haven't,' Patricia agreed. 'Not since the day I walked through that door nine and a half years ago. Before that I had my old mum to look after.' She pursed her lips. 'But I know one thing . . .'

'Oh?'

'I can't stay here. Not with that simpering female making goo goo eyes at him, I can't. She'd drive me mad. Waitress indeed! What is the man thinking of?' She narrowed her eyes. 'And if he thinks I going to teach her all I know, then he can think again.' She laughed wryly. 'So it looks as though we're both on the scrap heap, doesn't it, my dear?' She scowled fiercely and thumped her fists on the desk. 'Oh, sod. Sod Bertram Frizley!'

Josie stifled a laugh. The blasphemy coming from Patricia sounded so funny.

'What will you do?' she asked.

'Do? Oh, I don't know . . . go home and think. I suppose I could always go temping.' She paused thoughtfully. Rising from her desk, she walked slowly over and fingered the small silver Christmas tree she and Josie had decorated to make the office festive. 'I might just take this opportunity to have some time off. I might even travel. My mother left me a few bob and I've some savings of my own. I've always wanted to go abroad.'

Josie looked at her in awe. Travelling sounded so wonderful. 'Well, here's your chance. And you never know, you might meet someone.'

Patricia turned and smiled. 'You're just a romantic. But then, you could be right. Stranger things have happened. But to be honest, I'm not really all that concerned. This business has taught me a lesson. Besides, there's plenty more things in life than settling down. At this moment in time, Josie, all I want to do is get out of here.' She walked back to her desk. 'Come on. You can help me collect my things. My days at Frizley's are over. He's got some other daft bugger to do his bidding, and I'm not going to sit around and watch his downfall.'

Outside the main building Josie shook Patricia's hand firmly and they each said their goodbyes. Saddened, Josie watched as the other woman walked down the street laden down with her belongings from the office. She would miss Patricia. In a short space of time she had taught Josie so many things. Things that would hold her in good stead and things she would never forget. So another episode in her life was over. Things like this were becoming a habit just lately. As she set off for the bus station, she sincerely hoped the next episode lasted a while longer.

Chapter Ten

Josie stared out across the park. Christmas morning had dawned bright and clear and the frost that had turned the grass and leaves white during the night had melted. A wintry sun shone down from a cloudless sky but she felt no warmth. Her eyes alighted on several groups of children testing their Christmas presents and she drew her feet under the park bench as a young boy whizzed past on his new scooter, closely followed by another on a pair of roller skates, their whoops of delight rending the air.

She shuddered and huddled further down into the folds of her thick knitted scarf. She had never felt so alone in all her life.

The house had quickly emptied the previous day; all the other residents, including Sue and Peter, had dispersed to their various relatives. She had none to go to; none to share this special day with.

Memories of past Christmases flooded to mind. The paper trimmings hanging from the ceiling; the tree decorated to overflowing with baubles and lights, surrounded by brightly wrapped presents; a roaring fire piled high with coal and logs; the neighbours popping in for a festive drink and to express their good wishes. But most of all she remembered the happiness that had surrounded her. Even after the death of her mother, they had both, her grandmother and herself, striven to make Christmas special. She sniffed and blinked back a tear. Would she ever experience that kind of happiness again? At this moment in time she doubted it very much.

She briefly wondered how Marilyn was faring. For all the dreadful wrong she had done, Josie wished her no harm. And Stephen. How was he? She lowered her head and studied the wet path. All that was in the past. She had to think of her future. But at this moment she didn't feel she had one. Not one free from worry and lack of money at any rate.

What if she couldn't get another job? She shuddered. That didn't bear thinking about. Surely in these prosperous times there must be something she could get? It didn't matter what it was as long as she was paid enough to live on. She thought of her old colleagues on the markets but knew it was pointless approaching them. Any vacancies would have been snapped up by students and relatives desperate for work during the long holiday. A rush of resentment and anger rose as she thought of her uncle and wondered if he was sleeping peacefully at night. He didn't deserve to. As much as he wanted the house and stall, it wouldn't have hurt him to have given her time to sort matters out before he made her leave. He must have wanted them badly to act as he had. But why?

'Can't be as bad as all that.'

The softly spoken words echoed in Josie's ears and she turned abruptly to see a tiny, silver-haired woman sitting at the far end of the bench, busily knitting. The clicking pins paused momentarily as she stopped to tug more wool from the ball inside the pocket of her thick winter coat. Josie bit her lip, wondering if she had imagined the words. A brown and white Jack Russell bounded across the grass and dropped a rubber ball at the woman's feet. She picked it up and threw it. The dog leapt at it, slipping and sliding across the wet grass.

The woman laid down her knitting and turned her attention to Josie.

'Call me a nosy old woman but you do look the picture of misery, my dear,' she said kindly. 'Surely things can't be that bad?'

Josie breathed deeply. 'Can't they?' she answered abruptly.

The woman folded up her knitting, placed it in a tapestry bag and slid further up the bench. She eyed Josie closely.

'Things always look worse than they actually are.'

'And you would know?' Josie said flatly, not feeling in the mood for an old lady's chatter.

'Yes, I would. A problem shared . . .' Her sharp blue eyes twinkled. 'It helps to talk, you know, and I'm a good listener.'

Josie sighed deeply. Her privacy was being invaded. Not wishing to appear rude, she rose and opened her mouth to say her good-byes, but the old lady beat her to it.

'I lost my only daughter five years ago. She was coming over to spend Christmas Day with me, her and her husband and my little grandson. They were in a car crash. A drunk cut out in front of them and they were killed outright. They were all I had and I thought it was the end of the world.'

Josie froze. 'What?' she uttered as she lowered herself back on to the bench. 'Oh, I'm so sorry.'

'So was I, my dear. I thought I'd never get over it. But you have to carry on. You can't just give up.' She moved even further up the bench and patted Josie's knee. 'Luckily for me I had a friend who was determined not to let me wallow in self-pity. She insisted I join the voluntary services and soon I realised that many worse things can happen, although at the time of the tragedy I didn't think so.'

Josie sat speechless. Her problems seemed so trivial against this old lady's. Admittedly she had lost her beloved grandmother, but then she had lived a full and happy life. Hers hadn't been cut short so tragically as this lady's whole family's had. Josie was filled with shame.

'I've seen many sad cases over the years and could sit here all day and give you examples,' the old lady continued. 'Luckily, most people manage to conquer their hardships and grief. There's always an answer, you know. It's just a case of finding it. I found mine helping others.' She paused and placed her hand gently on Josie's arm. 'What is it, my dear? What's happened to upset you so much? Is it a boyfriend, is that it? Well, let me tell you, there's plenty more where he came from. You're a pretty girl, you won't have any trouble finding another.'

If only it was that simple, Josie thought. She sighed deeply and frowned. The old lady's story was a dreadful one, but she seemed to have coped. The grief of losing her own grandmother would lessen in time. Everyone had to face death, there was no escaping that, and as for her financial problems, well, something would turn up, as the woman had said. It was just a case of finding it. She had another two weeks before the rent was due again, and if she was frugal with her meals and the electric meter she would just about scrape through with the generous extra that Patricia had given her. Her heart lightened. It was about time she started thinking positively and it had taken this little old lady's tragedy to make her realise that. She breathed deeply and smiled.

'Nothing's the matter. I was feeling a bit down, but I'm fine now, thank you.'

The old lady smiled broadly. 'Good. I'm glad to hear it. I often come to the park if you ever need a chat.' She bent down to pat the dog who had arrived panting at her feet and watched out of the corner of her eye as the girl walked away. She straightened up and smiled to herself. Her daughter, bless her, would call her a wicked old woman if she ever heard the terrible lie she had just told. But she hated to see unhappiness and that young girl had reeked of it and needed to hear something profound to shake her out of the doldrums. She glanced at her watch. She'd better hurry. The mouthwatering dinner she had left them cooking would just about be ready for serving and she had promised her young grandson a story after the Queen's speech whilst his parents watched the film on the television. She clipped the lead on to the dog, gathered her knitting and set off for home. Old ladies had their uses sometimes. She was glad she had decided to give Jock a run around the park.

An hour later Josie stood before the table and blew into her hands. The room was freezing. She'd have been warmer staying outside, even if the fine morning had given way to rain clouds which now threatened to shed their load. Her eyes studied the table. Spread before her were the contents of her larder bought on her way home the previous day to tide her over until the shops opened again. Four skinless sausages, two faggots, three pounds of potatoes, a cabbage, one loaf of sliced bread – it went further than the uncut type which she preferred; a block of Stork margarine and a half pound of lard.

She thought deeply. If she had two of the sausages with boiled potatoes and some cabbage, the faggots could wait until tomorrow. She sighed. She had no gravy and the food would be dry and tasteless without something to accompany it. Some Christmas dinner, she thought ruefully. Oh, to hell with it. She didn't feel like cooking just for herself, and besides, she wasn't all that hungry despite having only a round of toast for her breakfast. She started to pack the food away. Maybe she'd feel more like eating later. Right now all she fancied was a cup of strong tea.

The kettle was just about boiled when she heard a car draw up and several moments later the front door bang shut. Who on earth could that be? To her knowledge all the residents, except herself, were away. She peered out of the window and saw Sue's bright yellow Mini Cooper parked outside under the street lamp. She ran to the door and yanked it open.

'Sue!' she shouted down the dark corridor. 'What on earth are you doing back? I thought you'd gone to spend Christmas with your parents?'

Sue pushed open her own door, withdrew the key and turned to face Josie. 'That was the intention,' she said. 'Look, come and have a coffee and I'll tell you all about it. I'm blooming frozen to the marrow standing out here.'

Josie smiled. Oh, for whatever the reason and however selfish it seemed, she was so glad her friend had returned.

'I've already boiled the kettle . . .'

'Oh, in that case, make the coffee and bring it through here. My room's warmer than yours.'

'Okay,' Josie replied happily.

By the time she arrived in Sue's room the girl had all the gas burners lit on the cooker and the electric fire on, the curtains drawn, and was sitting on a cushion in readiness. Josie handed her a mug, cleared a place and joined her. Sue pushed forward a biscuit tin full of mince pies.

'Compliments of my mother,' she said, biting into one.

'Well, what happened?' Josie asked keenly.

Sue swallowed hard. 'I shouldn't have gone home, that's what. My parents try, but it doesn't work. I love them dearly, Josie, but we just don't see eye to eye any more. They don't like the clothes I wear, don't like my friends, and haven't a clue what I'm talking about. We've nothing in common any more. Before I got into bed last night my mother and I had had a row and my father wasn't speaking to me. To top it all my brother brings home his new girlfriend. Well, talk about a dumb blonde!'

Josie nodded. She knew all about dumb blondes, remembering Bertram Frizley's new wife. 'She spent half the night in the bathroom tarting herself up then hadn't an ounce of conversation,' Sue continued. 'She just kept making eyes at my brother and I felt sick to my stomach. I couldn't put up with that all holiday. So here I am. I thought I may as well be miserable here as back there. At least I can play what I like on my record player without being told to turn it down.'

Josie grinned. 'Well, I'm glad you're back.'

Sue chuckled and rubbed her hands together. 'Well, I don't know about you but I'm starving. What have you got to eat? I didn't get anything in seeing as I was supposed to be away.'

Josie listed the contents of her larder.

Sue licked her lips. 'Well, that's settled then. We'll have bubble and squeak and sausages. Washed down with . . .' She rose and delved in a brown carrier bag. 'Da da!' she sang, holding a bottle of white wine aloft. 'Compliments of my father's drinks cabinet.'

Whilst Josie collected the food, Sue rummaged around and managed to find a blackened, battered frying pan and the other necessary plates and cutlery.

The meal was scrumptious and as they ate they chatted. Sue, having cleaned her plate, sat back and patted her stomach. 'I enjoyed that,' she said appreciatively. 'Have another mince pie?' She picked up the wine bottle and shared the remains between them.

Josie blew out her cheeks. 'Not for me. I'm full.' She picked up her glass and took a sip. 'I must say, though, I'm getting quite a taste for this.'

'Yeah, not a bad Château de plonk, is it? My father doesn't buy rubbish, I'll say that for him. Just hope he hasn't missed it.' She drained her own mug and eyed Josie thoughtfully. 'So that's you looking for another job. Shame really, that one sounded quite nice.'

Josie nodded. 'Yes, it was. Still, at least I managed to learn quite a bit from Patricia. I hope everything works out for her, she's a lovely woman. It's just a pity she spent all those years hankering after a man who didn't care tuppence.' She gazed down into her mug. 'Don't know what the hell I'm gonna do. I can't go back to that agency, that's for sure.'

'Oh, cheer up. You'll get something. I don't know much about employment agencies but you can't tar them all with the same brush. You'll manage, something will turn up.'

Just then they both looked at each other as they heard the sound of the front door closing and footsteps on the stairs. Sue jumped up.

'Who's that?' Josie asked. 'I thought everyone had gone away.'

'Oh, that'll be Tula,' said Sue, opening her door and disappearing out into the corridor. She returned closely followed by the most strikingly beautiful coloured woman Josie had ever set eyes on. Her dark skin was flawless and she was smiling, showing strong white teeth. She was dressed in a nurse's uniform, across her arm a dark blue cape edged in red.

'Meet Tula,' Sue announced. 'She lives in the attic rooms upstairs. You haven't met Josie, have you, Tula? She lives in Brian's old room. Been here just over a week.'

Tula held out her hand. 'Actually me name is Omotala Acabumdi but you English folks can't pronounce it, so Tula it is.'

Sue slapped the woman on the shoulder. 'You're in England now, Tula. You can't go round with a name like that. People'll think you're a packet of soap powder.' She giggled loudly, placed her arm round Tula's shoulder and squeezed her affectionately. 'I'm only joking, Tula. You know I love you really.'

Tula giggled also and accepted a cup of coffee. 'Sorry there's no wine left.'

'This will do nicely, ta very much. Coffee and bed, that's what I need. I've just done a double shift at the Infirmary and I'm on tonight at the old people's home. So much for my Christmas holiday,' she groaned. 'There's only two nurses on each shift and we're run off our feet.' She raised her head. Her dark brown eyes, although tired, twinkled merrily. 'Let's just hope no one gets sick, eh?'

The three laughed.

'So you've two jobs?' Josie asked.

'Yeah, I sure have. Nurse's pay ain't so good and I send money home to the folks in Jamaica. I came here to do me training and I ain't managed to go home yet. Some day, eh? When I've saved enough to buy me parents a little house, maybe then I get home. In the meantime, I keep workin'.'

'You hungry, Tula?' Sue piped up. 'There's some bubble and squeak left, if you fancy it?'

Tula's large brown eyes popped. 'Bubble and what? God, you English do eat some muck. No, ta. I'll get meself something later on.'

'Suit yourself.'

Tula turned her attention to Josie. 'You ain't a nurse, are yer?' she asked hopefully.

95

'Me? No. Why?'

'Just asking. We're short staffed at the nursing home. I could have got you some work, that's all.'

'Josie is looking for a job, though. Do they need any other staff?' Sue asked.

Tula thought. 'Yes, matter of fact, they do. Someone part-time to do the clearing up at night. Pay ain't bad either, 'cos they can't get no one to do it.'

Josie's eyes lit up. 'I could,' she volunteered.

Tula looked at her. 'I'll have a word tonight then. If the owner, Mrs Claymore, wants you, can you come along tomorrow night?'

'Yes, I can,' Josie said, smiling. This was a turn up. It was only washing up, but it was better than nothing. She sincerely hoped Tula could wangle something for her.

'Good, I'll see what I can do then.'

Chapter Eleven

The mention of Stoneygate to the people of Leicester conjured up a picture of wealth and prosperity. To afford or to have inherited one of the houses situated in this area meant that you were affluent. You had to be, the cost of their upkeep was enormous. Even the terraced houses on the outskirts of the district commanded a good price, and to say you lived there heightened your status.

Occasionally the cost was too high and a house was reluctantly converted into business premises. The Tory Party and the Prudential Insurance Society, to name just two organisations, had their headquarters in this area, their letter headings proudly announcing their prestigious address. Such was 152 Radcliffe Road. Mrs Greta Claymore, having lost her husband from overwork, trying to maintain his wife's escalating standard of living, had turned her house into a nursing home. Its five bedrooms, her own flat in the attic, and the extension, serving as a ward, provided her with an adequate income. Nothing like the one she'd been used to when her husband had been alive, but an income nevertheless.

She did not like old people. They were tiresome and a nuisance. But their money stopped her from losing her home altogether and she kept reminding herself of that as the smell of antiseptic and stale urine wafted towards her. She greeted Josie briskly, showed her where to hang her coat and took her through to the kitchens.

Piles of greasy dishes, pots and pans covered the dull stainless steel surfaces. Even the enormous sink was full to overflowing.

'Get these done,' she commanded. 'And if there's time you can help settle the residents down for the night.'

She left and Josie gazed around her. Taking a deep breath, she rolled up her sleeves and began.

Tula popped her head around the door and laughed at the sight of Josie up to her elbows in soap suds.

'How's it goin'?'

Josie turned. 'Fine, thanks.' She stopped her chores for a moment, wiped her hands on a large tea towel and rested her back against the sink. 'When I first saw this lot, I nearly died. I think I've just about washed every pot in the place.'

Tula grinned. 'I was just gonna ask if you could give me a hand to serve the cocoa and Ovaltine? Julie, the other nurse, hasn't turned up and I'm on me own. Madam,' she raised her eyes to the ceiling, 'is watching the television. She'll be down later, expectin' everyt'in' to be done.'

'Yeah, 'course I'll help,' Josie answered. 'I've nearly finished this lot anyway.'

Tula filled the large urn with water and switched it on to boil. 'If you could put the cups and saucers on the trolley and fill them jugs with the water once it's boiled. The cocoa and Ovaltine are in that cupboard. Bring it through to the ward. I should have them all in bed by that time.'

Josie smiled. 'Okay, leave it to me.'

Tula expressed her thanks then departed.

Half an hour later the kitchen was gleaming and the trolley loaded. It was heavy and Josie had a job to steer it properly. As she manoeuvred it into the dimly lit corridor, an old lady dressed in a long winceyette nightdress and walking with the aid of a Zimmer frame stopped her.

'What time is it?' she asked.

Josie looked up at the clock on the wall. 'Eight-thirty,'

'Oh, I'd better hurry,' she cackled. 'I'll be late for breakfast.'

Josie left the trolley and gently took hold of the old lady's arm. 'No, no. It's bedtime. Come on, come with me. Let's see if we can find your bed.'

'But I don't want to go to bed,' the old lady said in alarm. 'Once I've had my breakfast, I'm going out. My daughter's coming for me, you see. We're going shopping.'

'Oh . . . well, all right then,' Josie said, scratching her head. She thought it best to humour the old lady. 'Let's go and find your clothes and get you dressed. You can't go out with your daughter looking like that.'

The old lady's eyes lit up. 'All right. But I don't want to be late. What time is it?'

Once again Josie looked up at the clock. 'Just after half-past eight.'

'Is it?' the old lady said, bewildered. 'We should have had our cocoa by now. Where is it?'

'It's just coming. If you go back to bed, I'll bring it to you.'

'Oh, all right.' She paused and looked up at Josie enquiringly. 'Where is my bed?'

Josie suppressed a smile. 'I don't know. Tell you what, we'll find it together, shall we?'

The old lady smiled gratefully, and guided by Josie they slowly made their way down the corridor in search of Tula.

She was looking harassed and bathing several bed sores on an old man's backside. When she saw Josie's companion she ran her long fingers through her tight curls. 'Mildred! What a'you doin' outta bed? I've only just put you in it.' She looked at Josie expectantly. 'Her bed is in the ward, Josie. Can yer manage?'

Josie nodded and several moments later tucked Mildred beneath the covers.

'Now you stay there and I'll bring your cocoa.'

'Don't want cocoa,' Mildred sulked.

'Well, what do you want then . . . tea?'

'No. Don't want tea. They mek it too weak here. It's like summat the cat's done.'

'Milk. What about a nice glass of milk?'

She shook her head fiercely. 'No. Not milk. It'll curdle me stomach.'

Josie inhaled deeply. 'Ovaltine, then. Now that's nice and it'll help you sleep.'

'Ugh, no. I hate that stuff.' She paused. 'I know. I'll have cocoa. A nice cup of cocoa and plenty of brown sugar, mind. I like it sweet.' She grabbed hold of Josie's arm and pulled her closer. 'Keeps your bowels regular, does brown sugar.'

Josie smiled. 'I'll bear that in mind. Now you stay there. I'll be back with your cocoa in a jiffy.'

She hurriedly left, hoping the old lady would do as she was told long enough for her to get the trolley. As she turned the corner of the corridor that led to the kitchen, her eyes opened wide in alarm. Too late. The trolley that was thundering towards her hit her full force in the stomach, knocking the breath from her body, and she fell backwards with a thud on to the tiled floor. The corner of the trolley hit a wall and tipped over, a heavy object falling on top of her and winding her for the second time. The breaking of china and the clanging of metal rang loudly in her ears.

She tried to lift herself, but the object lying over her prohibited any movement. The object started to giggle and she realised it was an old man.

'My God!' Tula gasped, arriving on the scene.

She eased the old man off Josie, enabling the girl to raise herself into a sitting position. Josie gazed around. The trolley was on its side, two of its wheels still spinning. Cups and saucers lay broken and the tins of cocoa and Ovaltine had spilled their contents, some of which had scattered over her legs. Another old man was standing nearby, clutching the bottom of his long nightshirt, exposing his naked bottom.

'Jimmy,' Tula said sternly, 'what the hell have you bin up to?'

'Weren't me,' he said sulkily, pointing to the man sitting on the floor. 'It wa' Sid. He wanted a ride on the trolley.'

Suppressing a smile, Tula turned to Josie. 'You all right?'

She nodded.

Just then a screech rent the air and Mrs Claymore loomed before them, her face thunderous. She stared around her and her eyes settled upon Josie sprawled upon the floor.

'Get up and get out!' she screamed.

'But, but . . .' Josie started.

'I said, get out. And you!' She turned and addressed Tula. 'Get them into bed, clear up this mess and come and see me. Call yourself responsible! Just thank God no one was killed.' She turned and stalked off.

'What's the time?'

Josie turned her head to see Mildred shuffling towards her, the bottom of her nightdress tucked into her long woollen drawers. She was wearing a battered blue felt hat, a large black handbag swung from her bony arm and she was minus her dentures.

Uncontrollable mirth reared up in Josie.

Whilst she tried to clean herself up, Tula attempted to reason with Mrs Claymore but the woman was having none of it. Josie had been careless in leaving the trolley unattended, and to make matters worse Mrs Claymore had tripped and banged her leg on one of the jugs of water the two old men had unloaded so as to clear the top of the trolley for their escapade. But she had given Tula ten shillings for the work Josie had done. That was something.

Pulling on her coat, she made her way out into the cold dark road. With no buses running, this being Boxing Night, and no spare money for a taxi, she would have to walk home. She was getting used to walking, it was becoming an occupational hazard. How she missed the van! Her lips tightened. In three days she had lost two jobs. She hoped Tula didn't suffer the same fate. The woman needed the spare cash she made to send to her parents. Not knowing much about Jamaica, Josie visualised mud huts and bare feet. She started to smile, wondering if Tula had managed to get Mildred into bed at last. Oh, regardless of her lost job, the incident had been extremely funny. Sue would be beside herself when she related the story.

The cocoa and Ovaltine stains on her legs were still very much in evidence and she hoped that no one noticed before she got back to her bedsitter and had a proper wash.

Chapter Twelve

A heavy pounding on the door startled Josie. She had been standing looking out of the grimy window into the dark night reminiscing, and was feeling quite down. She rushed to open the door and was confronted by Sue.

'Come on,' the girl said, grabbing Josie by the arm and pushing her back inside. 'We're going out. So hurry up and get ready.'

'Going out?' Josie's stomach lurched. She had never been out on New Year's Eve before, having always spent the celebration with her grandmother when she had become old enough, sipping a glass of sweet sherry by the fire before retiring to bed. The prospect of actually going out to celebrate thrilled her beyond belief.

'That's what I said. We're going out,' Sue repeated.

'But I thought you'd be spending the night with your friends?'

'I am. With you.' She clapped her hands together. 'Come on. Get dressed. I'll be back in five minutes.'

They both heard the front door slam shut.

'Oh, maybe that's Peter,' Josie said hopefully. She was getting to like him very much. They got on well together and Josie was beginning to hope their relationship would develop into something more. Besides, it kept her mind from dwelling on Stephen. 'Maybe he'd like to come with us?'

'Oh, that won't be Peter. He's not due back 'til tomorrow. He's gone to stop with a friend.'

'Girlfriend?' Josie asked tentatively.

The smile on Sue's face froze. She thought for a moment, eyeing Josie warily as she decided whether to take the girl into her confidence. She made her decision, walked over and stood with her back against the electric fire.

'Josie, there's something you need to know.'

'Oh!'

'It's Peter. He's at a friend's, but it's not a girlfriend he's with.'

'Ain't it?'

'No.' Sue hesitated. 'It's a boyfriend, Josie. And this friend is a very good friend, if you know what I mean.'

Josie frowned. 'What, like you and me?'

'No. They're lovers. Well, at least, Peter's hoping they will be, given time.'

Josie's mouth fell open as slowly the truth dawned. 'You mean, he's . . .'

'Gay. Queer. Call it what you like. But, yes, he is.'

Josie ran her hand across the back of her neck. She would never have guessed.

'Look, Josie, Peter keeps that side of his life private. If anyone found out, he'd not only lose his job but he'd be hounded by the police and all sorts of people who don't understand. He can't help what he is and he's not on his own. There's many like him, women as well.'

Josie's eyes opened wide. 'You? You're not . . .'

Sue laughed loudly. 'No. I like men too much. But I'm only telling you about Peter because I think eventually you would have begun to realise something was different about him. I'm surprised you haven't asked questions already, considering the womanly mannerisms he has.'

Josie nodded. 'I did notice that, but just thought it was his way.'

'What, you thought all men from Manchester walked like that?' Sue guffawed. 'Well, anyway, I've trusted you with this knowledge, Josie. Please don't let it make any difference to your friendship with him. He's a great bloke and a very loyal friend.'

Josie smiled. 'No, I won't. To be truthful, I was getting rather fond of him.'

'I could see that. That's why I decided to tell you. Now come on and get ready or else it won't be worth going out.'

She left Josie and returned to her own room. Josie stood for a moment, stunned by the news about Peter. She found it difficult to comprehend and half wished she was still oblivious to the fact. Still, it took all sorts to make a world, and Peter was still Peter. Their friendship would not suffer because of her ignorance of such matters, she would make sure of that. It was up to her to work hard at understanding.

She suddenly realised that Sue's time limit was quickly running out so flew across to the recess and pulled back the curtain which hid her clothes. Having nothing much to choose from, she selected her black skirt and a white hand knitted jumper. She held the skirt up. It was well past its best but it would have to do. The elastic around the waist had slackened and she made a mental note to do something about it.

They arrived in the centre of town to find the place teeming with people all hell-bent on celebrating the coming of the New Year to the fullest. Very soon Josie and Sue were caught up in the high spirits. It had been an eventful year and 1967 promised to be even more so.

Josie had always been aware that the centre of Leicester sported numerous public houses, but she had never quite appreciated before just how numerous. It didn't take long for her to wonder if Sue was aiming for the record as to how many they could visit in one night. Not that they had many drinks. In most of the pubs you couldn't even see the bar, let alone get served. Oh, but she was enjoying herself! Josie's night out with Judy had been a nightmare and one she wanted to forget. Tonight she would want to remember for ever. Finally, at a quarter to twelve, they made their way towards the clock tower in order to wait for the famous landmark to strike the hour and herald the start of the new year. The clock was situated in the centre of Leicester and when they arrived thousands of people had already gathered there. They pushed their way towards the middle of the crowd in order to be in the thick of it when the clock struck.

Some bright spark was in the process of climbing the tower and as he hung a pair of bright red bloomers on the spire a huge cheer exploded. The giant Christmas tree standing to the right of the clock still twinkled brightly and Josie felt a surge of excitement. The crowd was at fever pitch as the clock's hands moved towards the allotted hour.

Suddenly, Josie's arm was grabbed and she felt herself swung round in the surging crowd. Her startled eyes rested on the person who had seized her. It was Stephen.

'Josie!' he shouted, his face full of delight. 'Where the hell have you been hiding yourself?' He grabbed her and hugged her tightly.

Josie's heart raced as she tried to keep her balance against the crowd. He pulled back slightly, his eyes searching her face.

'I've been to your house several times but your uncle says you're not seeing anyone. Did he give you the money?'

'What money?' she asked, bewildered.

'The money we collected for you. All the market traders chipped in and more besides. We got over thirty pounds.'

'You did!' Josie clasped her hand to her mouth. Thirty pounds was a fortune.

'We heard what Marilyn had done.'

'You did. How?'

'You can't keep things like that quiet, Josie. Will you be in tomorrow night if I come round? I want to talk to you.'

'Talk to me. What for?'

'Stephen, come on. It's just about twelve.'

Josie's eyes darted past Stephen to the girl who had shouted. She was a redhead and very pretty. Josie's heart plummeted.

Stephen ignored the girl.

'Will you be in?' he asked again.

Josie shook her head. 'I don't live there any more.'

'You don't. Why?'

Just then the clock started to strike twelve and the crowd cheered. She found herself being forced away from him. She fought to keep her stance but to no avail. Her eyes searched the crowd but he was gone. The next she knew Sue was grabbing her hand and they joined an enormous circle of people to sing 'Auld Lang Syne'.

After several choruses and a rendering of the 'Hokey Cokey', the crowd started to disperse towards the town hall square. Josie and Sue followed suit and spent a pleasant half hour mingling with them and watching the antics of several drunken students, jumping and paddling in the icy waters of the fountain.

It was well past two-thirty before they arrived back home. Josie gratefully accepted a hot cup of coffee and cheese sandwich from her friend. The bread was hard and the cheese stale, but to a ravenous girl who had had hardly anything to eat all day, the food tasted like nectar and she ate with relish.

Sue smiled fondly at her friend. 'Did you enjoy yourself then?'

Josie breathed deeply. 'Yes, I did,' she said with her mouth full. 'Thanks for taking me.'

'Who was the bloke?'

'Bloke?'

'Don't be coy with me, Josie Rawlings. The good-looking bloke who couldn't take his eyes off you at the clock tower.'

'Oh, him. That was Stephen. I've mentioned him to you before. He's a friend.'

She proceeded to tell Sue about the conversation they had had.

Sue's eyes opened wide. 'Why, that's great! That money will be a Godsend to you at the moment.'

'Yes, it will. But getting it will be another matter.'

'I can't see why,' Sue said matter-of-factly. 'You just go and get it. That money's yours, Josie. He's no right to hang on to it.'

'I don't think he'll see it that way,' she answered forlornly.

'I didn't like your uncle when you first told me about him, I like him even less now, if that's possible.' Sue sniffed disdainfully and paused in thought. 'Well, there's nothing for it, you'll have to go round and confront him.'

'I can't.' Josie lifted her eyes in anguish. 'You don't know what he's like. He always manages to frighten the life out of me. I daren't face him alone.'

'Then I'll come with you, and if you like I'll get some of the lads from College. We'll put the frighteners on him for a change. You can't let him get away with this. He's already got your house and

104

van and taken your livelihood away. I'm damned sure I can't sit back and let him keep your money.'

Josie sighed deeply. Talk was one thing when you had a drink inside you, having the courage to put that talk into action when sober was another matter. 'It was nice of my friends to collect it. I didn't realise they thought so much of me.'

'Well, it's about time you did. You're always selling yourself short and it's time you stopped.' Sue's face softened. 'I know I've only known you for a few weeks, but you're a great girl, Josie, and I'm proud to call you my friend.'

She fought back a lump in her throat but it was to no avail. Tears of anguish poured down her face. She sobbed and Sue sat back and waited, letting her give vent to her emotions.

Finally Josie stopped, wiped her face on the bottom of her skirt and raised her watery eyes.

'I'm sorry.'

'Sorry? You've nothing to be sorry about. I hope that cry has done you good.' She eyed Josie searchingly. 'This Stephen – are you sure he's just a friend?'

Josie sniffed loudly. 'Yes. Why d'you ask?'

'Nothing,' Sue answered flatly, not believing Josie for a moment. She was maybe trying to fool herself but she didn't fool Sue. This Stephen *was* more than a friend. 'Do you want me to come with you to see your uncle? I will, you know. You've only got to say.'

Josie raised her eyes. 'I'd like it if you'd come to the end of the street. Though facing him is something I must do by myself, but I doubt I'll get anywhere.'

'Well, if you don't, I'll just get the biggest friends I know to pay him a visit. He'll soon hand over that money, you see if he doesn't. When do we go?'

'Tomorrow,' Josie said slowly. 'We'll go tomorrow.'

She finally retired to her own room. She'd had a wonderful evening, and even seeing Stephen with that girl hadn't managed to mar her enjoyment. But she had a big challenge to face tomorrow and one she wasn't looking forward to.

Chapter Thirteen

Taking a deep breath, Josie knocked loudly on the door and stepped back. When nothing happened she repeated her actions. It seemed funny standing here knocking on her own front door. Was it only a few short weeks ago that she had lived and been happy inside these walls? The house seemed sad somehow, and uncared for, as though it knew what had taken place and didn't like it. She straightened her back. She was being silly. Houses were just bricks and mortar, they had no feelings. She stepped forward and knocked again.

'All right, all right. I'm coming,' she heard from within.

The door opened and her uncle stood before her. He was buckling up the belt on his immaculate blue trousers. He stared at her for a moment until it registered who she was.

'You. What d'you want?' he growled.

'Can I come in, Uncle Stanley?'

'No. Whatever you've got to say, you can say it on the doorstep. Now what d'you want?'

A movement from within caught Josie's attention. It looked like someone wearing a floral housecoat. Stanley noticed her quizzical look. He grabbed hold of the door and pulled it to behind him.

'Well?' he snarled.

Josie inhaled deeply, anger mounting. Her uncle had no right to be in this house, let alone keep her standing on the doorstep like a stranger. 'My money. I've come for my money.'

'Money! What money?' he sneered, squaring his shoulders.

'The money that was collected for me. Stephen Kingsman told me he gave it to you for safe keeping.'

Stanley ran his tongue over his lips. 'Oh, he did, did he? Well, he might have given me some but I used it to pay the bills you left.'

Josie narrowed her eyes. 'I left no bills, Uncle Stanley, you know I never. Gran didn't either. Now I want my money. It was collected for me, not you.'

'But it was given to me, wasn't it, and I used it to pay outstanding bills that were nothing to do with me. Now you prove otherwise.' He turned and walked inside, slamming the door shut behind him.

Josie stared at the door. With a sinking heart she hunched her shoulders and walked away.

She stopped and leant against a wall, squeezing her eyes tightly shut. This had all gone wrong. All that she and Sue had talked over the previous night, and the hints on how to tackle her uncle, had simply evaporated. She had stood there and let him cheat her, just as she had when he had turned up after her grandmother's funeral. She should have stood her ground then and refused to budge. But she hadn't. She had let him walk all over her. Just as she was about to retreat to Sue, who was waiting for her on the street corner, a surge of anger raced through her. She raised her head, her eyes flashing. This man had taken everything from her and now he was trying to get away with yet another devious act. Well, she wasn't going to let him.

With renewed determination, she walked back and banged loudly once again upon the door.

It flew open and he stood before her, glaring angrily.

'Didn't I tell you to clear off?'

Josie raised her head. 'I'm not leaving until you give me my money.'

A wicked smile appeared on his face. 'And I've told you my answer.'

'Okay,' she said more calmly than she felt, 'I'll go and get Big Jack and his sons. They won't take kindly to what you've done. Big Jack's been known to knock out a man with just one punch.'

She turned and began to walk down the street. How she managed to keep her legs from buckling, she'd never know.

'Hold on!' she heard her uncle shout.

She turned and retraced her steps. He disappeared back into the house, returning several moments later with an envelope which he waved menacingly in front of her.

'All right, you bitch. I'll swop you for the book.'

Josie frowned. 'You've asked me before for the book and I've already told you – I know nothing about a book. Now are you going to give me that or do I have to get Big Jack?'

Stanley's face clouded over. Josie gulped.

'If I ever find out you're lying to me, Josie Rawlings, you'll wish you hadn't.' He thrust the envelope at her. She grabbed it. 'Now get out of here and don't come back.'

Josie pushed the envelope deep inside her pocket and ran, not stopping until she was halfway down the street. She gasped for breath and tried to stop her legs shaking. She'd done it! She'd stood up to her uncle and she felt jubilant. She joined Sue who by now was impatient for news.

'I did it!' she cried.

Sue placed an arm around Josie's shoulders and hugged her. 'Good on you, Josie. You showed that bastard what's what. I'm proud of you. Come on, let's get home. But on the way we'll call into the off licence for a bottle of cider to celebrate.'

Josie lay in bed that night unable to sleep. She felt so pleased with herself. For once she had stood her ground. Well, that was a sign of things to come. Never again would she be walked over. A new Josie was beginning to emerge and she liked the feeling.

She smiled warmly. The money would come in so handy. She and Sue had talked half the night of things she could do with it. She knew one thing. Tomorrow she would go and buy some sheets, a pillow, and several blankets. Since she'd been in this room, not one decent night's sleep had she had because of the cold.

Her uncle's face loomed before her and she shuddered. So, he was now living in her grandmother's house? And what of her Auntie Hilda? The person she'd glimpsed on the dimly lit stairs when she had confronted him had been dark-haired. Stanley must have left her Auntie Hilda and moved in his fancy piece. Oh, her poor auntie. What she must have put up with all the years she was married to him! Maybe this was for the best, at least on her side. Well, Josie would go and visit her auntie and return the money that Hilda had given her. The woman would probably need it. As far as Josie knew she wasn't working. They had been supported all those years by the money they had received from Lily and now that had dried up she couldn't see her uncle supporting his estranged wife willingly.

As she turned over she wondered if they had yet heard from their elusive daughter. Well, she would hear all the news from her auntie. If there was any, that is.

'Well, isn't this nice?' Hilda Rawlings fussed as she handed Josie a cup of tea. 'Help yourself to a slice of cake,' she said, indicating a plate on the table.

Josie shook her head and took a sip of weak tea. She gazed around the room. It could have done with being decorated but it was homely. The imitation leather settee crackled beneath her as she shifted to a more comfortable position. A fire burned in the grate, illuminating a picture of The Crying Boy that hung above it. She tried to avert her eyes. The picture repelled her.

'You like the painting?' she heard her aunt say. 'I bought it just the other day.'

Josie took another sip of tea. Her auntie didn't seem at all perturbed by recent events. In fact, she appeared just the opposite. Stanley's departure had made her positively bloom. The woman seated before Josie wasn't the quivering wreck she had bumped into that awful night not so long ago.

'I'm selling the house,' Hilda twittered. 'Moving to Skegness. My sister's there, you know, and the air's ever so bracing.' She noticed Josie's quizzical frown. 'This house is all mine, dear. Nothing to do with . . . with . . . well, you know who.' Her eyes misted over and she turned and stared into the fire. 'I often wondered if he married me because I had this house.' She shook herself, picked up the plate and held it out towards Josie. 'Well, he didn't marry me for anything else.' Josie refused the offer and she put the plate back. 'I can only apologise for the way he's treated you, Josie. He'd no right to throw you out of your grandmother's house. But he's always been like that. No regard for people's feelings. I'd offer you a room. But, well – I don't expect to be here that long.'

Josie smiled. 'I hope you'll be happy in Skeggy, Auntie Hilda.'

'I expect I shall, dear. You can always come and visit, when I've settled. I'm getting a nice little flat facing the sea. My sister runs a cafe on the front and has offered me a job. To be honest, I can't wait. I hope this house doesn't take long to sell. I'd like to have moved before Easter.'

'Oh, it will sell, I'm sure,' Josie said reassuringly. 'It's a nice house.' She took another sip of tea and eyed her auntie thoughtfully as she wondered whether to ask several questions. If she didn't, she might never find out the answers. She decided on the easiest one first.

'Have you heard from Marilyn, Auntie Hilda?'

She raised her head. 'No,' she said slowly. 'I haven't heard a word from her. I do know she never went to Blackpool as she told me. Where she is, I don't know.' She smoothed her hands over her blue crimplene shirtwaister. 'I gave that girl everything and this is how she repays me. Well, she's on her own now. I'm going to think of myself for a change.'

Josie nodded in agreement. It was obvious her auntie hadn't a clue that Marilyn had stolen all her grandmother's money and she felt it best that the woman should stay ignorant. It was evident that she had not had an easy life with Stanley and Marilyn and she deserved some happiness now.

Hilda coughed discreetly. 'If Marilyn does put in an appearance after I've moved, will you tell her where I've gone?'

''Course I will,' Josie said quickly.

'More tea?'

'Please.'

Josie accepted the cup and placed it on the table.

'Auntie Hilda,' she began.

'Yes, dear?'

'Do you know why my grandmother and Uncle Stanley never spoke for years? I know I shouldn't ask, but I would like to know.'

Hilda sucked in her cheeks and clasped her hands together. 'I can't answer that one.'

'Why?'

'Because I don't know what happened.'

'Don't you. Oh!'

'All I know is that there was a terrible row. I did think it was something to do with money.'

'Did you?'

'Yes. I couldn't think it would have been anything else. 'Course, all this happened before I married him. I always hoped they'd make it up, but they never did. It would have been nice to have had a mother- and sister-in-law.'

Josie stared at her thoughtfully and reached for her cup. 'Did Uncle Stanley ever mention anything about a book to you, Auntie Hilda?'

Hilda frowned deeply. 'A book! What kinda book?'

'I've no idea. Just a book.'

'No. Why?'

'Uncle Stanley keeps going on about one and I don't know what he's talking about.'

'Neither do I.' Hilda patted her tightly permed hair. 'You will stay for dinner? I've a nice bit of haddock . . .'

'No, thank you. I must be getting back.' Josie put down her cup and saucer, reached for her bag and withdrew her purse. 'I want to repay you the money . . .'

Hilda held up her hand. 'I won't hear of it. You buy yourself something nice.'

Josie departed no wiser than she had been before her visit. But it was nice to see her auntie seeming so well and looking forward so much to her future. She hunched her shoulders against the biting wind. It was about time she stopped worrying about other people and started to be more concerned for her own future, just as Hilda had learned to be.

Chapter Fourteen

Josie hurried down East Bond Street, turned the corner and crossed the bottom of Churchgate. She stopped to hitch up her skirt and tighten her scarf. She had thought by cutting through the back streets she would reach the employment exchange on Charles Street quicker. But she had been mistaken. It had taken her twice as long and she was now freezing and badly in need of a cup of hot tea to warm her 'innards', as her old gran would have said. It was nearing the end of February, the weather had worsened and her job prospects were no better. She was getting desperate and her predicament was not from lack of trying.

Bending down, she pulled off her shoe and shook out the stone that had been nipping her. She pretended not to notice the hole forming in the sole or the ladder in her last pair of tights beginning to run up her leg. Straightening up, she made to start her journey again but something caught her eye and she turned and peered into the grimy window she had been leaning against. Funny, in all the years she had been coming into town she had never noticed this little greengrocery shop before. But then there was nothing peculiar about that as she didn't often come this way.

The outside of the shop was badly neglected and the inside didn't look any better. It was then she noticed the card: 'Help wanted. Apply within.' Josie thought hard for a moment, visualising what lay behind those filthy windows. She squared her shoulders. Who was she to be choosy? If they wanted help, then they'd got it. She just had to hope that no one had beaten her to it.

The bell on the door jangled as she entered and she blinked rapidly to accustom her eyes to the dim light. She gazed around.

Half-empty wooden shelves holding, she noticed, poor quality fruit and vegetables that she would have thrown out long since, lined the walls; several of the shelves housed an assortment of jams and preserves, their tops thick with dust. In the far corner, stacked at the side of an enormous pair of black iron scales, sat several hessian sacks of potatoes, carrots and cabbages. Josie wrinkled her nose. Something was off and had been for a long time by the smell of it.

Josie turned abruptly and her eyebrows rose. Through the door behind the worn wooden counter stood a woman, and for once Josie felt small and insignificant. The woman was at least six foot tall and solidly built, her body mass consisting mostly of hard muscle. It was difficult to determine her age, she could have been anywhere between thirty and fifty. Her raven-black hair was parted down the middle and coiled in two plaits around her ears. She wore a shapeless pale blue floral dress, a wrinkled pair of beige knitted stockings, and on her enormous feet a pair of brown, down-at-heel flat brogues. She wiped her large red hands on her stained white apron, her broad features spreading into a smile.

'Yes, me duck. What canna do fer yer?'

Josie cleared her throat. 'You have a card in the window . . .'

The woman's grey eyes opened wide. 'You've come to apply, 'ave yer?'

Josie nodded. 'But if the job's gone . . .'

'Oh, no, it's not gone,' she said hastily as she turned and shouted through the back: 'Dad. We've got someone applying for the job.'

'Eh?' a cracked voice replied.

'I said . . .' The woman sidled through to the back. The rest of her words were lost.

Josie turned and quickly eyed the door. Instinct told her to take this chance for escape but for some reason her feet were rooted to the dirty floor.

The woman reappeared. 'Come through. Come through,' she beckoned.

Josie hesitantly followed. The room she entered was even dimmer than the shop. In contrast, though, it was surprisingly clean, the assortment of good quality, old-fashioned furniture gleaming. Her eyes immediately settled upon the Victorian fireplace. She had only ever seen such a fireplace before in an old book of her grandmother's. It had been captioned 'a range'. Like the faded picture, this range also had a kettle swinging from a hook over the coals in the grate. Josie suddenly had an overwhelming feeling that she had stepped back in time.

She turned her gaze to the old man sitting in a horsehair armchair. In contrast to the massive woman, he was small and shrivelled, and for a fleeting moment she thought it impossible that such a tiny human being could have fathered such offspring.

The old man eyed her eagerly as he beckoned her over.

'Come 'ere,' he rasped. 'Me eyes ain't so good. I can't see yer properly. Come on,' he said, with laughter in his voice. 'I ain't gonna bite yer.'

The powerful woman gave a bellowing laugh at his words as she stood at the back of her father's chair, hands resting on her large hips.

112

Josie inched forward and stood before him.

'Sit down,' he ordered.

Josie sat down hesitantly on the edge of the chair opposite, clasping her handbag firmly to her chest.

The old man eyed her thoroughly.

Satisfied, he sat back and breathed deeply. 'Well, yer look all right ter me. What d'you think, Gertie?' She nodded eagerly in approval. 'Done this kinda work before?' he asked.

Josie swallowed hard. 'Depends what kind of work you're referring to,' she answered cautiously.

'Humping sacks of spuds and such like, and serving of course.' The old man tittered as he turned to address his daughter. 'Mek 'er a cuppa, Gertie. The poor gel looks frightened to death. Thinks we're gonna eat 'er for dinner.' Gertie obeyed his instructions and he turned back to Josie. 'That's right, ain't it? You think we're peculiar?' He sniffed loudly. 'I can't say as I blame yer, gel. We must look it. But let me tell yer – this place wa' a thriving business 'til me wife died, bless 'er, and me age got the better of me. Gertie can't manage by 'erself. Since me legs gave up, she's 'ad to do everythin' and it's too much. Ain't it, Gertie?' he shouted. 'I keep telling 'er, a woman of 'er age should be married with kids, not lookin' after 'er old dad.' He looked at Josie keenly. 'If we 'ad 'elp, she could spend more time lookin' for an 'usband . . .'

'Dad,' Gertie scolded as she strode forward with the teapot, 'this young woman doesn't want to 'ear you prattlin' on.' She turned her attention to Josie. 'A' yer interested, me duck? Only, bein' truthful, you're the only applicant we've 'ad. If you say yes, between us we could get the shop back to its former glory. I used to mek cakes and biscuits as well as jams and preserves. I could start that up again. It'll bring in new customers. People can't be bothered these days to mek things themselves, can they? But they prefer home-made to that processed stuff all the bakers sell now.'

Josie nodded in agreement.

'Well then, what d'you say?' she asked hopefully. 'We could just about manage four pounds a week, plus we'll throw in yer dinner, and yer can 'elp yerself to as much fruit and veggies as yer want.'

Josie breathed deeply. Four pounds was well below the going rate but that and a hot dinner each day wasn't to be sneezed at. The shop would need a thorough clean and if she offered to go down to the wholesalers and buy the produce herself, that side of the business would be enhanced also. She wouldn't like to hazard a guess as to where they bought their produce from, but it wasn't a good source. She quickly assessed them both as they waited patiently for her answer. They seemed quite nice people despite her first alarming impression. Both had a twinkle in their eye and they appeared honest enough. She could understand why they had had no other takers for the job. One look at these two and if you had any sense you'd run a mile! The beginnings of a smile started to form on her face. It wouldn't do any harm to give it a go. If things didn't work out, she could always leave. Besides, she had nothing else in the offing.

'I'll give it a try,' she said before she could change her mind.

'You will!' Gertie exclaimed. 'You 'ear that, Dad. She's gonna give us a go.'

William Waltham clapped his gnarled hands together in delight. 'Bless yer, gel. Yer won't regret it. When can you start?'

Josie left the shop, the bell jangling loudly behind her. Had she really agreed to work there? Sue would tell her she was crazy. A warm feeling rose within her. It felt right, and she knew she was going to enjoy the challenge. She quickened her step. At last she had a job and she couldn't wait to get started.

'I've got a job!' Josie shouted at the top of her voice as she burst through the door of Sue's room.

Sue looked up from the magazine she was thumbing through. ''Bout time.' She got up and hugged her friend tightly. 'What is it? When do you start?'

'First thing Monday morning, and it's an assistant in a green-grocery shop.'

'Oh, Josie. That's right up your street. I'm so proud of you.' Sue released her and clasped her hands together. 'This calls for a celebration. We'll have a party.'

'Party!'

'That's what I said. A party. And we'll have it this Saturday night.'

'Oh,' Josie murmured. A party. She'd never been to a party before. She'd always wanted to but had never been invited, and here she was going to one, and in her own honour.

'I ain't got nothing to wear,' she said, frowning deeply.

Sue tutted loudly. 'We'll soon fix you up.' She paused and looked at her friend critically. 'It's about time you had some new clothes, Josie. And some that suit you, not those baggy old things.'

Josie looked down at her black elasticated-waist skirt, grabbed the sides and held it out. 'It's not baggy.'

'It damned well is. The bloody thing is about falling off you.'

Josie hitched it up. 'I think I must have washed it wrong at the launderette.'

'Things shrink at the launderette, Josie, not get bigger. It's you. You've lost weight. Well, you certainly have since I met you, anyway.'

'Have I?'

Josie peered down at herself. Had she lost weight? Now how had that happened? She frowned deeply. She hadn't been eating half as much as she used to, and traipsing the streets day after day in search of a job had certainly given her much more exercise. She ran her hands over her stomach and her eyes widened in surprise. It had almost gone. That fat, flabby mound of flesh that used to wobble violently when she took off her clothes had almost disappeared. She ran her hands around. So had her big bottom. How come she hadn't noticed? Her eyes widened even further. It was the job. She had been too wrapped up in looking for one and worrying about her future to notice her changing shape.

Her face lit up. 'Do you really think I'm thinner?' she asked, feeling the need once again to clarify things.

'Heaps,' Sue responded. 'You'll have it confirmed when we go shopping. Have you any money?'

Josie grunted. 'Don't be daft. The money from the collection has just about gone keeping a roof over me head. That's why I'm so pleased about this job.'

'Well, not to worry. I've some.'

'You have?'

Sue grabbed her enormous shoulder bag and rummaged through it. She pulled out a cheque and waved it about. 'Courtesy of Daddy. The dear sent me my allowance today. We can spend some of that.'

Josie grimaced fiercely. 'You have to live on that for six months, Sue. You can't go round spending it willy-nilly.'

'Stop being so stuffy, Josie Rawlings. There's plenty more where that came from. If I'm really desperate I can always plead poverty. Anyway, you can pay me back when you make your fortune.'

''A' you sure?'

'I wouldn't be offering if I wasn't. Anyway . . .' She grinned wickedly. 'I can't introduce you to all my other mates with you looking like a rag bag, can I?' She slapped Josie on the shoulder, her face bathed in delight. 'That's settled then. We'll start making arrangements for the party and we'll rope Peter in. But first thing Saturday morning, you and I are going shopping. You're going to be transformed, Josie Rawlings. You see if you're not. Just leave it all to me.'

Josie exhaled deeply and flopped down on a cushion. 'I need a drink, Sue. This is all too much for me.'

Without further prompting Sue delved behind a pile of books stacked underneath the coffee table and pulled forth a half-empty bottle of cider. She split it between two mugs and gave Josie hers.

Just then the door opened and Peter walked through. He smiled at the sight that greeted him.

'Celebrating, are we?' he said, his eyes twinkling. 'I hope there's some of that for me. I could do with a drop after the day I've had.'

'None left, unless you fancy a trip down the offy,' Sue quipped.

Peter dug down into his pocket and pulled out some loose change. 'One bottle or two?'

'Two. And while you've gone, me and Josie will make some sandwiches and you can bring in your guitar. We'll have a sing-song.' She turned to Josie. 'Have you got any bread and something to put on it?'

Much later, Josie lay back against the cushions, mellow from the cider and comforted by the companionship of her friends. She listened enthralled as Sue sang 'The Times They Are A-Changing'. She had a good voice and Peter could certainly play the guitar. What an end to a perfect day. Life was beginning to change for the better and she felt excitement and well-being envelop her.

Chapter Fifteen

Sue gasped in delight. 'Oh, Josie. You look . . . You look fabulous!' she breathed.

Josie turned back to face the mirror. Was the attractive woman reflected there really her? Sue had said she was going to be transformed and she was right. The woman staring back was – dare she admit it – beautiful. Yes, she was – she was beautiful.

They had both risen early that morning but their first port of call had not been a clothes shop but a hairdressers. Sue had pushed Josie through the door and she had sat with eyes shut tight as the hairdresser had snipped away at her long shapeless tresses. When she had dared open them, she had gawped. Her thick dark hair was cut in a most becoming shape to just below her chin. She had wanted to hug the stylist in delight. Instead she just sat and stared at her reflection in disbelief.

Now here she was again, utterly speechless at the vision in the mirror. Never before had she thought it possible that good old Josie Rawlings could look like this. No one would recognise her, and to Josie it seemed nothing short of a miracle.

'Try the other on,' Sue nudged her, breaking her thoughts.

'Oh, no. I like this,' she whispered ecstatically.

She could not take her eyes off the black and cream crêpe mini dress. Nothing she would wear in the future would ever give her such a thrill. She would wear it tonight, along with her new black thigh-length boots and black tights. She finally forced herself to undress and pull on her old skirt and blouse. With head held high she followed Sue to the check-out and watched intently as the dress was carefully folded and put into a bag.

By the time the pair boarded the bus home, several bags holding a pair of camel hipster trousers, two mini skirts, the mini dress, three blouses and two jumpers, plus several pairs of tights, a pair of shoes and the boots, were being carried between them.

Josie sat down beside her friend and smiled warmly. 'I can't thank you enough,' she said sincerely. 'I'll pay you back as soon as I can.'

'No need for thanks,' Sue said sharply, beginning to feel slightly embarrassed at Josie's continuous gratitude. 'It was my pleasure.' She turned, and looking at her friend closely, took a deep breath. 'To be honest, you've made me realise how privileged I am.'

'Have I?'

'Yes.' Sue lowered her head, suddenly feeling an overwhelming need to get a few things off her chest. 'Josie . . .' she began falteringly. 'I've never had to struggle for anything. I only have to hold my hand out and it is filled. You've gone without food to keep a roof over your head. If I wanted, I could go home and be pampered. I only live here because it suits me.' She raised her eyes sheepishly. 'I take my parents far too much for granted. That business at Christmas when I arrived back early – it was all my fault.'

'Was it? You said it was because your parents were getting on your nerves.'

'Josie, my folks bent over backwards to give me a good Christmas and I repaid them by throwing a tantrum and storming out. My poor mother was really upset, but I didn't give a stuff about her feelings.' The bus turned a sharp corner and they both lurched to the side. Two of the bags fell on the floor and Josie bent to pick them up. When she had settled herself, Sue continued. 'Getting to know you these past months and listening to you has made me realise how selfish I've been.'

'Selfish, how?' Josie asked in surprise. 'I don't think you're selfish.'

'Oh, but I am, Josie. Look how you gave up your education to run your grandmother's stall when your mother died, and then you stayed at home to look after her. I wouldn't have done that. And then, instead of wallowing in self-pity when your uncle did the dirty, you picked yourself up and got on with things. You found yourself a room and now a job. I admire you, I really do. Because I don't think I could have done that on my own.'

'Oh, you could,' Josie said, lowering her head in embarrassment. 'I only did what I had to.'

'Don't sell yourself short, Josie. I'm telling you, I couldn't have done what you did. I'd have crumbled at the thought.'

Josie stared at her friend. No one had ever talked to her like this before. She was deeply moved and didn't know how to react.

She sighed. 'Do you realise that helping you get these clothes today has been the first time I've really helped someone? And it's given me more enjoyment than you'll ever realise. And I've made a decision. I'm going to treat my parents better from now on. Because, through you, I've realised that once they've gone, it's too late.' She tilted her head and let a slow smile spread across her face at Josie's bemused expression. 'Now that's enough of being philosophical. Here's our stop and we'd better hurry, we've stacks to do before the party starts.' Her eyes lit up in pleasure. 'I can't wait to show Peter your new clothes. He's going to be speechless when he sees your transformation.'

Josie was glad when all the preparations were finished and she could retire to make herself ready. And she enjoyed every moment of it from the scrub down in the sink to carefully applying the makeup Sue had lent her. Sue had also given her a pair of black plastic false eyelashes for a finishing touch. Josie sat before the mirror and applied a layer of glue on to the thin edge and painstakingly tried to put them on. She finally sat back and gave an exasperated sigh.

'That's me ready to knock them dead,' Sue said, breezing in through the door looking stunning in a microscopic red skirt, black tight-fitting jumper and chunky-heeled patent shoes. 'What's the matter?' she asked at the sight of Josie's troubled expression.

'I think there's something wrong with me eyes.'

'Something wrong with your eyes?' Sue advanced and stood at Josie's side, her face frowning in concern.

Josie looked up at her. 'It's these false lashes you gave me. I can't get 'em on. They don't seem to fit.' She handed the lashes to Sue. 'D'you think me lids are too big or summat?'

Sue examined the lashes, then gave a bellowing laugh. 'Oh, Josie, there's nothing wrong with your eyes.'

'Ain't there?' she said in relief.

'No. It's my fault. I only gave you one eyelash. It's broken, see. Snapped in two.' She held the pieces out towards Josie in the palm of her hand.

'Thank God for that. I was beginning to think I was deformed.'

Sue laughed again. 'I'll get you another pair.'

'No need, thanks. I'll make do with me own.'

'You don't really need them anyway. I'd do anything to have thick lashes like yours. Just put some mascara on, that's all you really need.'

Josie reddened, stood up and gave a twirl.

'Well, what d'yer think?'

Sue pretended to study her. She smiled. 'You look fabulous,' she said, hooking her arm through her friend's. 'Come on, let's get a drink before the gannets start to arrive and we've nothing left.'

Much later that evening, Josie flattened herself against the wall and scanned the roomful of people as she savoured the atmosphere. Sue had promised a party and some party it was turning out to be. She'd never thought it possible that so many bodies could be crammed into such a small space. Her own room had been cleared of furniture, which had been crammed into Peter's room to allow space for dancing, and at least thirty people were packed in there now, gyrating to the strains of a 'A Whiter Shade of Pale' booming from the record player sitting on the draining board next to the sink.

Sue's room held the food and drink. Each invitation was strictly 'Bring a bottle or no admission', and an assortment of cider and bottles of cheap wine filled Sue's small table. Plastic cups and paper plates had been elected to save on the washing up. Besides, between them they only had four chipped mugs and three decent plates.

Most of the crisps, sausage rolls and cheese sandwiches had been demolished, and overflowing ashtrays and crumbs lay scattered on the floor. But everyone looked happy and they were certainly enjoying themselves. Josie's eyes alighted on the darkened corner of the room. A couple smooched passionately, the man's hand edging further and further up the girl's thigh. She grabbed his hand, only to find it several moments later back where she had removed it from.

Josie jumped as a hand touched her arm. 'You haven't met Michael, have you, Josie?' Tula said, her large brown eyes staring fondly into the handsome face of the man standing beside her.

'No.' Josie accepted the large brown hand that was thrust at her and shook it warmly.

Tula leant over and whispered in Josie's ear. 'What d'you t'ink?'

Josie smiled. 'He's nice,' she whispered back. 'Is it serious?'

'I'm hopin' so. Like me, he's done all his trainin' in England and plans to go home at some stage and start his own practice. At the moment he's a locum at the Royal. I've bin seein' him for several weeks now.'

'You kept that quiet,' Josie chided, pretending to be hurt.

Tula gave a rich throaty giggle. 'I ain't so daft as to let him loose near you and Sue. Not 'til I was more sure.'

Josie felt flattered and laughed as Tula left her side and guided the handsome black man towards the drinks table.

She turned her head to find Peter standing at her side, taking large gulps of his drink, his face the picture of misery.

'What's wrong?' she asked.

'My friend hasn't turned up,' he muttered forlornly. 'And he promised he'd come.'

Josie laid her hand on his arm. 'Not to worry. There's plenty of girls . . .' She stopped abruptly, realising what she had said. 'Oh, sorry, Peter. I didn't mean . . .'

He laughed. 'I know you didn't.'

'There's still plenty of time. Maybe he'll come a bit later,' she said optimistically.

Peter shook his head. 'No. He won't come now.'

'Oh, well, maybe something important has cropped up.' She

studied him for a moment. 'Tell yer what. Why don't you bring him for tea sometime? Me and Sue could do one of our specials. I'd like to meet him.'

Peter eyed her fondly. 'In normal circumstances I would, darling. I'd love to introduce him to my two dearest friends. But, well,' Peter rubbed his chin, 'he's not the type to bring to tea, and especially not the type to eat off our chipped plates.'

'Ain't he? Oh! Well, what type is he then?'

Peter stared into space. 'Special, Josie. Very special. A one-off. And I feel so much for him that it scares me.' He sighed loudly. 'I'm not surprised he hasn't turned up. Things like this aren't his scene. But, well, I was just hoping.' He put his plastic cup to his lips and downed the contents. 'Oh, darling, I sometimes wish I could fancy girls, things would be a hell of a lot easier,' he said. His eyes brightened. 'If I ever did, it would be someone like you.'

'Me?'

'Yes, without a doubt. You're the kindest, most considerate person I know, and you look absolutely ravishing tonight, sweetie pie.' He leaned over and whispered in her ear, 'I'd give my right arm to have a pair of legs like yours.'

Josie giggled and slapped him playfully on the arm. 'Ged away with yer.' She grabbed his arm. 'Come on, this is a party. Let's have a dance. I'm not going to stand and watch you moping just because "he" couldn't be bothered to turn up.' Her eyes twinkled wickedly. 'It will give us both a chance to eye up the talent in the other room. You never know, Peter. There might just be someone else who'll catch yer eye.'

Josie jumped as a hand gripped her wrist.

'You're dancing with me,' a deep voice said.

She turned round. The voice belonged to a light-haired man of medium height. His face, although not handsome, had a kind of rugged attractiveness about it. His nose was long and straight and his piercing blue eyes were fixed upon her as he spoke. At one time he must have suffered from acne as his skin was badly marked, but this did not detract from his magnetism. She had not noticed him before and wondered if he had just arrived. She wanted to ask but her throat had dried.

His lips suddenly curved into a smile, revealing slightly crooked teeth, and without another word he guided her towards the music. The room was still full of people dancing and he had to push his way through to the centre of the floor. He stopped, turned and took her in his arms. So transfixed was she that she didn't even see Sue trying to catch her attention.

She closed her eyes as they swayed to the rhythm, unaware of anything or anybody. Her mind raced. Who was this man?

Several records were played but still they continued dancing. Finally he stopped, took hold of her hand and guided her back, depositing her against the wall. She watched him make his way over to the drinks table and pour two plastic cups of wine and then weave his way back. He held out a cup which she accepted. She took a sip, scrutinising him from under her lashes.

He gazed down at her, his eyes drinking her in. 'I'll pick you up tomorrow night about seven?' he said huskily.

Josie froze. Was this a date? It had sounded more like a command. But wasn't she supposed to be consulted first? And what was she supposed to say? Just yes? Wouldn't that sound too eager? She held her breath. He appeared so sure of himself. At this moment she doubted anyone had ever refused him. She felt his eyes boring into her as he waited for an answer.

'All right,' she said softly, raising her eyes to meet his.

He unexpectedly bent over and kissed her full on the mouth, then he was gone. Stunned, Josie stared after him.

'Who was that?'

Josie jumped. 'Eh?'

'I said, who was that?' Sue demanded.

Josie shook her head. 'I don't know. Isn't he one of your friends?'

Sue frowned. 'No. I've never seen him before. But he was rather dishy in a rugged sort of way.'

'Yes. He was, wasn't he?' Josie turned her attention to her friend and bit her bottom lip. 'He's asked me out. Well, it was more of a command, really.'

'When?' Sue asked, her face lighting up in delight.

'Tomorrow. He's picking me up at seven.'

'Phew! I wish it was me.' She slapped her friend on the back. 'See, I told you you'd slay them and I've been proved right.'

Josie laughed, but her mind was filled with questions.

The party finally ground to a halt just after four-thirty. Three bleary-eyed friends surveyed the mess.

'There's no way I can tackle this lot now,' Sue groaned sleepily. 'I vote we leave it and get some sleep.'

Peter and Josie agreed. Between them they sorted the beds, said goodnight, and all climbed gratefully under the sheets.

Josie woke with a start. Unexpected sunshine filled her room. She raised herself up on one elbow and stared around. She groaned loudly. The mess was frightening. It'll take weeks to clear this lot, she thought ruefully. Then there was Sue's room. Could that possibly be worse than this?

She slowly rose and sat on the edge of the bed. The sunshine that promised warmth did not materialise. The room was freezing and she hastily pulled the covers back over her legs. Screwing up her eyes, she fought to read the time on the old clock she had picked up from a junk shop. It said twelve-thirty. She sighed deeply. Sitting here wasn't getting this lot cleared up. If she didn't make a move soon, she'd be here until midnight.

Suddenly, the events of the previous night flooded back and she shuddered. She had a date, a date with a mysterious man, and she felt frightened.

Jumping up, she pulled on her old pink dressing-gown which, because of her much diminished size, now drowned her, and bounded out of her room. She hammered loudly on Sue's door. Then hammered again. After several moments she heard muffled sounds coming from within. A tousled-haired, red-eyed Sue opened the door.

'Huh,' she grunted. She tied the belt on her terry towelling dressing gown and rubbed her eyes. 'What time is it?'

'Never mind the time,' Josie cried impatiently, 'I need to talk to you.'

Sue half turned and glanced back into her room. She pulled the door behind her.

'It's a bit inconvenient at the moment. Give me ten minutes.'

Josie stared at her. Sue was acting very strangely. Why? Suddenly the truth dawned. She had a man in her room.

She gulped. 'Er . . . I'm sorry,' she began, inching back down the icy cold corridor.

Sue grinned sheepishly. 'Just give me ten minutes and I'll be all yours.'

Josie nodded. She arrived back in her room and placed the battered kettle on the gas ring. So Sue had spent the remainder of the night with a man? He hadn't been apparent after everyone had left. He must have been hiding. No wonder she'd wanted to leave all the mess until the morning, she had had more important things on her mind!

Eventually the front door slammed shut and several moments later her own door opened and Sue sauntered in, looking decidedly better than she had done a half hour previously.

'Sorry about that Josie. Now what's your problem?'

Pouring boiling water into a mug that already held a spoonful of coffee powder, Josie swallowed hard. 'Well, it's this date I've got tonight . . .'

'So!'

Josie handed Sue the mug, sat down next to her on the bed and absent-mindedly plucked at the bri-nylon sheets. 'Well, I don't know what to do or say.' She bent her head and studied the contents of her cup. 'I've never been on a proper date before,' she said softly.

123

Sue grinned broadly. 'Well, you've got to start somewhere, and what better bloke to do it with? He was gorgeous.'

Josie's face lit up. 'D'you really think so?' she said, then grimaced. 'But how do I act?'

Sue frowned deeply. 'You really are serious. You haven't been out with a man before, have you?'

Josie blushed scarlet. 'No, I haven't.'

'I don't believe it!' exclaimed Sue. She eyed her friend warmly. 'Just be yourself, Josie. The rest will come naturally. You'll be fine, trust me. What's his name, by the way?'

'I don't know. I don't know anything about him.'

'Mmm. Man of mystery, eh? I find this all quite intriguing.' Sue gazed across the still-littered room. 'I wonder where he'll take you? I bet it'll be somewhere nice.' She turned her attention back to Josie. 'What are you going to wear?'

She shrugged her shoulders. 'I don't know,' she said, looking at Sue for help.

'I suggest your hipster trousers and the black skinny rib jumper.'

'Oh, don't you think I'm still a bit fat to wear that? Me bulges will show.'

'Don't be stupid. A few more pounds off you and you'll give Twiggy a run for her money.'

Josie spluttered. 'That'll be the day. I'm too big boned to ever get as thin as Twiggy.'

'Josie,' Sue said sternly, 'stop bringing yourself down. You really have changed drastically since we first met and it's about time you started getting used to the idea. You're not big fat Josie any more. You're slim sexy Josie. Okay, you're right in that you'll never be as thin as Twiggy. You're a different build. But who wants to look like a clothes prop anyway? You look better than her, you've got some shape.' She giggled. 'Men don't really like women too thin. They like them to have some meat on them. Anyway, you wear the outfit I suggested and you'll have him foaming at the mouth. He won't be able to take his eyes off you. Mark my words.' She frowned deeply. 'I hope you're going to give that bag of yours a clear out before you go? You can't go out dressed up to the nines with a bag that looks like you've a month's groceries stuffed inside.'

'Oh.' Josie's eyes opened wide in alarm. 'I forgot about that. Ta, Sue.'

She rose. 'I'd better get back and start clearing up. Will you come through and give me a hand when you've finished in here? I'll give Peter a knock as well. It's about time that lazy devil was out of his pit.' She looked at Josie enquiringly. 'He didn't seem very happy last night. I never got a chance to talk to him. Do you know why?'

Josie nodded. 'His friend didn't turn up.'

'Oh, poor Peter.' She shook her head. 'I don't quite get this relationship of his. Peter's really cagey about it. But from what little he has told me, it seems pretty one-sided.'

'What d'you mean?'

'Well, this man, whoever he is, shouts and Peter jumps. I get the impression he's a lot older than Peter, and somehow . . .' She paused. 'Oh, never mind.'

'No, come on. What were you going to say?' Josie insisted.

Sue puckered her face. 'Well, I just think Peter's scared of him, that's all. I don't like it, Josie. I don't like it at all. But I have to be careful what I say. I don't want Peter to think I'm prejudiced against him being . . . well, you know. He can be very touchy sometimes. But then I suppose we all are on matters too close for comfort.' She yawned loudly. 'This isn't getting the clearing up done and I've got to meet some friends later.' She bent over and placed a friendly hand on Josie's shoulder. 'Don't worry about tonight. Just go out and enjoy yourself. Now hurry up and get cracking in here then you can come through and give me a hand.' She gave Josie a cheeky grin as she let herself out.

Josie let out a deep sigh. 'Don't worry?' she muttered. 'Who's she telling not to worry?'

She bent down and picked up her handbag and started to sort through it, then closed it and dropped it on the floor. It was too much of a task to contemplate at this moment, what with her room in such a state and the impending rendezvous on her mind. She'd find time later.

Chapter Sixteen

At two minutes to the allotted time Josie smoothed her hands over her camel hipster trousers and brushed away a fleck from her black skinny rib jumper. She was nervous; she had never been so nervous in all her life. She heard a car draw up and froze. A door banged shut and the vehicle moved away. She sighed deeply and wondered if she would ever make it through the night.

She tried to avert her mind and gazed around her room, now clear of the earlier debris. It was beginning to feel like home to her now that she had a few of her own bits and pieces dotted around. It still badly needed decorating but when she closed her door at night she felt safe, and knowing her friends were so close gave her added comfort. The events of a few months before seemed so far away. She felt that this was a positive sign. A fleeting picture of Stephen flashed through her mind. She quickly pushed it away. He belonged to the past. She must now look to the future and hope it held good things for her.

There was loud knocking on the outside door and she bit her bottom lip. This must be him.

She opened the door tentatively. He was standing before her, dressed in a pair of flared dark navy trousers, a multi-coloured tightly fitting tank top, a rounded-long-collared pale pink shirt stitched around the edges in black and a long dark navy Crombie coat. Josie stifled a gasp. He looked fabulous. Any girl would die to be seen on his arm, herself included.

His piercing blue eyes looked straight into hers.

'Ready?' he asked.

'Well,' Sue asked impatiently. 'How did it go? Where did he take you? What was he like?'

Josie clasped her hands together and smiled slowly. 'He was wonderful. He's in the process of buying a new car so we had to catch the bus into town. He took me to The Crown and Thistle on Loseby Lane.'

'Buying a car, eh! What sort is he thinking of getting?'

'I don't know. But I do know he's in partnership in a garage up the Aylestone Road, so I suppose he can pick and choose.'

'Partnership?' Sue said in awe. 'I'll bear that in mind when I come to change my car. Might get a discount. What's the name of this garage?'

'I never asked. It didn't seem right to pry too much on our first date. But I get the impression it's a really busy garage. He told me that he does all the mechanics whilst his partner does the selling and they both go all over the country to auctions. He says he's going to take me to one sometime.' She clapped her hands together. 'Oh, it sounds so exciting.'

'Hmm. It does,' Sue agreed. 'Where does he live?'

Josie shrugged her shoulders. 'I don't know. I didn't ask.' She eyed her friend sharply. 'You ain't half nosy, Sue.'

'No, I'm not. Just interested, that's all. Did he try anything on?'

'No, he didn't,' Josie answered crossly. 'He was the perfect gentleman. And he's not a "he", his name's Graham.' She shut her eyes tightly, a picture of utter bliss enveloping her face. 'Oh, Sue, he's wonderful.'

'He sounds it. When are you seeing him again?'

'I'm not sure yet. He's going to contact me. He's so busy, you see. Never knows from day to day what he's gonna be doing.' She grinned broadly. 'He said next time we go out, he'll take me for a meal. An Indian curry.'

'Very nice,' Sue said, impressed. 'Can I come? I love Indian food. I'll find a fella and we'll make a foursome.'

'No, you can't. I want to keep him to myself for a while.'

'Suit yourself,' Sue said, trying to sound hurt, but secretly glad for her friend. 'But you'll have to invite him in for coffee sometime. I must ask about his prospects.'

Josie gave her a friendly punch on the arm.

Sue suddenly grimaced fiercely and pointed to Josie's handbag. 'I see you never got around to clearing that thing out. I hope you didn't take it out with you?'

Josie smiled sheepishly. 'I never had time. So I just shoved my purse into my pocket. I'll do it tomorrow night after work. Now I have to get to bed,' she said happily, 'I've my new job to start in the morning. Though God knows how I'm going to get to sleep.'

'Dinner's up!' Gertie shouted loudly.

Josie stood back and admired her handiwork. 'Shan't be a minute,' she called.

In two short weeks the shop had been transformed. Gone was the dust and grime, in its place white paint and polish now made the shelves, walls and ceiling gleam. The floor had been scrubbed and the wood now shone. All this had happened while the trickle of customers still shopped and as Josie worked she also served.

. Gertie had been busy too and an assortment of home-made cakes adorned the top of the counter. As the different fruits and vegetables came into season, she would make a diversity of jams and pickles to add to the ones already on sale. Josie had been honoured with a glimpse of Gertie's secret recipes and she had been most impressed. Once Josie started to do the marketing for the vegetables and sold those instead of the second grade stuff they had been selling, business would certainly pick up.

She was paying her first visit to the wholesalers in the morning and although it meant a much earlier start she was looking forward to it. She might even see some of her old colleagues from the market.

When Josie had outlined her ideas, Gertie had taken her outside and, standing before an old lean-to at the side of the building, had wrenched open the doors and proudly introduced her to the 'company vehicle'. Josie didn't know whether to laugh or cry at the sight of the old Morris Traveller, covered in layers of dust and cobwebs. But to her amazement it roared into life with the first turn of the ignition. It was just what she needed to transport the goods.

Gertie called again and this time Josie obeyed the command. As usual the dinner was scrumptious. Josie was tempted to have another piece of the Jam Roly Poly that had been dished up covered in thick custard, but had resisted. She was so proud of her new figure that nothing would induce her to do anything that would make it return to its old shape. Not even Gertie's hurt eyes at her refusal.

The more she got to know this strange couple, the more she liked them. The old man would sit by the fire all day, amused by the carryings on around him, accepting the endless mugs of tea and samples of various mixtures that Gertie was in the process of making. Josie would often catch snatches of their conversation as she busied herself in the shop. The great affection between these two odd people was very obvious and to Josie it was lovely to witness.

Josie felt sad for the big ungainly woman whose body and looks defied the warm, caring person she actually was. She would make someone a lovely wife and some child a wonderful mother, but would she ever have the chance? Josie sincerely hoped so. Hopefully, some day, a nice man would look beneath the surface and snap Gertie up.

The only thing that niggled was that Graham had not yet been in contact again and Josie began to doubt her own attractiveness or ability to keep such a man interested. Sue had taken great pains, when Josie had divulged her fears, to tell her how stupid she was being. Men were an unknown quantity; they made promises and frequently broke them only to turn up when it suited them, bemused by your hurt responses. He'd contact Josie. He'd said he would and she would have to have patience and faith. As she had nothing else, she'd had to keep that to the forefront of her mind as the days passed silently by.

Just as she was preparing to leave that night, William beckoned her over and pressed two half crowns into her hand.

'What's that for?' she asked, shocked.

'For yer 'ard work, gel. You've done wonders with this old place and me and Gertie are ever so grateful. Ain't we, Gertie?'

She raised her eyebrows, smiled warmly and nodded in agreement.

Josie choked back a lump in her throat. Oh, these two lovely people, she thought.

On arriving home she turned into the pathway of the house and jumped as a figure emerged from the shadows. It was Graham and her heart thumped loudly.

'Have you time for a drink?' he asked, without a word regarding his absence or of the fact that he had startled her.

Josie stared up at him, the street lamp's light just catching his features. She noticed the way his long fair hair curled as it rested upon his shirt collar and wanted to reach out and touch it. Instead she just nodded in acceptance of his invitation.

'I'll wait for you on the corner.'

He turned and left and she hurried to tidy herself.

Breathless, she arrived at their appointed meeting place. Silently he took her arm and they walked to The Crow's Nest on the Hinckley Road, where he ordered the drinks. He put his hand in his pocket and frowned deeply.

'Damn,' he said.

'What's wrong?'

'I've left my wallet at work.'

'Oh.' Josie smiled as she delved into her purse and pulled out the two half crowns that William had given her earlier. 'I thought it was something serious.'

Graham accepted the money. 'I'll pay you back.'

'No need,' she answered lightly.

Seated in a discreet corner, he turned his full attention on her and smiled.

'So, what have you been doing with yourself?' he asked.

Josie related the past two weeks, enthusing over the shop and what they had achieved.

He nodded here and there.

'What about you?' she asked slowly.

He looked at his watch. 'God, is that the time? I have to be going.'

Josie's face fell. 'But we've not been here long.'

He took hold of her hand. 'I'm sorry, but I've a couple of cars I have to go and look at. I did try to get Melvyn, that's my partner, to go but he had other things on. And if I don't go tonight, I might miss them. Besides that I promised my mother I'd be home at a decent time. She's started to complain that she's forgotten what I look like.'

A warm feeling rose up in her. What a thoughtful man.

'I'm sorry our meeting hasn't been for long,' he continued, 'but I thought it better than nothing.'

'Oh, it is,' Josie cried.

Suddenly his arms were around her and he drew her close.

'Oh, Josie, Josie,' he murmured. 'I've thought of you constantly since we met. What are you doing on Sunday?'

'Nothing,' she said, raising her eyes to meet his.

'Good. I'll make arrangements so we can spend the whole day together.'

She thought she would explode with happiness. A whole day. A whole day spent with Graham. That would be heavenly.

She rose the next morning and sang softly as she dressed for work. It was five o'clock in the morning but that fact did not detract from her happy mood. It felt so good to be alive and nothing could take away her feeling of well-being. With a bounce in her step, she let herself quietly out of the house and walked down the damp dark streets. It was the beginning of March and spring was almost upon them. She noticed as she passed by a garden several daffodils about to burst into flower. After collecting the van, she arrived in good time at the wholesalers and deftly set about collecting the shop's requirements.

So wrapped up in her thoughts about the forthcoming Sunday was she that she clumsily knocked over a wooden box full of tomatoes as she was loading them on to the van. They spilled out everywhere and Josie watched in alarm as they came to rest, some badly squashed.

A man rushed forward, laughter in his voice as he offered his help. She stared up at him, her heart quickening. It was Stephen.

She said his name and he turned and looked at her.

'Josie?' he said in disbelief.

'Yes, it's me.'

'Well, I would never have recognised you.'

'You like the new me then?'

Stephen slowly nodded. 'I also liked the old one.'

Josie blushed as she put several tomatoes back in the box. Old feelings began to rise. Luckily, Stephen took control of the conversation.

'I searched high and low for you after we got split up on New Year's eve, but you'd vanished.'

Josie laughed. 'It wasn't hard. Most of Leicester must have been there that night.'

With all her goods loaded, she closed the van doors and smiled awkwardly up at him.

'Well, I must be off,' she ventured.

Was it her imagination or did Stephen seem on edge? She searched her mind for a reason but came up with no answer. Pulling her keys from her coat pocket, she made to unlock the driver's door. He looked at his watch.

'Have you time for a coffee?' he asked.

Josie thought rapidly. 'I'd love one, but it'll have to be quick.'

Stephen smiled broadly. They made arrangements to meet at a cafe they were both acquainted with and he set off towards a vehicle.

Josie frowned. 'Stephen,' she called, 'that van . . . It's my old one, isn't it?'

He walked back towards her. 'Yes. Your uncle sold it to me several weeks ago. Said you didn't need it any more. When I asked him why he told me in no uncertain terms to mind my own business. But I know a good bargain when I see one, so I bought it. Why? Is there something wrong?'

Josie tried to stem her anger. 'No. Not with you buying it. Just the fact that he sold it. He'd no right to.'

Stephen ran his fingers through his hair. 'I just thought, seeing as you weren't working the markets any more, you didn't need it and had given the go ahead for a sale?'

Josie placed her hand on his arm. 'Look, this is nothing to do with you. I'm glad you've got it.'

He searched her face. 'Josie, what went off between you and your uncle? Why did you leave home?'

She took a deep breath. 'Let's get to the cafe. I'll tell you all about it then.'

Sitting behind the wheel of the van, she stared straight ahead. She would have to tell Stephen the whole story. He was after all an old friend and deserved the truth.

Seated in the cafe with mugs of scalding hot strong tea, Josie told her tale. Stephen's face grew grim.

'Josie, why didn't you come and tell any of us about this? We'd have banded together and stood up to that man and sent him packing.'

'It all happened so fast. One minute I had a job and a home, the next nothing. Besides, despite me grandmother's wishes, she'd made no will and I hadn't a leg to stand on. Me uncle knew it. He's no fool.'

Stephen breathed deeply. 'But you've friends, Josie. Friends that'd move heaven and earth for you. Didn't you realise that?'

She lowered her head. No, she hadn't realised. At the time she'd felt she had no one in the world to turn to. She'd always thought people saw her as good old Josie, someone to ask to baby-sit or get the shopping in during illness. It never crossed her mind that anyone would actually care what happened to her or would want to help. Sue was right, she did undervalue herself and it was about time she stopped it. 'As I said, it all happened so quickly,' she said, raising her head. 'I'm fine now, though. I've a nice room, some new friends and a smashing job. It doesn't pay much but I manage.'

Stephen laid his hand on her arm and smiled warmly. 'Oh, Josie. What am I going to do with you, eh?'

She shuddered at his touch. Time had changed nothing. She still cared for him deeply. Thoughts of Graham were dispelled. This was the man she loved, would always love. Just his presence pushed everything else to the back of her mind. She wondered if he was involved with anyone, but truthfully didn't want to know. If he was, it would hurt too much.

'So,' she said airily, 'what's been happening with you? Still at the cafe?'

Stephen shook his head. 'No. Actually I've started my own little business. That's why I was down at the wholesalers.'

'Oh?' Josie looked at him with interest. 'Doing what?'

'Hot dog stall. I bought an old ice cream van cheap and me and a mate converted it. It's pretty smart and business is brisk. I go to all the football matches down Filbert Street and any other gatherings, and also have a regular round in Mowmacre Hill and the Netherhall Estates. That's why I bought your old van. I need it to collect my supplies and it's just the job for running about in.'

'Oh, Stephen. That's great.'

'Yeah. I'm pleased. 'Course there's some that don't like it . . .'

'Who?'

'The big boys. They're like the Leicester Mafia. Got their sticky little fingers into everything. They've got their own people and don't like outsiders coming in. I've been threatened once or twice . . .'

'You've not!' Josie said, aghast.

'I'll not let them stand in my way, Josie. I've as much right as they have.'

'Well, you just be careful,' she said, concerned.

132

She looked up at the clock on the cafe wall. 'Oh, God. I must be going.'

Stephen's face fell. 'Er, Josie . . . Sunday. If you're not doing anything, we could go to the pictures or something? It's the only free time I've got for a while now I've my business, and I still help the folks out in the cafe when they're short handed.'

Josie's throat tightened. How long she had wished for such an invitation. But she couldn't, she was seeing Graham. Why – why did it have to be Sunday? She had no way of getting in touch with Graham to change their arrangement and she couldn't stand him up. It wouldn't be fair.

She swallowed hard. 'I can't,' she said reluctantly. 'I've already got other arrangements. I'm so sorry.'

Stephen forced a smile. 'No problem. Some other time maybe?'

She slowly nodded and stood up.

'By the way, have you had any news of Marilyn?'

Josie's blood ran cold. So that was it! He still hankered after her cousin. Nothing had changed. He only wanted to meet her to glean information.

'No,' she said flatly. 'Sorry, I haven't. But if I do, I'll be sure to let you know.'

She turned abruptly and left.

By the time she arrived at the shop all thoughts of Stephen had been forcibly pushed to the back of her mind. She was greeted warmly as always and Gertie helped to unload the van and arrange the stock.

'Doesn't it look nice?' she enthused. 'This produce is much better quality than what we've bin sellin'.' She beamed at Josie in delight. 'Oh, I bless the day you walked through those doors. I do, gel, and so does Dad. Don't we, Dad?' she yelled.

'Eh!' came back the response. 'What's that yer said?'

Josie stifled a laugh as she opened the doors for business.

Chapter Seventeen

Relaxing back in her chair by the fire, Josie rested her feet on the old padded stool Tula had given her. The electric fire had now been fixed by a not too happy landlady who had moaned and grumbled about the cost, but the room felt decidedly warmer. It had been a glorious spring day which had brought all sorts of people out to enjoy the sunshine. The shop had been busy and the takings good. A bunch of unsold late spring flowers had been thrust upon her by Gertie, and they now sat wilting in a milk bottle on the mantel; several petals from a tulip had dropped on to the hearth and Josie bent to pick them up.

It was Saturday night. Sue was out with a lad from College, Tula with Michael, and Peter – she didn't know where Peter was. He hadn't elaborated but she presumed he was with his man friend. She was on her own and didn't know what to do with herself. It was a pity she couldn't afford a second hand television set, then she could have watched some of the programmes she used to enjoy. Still, she couldn't, so she would have to make her own amusement for the evening.

It was unusual for everyone to be out. Even the young married couple with the constantly shrieking baby on the middle floor had gone to visit relatives. For the first time in an age she felt lonely and didn't like the feeling one bit.

Her eyes alighted on her handbag and she sighed. Making a grab for it, she plonked it on her lap. Now was a good time to clear it out. She had her date with Graham the next day and would need to take it with her. Somehow she didn't feel so excited about their arrangement now and didn't need to ask herself why. Her chance meeting with Stephen had taken the thrill out of it.

She undid the clasp of her bag, opened it wide and stared at the contents. It was full of all sorts of items. Some rubbish, some she would need to keep, and the only way to find out which was which was to go through the lot. She knelt on the floor and tipped it up.

The contents scattered all over the threadbare carpet. Old biros, one of which had leaked all over the lining; several screws, for what she had no idea; numerous bits of paper; something sticky and

134

covered in fluff which she quickly discarded in the waste bin; an odd assortment of loose change, which if she had realised had been there would have been put to good use; an empty aspirin packet; several pieces of string and rubber bands; receipts and sale notices long past. And what was this? She picked up the long black pocket book and stared at it. It wasn't hers, so how come it was in her handbag?

She opened it and gasped in recognition at her grandmother's spidery handwriting. A memory flashed before her. She was bending down in her grandmother's bedroom on the night of her death. She snapped the book shut and held it to her chest, the feeling of being an intruder sweeping over her. She shook herself and forced herself to open the book again and scan the pages. She frowned, causing a deep furrow to cross her brow. Each page had a separate name, most of which she recognised, and figures and dates written in columns to the right.

What did they signify?

She continued to study the pages, thinking hard as she did so. Finally she closed the book and held it in her lap. So that was it. Her grandmother had been a money lender. That was how she had amassed all her savings and that was why Josie's uncle was so angry when he couldn't get his hands on the records. He would need this book to continue in his mother's footsteps. But from these records it didn't appear her grandmother had charged much interest. Sometimes payments hadn't been received for weeks.

She placed the book down on the arm of the chair, rose and put on the kettle. Armed with a cup of coffee, she resumed her task.

Gradually, like pieces of a jigsaw, Josie saw exactly what had transpired. Her grandmother's money lending activities were on a small scale. She would lend out amounts of several shillings to several pounds, each with a set interest rate according to how much the borrower could afford, and over the years she had put all the profits under her bed to help to secure her granddaughter's future. According to this book, it had gone on for many years and she'd had numerous clients. Josie forced back a tear. No wonder the old lady had been so well thought of. In times when loan sharks were bleeding people dry she had gone quietly about her business; a business aimed at helping the people who needed it the most and not at amassing a large fortune.

Her eyes narrowed and her face darkened. Her uncle's intentions wouldn't be so honourable. He wanted to pick up these outstanding debts, and put up the interest and bleed the debtors dry, she was in no doubt about that. Well, she would put paid to his plans. He might have got the better of her, but not of all these people, who were mostly friends and neighbours.

Putting the book aside, she set about sorting the other contents of her handbag, and whilst she worked formulated a plan. She had some work to do first, but once finished she would put that plan into action. Confronting her uncle upon completion would be pleasurable, very pleasurable indeed.

Just as she had finished she heard a hammering on the outside door. Thinking it would just be a visitor for one of the other tenants she went to open it. Before her stood a woman, a very attractive one, dressed in the best of clothes. She smiled kindly at Josie.

'Does a Susan Shaw live here?' she enquired.

Josie nodded. 'Yes, but she's out.'

The woman's face fell. 'Oh, dear. Still, I might have known she would be, it being a Saturday night.'

Josie looked at her quizzically and remembered the training Patricia had given her at Frizley's Finance.

'Can I tell her you've called?' she asked politely.

The woman smiled. 'I don't know whether that would be a good idea. She might move again to avoid me.' The woman laughed, an infectious sound that made Josie smile. 'I'm her mother, you see. And you must be Josephine?'

'Yes, I am.'

'I thought as much. Susan told me you were a very pretty girl and she was right.'

Josie blushed violently. She shifted awkwardly. 'Er . . . would yer like to come in?' she said hesitantly, knowing her room was not fit for a lady of Mrs Shaw's calibre. 'I don't know what time she'll be back, but I could make you a coffee.'

Mrs Shaw nodded her appreciation. 'That would be lovely. Susan's done her utmost to keep me in the dark about this place. I'm afraid my motherly instinct got the better of me and I just had to find out what she was up to.'

She followed Josie down the corridor and stood on the threshold of her room whilst Josie put on the kettle.

She eyed the woman for a moment. 'Would you like to sit down?' she asked.

'And what about you?' Mrs Shaw asked, looking at the single chair.

'Oh, I can sit on the floor.'

Mrs Shaw unbuttoned her coat, put down her black leather handbag and sat down. She stared around, then settled her gaze on Josie who was now sitting on the floor in front of her, cradling a mug of coffee between her hands.

'My dear, please excuse my choice of words, but is my daughter's room as bad as this?' She watched the expression on Josie's face. 'I see,' she said slowly. She took a sip of her coffee. 'She has a perfectly good room at home, you know. I can't understand why she chooses to live like this.' She laughed. 'Well, maybe I can. When I was her age I couldn't wait to leave home. I did at eighteen, but that was to get married.' She eyed Josie thoughtfully as she sat back and crossed her shapely legs. 'I envy you your freedom.'

'Do you?' Josie asked quizzically.

'Oh, yes. Not that I'm unhappy, far from it. But it would have been nice before I settled down to – shall we say – spread my wings a little, just as my daughter is doing. But in my day that would have been out of the question.'

Josie stared across at the woman and pictured her own mother sitting there. How would her life have turned out, she wondered, if her mother had still been alive to watch over and care for her as this woman obviously did for Susan?

'Is she eating enough?' Mrs Shaw continued. 'Only I do worry about that. You young girls skimp on food, don't you? You look to me as though you could do with a good feed. Get Susan to bring you round for a meal.'

Josie smiled. 'I'd like that.'

Mrs Shaw drained her cup and placed it down on the hearth. 'She's told me a lot about you, my dear. I can only say how glad I am that you two have met. Her attitude is much better. I put it down to the influence you are having on her. Her College crowd doesn't seem to have any sense of direction and I was beginning to despair. But now – well, let's say I'm more hopeful.' She picked up her handbag and rose. 'It doesn't look as if she'll be back for a while and I must be off. Her father will think I've left home. I told him I was only popping out for a while. I didn't want to tell him I was visiting Susan until I'd seen for myself where she was living. Now I've seen it, I'm glad I didn't. He would drag her back home without any hesitation. No wonder she's done her best to avoid me coming here!' She buttoned up her coat and straightened her hat. 'I've a few bits and pieces in the car for her. Would you give me a hand?'

Josie nodded and followed her out.

'Oh, no. That's torn it,' Sue grumbled. 'Why did you let her in, Josie?'

'I had no choice. Anyway, I wasn't about to leave her on the doorstep. Why all the fuss? Your mother seems a smashing person.'

'She is. But now she's seen this hovel, she won't rest until I'm out of here.' Sue started to rummage through the large brown carrier bag her mother had left. 'Oh, good old Mum. This lot'll keep us going for a while.' She split open a packet of toilet rolls and handed Josie one. 'I'm glad she's brought these, I'd been reduced to newspaper,' she said laughingly as she opened a packet of biscuits and crammed a bourbon into her mouth. She eyed Josie. 'I've been thinking.'

'Oh!'

'How d'you fancy sharing a flat?'

'A flat?'

'That's what I said.' She flopped down on a cushion. 'I think it'd work really well. We all get on.'

'All?'

'Yeah. Me, you, Tula and Peter. Think of the fun we'd have, and let's face it, between us we could afford something better than this. Besides, we spend so much time in each other's rooms we're practically all living together anyway. We could split all the living expenses and take it in turns to do the chores. And . . .' her eyes twinkled '. . . it'd keep the folks off my back.'

'Might have known you'd have an ulterior motive,' Josie said lightly.

'Well?'

She clasped her hands together. 'I think it's a great idea.'

'Good. We'll sound out the other two as soon as possible. Now if you don't mind, I need to get to bed. And you,' she said, winking wickedly, 'have a big day tomorrow.'

Chapter Eighteen

Josie glanced yet again at the clock. It was two hours past the time Graham had said he would call, and after inventing all sorts of excuses for his lateness she resigned herself to the fact that he just wasn't coming.

How dare he? she fumed inwardly. And after refusing Stephen's invitation! That part hurt the most even though she felt positive his invitation had been purely to gain information about the where-abouts of her cousin. But to spend time in his company would have been sheer heaven. Just then a light knock sounded on her door and it opened.

'The black woman let me in,' Graham said, smiling broadly at her. 'Sorry I'm a bit late. We had problems at the garage.'

Josie stared at him and all her anger subsided. He was dressed in pale fawn trousers, matching shirt, and a long chiffon scarf wrap-ped several times around his neck, the ends hanging down at the front. His black leather jacket looked expensive. In fact, his whole appearance radiated money.

'I know we planned a whole day together,' he was saying, 'but I can't I'm afraid. I have to get back.'

Josie tried to hide her disappointment.

'I thought we could go for a walk or something. How about the museum on New Walk? It's years since I've been there.'

Josie smiled, trying to hide her disappointment. He had said he was taking her for Sunday lunch; would book a table at a posh restaurant he knew of, and she had dressed herself especially for the occasion, blowing a good slice of her wages on a red jersey mini dress and matching boots. In anticipation of the meal she had not eaten any breakfast. She certainly wasn't dressed for a stroll around the museum and her rumbling stomach reminded her that she was ravenous.

'That'll be nice,' she said quickly. 'I'll just put on something more suitable.'

He eyed her. 'You look fine to me. Just grab your coat and we'll be off. I'm still not fixed up with a car, I'm afraid. I've been too busy. Besides, I thought the walk would do us good.'

Josie groaned. The walk might do him good but after racing around all week at the shop, exercise of that nature was something she certainly didn't need.

Nevertheless the afternoon passed extremely pleasantly. The more time she spent in Graham's company, the more Josie succumbed to his charms. And he was a charmer. He definitely had the knack of saying the right thing at the right time and he was very attentive. Had her grandmother still been alive, Josie felt sure she would have approved of him.

The trip to the museum was very informative and much to her pleasure Josie learned many things about the old Roman city she lived in that she hadn't realised before, which made her feel rather ashamed. After the museum they went for a cup of tea in a cafe and arrived back at her bedsitter in high spirits. She invited him in.

Placing the kettle on the gas ring, she turned to face him. He had discarded his jacket and was reclining on her bed, staring at her openly, and her heart thumped. He beckoned her to join him. She hesitated for a moment before doing so. He placed his arm around her and pulled her close.

'Oh, Josie,' he whispered huskily. He leaned over and kissed her full on her mouth. She responded, the thrill of his moist lips against hers sending urgent surges of feeling racing through her body. His hand found her breast and fondled it urgently. She pulled away sharply, jumped up and quickly busied herself making the tea.

'What's the matter, Josie? Don't you like me kissing you?'

'Yes, yes. 'Course I do,' she answered quickly without lifting her eyes.

'What's wrong then?' He rose and joined her by the sink, leaning his back against it. 'I thought you felt the same way as me?'

She raised her eyes to meet his. 'I do,' she said slowly. 'I like you very much.'

'Like? Is that all, Josie?' He paused and lowered his voice. 'I'm falling in love with you.'

Her body froze. She'd never thought she'd hear those words from any man, let alone one like Graham.

A slow smile appeared on his face. 'Relax, Josie. Let yourself go. I'm not going to hurt you. I'm not going to force you to do anything you don't want to.'

Her heart thumped so loud she felt sure he would hear it. But all this was too soon. She had given herself to Stephen and where had it got her? Nowhere. He couldn't even remember their lovemaking. And although this situation was entirely different, she didn't want to make the same mistake. She was frightened of cheapening herself. Sue was forever telling her that once a man got what he wanted, that was the last you would see of him. One-night stands were fine but if you wanted a longer relationship, keep him at arm's length for as long as possible and never declare your true feelings. That was a sure way to send him running.

She scratched her neck nervously and swallowed hard as she felt his arm tighten around her shoulder. She felt out of her depth. She needed help on this one and she couldn't ask him to wait whilst she went in search of Sue. She did know that she wanted something more with him, but how did she get that across without him thinking she didn't care, or worse still that she was frigid?

Just then the door burst open and Sue bounded in.

'Oh!' she said aghast, stopping abruptly. 'I'm so sorry, I thought you were on your own.' She began to back out of the door.

Josie pulled away from Graham. 'Come in, Sue, and meet Graham,' she said in relief. She had never been so glad to see her friend in all her life.

'If you're sure I'm not interrupting anything?' Sue said apologetically.

''Course yer not. Is she, Graham?'

Graham, doing his utmost to hide his anger, strolled over to the bed and picked up his jacket. 'I was just off anyway.'

'Oh!' Josie gasped in disappointment. 'You don't have to go just yet?'

'Yes, I do. My mother's not well and I need to get home and see if there's anything she needs.'

Josie walked with him to the front door. He turned and gathered her in his arms. 'I'll be in touch,' he said. He bent to kiss her, then turned and made his way out.

Sue eyed her friend cautiously when she arrived back.

'Josie, I'm so sorry. I'd never have barged in like that if I'd realised he was here. Only when I saw there was no strange car parked outside, I automatically thought . . .'

'It's okay,' Josie reassured her. She smiled warmly. 'Actually, you averted a sticky situation.'

'Did I? Tell me more,' Sue said keenly, making herself comfortable in the chair by the fire.

Josie related the day's events whilst Sue listened keenly.

'I think you rather like this guy, Josie Rawlings.'

Josie nodded. 'So do I,' she said slowly. 'But I'm not ready for that. Not just yet, anyway.'

'You're not keen on making mad passionate love to him then? I would be.'

'You keep yer hands off,' Josie spoke sharply.

'Only joking,' Sue laughed. 'But on a more serious matter, are you taking any precautions?'

'Precautions?'

141

'Yes. Look, Josie, you don't want to get caught out. It's easily done, you know.'

'Oh, I see what you mean.' She looked at Sue sheepishly. 'No, actually I'm not.'

'Good job I spoke up then. I'll fix an appointment with the Family Planning and come with you, if you like?'

'Yes, please.' Josie paused. 'A'you on the . . . um . . .'

'The pill,' Sue cut in. 'Of course I am. I'm not stupid, and neither are you. But don't you worry. We'll get you sorted.' She chuckled wickedly. 'Then you can bonk away to your heart's content.'

'Sue!'

'Just kidding.' Sue sat back in the chair and placed her hands behind her head. 'What's this about his mother? He doesn't seem the type of man who'd be that concerned.'

'Well, he is,' Josie retorted sharply. 'I think it's nice, personally. Shows he's got feelings. Not like some of the morons I could mention.'

'Yes, you're right,' Sue agreed, ashamed. 'I could tell you one or two who can't even remember their own names, let alone their mother's, and they have that many girlfriends . . .'

'Well, you can talk!' Josie cut in. 'You go out with that many different blokes you have to have a special book to keep track of them.'

Sue threw back her head and laughed loudly. 'Variety is the spice of life. Isn't that what they say?' Her face lit up in mischief. 'Oh, Josie, I haven't told you about the identical twins yet, have I?'

'Identical twins?' Josie said, raising her eyebrows. 'No, you haven't.'

'Well, I met this bloke at The Hole in the Wall club last week. You know, the night you didn't want to go out? I fancied him rotten and nearly died when he asked for a date. He was gorgeous, Josie. Blond hair down to his shoulders, legs up to his armpits, and a body on him that would . . . Well, he made my toes curl. He looked a bit like Mick Jagger but without the lips. Anyway, two nights later I was down the Palais giving my all on the dance floor when I spotted him supporting a pillar on the edge of the floor. So I put on my special walk, you know the one, and started chatting. I thought he gave me a funny look but I'd had a drink so I didn't take much notice. Anyway, Rita, the girl I was with, finished dancing with her bloke and came over to join us. I dropped several hints but she wouldn't budge, so I just said I'd see him Friday night at eight o'clock outside Woolworth's as we'd already arranged and off I went.' Sue started to laugh again and wiped away a tear of mirth. 'On Friday night not one hunky bloke strolls up to meet me, but two. I nearly wet myself, I can tell you. Thought I was seeing double – and I was.'

'What happened?'

'Not much. I slunk away before they could see me and left them to it. For all I know, they're both still waiting for me.'

Josie giggled. 'Oh, Sue. Shouldn't you have waited and told them about the mistake?'

'No. I know I'm good, Josie, but I couldn't manage two.' She put her hand up her sleeve and pulled out a handkerchief, blowing her nose noisily. 'I wonder if they'll ever know they were waiting for the same girl? Poor sods.' She burst into laughter again. 'So, when are you seeing lover boy again?'

'Not sure. He's going to contact me.'

'Oh, I hate that.'

'Hate what?'

'When they don't make definite arrangements and leave you hanging on, not knowing when they'll turn up unannounced. It means you have to look stunning all the time, just in case.'

Josie grimaced. 'Yeah, that's a problem. But he's very busy,' she said defensively. She drained her mug of coffee. 'Well, I must get on.'

'Get on?'

'Yes. I've something I must do.'

'What?'

'Can't tell you at the moment. But I will once it's all over.'

Sue rose, frowning hard. 'Sounds ominous. What are you up to, Josie Rawlings? It's not like you to be secretive. I thought we told each other everything?'

Josie rose to join her friend and slapped her playfully on the shoulder. 'Normally we do. This is just something I must do, and the sooner I get it over with the better. I'll explain all in due course.'

'You'd better,' Sue responded hurtfully as she departed.

Chapter Nineteen

'Well, I never!' Gwendoline Bates exclaimed as she stared at Josie standing on her doorstep. 'Come in, gel. Don't stand there like a stranger.'

Josie followed her old neighbour through into the back room and took a seat that was indicated, accepting the cup of tea that was thrust upon her. Big Jack, lounging in his chair wearing a string vest, the top button of his grey flannel trousers open, gawped in astonishment as he lowered the paper he was reading, taking several moments to recognise the young girl whom he had known since birth.

'Well, well. What a surprise. What yer done ter yerself, gel? Mind you, I'll say this, it's an improvement.'

'Jack!' Gwen exclaimed.

'Well, it is,' he said, folding up the paper and reaching for his pipe. 'I'd 'ave passed her in the street.' He ripped off a piece of paper, rolled it up and thrust it into the fire. Josie sat patiently as he proceeded to light the tobacco he had packed tightly into the pipe's bowl. That done, he sat back and eyed her thoroughly. 'Well, come on then. What's bin 'appening since we saw yer last? We got 'ell of a shock when we 'eard what Stanley had done to yer. Didn't we, Gwen? Always was a little sod, was Stanley. Never did take to him. Should 'ave been drowned at birth, that one.'

'Jack!' Gwen scolded severely.

'Well, it's true.' Jack spat as he shifted his large frame uncomfortably in his chair and puffed hard on his pipe. 'Yer look well, gel. I'll say that for yer. Mind you,' he said, winking wickedly, 'you'll catch pneumonia if you don't watch out by the length of that skirt yer wearin'. I've seen wider belts.'

Gwen tutted loudly. 'All the youngsters wear 'em like that these days. It's the fashion. And stop pretending to disapprove. I've seen the way your eyes pop out yer 'ead when they walk past the garage.'

Jack gave her an innocent look. 'Don't know what yer mean.'

Gwen frowned fiercely, then gave her full attention to Josie. 'So, 'ow yer bin keepin', love? We 'eard yer gorra job and a nice room. Seems yer doing right well for yerself.'

Josie nodded. 'Yes, I manage all right, thank you. How did yer know?'

'Stephen told us.'

'Oh!'

'Nice lad that, ain't 'e, Jack? Shame the way that cousin of yours treated him. Little trollop.'

'Well, what can yer expect? Look what supposedly fathered 'er . . .'

'Jack. I said less a' that. Have some cake, Josie?'

'Er . . . no, thanks.' She swallowed hard. 'I've come to ask your help. As well as to see you both,' she added quickly.

'Oh. And 'ow can we 'elp, me duck? If it's money, we can spare a few shillin', can't we, Jack?'

He nodded. 'Yeah. We'd do anythin' for you, Josie love, yer know that.'

'No, no. It's not money,' she said quickly. She took a deep breath and explained how she had found her grandmother's book and of her interpretations of its contents. 'You see,' she finished, 'I just wanted to know, before I went ahead, if my assumptions about what my uncle would do if he got hold of this book, are correct?'

Jack inhaled deeply and scratched his greying hairy chest. 'Yeah, they are. About yer granny and about Stanley. Yer gran got into this money lending lark by accident years and years ago. I'm surprised yer didn't know about it. Mind you, she was a bit of a dark 'orse. But always fair was Lily Rawlings. Never hassled for payments. That's why folks trusted her and they always paid up in the end.' His eyes darkened. 'Let 'im get his paws on that book and 'e'd fleece 'em all dry and drag her good name down in the process.'

'Yes, my thoughts exactly. Well, he ain't going to.'

Jack leant forward. 'Oh? What's yer intentions, then, Josie?' he asked keenly.

She took a deep breath. 'Firstly, I'm gonna visit all these people and tell 'em that their debts are clear.'

Jack and Gwen gawped at her.

'Then,' she continued, 'I shall take great pleasure in handing over the book to my uncle.' She let a slow smile spread across her face. 'Minus the pages, of course. Let's see what he makes of that.'

Jack fell back and guffawed loudly. 'I'd love to see 'is face.'

'So would I,' chipped in Gwen. ''Bout time someone gave that so and so what for.'

'Yes,' said Josie. 'And I'm that someone.'

Two weeks later Josie breathed deeply several times before banging loudly upon the door of her former home. She stepped back and waited.

Finally the door opened and her uncle stood there. Before he had a chance to speak, she held out the black book.

'Is this what you wanted?'

He eyed her cautiously before snatching the book, a satisfied smirk appearing on his face.

'Come to your senses at last, I see,' he said sarcastically.

His smirk quickly faded. 'What's this?' he growled as he realised he had been handed just the book's leather covering.

'Oh, I'm sorry,' Josie said more calmly than she felt. 'I forgot to mention. I burnt the pages.'

'What!'

She narrowed her eyes. 'Whatever you had in mind, Uncle Stanley, you can forget. Every name in that book has been contacted and their debts cancelled. When my grandmother died, her business died with her.'

'Oh, did it!' Stanley stepped forward, his face full of rage. 'We'll see about that.'

'There's nothing you can do. You have no evidence anyone owed me grandmother a penny, and that's the way she would have wanted it.'

Stanley knew he had been defeated. The bitch had got one over him and his fury mounted.

'I'll get you for this. You see if I don't,' he said icily. 'I'll make you rue the day you decided to cross me.'

Josie started to back away. 'I've no doubts on that score. Good-bye, Uncle Stanley.'

With his threat ringing in her ears, Josie turned abruptly and marched down the street. Well out of sight, she stopped to gather her wits. She had achieved her aim, but although she felt happy for the people she had saved from hardship trying to pay back the excessive interest rates she knew her uncle would have demanded had he gained access to that book, she worried about what his threats might hold. She hoped they were idle. After all, she had nothing he could want. He had already taken everything.

She breathed deeply. His threats were idle, she felt positive, and now that her actions had come to fruition she could put it all behind her and concentrate on her future. She had a lot to be thankful for. She felt she had come a long way since her grandmother's death and hoped the old lady would have been proud of her.

She hurriedly continued her journey, wanting to be home as quickly as possible. Further discussions regarding the sharing of a flat were taking place in Sue's room, and right now she wanted nothing more than to be with her friends.

Chapter Twenty

Josie tapped lightly on the door, opened it and poked round her head. She smiled fondly at the grey-haired old lady sitting in the worn armchair by the fire. The old lady put down her knitting, adjusted the straps on her old fashioned wrap-round floral apron and raised her head, peering over her National Health spectacles at the young girl and returning the smile.

''Ello, Josie. 'Ad a good day, me duck?'

Josie nodded. 'Yes, thanks. Shops been as busy as hell, but I ain't complaining. Be glad to get my feet up, though.' She gave a chuckle. 'That's provided Sue's not commandeered the living room again for a CND meeting. Some of them women don't look as though they've washed for weeks, and you should hear some of the remarks they come out with. I'd swear some of 'em were born with no common sense.'

Sophie Warrander nodded knowingly. She watched as Josie checked the coal scuttle to see if she had enough to last for the night. Although it had been a glorious sunny day, the evenings were chilly and her old bones needed the warmth the fire provided. A stir of well-being rose up and once again she blessed the day young Josie had knocked on her door and enquired about renting her upstairs flat which she had heard about through local gossip.

Sophie hadn't made the decision lightly, having had no intention of re-letting, much preferring the house to herself after all these years, and thoughts of hordes of boyfriends, late night parties and marijuana did cross her mind. Her cronies down at the old people's centre had also expressed their deep reservations. But she had told them straight. She would have who she damned well liked to lodge in her house, and their narrow-mindedness would make no difference to her decision. Besides, she had taken to Josie; the young girl reminded her of one of the many daughters she had hoped to have. And she had never once regretted her decision. The three girls were so full of life. She enjoyed nothing more than to listen to their daily trials and tribulations, and never hesitated to stick in her own twopenn'orth. Sophie felt she had a lifetime of experience behind her, and young girls needed an older person's viewpoint to put a different perspective on matters.

In return the girls happily collected her shopping and library books, and invited her up for coffee, laughingly telling her they knew she only accepted so she could inspect the premises.

Yes, Sophie mused thoughtfully, they were good girls. A bit boisterous sometimes though what young people weren't, and the flat at times could be tidier. But what the hell? Cleaning was a soul destroying occupation at the best of times and would still need doing long after they had all gone. Anyway, the sounds coming through the ceiling were a welcome reminder that she wasn't on her own, that she only had to call out and a friendly face would appear at her door. It made a change from her last tenant who had outstayed his welcome for over twenty years.

What a surly old devil he had been. Unkind or not, she was glad when he had been carted off to the home, though not without a fight. The Social Services had fully expected her to care for him in his dotage, and without any remuneration. She had struggled to do so, even though at seventy-nine she was ten years his senior. Luckily, a mini-skirted, raven-haired, twenty-two-year-old social worker had spotted her plight and arranged his removal to a home despite his loud protests, and the flat had become free for the first time in over twenty years.

From the day the three young friends had moved into the old Victorian three-storey house on Fosse Road Central, it had come alive to their happy sounds. They had set to and painted the walls, scrubbed all the furniture and cleaned the floors. The windows had been thrown open and popular music sailed continuously out. In the six short months the girls had been there, Sophie's mundane life had been transformed. Any reservations she might have had were quickly dispersed. Her only worry was that they might eventually decided to move on. She shuddered. No, it didn't bear thinking about. She would miss them dreadfully, and all the friends that came calling.

She did have one slight worry. That pretty black nurse with the infectious laugh had a secret, one that Sophie had been asked her opinion on and entrusted with. She had felt honoured to be consulted and readily talked long into the night with the girl. She sincerely hoped this was not the start of a trend. Still, time would tell. But she would have to wait for the others' reaction until Tula told them.

She realised Josie was speaking to her. 'Pardon?' she said.

'I was just saying, you seem distant tonight.'

Sophie smiled. 'Do I? Just thinkin', me duck, that's all.'

'Oh!'

'Yes, about you three and what a difference you've all made to me life.'

Josie bent over and kissed her on the cheek. 'And we appreciate you. You're just like a mother to us.'

Sophie blinked back a tear.

'Anything else yer need?'

She shook her head.

'Well, I must get off upstairs,' Josie said, yawning loudly. 'I fancy a quiet night tonight.'

Sophie grinned. Quiet night? Those girls didn't know the meaning.

She picked up her knitting and inserted the silver needle through a stitch. Yes, the girls had surely made a difference.

She and Albert had scrimped and saved to buy the house not long after they had married in the early 1920s. It had been a grand gesture on their part. Their respective families had scoffed. 'Gettin' above yerself, ain't yer?' they had grumbled jealously from the damp, depressing, overcrowded rooms of their little terraced houses. Maybe they had been. Sophie smiled, but she and Albert had wanted plenty of space to bring up the large family they had planned to have, and were prepared to work long and hard to do so. But the family had never materialised and her beloved Albert had died in his early-forties from years of kneeling on roof tops, frozen with cold and wet through from his job as a slater.

To keep the house and body and soul together, Sophie had had the rooms on the middle floor converted into a flat and had also taken in lodgers in the attics. Finally, after years of running after other people, she had managed to pay off the mortgage. The rambling Victorian dwelling was now all hers, even if it had taken a lifetime in which to achieve it. But what had it all been for? She had no one to leave it to; no offspring would be fighting over their share when she died. Had it all been worth it?

She dropped a stitch, her failing eyesight missing the ladder it caused as it ran the length of the knitting. She thought of Albert with his shock of jet black hair and laughing eyes. Yes, it had been worth it. They had brought this dream together in the first flush of their youth when their lives had stretched endlessly before them, neither visualising they would go through two world wars and a dreadful recession. She had seen neighbours come and go; vast areas of surrounding properties demolished to make way for more modern buildings; and fashions change out of all recognition. In her day, ladies did not show their ankles, let alone their underwear. What next? she sometimes wondered.

But still she stayed put, surrounded by the walls that knew her, and felt sure Albert would be resting easy, knowing the roof over her head was hers and that nothing could take it away. She had her memories here. If she sold up and moved into a smaller place, they might fade. Besides, the thought of an old people's dwelling did not appeal in the least, with one of those wardens fussing around all the time and only other old people for company. No, she was content. It was just a pity she had not thought of having young people to stay years ago instead of the upright solid citizens she had had, whose idea of an entertaining evening was sitting bolt upright in one of her uncomfortable dining chairs, grumbling about the rising cost of living or the youth of today.

What would some of her past lodgers, the formidable Major Thompson or the fanatically religious Matilda Cardew, have made of her three new residents? she thought wickedly. She smiled. They would have turned up their noses in disgust, that's what, and their narrow minds and bigoted opinions would have sent them packing long since. Especially when at the outset there was going to be four of them sharing the flat and one of them being a male. The lad, Peter, such a nice young man, had in the end decided to stay put in Wentworth Road. Maybe that had been for the best. The flat, after all, had only two bedrooms. She smiled again. That really would have caused a stir at the centre should it have happened! She would have been accused of singlehandedly encouraging the demise of moral standards.

She frowned deeply. It was about time the older generation woke up and realised that times had changed, out of all recognition in fact to when she had been young, and the sooner they did, the better it would be all round.

She knew she was in the minority with her outlook on life and always had been. Unlike her restricted youth, young people today enjoyed their freedom, and why not indeed? They had no wars or recessions to hinder their enjoyment and make them old before their time. But they needed someone like her to exert just a little steadying influence on their lives and make sure they ate regularly, as Mrs Shaw had requested, unbeknown to her daughter.

What a nice woman that Mrs Shaw was, and how thoughtful of her to insist she pay to have a telephone installed just in case Sophie or the girls ever needed it. Not that she was to tell them of her generosity, that had to be their secret. But a telephone was a comfort for cases of emergency. Sophie had no doubts as to how much Mrs Shaw cared for her daughter's welfare and that of those around her, but like most of the young who baulked at the idea of having caring parents, all the little things Sophie had been able to do for the girls through Mrs Shaw had to be done on the quiet. Like the fitting of a shower in the tiny bathroom and a second hand carpet in the living room in place of the ancient threadbare one.

She folded up her knitting and put it in the faded tapestry bag at the side of her chair. The appetising smell of the beef skirt casserole, packed with all those tasty vegetables that Josie kept her continuously supplied with, wafted towards her. She rose awkwardly and made her way over to the old walnut wireless sitting on top of the oak sideboard and switched it on. If she hurried she could eat while listening to Victor Sylvester and his band playing on the BBC's Third Programme, and just maybe one of the girls might pop down for a chat later on.

Josie opened the flat door and grimaced as an unpleasant smell hit her full force.

'Phew! My God, what's that stink?' she said in disgust.

Sue, lolling in a chair reading a novel, her legs resting over the arm, looked up. 'Stink! That's no stink. It's my joss sticks,' she said indignantly. 'They're the "in thing" at the moment.' She flicked back her long hair and returned her attention to her book.

'That's maybe the case, but I can't live with that smell, or the smoke come to that, so put 'em out.'

'Ah . . .'

'Ah, nothing, Sue. There's three of us live in this flat. Not just you. Now put 'em out.' Josie pulled off her green Trevira jacket and hung it up. 'And while we're at it, it's your turn to cook the dinner. So what we having?' she asked, sinking down in the other armchair and resting her feet on the small stool.

Sue looked at her blankly. 'Is it?'

Josie pursed her lips. 'You know fine well it is. Tula will be home soon, and don't forget you invited Peter round, so you'd better get cracking.'

'Bloody hell! I forgot.' Sue gave her a pleading look. 'Will you help me, Josie?'

She shook her head. 'No, I'm bushed. I've been on me feet all day and I ain't doing another thing.'

'Ah, please, Josie,' Sue cried, jumping up. 'I'd do it for you.'

Josie laughed. 'No, you wouldn't.' She slowly rose, her better nature taking over. 'All right, but this is the last time. I'll peel the spuds and you can do the rest. I don't know why we keep that damned roster. It's only me who sticks to it.'

Sue put an arm around Josie shoulders. 'You'll make someone a wonderful wife, Josie Rawlings.'

She glowered fiercely as she shook the arm free and made her way to the kitchen.

After clearing the mess left from that morning and then peeling the potatoes, for once Josie kept her word and, much to Sue's dismay, left her to cope on her own whilst she took a welcome bath. She gently lowered her body into the hot water and sighed in pleasure as the soothing liquid enveloped her. She lay back and sipped at the cup of tea she had taken through with her and let her thoughts flow.

She was certainly living life to the full at the moment. Sharing the flat with Sue and Tula was proving to be one of her better decisions. There was always someone dragging her to a party or a dance and always someone around to discuss and share problems with. There were plenty of laughs; with three girls and numerous friends calling at all hours, crises came thick and fast. Constant disputes over daily chores were becoming legendary and were even discussed at the local launderette. Luckily these disputes were quickly forgotten and always ended amicably – until the next time.

Her continually expanding wardrobe to clothe her new slim frame gave her constant pleasure and the thrill of trying on different styles never wavered. She only wished she had not had to endure the endless taunts about her size during her teenage years. Maybe then they would have been more pleasurable. But, she would often wonder, had those years of suffering helped to make her tolerant of other's failings? If so, maybe her experience wasn't such a bad thing.

Then there was Graham. The thought of him brought a sparkle to her eyes. She was glad she had taken Sue's advice and gone on the pill. Sexually they were well suited and Graham had taught her so much. With his help she had learned to express her feelings and be proud of her body, and she enjoyed their lovemaking to its fullest, feeling neither ashamed nor guilty. The more she saw of him, the more painful their partings were. Their meetings were irregular – too irregular for Josie's liking, but something she had to endure. She was falling deeply, and she knew it. To insist on a more regular relationship might rock the boat. That was the last thing she wanted. Graham was busy and had problems with his business to contend with. He wouldn't want her to start laying down the law. So she contented herself with what came her way and relished every minute. That there was plenty of time for them she had no reason to doubt.

The greengrocery shop was thriving. Gertie and William were a pleasure to work for and Josie thanked the day she had happened upon them. Her duties had increased, along with her remuneration. She was now fully responsible for the shop and what it sold, and the three would often sit after closing time and discuss any further enhancements she recommended. It was in her mind to broach the subject of van sales, as her uncle had done from the market stall. She felt positive business would double if they got the right person to handle it. She would mention the prospect at the right time. Only William had not been too well of late, so she felt it better to wait.

She felt saddened as a picture of Marilyn rose before her. To her knowledge no one had heard a word from the girl since the day she left, and despite what she had done, this lack of news worried Josie. She took a sip of tea. How was she? Had she managed to find work in the fashion business? If not, how was she surviving? London was not paved with gold, and she wondered how long it had taken Marilyn to find that out.

She trailed her hand through the hot water, sending waves of comfort over her naked body as she remembered incidents from her past. She smiled ruefully. Marilyn was a survivor. She was single-minded to the point of ruthlessness and would let nothing get in the way of what she wanted. Josie wondered how many people she had hurt as she had trampled over them in her efforts to succeed. Just like her father. At the thought of him, Josie shivered and sat up. Well, one thing was for certain: if Marilyn returned now she would not find the old Josie waiting to be used and manipulated. She would give Marilyn all the help the girl asked for, but that was all she would give. She had stood up to Marilyn's father and she would stand up to her.

She drained the cup and, hanging over the bath, sat it upon the floor, then sank back, closed her eyes and let the water once more flow over her. Yes, this last nine months had changed her. After what she had faced she was stronger and wiser. She now felt so much a part of it all. No longer was she sitting on the sidelines, living her life through others. She was in the thick of it and enjoying every moment.

'Have you drowned in there?' Sue's voice cut through her thoughts as she shouted from outside the bathroom door. 'I'm about to dish up, and if you're not out in ten seconds it'll go cold and you needn't blame me.'

Josie smiled as she leaned over and grabbed a towel. There was one thing her life never was now, and that was dull.

Chapter Twenty-One

The autumn night was warm and clear. A full moon lit the deep blue, star-laden sky, the reflections sparkling brightly upon the water of the river. A slight breeze wafted through the thick hedges hiding fields of newly cut corn, and the scent of the last summer flowers filled the air. Peace and tranquillity surrounded the couple as they walked silently down the rutted towpath. There was no need for words – the atmosphere said it all.

Josie felt the pressure of Graham's hand on hers and she smiled. It was just the type of night to be out strolling with someone you cared very deeply for.

They had spent a wonderful evening together, arriving in style in a Ford Granada Graham was debating whether to buy. They had dined on appetising food offered by the amiable publican of The Riverside Inn and were now ambling slowly along the picturesque waterside. They were by no means alone, the area was filled with courting couples, but for Josie, the only presence she noticed was Graham's.

He suddenly stopped and looked at her, 'I love you, Josie.'

His words, so softly spoken, made her gasp.

'Will you marry me?' He took her in his arms. 'Say you will, please. Say you will, Josie?' His pleading eyes searched her face as he waited for her answer.

Josie held her breath. His proposal was most unexpected. She knew Graham was very fond of her, he'd even told her he loved her on several occasions, but marriage . . . well, she had never expected that. Suddenly a picture of Stephen flashed before her. Why? she groaned inwardly. She hadn't seen him for several months so why should she think of him at a time like this? Stephen was not for her and never would be. Graham was here now, holding her tight, asking her to marry him. With all her strength she pushed Stephen's face from her mind and gazed lovingly up into Graham's.

'Yes. Yes, I'll marry you,' she said eagerly. 'If you're sure?'

The look on his face told her all she needed to know and she sighed with happiness as he kissed her deeply.

'I've never been so sure about anything. I'll make you happy,

Josie, I promise.' His face clouded over. 'My mother has to go into hospital for an operation, it's nothing serious, something to do with her varicose veins, but as soon as she's recovered I'll take you to meet her and we can make plans. You'll like my mother, Josie. She's a wonderful woman and I've no doubt she'll love you.'

She felt a thrill rush through her. To be asked to marry a man such as Graham was every girl's wish, and she knew how lucky she was.

'The garage has a cash flow problem at the moment,' he continued. 'But it's only temporary and as soon as it's sorted out I'll buy you a ring.'

'Oh, don't worry about that, Graham. Your business comes first,' Josie said hurriedly, though in her mind's eye seeing diamond rings flash before her eyes. 'I can get a ring any time.'

Graham's eyes filled with tenderness. 'I knew you'd say that. You're so thoughtful, Josie. But I want to buy you a ring. I want everyone to know you belong to me.'

She hugged him tightly and rested her head on his shoulder. 'Oh, Graham, you don't know how happy you've made me.'

He kissed her cheek. 'There's just one thing I ask.'

'Oh!' She drew back and looked up into his eyes.

'Only that we keep this to ourselves until after my mother has been told.'

'You want to wait until after she's recovered from her operation?' she asked hesitantly.

'Yes.'

Josie breathed deeply. 'Okay, Sue and Tula won't breathe a word . . .'

'I said no one, Josie.'

'Oh, but I can tell my friends, surely?'

'I'd prefer it if you didn't. You know how news travels. It won't be for long, Josie, I promise. Then you can tell who the hell you like.'

She reluctantly agreed.

How she managed to continue to walk sedately down the path she never knew because all she wanted to do was run and skip and tell the world her news. She silently scolded herself. She was being selfish, she would have to be patient, but hopefully not for long.

'Can you keep a secret?'

'What?'

'I said, can you keep a secret?'

Josie sat perched on the edge of her chair and looked at Sue keenly. The girl was surrounded by all manner of nail care equipment and assorted bottles of polish. As Josie spoke she was

155

deliberating between a bright yellow or stark jet black to paint on her long, perfectly filed nails. Josie twitched excitedly. She had kept the news of her engagement to herself for three whole days and she was at bursting point. She just had to tell somebody and Sue, being her closest friend, was the one.

Still concentrating on her nails, Sue's eyes narrowed with interest. 'Yeah, sure. What is it?'

Josie breathed deeply. 'First I must have your promise you won't tell a living soul?'

Sue stopped filing her nails and gave Josie her full attention. 'It must be something good then. Come on, what is it?' she asked excitedly.

'First your promise.'

'Okay, okay. I promise, I promise. Now what is it?'

A slow smile spread across Josie's face. 'I'm getting married,' she breathed.

'Married! What do you mean, getting married? What – like in . . . marriage you mean?'

Josie nodded. 'Yes.'

Sue's mouth gaped. 'To Graham?'

Josie nodded again. 'Yes. Only you mustn't say a word until we've had a chance to tell his mother.'

'Say a word about what?' Tula asked as she came through the door, discarding her cape on the back of the chair.

The other two girls looked at each other. Josie clasped her hands together. She'd already broken her promise to Graham once and supposed telling Tula would not make any difference.

'First you must promise . . .'

Sue tutted loudly. 'Oh, we're not going through all that again, Josie.' She turned her attention to Tula. 'Josie's getting married, only we haven't to say a word to anyone because it's a secret.'

Tula clapped her hands together in delight. 'Oh, Josie, I'm so pleased for you. When's the big day?'

'That's just it. We're just unofficially engaged at the moment, 'til he breaks it to his mother.'

'Oh, I see. Well, congratulations anyway. I t'ink it's wonderful news.'

Josie sprang up and started to do a jig around the room. 'Oh, I can't believe it. I'm so excited,' she sang. 'I want you both to be my bridesmaids.'

'You try and stop us,' Sue shouted, jumping up to join her friend. Soon they were all jumping up and down in excitement.

'Wow. This calls for a party,' Sue shouted.

'No, no,' Josie said, backing away from the others. 'I told you, my engagement's a secret.'

'Spoilsport,' Sue grimaced. 'Well, tell him to hurry up and tell his damn mother. But in the meantime, we could still have a party. We don't have to tell anybody what it's for.'

A knock sounded on the outer door and Sophie shuffled through.

'What's all the bangin'? Sounds like someone's comin' through the ceilin'.' She eyed the girls. 'You're not on that "mariarna" stuff, are yer? Only summat's goin' on. I can tell by the look on all yer faces.'

Sue looked at Josie. 'You'll have to tell her, or she won't sleep tonight.'

'Tell me what?' Sophie asked as she settled herself into an arm-chair by the gas fire. 'And while yer at it, a cup a' tea would go down nicely.'

'Oh, all right. But you have to promise not to say a word, mind,' Josie said.

'Why?' Sophie asked.

'Oh, just tell her, Josie,' Sue cried.

She hesitated before she spoke. 'I'm getting married. Only it's a secret for the time being, 'til Graham tells his mother.'

Sophie's eyes lit up in pleasure. 'Oh, I am pleased for yer. From what I've seen of him, he seems a nice enough lad. I'll be sorry to lose yer, but a pretty gel like you, it was only a matter of time. I wish you the best, really I do.'

'Thanks, Sophie.'

She looked quickly at Sue. 'You won't be long behind, mark my words.'

'Not me,' Sue guffawed. 'I'm not that stupid. I've not finished testing the market yet. What about you Tula? Tula – what's wrong?'

Sophie sniffed loudly. 'I think you'd better tell 'em your news, gel. Now's a better time than any.'

'Yes, yer right,' Tula said slowly.

'Tell us what?' Josie asked, sensing a feeling of sadness in her friend.

Tula sat down slowly and the others followed suit. She clasped her hands together and lowered her head. 'I'm pregnant, an' I'm goin' home to have me baby. Michael don't want no part of it. He say it my fault and I do what I wanna. I wanna go home to Jamaica and keep me baby.'

Josie and Sue sat in silence for several seconds whilst the news sank in. Josie was the first to speak.

'Michael doesn't want any part in it? I don't believe it, him a doctor an' all! I thought he was such a nice man.' She frowned deeply. 'A' you sure Tula? A' you certain you ain't took him wrong?'

'I know what he say. Besides, I ain't seen the man since I broke the news. He's took sick leave from the hospital and no one knows where he's gone.' She wiped her brimming eyes. 'That says it all, don't you t'ink?'

Josie choked back a lump in her throat. 'Oh, Tula. I'm so sorry. I just can't believe it all. I really can't. But you can stay here. We'll help you, won't we?' she said, looking quickly at Sue and Sophie. 'We'll all pitch in and help you take care of the baby. You can't go home, Tula, we'd miss you too much,' she pleaded.

Tula smiled. 'T'anks. I do appreciate your offer. But I made me mind up. I'm goin' home. Me parents are expectin' me.' She pulled out a large white handkerchief from her pocket and blew her nose. She looked at each of her friends in turn, friends she would miss badly in the future. 'I am happy, you know. Admittedly it was a hell of a blow when I realised what Michael was really like, but now I've got used to the idea, I'm pretty thrilled about it all. And me parents are goin' to stand by me, and once the baby's bin born I can return to nursin' and they'll help me look after it. I'm lookin' forward to it. It'll be nice to get home and feel warm for once.' She gave an infectious laugh. 'Your English weather would have bin the death of me in the end.'

They all laughed loudly.

'You're right. I think I'll come with you,' Sue quipped. 'I quite fancy all that tropical scenery.'

Josie turned to Sophie.

'You're not saying much.' She narrowed her eyes. 'You knew about this, didn't you?' she accused.

Sophie sheepishly nodded. 'Tula took me into her confidence a while ago. She was in quite a turmoil, poor gel. Didn't know what to do for the best. But it's all straight now. And the main thing is that Tula's 'appy.' She smiled and rubbed her gnarled hands together. 'Forget the tea. I've a bottle of sherry in the kitchen cupboard, I think we could all do wi' a drink. It's only cookin' sherry,' she laughed. 'It's well matured, I've had it several years. But it's the best offer you'll get tonight. So if someone'll go down and get it, we'll have a toast to celebrate. 'Cos it *is* a celebration. A baby and a weddin'. Even if the weddin' is 'ush 'ush for the time bein'.'

The sherry was poured out and all four sat sipping at the strong dark brown liquid.

'Sorry if I spoiled your news, Josie,' Tula said softly.

'Spoiled it. Don't be daft, woman. We're all just glad the situation's been resolved. But you could have told us before. A problem shared and all that. Still, at least you had the sense to tell Sophie.' She turned her head and winked at the old lady. 'When a' you planning to leave us?' she asked slowly.

'Next week. Monday to be precise.'

'Next Monday! But that's no time . . .'

158

'I'm sorry, Josie. I kept putting off tellin' yer . . .'

'Ah, well, not to worry,' Sue said, grabbing hold of the sherry bottle and draining the dregs. 'We'll just have a damned good bash before you go to make up for it.' She raised her glass. 'To Tula and Josie,' she toasted.

'Tula and Josie,' they all chorussed.

'Now,' Sue piped up, 'when are we having this "do"?'

It was two tearful girls who saw their friend off from the bus station bright and early the following Monday morning, on her way to Southampton to catch the boat back to her home in Jamaica. Josie choked back a sob as the bus turned the corner and Tula disappeared. They would all miss her pretty dark face, sharp tongue and huge, worldly wise brown eyes. She hooked her arm through Sue's and the pair walked silently out of the bus station and down the street.

Sue frowned deeply. 'I don't know why we didn't have a proper 'do'. Doesn't seem right somehow, just the four of us sitting in Sophie's living room with a bottle of cider and some sandwiches. It's a shame too that Peter couldn't manage to come. I missed his company.'

Josie squeezed her arm. 'Me too. But that's what Tula wanted. No fuss. And let's be honest, Sue. It was a great night, wasn't it?'

Sue nodded and smiled in agreement. 'Yes, it was.'

'Well, then.' She started to quicken her pace. 'Come on, I told Gertie I wouldn't be later than nine and it's nearly that now.'

Chapter Twenty-Two

Josie twisted the corners of the brown paper bag and handed it to her customer.

'Anything else, Mrs Biddle? How about a freshly made fruit cake or a pot of rhubarb and ginger jam? Mr Biddle is partial to a pot of Gertie's jam and we've only a couple left. We've had a run on 'em just lately.'

'Oh, go on then. Give us a pot or I'll never get out of 'ere.' Mrs Biddle accepted the jar from a smiling Josie and placed it along with her other purchases. 'You'd sell whisky to the Scots wi' your patter.'

Josie chuckled as she put the money in the till and watched as the woman departed. She stifled a yawn and picked up the mug of tepid tea that Gertie had brought through over half an hour before. The shop was empty for the first time that day, and as she gulped at the cold contents of her mug she eased herself down on the stool that was kept at the back of the counter and hoped that no one would come in until she'd had time to catch her breath.

Gertie popped her head around the opening at the back. 'All right, Josie love? Only I'm just going up to sit wi' Dad for a bit.'

Josie nodded and smiled affectionately at the other woman. 'Tell him I'll be up before I go tonight.'

'That'll cheer 'im.' Gertie paused thoughtfully. 'Look, why don't you stay for a bit of supper tonight? I could do wi' the company,' she asked hopefully.

'Yeah, okay,' Josie responded listlessly.

Gertie eyed her sharply. 'What's up, Josie?'

'With me? Nothing.'

'Yes, there is. It's not like you to be grumpy. So what's the matter?'

Josie let out a long sigh. 'It's nothing much, honest, Gertie. I'm just missing Graham, that's all. He's been attending auctions all week and I never saw him at all last weekend because there was so much to do at the garage. I thought he might telephone, but he ain't.'

'I take it 'e still 'asn't told 'is mother about yer engagement?'

Josie shook her head. 'Not to my knowledge. In fact, since he

160

asked me we've hardly mentioned the subject again. I find that very strange. Either you want to get married or you don't.' She raised worried eyes to meet Gertie's. 'Maybe he's changed his mind and daren't tell me?'

'Don't be daft. A man like 'im would 'ave said.'

She sighed deeply. 'Yeah, I suppose. But to be honest I'm getting a bit fed up. I've even stopped looking in the jewellery shop windows. I'm beginning to think I'll never get a ring.'

'Maybe 'e can't afford it and feels embarrassed. You did say 'is garage 'ad money problems.'

'Yes, but that was last September. It can't still be in trouble. He goes to enough auctions and he's certainly busy enough in the garage, judging by the amount of time he tells me he spends there. He must be making some money or why bother?' She lowered her eyes and studied the contents of her mug. 'Anyway, it's not as though I'm after a dear ring, a cheap one 'ud do. Just something I could show off.'

Gertie smiled. 'You told me you weren't bothered about a ring.'

Josie pouted. 'Yeah . . . well . . . that was before. I've changed me mind since then.' She raised her head. 'Gertie, you do realise I've been secretly engaged for over six months and I'm no further forward than I was when he first asked me. We've never looked at houses or furniture together and it's only me who's been collecting for me bottom drawer. I've that many pots and pans I could stock a shop. Even Sue's started to complain about the space I'm taking up.' She sniffed loudly, banged down the mug and folded her arms. 'I'm gonna tackle him, Gertie,' she said defiantly. 'I'm gonna get something fixed up, you see if I don't. I ain't gonna be sitting here in twenty years time wondering when me big day's gonna be.'

Gertie frowned, horrified. 'Oh, I shouldn't do that, gel.'

'Why not?'

'Well, women don't, do they?'

'Don't they! Well, this one does. I've been patient for too long. And I ain't spending another Christmas like the last. I hardly saw him. If it hadn't been for Sue's mother inviting me over, I would have been practically on me own all the holiday.' She scowled fiercely. 'He won't let me near the garage. I've offered to take sandwiches or just pop by for a chat but he always makes some excuse. I'm beginning to think he's ashamed of me.'

Gertie gasped. 'Don't you think such a thing. That lad's lucky to 'ave yer and 'e knows it. More than likely 'e doesn't want that partner of 'is to clap eyes on yer. He sounds like a bit of a jack the lad. I think Graham just wants to keep yer to 'imself.' Her eyes lit up as a thought struck. 'Look it's yer twenty-first in a few weeks. Maybe 'e's biding 'is time 'til then?'

161

A smile spread over Josie's face. 'Yeah. Maybe he is. I never thought of that. Maybe he's planning a surprise engagement party. Oh, bless him. Yes, that's what it'll be. Oh, thanks, Gertie. And there was me thinking all sorts of things. I'd better get something really nice to wear.'

Gertie grinned. Josie had more clothes than she knew what to do with. But, she supposed, if she had a figure like Josie's she'd want to dress in the latest fashions and flaunt it. She quickly glanced down. Life was unfair sometimes. Whoever it was up there that dished out the looks and bodies needed a reprimand, as all the cast off bits that were of no use to anyone had been thrown together to make her, and no amount of attention she cared to lavish upon herself would make her any more attractive.

She returned her gaze to Josie who was gazing into the distance, deep in thought.

'I'd better get off upstairs. Dad'll think I've forgotten him.'

Josie nodded absent-mindedly.

Several moments later the bell on the shop door jangled and a tall, exceptionally thin, middle-aged man wearing a black suit smelling of mothballs walked through. Josie rose stiffly. Mr Snell who owned the newsagents further along the road was a tyrant, disliked intensely by all the shop owners in the immediate vicinity and by most people who knew him.

His brusque manner had lost him many a customer; school children bought their comics, crisps and sweets elsewhere having long since got sick of his accusations of shoplifting and time wasting, and since the death of his long suffering wife a year previously his attitude had become worse, if that were possible. To Josie, shopkeepers were jolly people who were polite and accommodating. This man was even too depressing and surly to have been an undertaker, she thought unkindly.

She saw his small grey eyes narrow with distaste as they settled upon her and her hackles rose.

'Miss Waltham,' he barked rudely.

It was on the tip of Josie's tongue to say 'What about her?' But she thought better of it.

'She's with her father at the moment.'

Mr Snell glared at her through his thick round glasses and ran his hand over his thinning Brylcreem'd hair. 'Don't just stand there, girl. Tell her I'm here.'

Josie slowly rose and walked through to the back. What could the horrible Mr Snell possibly want with Gertie? Josie summoned her and showed the man through.

Sitting once more on her stool, her thoughts returned to the surprise engagement party. She was just going through the guest

162

list, hoping that Graham would forget no one when the door bell jangled again.

She lifted her eyes. 'Stephen,' she gasped.

'Hello, Josie,' he replied as he closed the door and took several strides to stand before the counter.

Josie rose, aware that he was gazing at her intently.

'You look . . . good,' he said appreciatively.

She bowed her head slightly. 'Thank you,' she answered, feeling anything but good in her stained white overall. 'What can I get you?' she asked, trying to steady her shaking legs.

Stephen cleared his throat. 'Nothing, actually. I dropped in to see you.'

Josie reddened. 'Oh!'

'I've a favour to ask, but I thought I could ask you over a drink tonight. Are you doing anything? We could take a drive into the country and find a nice pub. That's if you don't mind the old van?'

Josie's stomach lurched. The idea sounded wonderful. But she was an engaged woman, albeit unofficially still. Besides, she already had a commitment and couldn't let Gertie down this late in the day.

'I'm sorry, Stephen,' she said remorsefully. 'I've promised to have supper with Gertie . . . Miss Waltham.' She was bemused by the hurt expression that clouded his handsome features. 'It's not an excuse, honestly,' she added quickly. 'I'd have loved to if Gertie hadn't ask me earlier.'

'No matter,' he replied lightly, plunging his hands into his jeans pockets. 'Some other time, maybe.'

Stephen stared around him, pretending to be deeply interested in the improvements to the shop. He felt anger rising. Every time he plucked up the courage to speak to Josie, either someone or something got in the way. And what he had to say to her was so important. If those rumours he heard were true, he needed to speak his mind now or it would be too late. He turned his head slightly and looked at her out of the corner of his eyes. It was either now or live with the consequences.

As he stood, legs astride, glancing around the shop, Josie quickly scanned his features. His physical appearance had changed little since the last time she had seen him. His face was still as handsome as ever, he had grown his sideburns long which was the latest style and it suited him; but there was something else, something different that Josie couldn't fathom.

As she studied him it struck her. This wasn't the same Stephen who had drunk himself into a stupor over her cousin, and made love to her and not been able to remember. He had matured. Gone was his youthful look. Standing before her was a man in charge of his own destiny. Someone who knew what he wanted out of life and was striving to get it.

She searched his face. Did he see a difference in her, and not just a physical difference? she wondered. Did he see that she had changed? Did it matter to him? Was she destined to be just his friend and nothing else? And why did she still feel like this when she had Graham?

She fought desperately her compulsion to divulge her innermost feelings. Once and for all to tell him how much she cared and be rid of the spectre that reared itself whenever they met. She quickly decided. It was now or never.

Simultaneously they both opened their mouths to speak and laughed as inaudible gabble burst forth.

They both knew the moment had gone.

'You first,' Josie said.

'No, you,' Stephen replied politely.

'Well, er . . . I just wondered what this favour was?' she asked slowly.

Stephen looked blankly at her. 'Favour?'

'Yes, the one you came to ask me.'

'Oh, that.' He sighed deeply and squared his shoulders. 'I just wondered if you fancied a part-time job helping me out on the 'dog van? If . . . er . . . you can't help me out on a regular basis maybe you could just now and again when I'm pushed for staff. A couple of my regular lads have let me down lately and you can't take just anybody on. You need people you can trust and I thought of you. I'll pay you, of course.'

Josie smiled weakly. She knew she should turn down his proposal. The only way she would ever be able to bury her feelings completely was to avoid him whatever the circumstance. But he needed her help. He had turned to her because he trusted her and she knew, as much as she wanted to, she could not refuse him.

'I can't manage on a regular basis, but now and again would be all right.'

'You would?'

'Yeah, I'd love to. It sounds fun,' she said, trying to sound sincere. 'The extra money'll come in handy,' she added.

'Good. That's settled then. I'll be in touch nearer the time to make the arrangements and explain things.' That was one thing. At least he knew he had an excuse to see her again. All might not be lost.

'I'll look forward to it.'

He gulped hesitantly. 'Er . . . Josie. Is it true what I've heard?'

'Is what true?'

'About you getting engaged?'

Josie gawped. 'How on earth did you hear about that?' But more to the point, how come Stephen seemed bothered about it? And he was bothered, she could tell by the look on his face and the tone of his voice.

'So it's true then?' he said tonelessly.

'Yes. But it's unofficial at the moment. Just one or two things that need sorting out first. Nothing major.' She smiled. 'Don't worry, I won't forget you when we send out the invitations.'

He stared at her quizzically then forced a smile to his face.

'Congratulations. I hope you'll be happy. Who's the lucky fella?'

'No one you know. His name's Graham and he's a partner in a garage,' she said proudly. She cleared her throat, wanting desperately to change the subject. 'Have you heard anything from Marilyn?' She asked the first thing that came to mind.

Stephen's face darkened. 'No. Should I?'

Josie was surprised at his abrupt response. 'I just thought, with you being so close at one time, she might have contacted you.'

'As you said, at one time. And that time was long ago. Marilyn was never for me, Josie. It was just young love, and that one-sided. All on my part.' He looked straight into her eyes and took a deep breath. 'It's you that . . .' But he did not have time to finish, as Gertie came through, followed closely by Mr Snell.

Stephen swallowed hard. 'I'll er . . . be in touch,' he said flatly.

Josie stared at him as he walked quickly out, Mr Snell following suit. She frowned. What was Stephen about to say before they had been interrupted? Several possibilities came to mind. She breathed deeply. She needed to sort things out with Graham and put all her energies into their relationship. She would tackle the subject when they next met.

She became conscious of Gertie standing beside her. She turned and quickly took in the woman's excited state.

'Oh, Josie,' she breathed ecstatically. 'I've just been invited to the Small Shopkeepers' Federation annual dinner.'

Josie managed to stop herself from saying 'What, with him?' Instead she smiled. 'Gertie, that's wonderful. But that's tonight, ain't it?'

'Yes, and I've n'ote to wear.' Her face fell. 'Oh, Josie, what am I gonna do? I've got to look nice. I couldn't possibly show Mr Snell up, not after 'e's took the trouble to ask me.'

Josie thought rapidly. It was quite possible that Gertie was the only female who would have consented to accept his invitation, and he knew it. Regardless of whether Gertie was aware of this fact or not, Josie felt determined that by the time she was finished, the woman would feel like a million dollars.

She placed her hand on Gertie's arm. 'Don't you worry. Just leave it all to me.'

'How . . .'

'Trust me,' Josie cut in, praying that her old friends on the market would come up trumps. 'Close up the shop, it won't hurt for once, and go and get Jackie across the road to do your hair. Tell her I sent yer and you don't care whether she's not got any appointments left, she's to fit you in,' she shouted as she raced through the back and grabbed her coat and bag. 'Then have a soak in the bath. By that time I should be back,' she said, racing out of the door.

Gertie stared agog, then proceeded to do as she had been told.

Gertie stared into the mirror. 'I do look nice, don't I, Josie? D'you think Mr Snell will think so?'

Josie nodded. 'Him and the rest of them. You'll knock 'em all for six, Gertie.'

She nodded in agreement. The long black velvet evening skirt and silver lamé over blouse had worked wonders. Jackie had performed a miracle and Gertie's hair was now piled up into layer upon layer of coils which sparkled brightly from the silvery spray that had been used as a finishing touch, and with her mother's diamanté necklace and matching earrings, she was now ready for her first ever evening out with a man.

'However did you manage to get these clothes to fit me?' she asked in awe.

'From an old friend on the market. She carries lots of things for the woman with . . . with the fuller figure,' said Josie carefully so as not to hurt Gertie's feelings. 'I'll take you to see her.'

'Oh, I'd like that. I've always run things up meself before now. I thought I was too big to buy anything ready made.'

'Well, yer not. Now come on, Mr Snell will be here in a minute and I'd better make myself scarce.'

Gertie turned and gave Josie a hug. 'Thanks, and yer sure you don't mind sittin' wi' Dad?'

'Not at all. You just go and enjoy yourself.'

'I will. I will now I look like this!'

Josie smiled, knowing just how she felt. Sue was right. It was a nice feeling being able to help someone.

When she arrived home very late that night she was greeted by a delighted Sue waving a letter under her nose.

'It's from Tula. And guess what?' she cried happily. 'She's had the baby. A little girl, and she's called it Josu after us.'

Josie clapped her hands together. 'Josu,' she repeated softly, visualising the baby, the image of her mother, lying cooing in a wicker cot, the tropical sun warming her pretty brown face, tight wiry curls springing up from her head. 'Oh, fancy Tula doing that. I feel so honoured. What else does she say?'

'Oh, that everything is going well. The baby is healthy, her parents have come up trumps and she's working in the local hospital.' Sue frowned slightly. 'No mention of a man as yet, but I suppose there's time.' She grinned. 'She also says we can go over any time we want. And I want to go, Josie. Now!'

Josie laughed loudly. 'And you would, wouldn't you? You'd drop everything? Now gimme that letter and go and make a cuppa tea, so I can get some peace to read it properly.'

Tula sounded so happy. She loved being a mother and one day hoped to present little Josu with many brothers and sisters, provided she could find the right man. At that Josie smiled. She couldn't imagine Tula having any trouble in the man department, despite the fact she already had a child.

As she read on, Josie sighed. Tula's existence back in her home country sounded so idyllic that momentarily envy rose up in her. Like Sue, she suddenly wanted to drop everything and go and spend a few weeks with her friends in the tropical paradise. But for many reasons, money being the most apparent, it was not possible. But she did wonder if she and Graham could scrape together enough to go over for their honeymoon. She doubted it, but it was worth a mention at the right time.

She folded up the letter and accepted the mug of tea which Sue thrust at her.

'Do you think my father will lend me the money?'

Josie raised her eyebrows. 'What for?'

'The plane fare to Jamaica.'

'No, I don't,' Josie scolded. 'You can pay for yourself when you land a good job after passing your exams. Now I'm off to bed. Goodnight.'

Chapter Twenty-Three

Josie stared around the public bar of The Navigation Arms and
sighed. A group of loud-mouthed youths were playing darts, spill-
ing their beer over the floor as they shouted obscenities to each
other, spoiling for a fight. A couple of old ladies sniffed in distaste
as they supped their milk stouts. Several older men, still dressed in
their work clothes, played cribbage, and another lot dominoes.
Elvis Presley's 'Love Me Tender' came from a juke box in the
corner, a remnant of the fifties, while a drunk lolling across the top
shouted tunelessly along with the words.

She groaned softly. The Navigation Arms was not her choice for
a Friday night out. It had been Graham's. He had been almost
insistent, dismissing completely anywhere else she had suggested.
She had wanted to go down the town to mix with the crowds of
teenagers on their way to the dance halls and clubs; to savour the
atmosphere and excitement they felt after being cooped up in their
work places all week.

For a fleeting moment she missed it all. The thrill of getting
ready, the rush for the bus, the banter, the jollity, the crush on the
dance floor as they vied for a spot, and the anxiety as to whether
the lad you fancied would ask for a date. She suddenly felt old. It
seemed to her that she had just been introduced to this wonderful
freedom only to have it swiftly taken away. Was she ready for
marriage, for the commitment it entailed? Should she really go
ahead with the speech she had so carefully planned? A speech that
would finalise things once and for all.

She turned and looked at Graham who was lighting a cigarette.
She watched as he blew the smoke into the air. He seemed content
and so should she be. After all, she had readily accepted his proposal. If she had had any doubts, she should have expressed them
at the time. But it seemed to her that the doubts she had, had only
surfaced since her last encounter with Stephen. Before that it
hadn't mattered where Graham had taken her. So long as she
was in his company she hadn't minded the location. So what
had changed?

She didn't know the answer, she just knew that she had to get matters sorted between them, and the sooner the better.

'Graham?'

'Mmm?'

'We need to talk. I need to know how things stand between us and I want to know when we're going to set a date for our wedding?'

For a fleeting moment a look of horror crossed his face, then it was gone. 'Josie,' he said, swallowing hard. 'There's . . . there's something I have to tell you.'

'Oh!'

He gulped again and shuffled nervously on the red plastic-covered bench.

'I'm broke, Josie. My business has gone bust. I've lost everything. Everything I worked for.'

'Graham!' she uttered, dismayed. 'Why didn't you say something?' She suddenly felt very guilty for her previous feelings.

'I . . . I couldn't.'

'Why?' she cried. 'I could have helped. Why didn't you tell me?'

He smiled wanly at her. 'I thought I'd lose you.'

'Oh, Graham,' she said softly. 'It's you I want, not your money.' She looked at him for several moments. 'How did it happen? I thought you were doing so well. You worked all the hours God sends . . .'

'Too much competition and cowboys willing to do a job for a fraction of the true cost,' he cut in. 'No overheads, you see. No premises to pay rent on, not registered for tax . . .'

'I see. But surely all your old customers will stand by you? You've told me often how much they praise your work, and the cars you've sold have always been good ones . . .'

'You don't see, Josie,' he snapped. 'I've lost everything, even my tools, and I've nothing to start up with again. By the time we'd paid all the creditors, there was nothing left. Melvyn walked out with the same as me. Not a penny. We've talked 'til we're blue in the face on how we can start up again but 'til we've some money behind us, we ain't got a hope.'

Josie's shoulders sagged. 'Graham, I'm so sorry. After all that hard work.' She wrung her hands together. 'Is that why you've never mentioned again about us getting married?'

He nodded.

'And I thought you'd gone off the idea and didn't know how to tell me.'

'Never,' he said, grasping her hands. 'We'll just have to wait, that's all. That's providing you will?' he added softly.

'Of course. Of course I will. And I don't care for how long. How could you think I wouldn't? I just wish you had told me about all this instead of worrying about it yourself.' She paused and studied

169

him. 'We don't need to wait. We can still get married. We could get a rented flat, and they do say two can live as cheaply as one.'

'No. No. I want to do it right, Josie. I'll not marry you while I haven't a penny to my name.' He reached for another cigarette. 'It won't take me long to get a job, and once I've some money at the back of me . . .' He grinned. 'I hope it doesn't take me long to get used to taking orders from other people. I hope I can stand it.'

She sat silently as he rose and made his way towards the bar.

It wasn't fair, she fumed. After all his hard work, to have this happen. Suddenly an inspiration flashed into her mind and she sat for a moment and examined the idea. When he came back to rejoin her she eyed him keenly.

'What would you need to get started again?'

'Eh!'

'I said, what would you need? Maybe a small building big enough to work on one car at a time and a few bob for tools and such like 'til you could afford to expand?'

'Yeah, I suppose. Why?'

'What if I knew of a building that would suit and could get hold of the money? Would you start again?'

'Er . . . I don't know, Josie.' He shook his head. 'I need time to think.'

'Well, if you think for too long you'll lose all your old customers, then you'll never be able to start up again. It'll be too late.' She smiled broadly and sat back. 'You leave it all to me. I'll have you back in business before you know it.'

'Josie . . .'

'Graham. You can't sit back and let what's happened ruin your life. You're a hard worker and deserve better than slaving for someone else. Now finish your drink. I hate this pub. Let's go somewhere else.'

Josie lay in bed that night and stared up at the cracked ceiling. She hoped that she hadn't spoken out too soon and that she would be able to fulfil her promises. She chewed on her bottom lip and her eyes traced the large yellow stain on the faded blue-flowered wallpaper. Although she had some money in her post office savings account, that was to have been used for her wedding. She did not know if it was enough to buy even the most basic of tools. And what if William and Gertie didn't like the idea of their lean-to being used as a garage? She calmed her own fears. They would. They were a good-hearted couple, and once she had told them the story they would be only too willing to help.

All Graham had to do then was drum up some trade and he was in business again. She would help. She could do all his books and make sure he got in his money. It sounded simple. Too simple.

She grimaced. She had been rather bold. She had given Graham no room for objections to her plans. Maybe he did need time before he started another venture? She thought of her grandmother's stall and how she had felt when it had been taken away from her. How it still hurt, in fact. If someone had come to her aid then she would have jumped at it. Yes, she felt positive that that was the way Graham would feel once it was all finalised.

She turned over and pulled the covers over her ears. If she didn't get to sleep soon she'd be in no fit state to put any plans into operation and that wouldn't do. She had made promises that one way or another had to be kept.

The next morning at breakfast Josie looked with concern into Sue's ashen face.

'I don't know what my parents are going to say. Oh, Josie, I've let them down badly. What the hell am I going to do?'

Josie jumped up from the table, raced round and placed her arm around her friend's shoulder. 'Look, it ain't the end of the world. It's only some stupid exams and I'm sure you'll pass . . .'

'That's not what my tutors are saying.'

'Well, prove 'em wrong. You've still time before your exams start. You'll just have to stay in and study, that's all.'

'I wish it was as simple as that.'

'It is as simple as that,' Josie said sternly. 'You're just gonna have to learn to say no to any invitations you get and knuckle down.'

Sue sniffed loudly. 'Will you help me?'

'If I can,' Josie answered dubiously. ''Course I will.'

Sue smiled gratefully. 'Thanks, Josie.' She eyed her friend warily. 'I've quite a lot of revising to do. I've not really done much on the Renaissance period . . .'

'The what?'

Sue frowned deeply. 'Josie, are you sure about this?'

'I'm sure. It was just my fun. I know all there is to know about the Renaissance period,' she lied flippantly. 'Now you get cracking. I've to get to work, and tonight I'll start to test you.'

'Okay. And not a word to my mother.'

'Not a word.'

Josie returned to her cornflakes, hoping she had enough time to spread equally between the people who at this moment needed it so badly.

Later that day she approached Gertie with her ideas.

Gertie listened in interest. 'Sounds fine to me, love, and I'm sure Dad won't object. We'll just have to keep the van on the front, that's all.'

'Thanks, Gertie,' Josie said gratefully. 'He'll pay you back rent as soon as he's able.'

'We'll talk about that when the time comes. It's not as though it's puttin' me about. And besides, all the work you've put in 'ere, it's nice to give yer somethin' back.'

Josie smiled. 'You pay me ample for what I do and I love working for you both. How is Mr Waltham this morning?'

'Bit perkier today, thanks, Josie love. 'Is chest is still bad. Sometimes I think he's tryin' to cough 'is boots up. But, yes, on the whole I think 'e's on the mend. But you can go up and see fer yerself. 'E likes a chat wi' you. Looks forward to it, 'e does.'

'I'll go when we have a quiet spell.' She eyed the woman for a moment. 'How's Mr Snell?'

Gertie blushed. 'Very well, thank you. I'm goin' for tea, tomorrow.'

Josie grinned. 'Tea, eh! Watch it, Gertie, he'll be proposing next.'

'Ged away wi' yer. We're just friends, that's all. 'Is wife would turn in 'er grave if she 'eard yer say that.'

Josie laughed as she made her way out into the shop. She felt light-hearted. Everything was going to work out fine. Gertie had readily agreed to Graham's temporary use of the lean-to. All they had to do now was get some tools and he was on his way, and whilst he worked the long hours she knew he would, she could help Sue with her studies. Humming softly, she picked up a duster and started to polish the counter ready for the neverending onslaught of customers who would descend to collect their weekend supplies.

That night Josie hurried home as fast as she could. She arrived out of breath, dumped her bags on the gate-legged table and addressed Sue who, keeping true to her word, had piled high her books, and was reading at a furious rate.

'Has Graham called?'

'No,' Sue answered without lifting her eyes. 'Should he have done?'

Josie frowned. 'Well, yes. I thought he would be waiting for me, to see how I'd got on regarding the garage.' She sighed. 'No matter, he'll probably call later.'

Just then a knock sounded on the door and her face broke into a grin.

'That'll be him now,' she shouted as she rushed to open it. She tried to hide her disappointment when she saw it was Mrs Shaw.

'Hello, Josephine. Is my daughter at home?'

Josie smiled in greeting as she stood aside. 'Hello, Mrs Shaw. Come in. Sue's in the kitchen.'

Mrs Shaw's eyebrows rose. 'Not cooking by any chance?'

Josie giggled. 'No. She's studying.'

'Even better. I never thought I'd see the day. Hello, Susan. How are you?' she asked, taking off her gloves and placing them neatly across her handbag. She sat down.

172

'Fine, Mother dear,' Sue replied without looking up. 'What brings you here?'

'Do I have to have an excuse to see my daughter?'

Sue raised her eyes and looked at her mother fondly. 'No. Of course you don't.' She leant on the table and narrowed her eyes. 'Unless, that is, you've come for a snoop.'

'Snoop? Daughter dear, how could you even think such a thing?' she said, her eyes twinkling. 'Actually, I have come for a reason.'

'Oh?'

'I need a favour. Thanks, Josie,' she said, accepting a mug of tea.

'What sort of favour?' her daughter asked quizzically.

'Well we're a bit short of items to sell at the bazaar next Saturday and I was wondering if you would see what you had lying around, and . . .'

'And what?' Sue asked sharply.

'I was hoping you would volunteer to go door to door collecting.'

'What? Oh, Mother! Haven't you got your regular helpers to do that sort of thing? I wouldn't be seen dead collecting junk. What if anyone saw me?'

'Susan Shaw, I never realised you were such a snob. What have I raised? I ask myself. It is for charity after all. For people less fortunate than yourself. Surely you can lower your standards just this once? I wouldn't have asked if I wasn't desperate.'

'I'll go with you,' Josie offered.

'Oh, Josephine. How kind of you. See, Susan. Josephine is quite willing . . .'

'I haven't the time,' Sue cut in. 'I've all this studying to do.'

Mrs Shaw leaned forward. 'I can only say that if you had put your mind to it in the first place, and not gone gadding about with all and sundry, you wouldn't have all this work to do so near to your exams.'

Sue pouted. Her mother was right and she knew it.

'I'll see what I can do.'

Mrs Shaw leaned back and smiled. 'Thank you.' She looked across at Josie and winked.

Josie joined them both at the table and looked at Sue keenly.

'It'll be fun, you'll see, Sue. I could make a start on my half day on Wednesday and you could join me after you've finished College. I'll borrow the van and we can pile everything inside and sort it out when we get home.'

Mrs Shaw rose. 'I can see you are very organised, Josephine. I'll leave you two to it.' She laid her hand on Josie's arm. 'Thank you. And see my daughter does her share,' she added softly.

Josie parked the van down a side street at the back of the

Braunstone Gate, locked it securely and headed towards a long row of terraced houses. She had been out for several hours and was feeling very pleased with herself. The back of the van was three-quarters full of all sorts of things suitable for resale; a good selection of second hand clothes, several lampshades, old boots and shoes, pots, pans and ornaments, a large selection of books and a collection of Country and Western LPs, all of which would add a good few coppers to the overall total of the bazaar's takings. She hoped Mrs Shaw would be pleased with her efforts.

Sue had promised to join her but as time wore on, Josie realised that her friend had obviously managed to think up some good excuse for her absence. Still, it was of no consequence. Mrs Shaw's request had been fulfilled and if Josie was honest she had really enjoyed herself. She had encountered all sorts of people and had been overwhelmed by their generosity, regardless of their status.

A light drizzle was beginning to fall and she pulled up the collar on her red plastic mini mac as she knocked loudly upon the brown-painted door of number seven Briton Street. The door tentatively opened and a young woman in her early-twenties peered out. In her arms she held a young child, a pink dummy firmly planted in its mouth. To her side stood a slightly older child, naked except for a short grubby vest. His face was streaked with the remains of tears and beneath his nose ran two hardened mucus tracks. He was holding on tightly to his mother's skirt, looking at Josie through large blue eyes.

'Yeah?' the woman asked quizzically.

Josie put a smile on her face. 'I'm collecting for a church bazaar. I wondered if you had any old clothes or odds and ends you no longer wanted?'

'Huh!' the woman replied. 'I'm wearing me old clothes and as for odds and ends . . .' She breathed deeply and paused in thought. 'I suppose yer can 'ave that pile a' books that's clutterin' up me passage. I've read 'em all at least three times so they're of no use to me any more.' She moved to the side and nodded towards a precariously stacked pile of books beneath the stairs. 'Can yer manage 'em yerself, only if I put the baby down she screams 'er 'ead off?'

Josie nodded. 'Thank you. Those'll be ideal. Go a treat do books.'

The woman smiled. 'Yeah. I always mek for the book stall meself. Avid reader I am.'

Josie followed the woman through and knelt down in order to arrange the books into manageable piles. She suddenly stopped and gasped in delight. 'Oh, I don't believe it. I've been wanting this book for ages.' She rose and clutched the book to her chest. 'I was engrossed in this once and when I got to the last few pages, someone had ripped them all out. I've been wondering ever since what happened to Angelique.'

The woman smiled. 'Oh, *Angelique and the Sultan*. I've read that several times. In the end the Sultan . . .'

'No, no,' Josie cried. 'Don't tell me. I'm gonna take this home and read it tonight.'

The woman frowned. 'But I thought these were all for the bazaar?'

'Oh, they are,' Josie said hurriedly. 'But I'll finish this well before they're to be collected from me. Nobody'll know.'

The woman eyed her. 'Have you any more books besides these?'

'Yes, quite a few on my van. Why?'

'Well, in exchange for this lot, you can give me a couple of yours.'

Josie frowned, then smiled. 'Okay. I don't see why not.'

'Oh, ta,' the woman said excitedly, hitching the child further up on to her hip. 'Readin's me lifeline. Since the kids came along money don't stretch to luxuries, so I can't afford to buy any new 'uns. D'you mind if I pick one or two?'

'Help yerself,' Josie replied. 'I'll go and get them. No, better still, I'll stay here and mind the kids while you take five minutes to choose what you want. The van's just a few yards away. You can't miss it.' She held out the keys which the woman took.

'Oh, ta again.' She walked through to the living room and put down the child, wrenching the other's hand from her skirt. 'You stay 'ere with this nice lady. I won't be a tick.'

She ran out, leaving Josie standing in the middle of the shabby living room, two small children staring at her wide-eyed. The baby's lips puckered and she let out a howl of protest. Josie looked at her for a second then bent down and scooped her up.

'There, there,' she soothed. 'Your mummy won't be a minute.'

She found another dummy on the arm of the faded maroon moquette armchair and picked it up, gave it a wipe with a clean tissue from her pocket and pushed it into the baby's mouth. The howls stopped and Josie sighed in relief. The nearly naked little boy pulled at her mac and held up a toy.

'Car,' he said proudly, wiping the back of his other hand under his nose.

Josie sat down on the chair, settled the baby on her lap and took the Dinky replica of a Ford Prefect.

'Oh, that's very nice. Have you any more?'

The boy nodded and proceeded to drag a box from behind the settee and tip the contents all over the floor. Josie grimaced as all manner of children's toys scattered across the worn carpet. Just then his mother appeared, her arms laden down with books.

'Nathan,' she shouted, 'yer can put that lot back! Yer know what yer dad's like. 'E'll go mad when 'e sees that mess.' She turned to Josie. 'Is this too many? Only I think I got carried away.'

Josie smiled and shook her head. 'No. You've given me more than double in exchange.'

The woman smiled gratefully as she put down the books and took hold of the baby. 'Fancy a cuppa?'

Josie made to rise. 'No, thanks. I must get on.'

'Oh, stay. It's not often I get company and the babies both seem to 'ave taken to yer. Normally our Gemma screams 'er 'ead off at strangers. You needn't worry, I've locked yer van. It's quite safe.'

'Oh, go on then. I could murder one.'

The woman disappeared and returned shortly with two mugs of tea and a bag of sugar which she placed on the coffee table.

''Elp yerself to sugar,' she said. 'My name's Gilly, by the way. What's yours?'

'Josie,' she replied, putting in two spoonfuls of sugar and stirring it well. She sat back in her chair and looked around. 'Nice houses these. I used to live in one just like this myself until a couple of years or so ago.'

'Did yer? I can't wait to get out meself. We're down for a council 'ouse but it takes forever. I wouldn't mind if we owned it, it'd be worth our while sprucing it up. But I ain't putting good money in the landlord's pocket. Besides, it's full a' damp. It'd cost us a fortune to get it sorted, and to be 'onest, my Terry's no 'andy man.'

'Terry?' Josie asked out of courtesy. 'Is that yer husband?'

'Yeah. Bin married three years. 'Ad to, wi' im.' She nodded in the direction of the young boy. 'A' you married?'

'No, but I'm engaged.'

'I'd stay that way if I were you. Marriage ain't all it's cracked up ta be.' She looked fondly down at her daughter who had fallen asleep in her arms and then across at the little lad playing happily with his toys.

'Oh, I don't know,' Josie said, shrugging her shoulders. 'It's what you make of it surely, and of course who you marry. I know I'll be happy with Graham.'

Gilly turned her attention back to Josie and tutted. 'That's what I thought. Soon 'ad the stuffing knocked out of me. It weren't long afore me and Terry were at each other's throats. Mind you, 'e's always been a bugger and I can't pretend I didn't know what kinda bloke 'e wa' before we married. But when you're pregnant you ain't got much choice, a' yer? Either way you suffer the consequences.' She sniffed loudly. 'To be 'onest, I don't think I'd 'ave married 'im if I'd known 'e wa' such a liar. I thought 'e'd got good prospects. Told me 'e owned a garage wi' 'is mate Melvyn, and me bein' so

176

gullible believed every word.' She rolled her eyes. 'I thought I'd landed the big 'un. Not only was 'e a looker but 'e had 'is own business as well. Soon found out the truth, din't I? Soon found out that 'e were only a mechanic and all the cars 'e used to bring 'ome weren't 'is, they were borrowed, and 'e could 'ave bin sacked if anyone had found out. The garage lark wa' just a line to pull the birds. Only 'e never reckoned on landing me in the family way.' She inhaled sharply. 'I blame the fact 'e's an orphan. It's 'is way of copin' wi' bein' abandoned as a baby,' she said matter-of-factly. She smiled warmly. ''Nother cuppa?'

'Oh, no thanks. I really must be going.'

'Stay a few more minutes, please. I'm enjoyin' our chat.'

Josie relented. 'Okay. But not for long. I've some more houses to visit before it gets dark.' She was frowning, though. Gilly's story was sounding horribly familiar.

'Terry won't be 'ome for ages yet. That's if 'e does come 'ome. 'E spends most of 'is time down the pub wi' 'is mates. Mind you, that's what 'e tells me. Personally I think 'e's got some other woman on. Comes 'ome wi' that look, if yer know what I mean, and smellin' like a brothel.' She narrowed her eyes. 'Just let me catch 'im wi' 'er, that's all I can say. I'll cut 'is bloody balls off.'

Josie shuddered at her bluntness.

'Er . . .' she started hesitantly. 'Did you say your husband told you he owned a garage and that his partner was called Melvyn?'

'Yeah. Why?'

'Oh.' Josie gulped. 'Well, it's maybe a coincidence but my Graham was 'til recently in partnership with a man called Melvyn and that was in a garage.'

Gilly frowned. 'This Melvyn . . . is 'e tall, black-haired and shifty-eyed?'

Josie shook her head. 'I don't know. I've never met him.' She laughed ruefully. 'It won't be the same man, it's just a coincidence.'

'Well, I'd watch out, 'cos the Melvyn my Terry pals around wi' is a right bastard. 'E lived wi' a girl once and she got 'ome one night from work and 'e'd scarpered – but not before 'e'd sold every stick of furniture in 'er 'ouse. Poor gel were left wi' n'ote but the floorboards.'

Josie's face grew serious. 'I hope it isn't the same man. Graham's talking of starting up again with him. Maybe he doesn't know what he's really like? I wonder how I can find out without . . .'

''Ang on,' Gilly interrupted. 'I've a photo of 'im somewhere. Not that it'll be of much use to you. But you'll certainly know him again, should you meet him.'

She carefully placed the sleeping baby down on the floor and went over to the sideboard, pulling open one of the cupboard

177

doors. Several items fell out which she ignored as she delved under a pile of objects. She pulled out an album.

''Ere it is. If I remember right 'im and Terry had one took together when we all went to Mablethorpe for the day last year.' She knelt on the floor to the side of Josie's chair and leafed through the book. 'Oh, look, there's me and the kids.' Josie smiled at the picture that Gilly was pointing at. 'It were a lovely day,' she continued. 'The kids really enjoyed it.'

Just then they both heard the front door slam shut and Gilly jumped up.

'Bloody 'ell! That must be Terry now,' she said in alarm. 'And look at this mess. Quick, Nathan, get these toys cleared away before yer cop it from yer dad.' She bent down and began to throw the scattered toys into the cardboard box, Nathan, his large blue eyes wide, looking on.

Josie rose. 'I'd better be going . . .'

'Gilly,' Terry's voice boomed from the hallway, 'our bloody Nathan's wee'd, dirty little bleeder, and I've just stepped in it. Ain't you got no control over these kids?'

The menacing voice of her father awoke the baby and she began to howl. He appeared in the doorway waving a wet sock in the air and scowled down at the baby. 'And you can shut yer racket,' he hissed.

For the first time he sensed Josie's presence and raised his head. Their eyes locked.

Simultaneously they both froze in recognition.

Josie grabbed the side of the armchair for support. Before her stood the man she loved; the man she was betrothed to; the man she knew as Graham. Her blood ran cold and she felt in grave danger of collapsing.

Gilly appeared at her side. 'Terry, this is Josie. She's collectin' for a jumble sale. I've give 'er that pile a' books under the stairs.'

Terry took a breath, planted a smile on his face, strode forward and held out his hand. 'Pleased to meet you,' he said politely, putting on a refined accent. The accent he had always used when in her company.

Josie's eyes fell upon his hand and she stared at it. A wave of anger and humiliation rose up. Somehow she mustered some strength, and ignoring his outstretched hand made a grab for her bag. 'I must be going,' she blurted, desperately wanting to get away from this house; away from this man and anything connected with him.

Gilly turned to her, her face wreathed in confusion.

Before either Gilly or Terry could say another word, she had grabbed the van keys from the coffee table and was charging towards the front door.

'Yer books,' Gilly shouted after her.

But Josie did not hear.

Josie gulped down the last of the cider in her glass and picked up the bottle and shook it. It was empty. Wiping her eyes on the back of her sleeve, she struggled up and headed for the kitchen where she gratefully unearthed a bottle of wine and re-filled her glass. She eyed the glass before she took a mouthful. For all she had drunk, the pain was not lessening. She grabbed the bottle and stumbled back, collapsing heavily into the chair.

She stared blindly into the flames of the gas fire and choked back a sob. She felt gutted, filled to overflowing with desolation and sorrow. How could he have done this to her? He knew how she felt so how could he have continued the lie? If he had had any common decency he would have come clean. But like that poor woman had said, he had none. He was a liar, only out to impress, and he had left her with nothing, not even her pride. How long would the lie have gone on if she hadn't happened upon his wife?

She shuddered. She was just glad that no one was around to witness her misery. She just wanted to be alone; to finish this bottle of wine, then curl up and die.

She heard the door open and raised her head sharply. Through a haze she saw Graham walking towards her.

'Josie,' he began. 'Please, let me explain.'

She jumped from her chair, sending the glass of wine crashing to the floor. 'You!' she cried. 'What are you doing here? How dare you . . .'

'Josie,' he spoke in a pleading voice as he grabbed hold of her arms, 'I love you. I couldn't tell you I was married, could I? I'd have lost you.'

'Love me? Love me!' she spat. 'You never loved me. All you love is yourself.' She wrenched herself free from him, swung back her arm and struck him hard across his face. 'And that's for all those lies you told me.'

He recoiled in shock and placed his hand to his smarting cheek. 'Josie, please . . . I'm going to divorce her . . .'

'Divorce her? You bastard. And what about your children? Are you going to abandon them as well?' She clenched her fists into a ball as she shook in anger. 'Get out,' she hissed.

'I'm not leaving, Josie . . .'

'I said, get out!' she screamed. 'And if I ever see you again and you're with anyone else but your wife, I'll go straight round and tell her. Is that clear? Is it?'

He stared at her, his face ashen. Resigned to defeat, he turned from her, hunched his shoulders and walked out.

She stood for several moments staring blindly at the door before she fell to the floor, bursting into uncontrollable sobs of grief.

Josie gradually awoke. A smell of stale vomit stung the air and she shivered violently, her body stiff with cold. Her stomach felt nauseous and her head swam. It took her several moments to realise she was naked and that the smell of vomit was her own. She struggled to rise, her head throbbing relentlessly as she tried to accustom her eyes to the darkness. Slowly it dawned on her that she was in a bathroom, a filthy bathroom by what she could detect. But whose bathroom? It was certainly not one she had ever been in before.

She groped around and found a towel which she wrapped around her as best she could whilst struggling to remember how she had come to be in this predicament. But nothing came. Her mind remained a blank.

Unable to stand, she crawled slowly out of the bathroom, stopping several times to take deep breaths to calm her stomach which threatened once again to empty what was left of its contents. A door to her left was ajar and she inched her way through. The room held a bed, and the bed, a body. The body moved, grunting as it rolled over, and pulled the covers over its head.

Josie froze as realisation swept over her. She had spent the night with a man – a strange man. Her stomach no longer remained under her control and she made a dash for the bathroom.

She felt wretched. At this moment death would have come as a welcome release. But death did not come. She was alive, the pain in her head and the heaving of her stomach were there to remind her. Praying for a miracle, that the man would not wake, she hurriedly dressed, stuffing her underwear into her handbag which she found under the bed next to her shoes. Then she made her way down the stairs and out into the cold morning air.

It seemed she would never get home. Unfamiliar streets stretched endlessly in all directions and it took her a while to get her bearings. It was with a sigh of relief that she finally let herself quietly into the flat and pressed her back against the door. Suddenly light flooded the passage.

'Josie!' Sue cried. 'Where on earth have you been? I've been worried to death.' She stopped, gasping in horror at the dishevelled state of her friend, the ashen face staring blankly back. Rushing forward, she threw her arms around the girl and ushered her through to the living room, seating her before the gas fire. Quickly she made a pot of tea and thrust a cup into Josie's hand.

'What happened, Josie?' she asked softly.

She waited patiently, filled with worry over what terrible catastrophe had befallen her friend. She saw Josie's eyes brim over with tears which overflowed to roll down her face.

'Oh, Sue. Sue,' she sobbed.

Sue quickly wrapped her arms around her and hugged her tightly. 'That's it, let it all out,' she soothed.

An hour later she sat back and sighed. 'Oh, Josie, Josie love. What can I say?' She placed her head in her hands and sighed loudly. 'Oh, if only I hadn't gone around to see Peter I would have been here for you.'

Josie managed a smile. 'You weren't to know.' She wrung her hands together in anguish. 'It's not what Graham did to me I'm concerned about. It's what *I* did.' She raised her eyes. 'I slept with a man I didn't know. And I can't even remember how I met him! The last thing I recall is grabbing my coat and heading for the off licence, worrying they might be shut. Oh, Sue, I feel disgusted with myself. I feel I'll never be able to hold my head up again. I know everyone will be pointing at me.' Her voice rose. ' "There she goes," they'll be saying. "That's the slag that picks men up . . ." '

'Stop that. Stop that nonsense this minute. You've done nothing wrong. I'd probably have done the same in your position.'

'Would you?'

'Too right.' Sue lowered her voice. 'If I'm honest, I've probably done worse.' She paused. 'You're hurting, Josie, and you sought the comfort of a man – any man, what did it matter? You're not the first to react this way and you won't be the last. If you were a man and had slept with a strange girl, you wouldn't even be questioning yourself.'

'That still doesn't excuse what I did.'

'No. But then we all have a lapse now and again. We are allowed, you know. Nobody can be saintly all the time.' She shook her head. 'I should have twigged there was something funny going on.'

'What d'you mean?'

'Well, when you think about it, he never really took you out except to crummy pubs or for a walk. He never even introduced you to his mates, and you were always lending him money.'

'I wasn't,' Josie said defensively.

'You were. You were always telling me for one reason or another you paid for the drinks or the bus fare or whatever.'

'Yes,' Josie relented. 'You're right, I was. But I won't get caught like that again. I've learned my lesson.'

'Good. But just pray that I never bump into that Terry. He'll not live to regret what he's done to you.'

Josie raised her hand. 'Enough. Please, Sue, I don't want any retaliation in case it ever gets back to that poor wife of his. And to be honest, I don't want to talk about it ever again. I want to forget . . . if I can.'

Sue smiled fondly. 'Okay. Go to bed and try to sleep.'

'Yeah,' Josie replied forlornly. She rose and kissed Sue lightly on the cheek. 'Thanks,' she said sincerely.

'Thanks?'

'For listening and waiting up, worrying about me.'

She made her way into her bedroom, undressed and climbed under the covers. She closed her eyes and tried to block out the desolation that overwhelmed her.

In several days' time she would be twenty-one. Twenty-one years old and what had she got? At this moment it felt like nothing. Twice in her life she had loved and, for whatever reason, had it thrown back in her face. She was hurting now as she had never hurt, and before she slept she made a vow. Never would she let a man cause her so much distress again. If that meant spending the rest of her life alone, then that's how it would be.

Chapter Twenty-Four

Josie carefully opened the envelope, took out the birthday card and read the verse. 'Thanks, Sue,' she said sincerely as she placed it on the fire surround along with the others.

'Don't screw up the envelope, there's something else inside.'

'Is there?' She frowned. 'What?'

'Why don't you look and see?' Sue replied, trying hard not to show her excitement.

Josie did as she was told and pulled out two pieces of card. 'They're tickets,' she exclaimed.

'Yes, train tickets. We're going to London.'

'London?'

'That's what I said. A day in London is just the tonic you need.'

Josie sighed. 'Thanks, Sue. I do appreciate the offer. But, no. I'm not really in the mood. All I want to do is go to work and come home.'

'Oh, for God's sake, Josie! It's your birthday today. You're twenty-one, not forty-one. And we've all respected your wishes, we've not even bothered to make you a birthday cake. But you've got to draw the line somewhere. You can't hide for the rest of your life because of what that Terry did to you.'

Josie looked at her, ashamed. 'I'm sorry. I didn't mean to hurt you.' Sue, Sophie and Gertie had been so good to her over the past few weeks, doing everything they could to ease the pain she was going through, and now she was insulting Sue by turning down her offer. Her friend would have gone without to scrape the money together for the tickets. It would be a terrible thing on her part if she refused. She raised her eyes. 'Yes, a day in London does sound nice. When are we going? Sunday?'

'Sunday! Who wants to go to London on a Sunday? No, we're going this coming Saturday.'

'Oh, I can't. I work, remember?'

'That's all sorted. I've had a word with Gertie, and like me she agrees a day away from it all will do you good. Have you got any money?'

'Yes. I've some in my post office account. It was money

I was saving for . . . saving for . . .'

'That'll do,' Sue cut in. 'Draw it all out and we'll blow the lot.'

Josie smiled broadly. 'Yes, you're right. That's a good idea.'

Sue slapped her on the back. 'I'll take you to Carnaby Street, then the Kings Road, and how about the markets? You can get some smashing bargains on the markets, especially Camden and Petticoat Lane.' She grinned broadly. 'If we're lucky, we might spot some pop stars.'

'Might we?'

'Yeah. They have to do their shopping as well. We'll catch an early train then we'll have all day to please ourselves. Oh, I don't know about you, but I can't wait! It's ages since I've been up to the capital. The last time I went was with my mother, Christmas shopping.' She frowned. 'That's not the same as going with one of your friends.'

Josie laughed. 'I bet it's not! Okay, you've won me round. I'm looking forward to our trip. It might do me good,' she said.

'There's no might about it. It will do you the world of good. Trust me.'

Later that day Josie alighted from the bus and walked slowly towards the house. It had been like any other ordinary day. But this wasn't an ordinary day, this was her birthday, a very special birthday, and apart from the few cards and the forthcoming trip to London, nothing else to mark the occasion had happened. Even Gertie had slipped away early without a word of explanation and she had been left to clear up and lock the shop, having first waited for a neighbour to arrive who was very kindly keeping an eye on William until Gertie returned. That hurt. Gertie usually asked Josie first, before anyone else.

Why was she feeling so sorry for herself? In view of recent events she hadn't wanted any fuss and had expressed that wish loud enough. She should be glad that her friends had complied. She made a decision. A hot bath and bed. That way she could get the day over with.

She let herself in, knocked loudly on Sophie's door and tried the door knob. It was locked. She frowned. It was very unusual for Sophie to be out. Oh, well, maybe she had gone to visit one of her cronies and stayed on for supper. She would just have to check on the old lady later. She climbed the stairs and paused before the flat door. That was strange also. Usually by now Sue was home, playing her music at full volume. Where had everyone gone? She opened the door. Before she had a chance to switch on the light a loud cheer rose, light flooded the room and several people rushed towards her, shouting a greeting.

Stunned, Josie was pulled towards the living room. Here the old gate-legged table had been pulled into the centre of the room and was filled with plates of sandwiches, a huge trifle, sausages on sticks and other bits and pieces. In the centre sat a decorated cake adorned with candles. All around the room were balloons and streamers, and on the coffee table sat several gift wrapped parcels. She stared at the smiling faces of Sue, Sophie, Gertie, Peter, and several other friends. She was speechless.

Sue grinned at her. 'Happy Birthday, Josie.'

Dressed in a short yellow, orange and lime green psychedelic-patterned halterneck dress, yellow tights and matching platform shoes, and with her savings tucked well down inside her black, imitation leather shoulder bag, Josie hurried out of St Pancras station, arm in arm with Sue, into the brilliant sunshine. The noise of traffic and the hustle and bustle of the capital city filled the air.

'Great, isn't it?' Sue beamed. 'Come on, let's find the underground. First stop, Carnaby Street.'

Several hours later Josie gingerly lowered herself down on to a bench on the Thames embankment, put down her packages and leaned over to rub her legs.

'They're killing me,' she grimaced. 'I don't think I've ever walked so much. I don't know about you but I'm knackered.'

'We've hardly begun.' Sue laughed loudly as she sat down next to her friend. 'We still haven't been down Oxford Street or to Trafalgar Square.'

Josie looked at her watch. 'But will we have time? It's past four o'clock.'

'Of course we will. Stop worrying.'

'But what about the train . . .'

'Oh, there's plenty of those. If the worst comes to the worst we can always catch the mail train home. That doesn't leave the station 'til two. We'll be able to wish the milkman good morning. I've always wondered what he looked like.' She jumped up and grabbed Josie's arm. 'Come on. We're wasting time. Let's get something to eat from one of those stalls and we'll be off.'

At nine-thirty that night they both stood in the middle of Trafalgar Square. Josie stared around in awe. The square was crowded with people, either scurrying towards other destinations or dawdling with a loved one hanging on their arm. A policeman nearby was directing several foreigners, and hundreds of pigeons flew down looking for crumbs or to find a place to settle for the night. The atmosphere was magical and she stood and savoured it for several moments before she turned to Sue, standing by her side.

'I've had a wonderful day. Thank you.'

'My pleasure. We'll have to do it again sometime.'

'Yes, please.' Josie answered sincerely. She yawned loudly. 'I hope I've enough strength to carry this lot home.'

Sue gazed down at the array of bags at their feet. 'I told you not to buy that wicker bird cage.'

'Oh, but I wanted it, Sue. I thought I could fill it with plants and put it on the window sill in the kitchen.'

'Mmm. Yes, it will brighten the place up a bit.'

'And I just had to get that hat,' Josie continued. 'Don't know if I'll ever wear it, though. But I can always stick it on a wall as a decoration. Anyway, you can talk. Look at all the stuff you've bought.'

Sue stuck out her tongue. 'Touché.'

'Right then,' Josie spoke hopefully, 'shall we make tracks for the station?'

'Not just yet.'

'But surely there's nothing left for us to see? We've been round London twice as it is.'

'Hardly.' Sue grinned. 'It would take a month of Sundays to do that.'

'Well, where were you thinking of? It's nearly ten, everywhere will be shut, won't it?'

'Nothing shuts in London, Josie.' She paused, eyeing her friend warily. 'There is just one place I've always wanted to visit.'

'Where's that?'

'It isn't far.'

'What isn't far?'

'Soho.'

'Soho! Isn't that the place where . . .'

'Yeah. People go in search of a good time, and I fancy taking a look. It won't do any harm. I've read so much about it in magazines and it really intrigues me.'

'I've read about it as well,' Josie said, sternly. 'What if we're picked up by the police?'

'Oh, stop being so stuffy. How on earth can we be picked up for walking down a street? This is England, Josie, not Russia.'

She studied the pavement. The thought of a visit to Soho intrigued her also, but she was not about to admit the fact to Sue.

'Okay. But just a quick look, mind, and if we're picked up it'll be your fault.'

Josie stuck as close to Sue's side as her bags would allow as, wide-eyed in amazement, they walked slowly down a busy narrow street in the centre of Soho. A steady stream of girls, cleavages exposed, wearing black fishnet stockings and skirts no longer than curtain pelmets, their heels clicking rhythmically along the pavement, eyed them cautiously.

'They think we're rivals,' Sue whispered laughingly, nudging Josie in the ribs.

She hitched her bags further up. 'I hope not,' she answered grimly. 'I don't fancy getting into a fight with one of them.' She paused before a doorway, letting several people pass by. Her eyes caught the display board on the wall. Several naked females in sexual poses stared back. She gulped.

'I don't know how anyone could do that,' she said, horrified.

'It's good money, Josie.'

'It might be, but personally I'd sooner starve.'

She sharply turned her head as several men walked by and eyed them both keenly. One man stopped, turned and made to approach. Josie quickened her pace.

'Let's get out of here, Sue. We've seen enough now.'

'Not yet,' she replied.

Josie stopped again as a group of people pouring out of the doorway of the Pink Panther Club blocked her route. A man from the group hailed a passing taxi. Josie waited as the taxi stopped and several of the crowd climbed aboard. A woman sat down in the window seat facing her, her profile clearly visible through the glass. Josie stared transfixed as the taxi pulled away.

'What's the matter?' Sue asked.

Josie jumped and turned to face her. 'That woman in the taxi. It was my cousin, Marilyn. I know it was!'

'What, the one who stole all your grandmother's savings? Are you sure?'

'Of course I'm sure,' Josie snapped. She let several of her bags slip to the pavement. 'Oh, Sue, what was she doing in these parts?'

Sue shrugged her shoulders. 'I don't know. What do you think?'

'I daren't think, that's the trouble,' Josie said as several possibilities raced through her mind. 'Oh, my God, Sue! You don't think she's . . .'

'I don't think anything, Josie. For all we know she was just on a night out with some of her friends. But I'd pick up your bags if I were you before someone steals them.'

Josie bent down to retrieve her belongings. She straightened up and looked at Sue in alarm.

'I'll have to try and find her, Sue. I can't go home and leave her here. What if she's in trouble? Did you see those men she was with? They looked like thugs to me. What if she's their prisoner? I've read about things like that. Oh, I must find her. I must.'

'And how do you propose to do that? London's a big place, Josie, she could be anywhere.'

'I don't care. I have to find her.'

Hitching up her bags, she rushed towards the bouncer guarding the entrance of the Pink Panther.

'You can't come in with all those bags.'

'I don't want to come in. I want to know where those people just went in that taxi?'

'If you're not coming in, move on,' the bouncer said nonchalantly. 'I'm only interested in the people coming in, not where they go afterwards.'

'Oh, but . . .'

'I said, move on. You're blocking the pavement.'

A man appeared at the door, a large cigar hanging from his mouth. He stretched and looked at Josie apathetically. 'Trouble, Brett?' he asked the bouncer.

'No, Boss,' came the reply. He looked at Josie and jerked his head to the side, warning her to move on.

Sue came up and nudged her hard. 'Josie, come on. You'll cause trouble. These men don't mess about, you know.'

'I can't just leave. That man's the only chance I've got of finding out where that taxi went.'

'Don't be daft. How will he know?'

Josie's shoulders sagged, then her face brightened. 'I know. Let's get a taxi and ask it to follow the other one. I've seen that done in films. We're sure to find her then.'

'That taxi will be miles away by now. Besides, I've not enough money left for a taxi. Have you?'

Josie shook her head. After all her purchases she had only loose change left in her purse. She knew deep down the situation was hopeless. They hadn't a hope of finding that taxi.

'I don't know why you're so concerned about her, Josie. You told me she treated you like dirt.'

'So she did. But that's not the point. Marilyn's my cousin and she might need my help.' She bit her bottom lip. 'She was wearing a fur coat.'

'Who was?'

'Marilyn. She was wearing a fur coat.'

'Well, she must be doing all right to afford one of those.'

'Yeah, I suppose you're right. I'll just have to hope that it's not by doing anything illegal.'

'If it is, there's not much you can do about it.'

'I could talk to her. Tell her to come home.'

'And do you think she'd listen?'

Josie shook her head.

'Well, then. Come on. Let's go and catch our train. There's nothing you can do here.' Her eyes twinkled mischievously. 'Unless you fancy picking up a couple of blokes and making some money?'

Josie giggled. 'Trust you to come out with something like that.'

She paused. 'How much d'you think we'd make?' she asked in all seriousness.

Sue frowned thoughtfully. 'Not much in your case. You'd need to give them change out of a tanner.'

'Cheeky devil! I'd bet I'd make more than you.'

'You're probably right.' She yawned loudly. 'Just now I'm too tired to do any more than lie back and think of England.'

'Same here,' Josie answered with a twinkle in her eyes. 'Let's leave it for some other time.'

They arrived at St Pancras just in time to catch the one-fifteen back to Leicester. Both girls settled in their seats and Sue yawned loudly.

'Been some day, hasn't it?' she said.

'Yes,' Josie agreed. 'It certainly has. And one I won't forget in a hurry.'

As the weeks passed by, Josie began to heal. With the help of her friends she had little time to dwell on thoughts of Terry, they each saw to that.

Gertie constantly had her re-arranging the shop, leafing through old recipe books or making endless trips up and down the stairs on errands for William. Sue commandeered her early evenings with her revision and through this opened up a world that Josie had never realised existed before and one which, to her pleasure, she found enthralling. She now knew the names of various artists and could accurately pinpoint a particular work from just a description; no mean feat for one who'd known only the rudiments previously. Sophie taught her to crochet and she jubilantly produced several colourful table mats for the old people's Bring and Buy sale, and whilst they worked Sophie chatted and Josie marvelled and laughed at all her tales and anecdotes.

She was blessed, she knew. Without her friends she would never have coped.

Chapter Twenty-Five

The final days of July brought a heat wave of stifling intensity. Everything solid was either melting or wilting under the relentless blazing sun. The nights were only slightly cooler than the days, and tired from lack of sleep and listless from lack of cool air, the people of Leicester, for once, were willing the onset of autumn.

Josie rose late one morning after a fitful night's sleep to find Sue sitting stiffly at the kitchen table. She held a piece of paper in her hand and Josie eyed it hesitantly, knowing instinctively what it was. They had both been waiting anxiously for this news and Josie felt suddenly frightened.

She quickly poured herself a mug of tea and sat down opposite her friend.

Sue raised her eyes. 'I went down to the College at the crack of dawn for my results.'

'And?' Josie said slowly, fanning herself with a tea towel.

'I failed.'

Josie inhaled sharply, unable to find the right words. After all the hard work Sue had done, her failure seemed an injustice. But on reflection, her hard work had begun too late in the day, even Josie knew that.

She leant her arms on the table. 'Never mind. There's always next year.'

'No,' Sue replied flatly. 'I've finished with studying.'

Josie stared at her blankly. She could not visualise Sue now without a pencil in her hand or her nose in a book; all the rooms cluttered with her paint pots and paraphernalia. It wouldn't seem right not to have these things lying around to fall over. It didn't seem right that Sue should give up, not after she had finally made so much effort.

'Oh, come on. Don't let that piece of paper get you down. Once the new term starts you'll feel better. You'll soon be in the thick of it. But now things will be different. You know where you went wrong the last time.'

Sue breathed deeply. 'I meant what I said. I've finished with studying, and nothing that anybody says will make any difference.'

She folded her arms and leant on the table. 'You see, Josie, I didn't just fail, I failed miserably, and I'd already made a promise to myself that if I didn't get a certain pass rate then I would pack it all in. I'm over twenty-one and I can't go on studying forever.'

'But that's silly . . .'

'No, it's not. I'm sensible enough to realise that I would never amount to anything in the art and design world. I haven't got what it takes and now's the time to call it a day.' She smiled at Josie's dismayed expression. 'Don't be upset. I only achieved what I did through your help, and if you remember rightly, I only studied for this degree because it seemed the easiest option. I was wrong. I was wrong to take it in the first place and wrong to think I could breeze through it.'

Josie sighed. 'I suppose you know best. But what will you do?'

'Workwise, I don't know. But I have made some plans for the mean time.'

'Oh?'

Sue picked up the spoon from the sugar bowl and played with it. 'I'm off to France.'

'France!'

'Yeah. And maybe Italy. I've made some arrangements with College friends who are back-packing across Europe. I'm joining them for a few weeks of fun before I have to find myself a job.'

'Back-packing! You mean camping?'

Sue laughed. 'You make it sound like a Girl Guides outing. But yes, camping, if that's what you want to call it. Going wherever the road takes you. Picking up work here and there, and meeting other travellers on the way. I could end up anywhere. It doesn't matter really. It'll just be fun and I can't wait.'

Josie sighed. 'It sounds wonderful. I wish I could come.'

'Why don't you?' Sue exclaimed. 'You'd love it. All that freedom. No one to care about but yourself.'

'I can't. I can't leave Gertie, not while her dad is so poorly. We thought he was on the mend but he's slowly getting worse.'

'It's only a job, Josie.'

'Not to me. Gertie's a friend.'

'Yes, she is,' Sue replied sincerely. She thought for a moment and her eyes sparkled. 'She'll keep the job open for you. I'm sure she would if you asked.'

Josie shook her head. 'I couldn't expect her to do that. No, I can't come, Sue, as much as I'd love to.' She paused thoughtfully. 'You can keep me informed by sending me postcards. I'll look for the postie every morning.'

'Yeah, and I'll take lots of photos.'

'Oh, do that. It'll be just like I was there. When are you going?'

'Tomorrow. No sense in wasting time.'

'Tomorrow! Oh, I didn't realise you'd be going that soon.'

'Well, the new term starts in September and the College crowd will have to be back by then. That gives me at the very most four weeks.'

'Oh.' Josie smiled in relief. 'Not as long as I feared. I thought you'd be away for months.'

'Fat chance. Besides, I still have to keep up with the rent while I'm away. Don't want to come back and find you've re-let my room.'

'I wouldn't do that. And you can forget paying the rent. I'll pay for us both. It'll be a holiday gift from me.'

'Oh, Josie . . .'

'Don't say another word. It'll be my pleasure. Besides, I owe you a fortune one way or another.' She rose and re-filled both their mugs from the tea pot. 'What about your parents? Have you told them yet?'

Sue shook her head. 'No. I did think of just slipping away. Then I thought that wouldn't be fair. They've supported me all this time and I would only have to face them when I came back.' She sighed deeply. 'I don't know what I'm going to say. I feel I've let them down badly. A couple of years ago I wouldn't have given a damn, but I do now. Funny, isn't it?'

'Not really. You've just grown up that's all.'

Sue smiled, finished her tea and scraped back her chair. 'I have to start my packing and practising my speech to my parents. Wish me luck.'

'I do.'

She paused by the door. 'Do you fancy a bottle of cider tonight? We could get fish and chips and sit and have a good chin wag.'

'Wonderful idea.' Josie beamed. 'I'll look forward to it.'

Early next morning Sue departed on her travels with everything in her rucksack but the kitchen sink. Josie marvelled how such a seemingly small bag could hold so much, and wondered how long Sue would manage to walk through the wilds of the French countryside with that weight strapped to her back. She managed a cheerful wave as she saw her friend off, but stared forlornly down the street long after she had disappeared around the corner.

Finally she closed the door and stood for several moments with her back against it, listening to the silence. Several months ago three friends had shared this flat, now there was only her. She managed a brave smile. Four weeks was no time at all. Before she knew it Sue would be back, music blaring, rooms cluttered with her belongings, and Josie would be roped into helping her find a job. It would be as though she had never been away. Even so, Josie would miss her and hoped the time would pass quickly.

She hurried to dress. Work beckoned, and when she returned she had promised to help Sophie clean under her monstrosity of a bed.

Several nights later Stephen drew his van to a halt and gave the horn a loud blast. Josie jumped and nearly fell over in shock. She had just finished for the night and was hurrying for her bus when the sound of the blaring horn startled her.

'Sorry, Josie, I didn't mean to give you a fright,' he shouted through the open window. 'Only I was hoping to catch you.'

'Oh?'

He leaned upon the window frame and watched as she walked hesitantly towards him. 'Still interested in helping me on the 'dog stall?' he asked.

Josie swallowed hard. 'Yeah. But . . . well . . . I don't know anything about cooking hot dogs.'

'Oh, it's as easy as anything, and to you it'll be nothing at all. You always were a dab hand in the kitchen. Smashing cook, you are.'

Josie reddened at the compliment. 'That's different,' she replied, turning the praise aside. 'You can't compare cooking in a kitchen to a van. I'll need intensive training.'

'Stop worrying, Josie. Half an hour is all it'll take and I'll be with you anyway, should anything go amiss.'

'Will you? Oh, but I thought I'd be on my own. You said you were getting another van.'

'That was the original plan. But I've had a few hiccups so it'll just be me and thee, I'm afraid. That's all right, isn't it?'

Josie cleared her throat. 'Yeah, 'course it is,' she said lightly. 'So, when d'you want me?'

He looked quickly at his watch. 'Get in. I'll give you a lift home and we can discuss it.'

She hesitated before walking around, opening the side-sliding door of her old Bedford Commer van, and climbing aboard.

'Be careful of that door. It doesn't lock properly and slides open when I go round a corner,' he laughed. 'I don't want you falling out.'

'Oh, don't mind me,' she bantered to hide her nervousness. 'Just leave me in the road. Some kind soul is bound to stop and take my broken bones to the hospital.'

Stephen laughed again, then his face grew sombre. 'How are you, Josie?'

'Fine, and you?'

'Can't grumble.' He revved the engine and guided the vehicle into the traffic. He glanced again at his watch. 'We could discuss the details over a drink if you fancy? That's if you're not in a hurry to get home.'

'Not particularly. A drink sounds fine.'

'Good.'

They both lapsed into silence as Stephen negotiated the traffic. Josie sat stiffly, determined not to let her feelings show. Finally he pulled into The Huntsman on the Narborough Road and switched off the engine. 'After you,' he said. He watched as she slid out of her seat, then locked the van and joined her.

Seated at a table, Josie took a sip of her cider. 'So, when d'you want me?' she asked casually.

'Oh, Wednesday night if that's convenient. Leicester City are playing a big charity match and there's bound to be a massive crowd of hungry supporters. I know it's a bit short notice . . .'

'Oh, that's all right. I've nothing planned for Wednesday and it's my half day anyway.'

He looked at her quizzically, noticing the flat tone of her voice. 'I was worried you'd be busy. Aren't you seeing your fiancé?'

She breathed in sharply. 'Er . . . no. He's working,' she lied. 'He's a very busy man.'

'He must be if he's working nights.'

'You do.'

'Touché,' he said, smilingly. Then the smile vanished. 'When's the wedding?' he asked.

Josie raised her head and stared straight into his eyes. 'We haven't made definite plans. We want to buy a house. Not an ordinary house but a nice one. That's why he's working,' she lied again. She lowered her gaze and picked up her drink. Why had she lied? Why could she not have told him the truth about Graham? Well, it was too late now. She couldn't take back what she had said without looking stupid. 'The money you pay me will come in handy. You do pay well, I hope?' she said, marvelling at her own calmness and how the words were slipping so easily off her tongue.

'I'll pay you well, Josie,' he said flatly. 'And I'll add a little extra so you can buy something nice for your bottom drawer.'

She flinched at the sarcasm in his voice and noticed with concern the sadness that flitted briefly across his face. The mood passed as he took a gulp of his beer and smiled broadly at her. 'How's the job going? Still enjoying it?'

'Yes, I am, thank you. I expect I shall have to give it up, though,' she added, before she could stop herself.

'Give it up?'

'Yeah, when I get married.'

'Oh. Yes, of course.' Again he gulped at his beer. 'Another?' he asked rising.

Josie shook her head. 'I'd better be going soon.'

'Yes, er . . . okay. I'll have another quick half, though, if you don't mind?'

She shook her head and watched as he strode towards the bar. He recognised one of the customers and stood and chatted whilst his drink was poured by a comely barmaid. Josie smiled as his long fingers raked absent-mindedly through his hair; she saw how his face lit up when he laughed, and how his eyes twinkled merrily, and the ease with which he spoke, commanding his audience. She swallowed hard and averted her eyes, wishing with all her might she had not agreed to help him. Being his friend was proving extremely difficult and something she knew she was not strong enough to handle at this moment.

She shuddered as she remembered the savage pain she had suffered after Terry's betrayal; the endless stream of tears, the hours spent locked in the bathroom soaking in cooling water, analysing the whys and wherefores, and also the terrible futile longings she had felt for Stephen over the years. She knew she could not endure it again.

She realised then why she had lied to him earlier. It had been to put a barrier between them. It was her safety net. She had pulled down the shutters, and to survive they must stay down. Not only with Stephen. It would be the same with any man who made the slightest advances towards her.

As he approached, she slowly lifted her eyes.

'We'd better make the arrangements for Wednesday. I really must be going,' she said coolly.

Wednesday dawned bright and clear. It was one of those September mornings that give a gentle reminder that summer is on the wane. The grass sparkled with dew, spiders' webs hung miraculously from branches, and the chill in the air sent you scurrying back for a warm jumper to pull over your summer top.

The postman had delivered a picture postcard from Sue. Josie gasped in delight at its arrival and then tried desperately to decipher the French words inscribed above a cartoon picture of a man wearing typical French dress, a string of onions draped around his neck. Josie knew it was rude, it had to be coming from Sue, and the suspense of not understanding it drove her to distraction.

Sue was enjoying herself and would see her soon. Josie fumed. Her friend had been away for over six weeks, much longer than she had said, and not one word of explanation for her prolonged absence. Boy, would she get it on her return.

The day passed quickly enough. The shop was extremely busy and Josie wondered if the neverending queue of customers would ever lessen. It was early closing day but in the end she had to stay open over an hour longer than normal, and by the time she had tidied up and had a natter with Gertie and William, it was getting on for her usual home time. She had been glad about the way her day had gone, though. If she was honest, despite her resolve, she was nervous of her forthcoming encounter with Stephen, and keeping herself occupied gave her less time to dwell on it.

At seven-thirty that evening, as the twilight faded, she turned the corner of Filbert Street and made her way towards Leicester City football ground's entrance where she had arranged her rendezvous with Stephen.

As she approached she saw him and he was not alone. With him was a girl, a very attractive girl. She was tall and dark, dressed in a black midi coat, long black boots and red satin hot pants. She had her hands on Stephen's arms and was looking adoringly up into his face. Josie stiffened at their intimacy and stopped abruptly as she saw him bend and kiss her lightly on the lips. He stood and watched as the girl turned and walked away. As she passed, Josie noticed the look of happiness written across her face. She winced. The scene she had witnessed hurt. It hurt more than she dared admit and she wanted to turn and run away.

Before she had chance Stephen spotted her and beckoned her over, beaming broadly.

'There you are,' he called to her. 'I was beginning to think you weren't coming.'

Breathing deeply, she forced her legs to move. By the time she joined him she was smiling as broadly as he was. She stared at the van in admiration. Stephen had had it customised with various illustrations of the items he sold, plus in bold lettering the words 'Dogs Galore'.

She laughed in approval. 'I like the name. Very catchy. Right,' she said, rubbing her hands together, 'you'd better give me the instruction manual.'

Amid the handful of supporters who had started to arrive, wearing the familiar blue and white striped hats and scarves and shouting loudly 'Up the City', Stephen quickly showed Josie the workings of the van.

She stood and listened intently. He was right. It was easy. She felt enthusiasm flow through her. She would enjoy tonight. She loved people and would enjoy the banter and good humour she knew the supporters would throw at her. The fact that Stephen was beside her was of no consequence, she told herself.

Just before the match started she saw him frown and lean out of the serving window. She followed suit. Another van had arrived.

'Competition?' she asked.

'Mmm,' Stephen replied grimly. He pulled himself upright. 'It's of no importance. I got here earlier and secured the best pitch. And besides,' he grinned, 'my "dogs" are cheaper and I don't use stale rolls.'

Josie continued to stare out across the tarmac towards the other van. She didn't like the look of the two men staring back. She hurriedly withdrew and proceeded to split open another two dozen rolls in readiness.

She turned to Stephen thoughtfully. 'You've put a lot of thought and effort into this business, haven't you?'

'Sorry?' he replied absent-mindedly as he lifted the cover on the broiler to check the sausages and then proceeded to light the gas under the large urn full of water. 'Sorry, Josie, what did you say?' He leaned back against the tiny sink in the corner of the van, wiping his hands on a tea towel, and gave her his full attention.

She repeated her observation.

'Yes, I have,' he replied proudly. 'Eventually I'd like to open my own restaurant but I thought this would give me a good grounding in the business sense. You still have to keep books and do tax returns, and also with only the van to worry about, I don't have such big overheads. That's what swayed me in the end. The restaurant can wait while I'm having fun with this venture.' He laughed. 'It still gives me a headache, estimating how much perishable stock to buy. I mean, it would be pure madness on my part to buy thirty dozen rolls and then have to throw half of them away the next day because I calculated wrong. Luckily, up to now I've been pretty accurate.' He paused and stared at her for several seconds. 'Have you ever thought of doing something for yourself?'

'Me?'

'Yes, why not? You practically run the greengrocery shop, and you certainly did your grandmother's stall before that. Marilyn wasn't much help, was she? Running your own business would be nothing to someone like you.' He grimaced and turned away from her. 'Sorry, I forgot,' he mumbled. 'You'll soon be up to your neck in housework and nappies. You won't have time for anything else.'

Josie was spared having to reply by her first customer who wanted some crisps to eat whilst watching the match.

The City team scored several goals against the opposing side and the ecstatic cheers from the twenty thousand odd crowd could be heard several miles away. The match finished in a home win and the delighted crowd swarmed through the gates. It seemed to Josie that they all surrounded the van, demanding 'dogs with onions, 'dogs without, red sauce, brown sauce, no sauce, and one young lad, his hat pulled right down over his forehead, even asked for fish and chips. All Josie did as she worked side by side with Stephen, delivering an endless supply of food to the hungry horde, was worry that they would run out and the crowd would run amok.

Finally, the last of the masses were fed and with only two rolls and one sausage left, Josie flopped back against the counter and exhaled deeply as she wiped the sweat from her brow. Stephen smiled at her.

'Well done, Josie. You did me proud.' His eyes twinkled. 'Fancy a 'dog?' he chuckled.

Josie shook her head. 'I don't care if I never see another one as long as I live.'

'Oh, I hope not, Josie,' he said in dismay. 'I was hoping you'd help me out again.'

'I might,' she said. 'I'll see how I feel when I get the feeling back in me legs.' She turned and stared out into the dark night. The row of entrance lights had been switched off and the surrounding area was pitched into darkness. She turned back and shivered. 'We'd better start clearing up 'cos I don't know about you, but all I want to do is climb into bed.'

Stephen laughingly agreed as he climbed out of the back of the van and proceeded to close the large metal shutter that covered the opening.

'Shoot the bolts, Josie,' he shouted from outside.

Josie did as she was bidden, flicking the large bolts across and securing the flap. As she shot the last bolt home she heard a shout, then a loud thud as though someone had fallen against the side of the van. Then more shouts followed by silence. Panic raced through her. They were being attacked or, worse, robbed! Grabbing the bread knife, she rushed for the door only to be thrust back inside by a heavy object. The knife was wrenched from her hand, a leg shot out tripping her up, and she fell heavily upon the floor. She cried out in pain as she caught her knee awkwardly on the metal door of the cupboard underneath the counter.

Stunned, she raised her eyes to see a large figure wielding a thick stumpy stick looming over her. He was dressed completely in black, a balaclava pulled down over his face, his glaring blue eyes staring out. He froze for a second, hesitating before he bent down, grabbed her shoulder and pulled her up, thrusting a cloth bag into her face.

'Money,' he growled. 'In 'ere, and quick about it.'

She shook, her eyes darting towards the open door. Stephen? Where was he? Her mind raced frantically.

The man thumped her on the shoulder, jerking nervously. 'Josie. Put the fucking money in the bag unless you want a taste of this,' he shouted, shoving the stick beneath her chin.

Frightened, she grabbed the bag and with shaking hands started to stuff it with the notes and coins. It was then that it struck her. The man had called her by name. He knew her. Her eyes darted sideways and she noticed him glance briefly towards the open door, checking that the coast was still clear. Without a thought, she seized her chance. Twisting the top of the bag around her head, she turned, swung back her arm and hit him on the side of the head with all the force she could muster. Taken off guard, he stumbled and she lunged for the bread knife he had discarded on the work surface. Shaking uncontrollably, she jerked the knife towards him, made a grab for the balaclava, and before he could stop her had wrenched it from his head.

She stared in horror.

'You!' she gasped.

The man held up his hand. 'Josie, just hand me the money and you won't get hurt . . .'

'You bastard!' she screeched, jabbing the knife in the air between them. 'You filthy rotten bastard!'

He made to grab the knife and Josie stepped back, still brandishing the weapon towards him.

Her anger rose. 'Don't come any closer,' she said hysterically, stepping as far back as she could. 'I'll use it.'

His shoulders sagged. He cocked his head to one side and smiled. 'You wouldn't. Not on me.'

'Try it. Just try it, Graham, or Terry, or whatever you happen to call yerself. I'd stick this in you without a thought.'

The tone of her voice left him in no doubt she meant business.

'This isn't my doing, Josie,' he pleaded. 'I was forced into it. I owe people money . . .'

'I don't want to hear your lies. Now get out of here!'

'Josie . . .' he began, advancing towards her.

'I said, get out!' she screamed, thrusting the knife just a little too hard. The sharp edge pierced through his jacket and into his side, cutting his skin.

He looked at her and placed his hand over the wound.

'You stabbed me,' he said in bewilderment.

Josie looked down at the knife smeared with blood. She raised her head. 'I'll do it again . . .'

'Okay, okay,' he spluttered.

He quickly turned and ran out of the van into the night.

Josie stood open-mouthed for several moments. The knife dropped from her hand, landing with a clatter on the floor, and she sank down on to her knees and groaned loudly. She clutched her stomach, forcing away the nausea that threatened. For several moments she rocked backwards and forwards, shaking in delayed shock as she re-lived the horror. Suddenly she stopped. Stephen! Oh, God, what had happened to Stephen?

She pulled herself up and, despite her throbbing leg, ran from the van into the darkness, shouting his name at the top of her voice.

She knew the huddled shape lying in the middle of the path was Stephen long before she reached him. A sob caught in the back of her throat. Blinded by tears, she threw herself down beside his crumpled body. There seemed to be blood everywhere. He was covered in it. She gently lifted his head on to her lap and cradled him in her arms.

'Oh, Stephen, Stephen,' she cried hysterically. 'Please don't die. Please, please.' She placed her face next to his. 'I love you, Stephen. I love you so much.'

The wail of sirens reached her ears and she felt herself being gently eased away by unseen hands.

'No. No,' she wailed as she struggled against them.

'Come on now, love. Let them see to him,' a soothing voice said.

She lifted her eyes. An ambulance and a police car, both with flashing blue lights, were parked close by and several medics were milling around Stephen's body. She saw him being lifted on to a trolley and into the back of the ambulance.

She tried to break free. 'Let me go with him, please. Please let me go with him.'

'Don't worry, love. We'll follow them down,' came the soothing reply.

She turned and buried her head in the shoulder of the policeman who was holding her tightly.

'Please, tell me he's not dead,' she cried. 'Please tell me he isn't. I couldn't bear it.'

She felt a hand on her head, gently smoothing over her hair.

'Let's lock the van and collect your things and I'll take you to the hospital. Come on now.'

Josie stepped back and raised her tear-filled eyes.

'Thank you,' she managed.

The policeman took her arm and guided her towards the van.

'We'll need a statement from you,' he said gently. 'But first we'll find out how your young man is.'

Josie, hands clasped in her lap, face ashen and drawn, sat opposite the two policemen across the chipped wooden desk in the interview room at Charles Street Police Headquarters. The last few hours had been a nightmare and without the kindly attention of the police and the hospital staff she did not know how she would have coped.

On his arrival at Leicester Royal Infirmary, Stephen had been rushed straight into the theatre for emergency surgery. Reluctantly, Josie had had her badly bruised knee bandaged and been given a tetanus injection. All she could think about was Stephen. He could not die, not her Stephen. Life would be meaningless if anything happened to him, though at this moment the doctors were unsure of the full extent of his injuries. She could only wait and pray like the rest of his family.

His parents had been summoned and they were at the hospital now, pacing the waiting room, eager for news of their eldest son. Whilst Josie sat struggling with her conscience in a small square room on the other side of town.

The elder of the two policemen, Detective Inspector Mason, a solid middle-aged man, heavily lined face portraying the toll of his years in the force, lit his pipe and puffed for several moments until he was satisfied it was lit. Josie felt his kindly eyes resting upon her. She raised her head, noticing that the stitching around the leather patch on the left sleeve of his sports jacket was coming undone.

Mason scratched his nose and eased the pipe from his mouth. 'Nasty business,' he said gravely. He leaned forward. 'Now are you positive you cannot identify any of the attackers? Did you see anything suspicious before the event? It's very important, so take your time.'

Josie stared blankly at him as a picture of Terry's face swam clearly before her. He knows, she wanted to shout. Terry knows who did it. He was part of the gang. But she suppressed that longing. All she could think of was his poor unsuspecting wife and those little children. How they would suffer when they found out their father was nothing more than a thug! But what about Stephen, fighting for his life on the operating table? Stephen, who until a few hours ago had his future mapped out. What was in store for him now? Whoever did this had no right to expect any compassion. They hadn't shown any when they had beaten Stephen to a pulp. If they were not caught and punished, they were free to terrorise again.

'Terry,' she whispered faintly.

Detective Inspector Mason leaned even further forward. 'Pardon, my dear?'

Josie raised her head. 'The one that attacked me is called Terry and he lives at number seven Briton Street,' she blurted before she could change her mind.

He sat back and inclined his head knowingly towards his younger colleague. 'Terry Bradley,' he said. 'Get the mug shots.' He turned back to Josie as the constable departed. 'You know Terry Bradley, I take it?'

Josie nodded. 'Yes. But I didn't know he was capable of anything like this. I never dreamt . . .' She looked at the man facing her. 'What will happen to his wife and children?'

He breathed deeply and eyed her sternly. 'I wouldn't concern yourself about them, my dear. I would worry more for your young man in hospital, fighting for his life.'

The constable returned with a large book and placed it in front of his boss. He flicked over several of the pages, stopped at one, turned the book round to face Josie and pointed at a picture. 'That him?'

She stared down. She would never forget that face. Cold menacing eyes glared back at her, eyes that once she had loved to look into. She averted her gaze and squeezed her own eyes tightly shut.

'Yes, that's him,' she said firmly.

When satisfied Josie had given them all the information she could and she had signed her statement, they returned her to the hospital. As desperately exhausted as she was, she could not go home. She would wait in the hospital, for the duration if necessary.

She was met by Stephen's mother.

'Josie, me duck,' she cried, rising awkwardly from her chair. She placed her arm around the girl and guided her towards a bench. 'Sit down, Alf will get you a cuppa.' She sat next to Josie and stared helplessly for several moments into her face.

'Any news?' Josie asked hesitantly.

Rene Kingsman shook her head, a tear escaping down her cheek. 'Not yet,' she uttered. She wiped the back of her hand across her face. 'I dunno,' she said. 'You give birth, nurses 'em, smacks their bums when they're bad, and you pray each day that they'll turn out good solid citizens. And when summat 'appens it tears yer guts like it's 'appened to you.' She sighed and looked at Josie fondly. 'But then you'd know what I was talking about, wouldn't you, love?'

Josie frowned.

Rene placed her arm around Josie's shoulder and squeezed her tightly. 'You've always been fond of our Stephen. Right from being babies when you used to play 'ide and seek amongst the market stalls. And you still carry a torch, I can see it in yer eyes. A mother knows, me dear.' She sighed deeply. 'If truth be told, I'd say you're suffering just as much as me. Well, do like me, Josie love, and 'ave faith in 'im up there. 'E'll pull our Stephen through. 'E's got to. There's too many people that'd miss 'im.'

Just then Alf returned and silently handed her a plastic cup of tea. Josie nodded. As she sipped at it her mind raced. Was she really as transparent as that? She must be if Rene had always known of her feelings towards her son. Had she ever mentioned the fact to him? Her shoulders sagged. Did it really matter? What mattered most was Stephen, struggling for his life.

Her thoughts were interrupted by the arrival of a doctor. He paused before them, a grave smile upon his face.

'Mr and Mrs Kingsman,' he said, addressing the other couple.

Rene froze and Alf slowly rose. 'Yes, doctor,' he answered.

'Your son is out of the theatre and in intensive care. He has a fractured skull, several broken ribs, one of which had punctured his lung, and nasty bruising on his legs and arms. He's still unconscious, I'm afraid. But he's stable.'

'And . . .' Rene began hesitantly. 'Will 'e be all right?'

The doctor smiled reassuringly. 'It's early days, but we're hopeful. The next twenty-four hours will be crucial. That's as much as I can say at the moment. Now if you'd all like to go home and get some sleep, we'll contact you if there's any change.'

'Can I see him?' Rene asked.

The doctor eyed her cautiously. 'He's . . . well, it could be upsetting for you.'

'I don't care, doctor, please let me see my boy?' she begged.

He nodded. 'Okay, but just for a moment, through the glass window.'

Josie blinked away the tears and swallowed hard to rid the lump in her throat as she stood stiffly before the glass window of the intensive care ward.

Stephen lay motionless, the untortured parts of his skin not much darker than the sheets he lay upon. Tubes seemed to protrude from everywhere, monitors bleeped above him and nurses bustled around. She turned and dragged her feet slowly down the maze of corridors and out into the early morning chill. It was at this moment that she wished that she smoked. She longed to feel the nicotine flow through her veins and ease her fraught nerves. She leant against the red brick wall at the entrance of the hospital and raised her head towards the lightening skies.

'Oh, God, please,' she pleaded. 'If you're up there, please don't let him die.'

She felt a hand on her arm and turned abruptly, her face wreathed in confusion.

'Gertie,' she uttered. 'What are you doing here?'

The large woman looked at her blankly, her kindly eyes filling with tears. She clutched her handbag to her chest and took a deep breath.

'It's Dad, Josie. 'E's gone.'

Chapter Twenty-Six

'You'll get it down yer and do as yer told!'

Josie raised her eyes to Sophie pathetically. 'But I'm not hungry,' she said, pushing the bowl of home-made chicken soup away.'

Sophie shoved it back. 'I said, eat it.'

Josie reluctantly picked up her spoon and put it in the bowl. She knew it was pointless arguing with Sophie. Besides, she hadn't the strength. She stirred the soup round for several moments before she took a mouthful. It was good and, surprisingly, she began to feel hungry.

Sophie sat back in silence and watched whilst Josie ate. Poor girl, she thought sadly. The last few weeks had been a living hell; it was a wonder she was getting through it all. First there was that young man who, although Josie had never said as much, she was so obviously very fond of, being attacked so brutally. Although conscious now, he was still very ill. Then to have her employer die at the same time. And to top it all there had been no further word from Sue since her postcard and she knew Josie was worried about her friend's whereabouts. Sophie shook her head. It was a shame, it really was, for such a young woman to have so many burdens all at once.

The distraught girl had been dividing her time tirelessly. When she wasn't at the hospital, she was consoling Gertie. If she carried on like this she'd make herself ill. Sophie gazed at her with concern.

'Why don't yer go and 'ave a lie down? It'll do yer the world a' good,' she suggested.

Josie put her spoon into the empty bowl and sighed. 'I can't, Sophie. I promised I'd sit with Gertie for a while. Then it'll be time to go back to the hospital.'

Sophie blew out her cheeks. 'Gertie seems to be well and truly taken care of, if yer ask me. Don't know why yer bother,' she said sharply.

'Oh, it's not her fault. It's that weasel, Mr Snell. Poor Gertie doesn't even know what time a' day it is. She's in no frame of mind to see clearly regarding him. She's just so glad to have someone else take over all the arrangements. And to be fair, he did a good job.

The funeral was well organised and there was a good turn out.'

'You were doin' very well on that score 'til 'e poked his nose in. Nasty little man. I hope Gertie knows what she's doin', that's all I can say.'

Josie frowned. 'I don't think she does. Oh, Sophie, I've a terrible feeling . . .'

'Terrible feeling? What about?' she cut in.

Josie shook her head. 'Oh, nothing. It's just a feeling, that's all.'

'Well, you'll 'ave to finish now. You can't make statements like that and leave 'em in the air.'

Josie picked up a piece of bread and absent-mindedly began to pull it apart. 'I feel Mr Snell is musclin' in.'

'Musclin' in?'

'Yes. On Gertie's bereavement. He's using it to catch her offguard.'

'To do what?'

Josie shrugged her shoulders. 'I don't know. But I suppose I'll find out soon enough.' She stared down at the broken pieces of bread and the crumbs that had scattered over the table. 'Oh, I'm sorry, Sophie. Look what a mess I've made.'

'No matter,' she replied flatly. 'The birds will benefit.'

Josie rose. 'I must get cracking. I'll wash these dishes, then run and change. Gertie will wonder what's happened to me.'

'Leave the dishes. Just you get off.'

Sophie watched Josie depart and thoughtfully collected the dirty dishes.

Two hours later Josie approached the door at the side of the shop that led to Gertie's living accommodation. Before she had time to ring the bell, the door was thrust open and Mr Snell stormed out, knocking her on the shoulder as he pushed past and marched down the street. She recovered her balance and with raised eyebrows stared after him. Then she turned and rang the bell.

Gertie appeared, her face full of excitement, and ushered Josie through.

'What a' you ringing my doorbell for? You can come in any time, you know that, Josie love. Anyway, sit down by the fire. I've a pot of tea already mashed. I'll just fetch another cup.'

Josie sat down slowly and warmed her hands before the flames. She frowned. Gertie's obviously happy state did not reflect Mr Snell's and she wondered what was going on.

Gertie returned. She poured out the tea and pushed a plate of cake in Josie's direction.

Sitting down, she addressed her. 'Now, 'ow's that young man?'

'Getting better, thanks. I'm off to see him later . . .'

'Good,' Gertie cut in. She put down her cup and saucer on the small coffee table and clasped her hands together. 'Oh, Josie, I've got to tell yer. I can't keep it to meself any longer.'

Josie raised her eyes keenly and with bated breath waited.

'I'm gettin' married,' she blurted.

Josie gulped. This was the last thing she had expected. Her heart sank and she gasped for breath.

'Oh! Oh, er . . . Gertie, that's wonderful news,' she managed to splutter, forcing a smile to her face.

'It is, ain't it? Who'd a' thought a big lump like me would be gettin' married, eh? Oh, Josie, I'm so 'appy. 'E's such a lovely man. Kind and considerate. In't I a lucky woman?'

Josie looked blankly at her, unable to control her dismay. Gertie couldn't possibly be serious? She couldn't marry that man. She would have a life of hell with him. But how could she talk some sense into her friend without hurting her feelings?

With the cup rattling loudly in its saucer she placed it on the table and looked up. 'Gertie. Are you sure this is what you want?'

'Oh, yes, yes, Josie. I've never wanted anythin' so much in all me life.' She blinked back a tear. 'I miss me dad somethin' terrible and I need someone to care for, Josie.' Her face lit up. 'You never know, I might even be blessed with some kids. It ain't too late, yer know.'

Josie groaned inwardly. This was getting worse. Gertie had fallen badly for this man and was being blinded to his real nature by love. She had to stop it. She couldn't sit back and see her friend condemn herself for life like this. She felt so strongly that Gertie was making a terrible mistake. It was because she was bereaved, it had to be. Gertie was normally such a sensible woman, so how come she had been taken in so easily by this tyrant of a man?

'Gertie,' she blurted, 'I can't let you do this.'

She raised her eyebrows in surprise. 'Eh! Why not? I thought you'd be 'appy for me. What's wrong?'

'You don't know this man, Gertie. He treated his wife terribly and nobody likes him. Can't you wait a while and get to know him better before you take the plunge? It's a hell of a big decision you're making.'

Gertie's mouth set firmly. 'I know it is, Josie. I wouldn't 'ave agreed if I wasn't sure. But there's summat you've got wrong. 'E's never been married and 'e's got lots of friends. I should know, I've met some of 'em.'

'He has been married. His wife died last year.'

'No 'e ain't,' Gertie said with conviction. She paused and eyed Josie questioningly. ''Ow come you think you know so much about Mr Timmins? I 'adn't realised you knew 'im?'

'Mr Timmins?'

'Yes. Me fiancé.'

Josie's mouth dropped open and she fell back in the chair in relief. 'Oh, Gertie. I thought you were talking about Mr Snell.'

Gertie threw back her head and guffawed. ''Im! You must be joking. That man's a 'orror. I wouldn't marry 'im if me life depended on it.'

Josie sank against the back of the chair in relief. She started to laugh. She laughed so much the tears rolled down her cheeks. Gertie just stared at her. When she managed to control herself, she wiped her eyes with her handkerchief and blew her nose.

'What's he like then? Come on, Gertie, I want to hear all about him.'

She beamed in pleasure. 'I've known him for years, on and off. 'Is mother always used to buy her greens from us.'

'Oh, Mrs Timmins, that nice old lady that came on a Friday morning?'

'That's 'er.'

'Well. I'll be blowed. She always talked very highly of her son. He's a clerk, isn't he?'

'That's right. At Goodwin and Barsby's, the engineering people. Quite a good job 'e's got. You'll remember the old lady passed on a while ago?' Josie nodded. ''E's been livin' on 'is own since then. I used to see 'im quite often in Sainsbury's, that new supermarket in Lee Circle, and we'd always stop for a chat.'

'You never said?'

'I never thought to. Anyway, Mr Timmins made a point of droppin' round when me dad died to pay 'is respects, and well . . . things went on from there.'

'Gertie!' Josie exclaimed. 'You dark horse. Fancy you not telling me.'

Gertie grinned. 'I suppose I didn't want to tempt fate.'

'So when am I going to meet this wonderful man?'

She looked up at the clock. 'Any minute now.'

Josie smiled. 'I'm looking forward to it.' She gave a giggle. 'So that's why Mr Snell stormed out, knocking me flying? You told him, didn't you?'

'Yeah, and 'e wa' fumin'. Said I'd led 'im on. Lettin' 'im arrange all the funeral and so forth. But 'e insisted, and who was I to argue?' She bit her bottom lip. 'Oh, dear. 'E was so angry. Said 'e'd sue me for breach of promise. But I promised 'im n'ote, 'onest, Josie.' She grimaced. ''E were only after me shop and me as 'ousekeeper. Must 'ave thought I wa' stupid or summat. I soon cottoned on to 'is little game.'

'Serves him right. He can't sue you anyway. He would know

that. He's all wind and hot water. But I can tell you, I'm relieved. I nearly had a heart attack thinking you were about to marry him. Gertie, you didn't half give me a scare.'

'Not as much as 'e did me when I realised what 'e were after!' Gertie answered, laughing.

Just then the doorbell rang and she jumped up to answer it.

Several moments later she came back brandishing a bunch of flowers. She stood aside to allow her fiancé to enter.

'This is Mr Timmins, Josie. Brian, meet me good friend, Josie.'

She smiled warmly as a man of medium height walked towards her, his hand held out in greeting. His brown suit, although well worn, was immaculate, his shoes highly polished; he was clean-shaven with a shock of thick grey hair, and as he bent to grasp her hand Josie caught the smell of Old Spice aftershave. His hazel eyes twinkled merrily as he shook firmly.

'Hello, Josie. I'm very pleased to meet yer. Gertrude has told me so much about you.'

Josie felt a weight lift from her shoulders. She knew instantly that her friend was in good hands. Brian Timmins reminded her so much of Gertie's father, and the way he looked at Gertie left her in no doubt of his feelings towards the big woman. They would make a lovely couple. Oddly matched in appearance, but so suitable in every other way.

Later that afternoon she walked towards the hospital with a spring in her step as she planned what to wear for the wedding. She had promised to take Gertie shopping for her trousseau and was so looking forward to it. Her friend deserved some happiness and was receiving it in abundance. Even more exciting, Gertie had asked her to be her witness at the service, and Josie, overwhelmed, had willingly accepted.

Josie arrived at Stephen's bedside just as a chirpy young nurse was pulling back the curtains surrounding his bed. She straightened his covers.

'There you go. Nice and clean for your lady friend.' She patted his bed, smiled at Josie and pushed away the stainless steel trolley.

Josie sat down. 'You look better today,' she said softly.

He smiled up at her. 'Yeah, I am. Although I'm a bit tired. They had me sitting in the chair today while they changed my bed. I didn't realise what an ordeal it would be. It's fair took it out of me. The doctors are pleased with my progress, though. Say if I carry on like this, I'll soon be chasing the nurses down the ward.'

Josie smiled. 'Any idea yet when you'll be allowed home?'

'About a couple of weeks. Then I've to spend several more recuperating before, hopefully, it's back to work.'

'Back to work! Surely you should be thinking of taking a holiday or something first. With the takings we managed to salvage, you can afford it.'

'I'll be taking no holiday, Josie. I've had enough of lying around to last a lifetime. At the first opportunity I shall be taking the van out.'

'What?' she said, aghast. 'You surely can't mean that, not after . . . Look, what if you get done over again?'

'Josie, I'm not afraid. If I let them think they've scared me off, then they've won. And what about the next poor devil who wants to make an honest living? They'll do the same to him. Only next time they could go too far, and it could be murder.' He made himself more comfortable against the pillows, wincing sharply as a stab of pain shot through his side. 'Anyway,' he continued, 'according to Detective Inspector Mason, they caught the whole gang and they're awaiting trial.'

'Mmm.' Josie frowned deeply. 'But he wasn't convinced they had caught the man behind the gang. Mr Big, as he put it.'

'There's loads of Mr Bigs out there, Josie. Men who think threats and a good going over solve all their problems. Well, they're not going to get the better of me. As soon as I'm fit enough I'm taking the van out, and when the time's right – for me – then I'll stop and open my restaurant.'

Josie stared at him in admiration.

'Just don't mention this to my mother, Josie. She'd have a fit.'

'No, I wouldn't dare,' she agreed.

'So what's been happening in the great outdoors?' he asked keenly.

Josie proceeded to update him and also told him of Gertie's good news.

He gazed at her thoughtfully. 'So what will you do now?'

She shrugged her shoulders. 'Do now? What do you mean?'

'Well, it just crossed my mind, with Gertie getting married, you might not have a job for much longer.'

'What makes you say that? Do you think they'll get rid of me, then?'

'I don't know. But what if Gertie decides to sell up?'

Josie's mouth dropped open. 'To be honest, that thought never crossed my mind. But if she does decide to do that, then I suppose I'll just have to get another job.'

'Get another job?' Stephen exclaimed. 'Josephine Rawlings, is that the best you can come up with?'

She looked enquiringly at him.

'I would have thought this was the ideal opportunity to do something on your own. Haven't you ever had any ambition to start your own business? It's much better than working for someone else.'

Josie ran her eyes across his still heavily bandaged body. 'Yeah, I can see that,' she said sarcastically. 'And you get everything else that comes with it.'

'Don't be cynical. What's happened to me isn't typical, Josie, and you know it.' He eased himself up again. 'Look, all I'm saying is to give it some thought, just in case the worst happens. You have the brains and the know-how to go it alone. You just need the right opening.'

Josie pursed her lips. 'Well, there is one idea I have. Although I never took it that seriously.

'Oh. Let's hear it then?'

'Well,' she began, 'I met this woman once and she told me that she loved to read but couldn't afford to buy new paperbacks all the time.' She paused for a moment as she remembered Gilly and wondered how she was coping now that her husband had been arrested. She mentally shook herself. 'Well, it just got me to thinking, that's all.'

'Thinking what?' Stephen asked, his face wreathed in interest.

'What people do with all their books once they've read them? I know they keep some to read over again, but what about all the others? I suspect they get shoved in the cellar or under the stairs or just thrown away. I was wondering whether I could buy these books cheaply and then re-sell them.'

'What, like a second hand book shop, you mean?'

'Similar. But not specialising in expensive hardbacks and works of literature. It would be dealing with your ordinary novel, love stories, westerns, that kind of thing. I could buy them for a few coppers, re-sell at a few coppers more, and buy back again when the customer had read them. Provided they were still in good condition, that is. And there must be other things people use once or twice then push into a drawer. Knitting and dress making patterns, for instance.'

A broad smile spread over Stephen's face. 'I'm sure there's a need for something like that in Leicester. There's not a shop like it, not to my knowledge. My mother has piles of books. She for one would be a good customer.'

'So you think it's a good idea then?'

'I think it's brilliant. When are you going to get started?'

'Oh, I don't know. As I said, I'm only thinking about it at the moment.'

'Well, stop thinking and put your plan into action. You need to find some premises. A small empty shop in a good location.'

'Shop? I was thinking more of a market stall . . .'

'No, no, no,' Stephen cut in. 'You want a shop. Somewhere where people can browse around at their leisure.'

'Mmm. I see what you mean,' she said thoughtfully.

'So?'

'So, what?'

'When are you going to get started?'

'Oh, Stephen, stop badgering. Let's see what happens with Gertie first. I wouldn't leave her in the lurch, not while there's so much going on. But it's something to consider should anything change. Besides, you need money to do things like that.'

'I could help in that department. I've put some aside for the restaurant. You could have that.'

Josie smiled warmly. 'I'll keep that in mind, thank you.'

'Yeah, well, you make sure you do. And keep me informed. That idea of yours is a good one and I want to see you carry it through.'

She watched as his eyelids drooped then closed, and sat in silence whilst he dozed. Several nurses passed by and acknowledged her. She was becoming part of the furniture after all her visits. I wonder how much they read? she thought.

Moments later she felt a presence at her side and turned to find the girl she had seen Stephen with on the night of his attack. The girl smiled fondly at him.

'He's asleep, poor love,' she said with a catch in her voice. She walked round and placed a brown paper bag of fruit, some magazines and a bottle of orange squash on his locker.

'You must be Josie?' she said.

'Yes, I am.'

'Stephen's told me a lot about you,' she whispered so as not to wake him. 'In fact, I used to get quite annoyed until he finally convinced me that you were just a lifelong friend. He also told me you were getting married. Is that right?'

Josie smiled weakly, not knowing what to say.

The girl took the smile to mean yes and looked relieved. 'I was being silly, I see I was. But you know how it is when you're really fond of someone?' She smiled down at Stephen again, love radiating from her eyes. 'I expect he's told you a lot about me?'

Josie swallowed hard. Stephen had never mentioned her. She managed another weak smile.

'I hope it was all nice things,' she said happily. 'I'm Sally.' She held out her hand. Josie accepted it. 'Look, d'you fancy a cuppa? Only I'm parched. It's a good trek to the hospital from where I live. We could pop down to the canteen and leave him in peace for a while.' She laughed. 'You can tell me what he got up to when he was a small boy.'

'Yes, okay,' Josie said flatly.

She sat facing Sally across a beige formica table, nursing a cup of tea, an unappetising slice of apple pie topped with synthetic cream in a dish to the side of her. She looked at the girl through her lashes as she tucked hungrily into a ham sandwich. She seemed very nice. Not only was she attractive but she also had a friendly personality. In fact she was just the right type of person for Stephen.

Josie's heart sank. She should have been prepared for this. It was only a matter of time before she met the girl with whom he would share his life. She should be happy for him. But she wasn't. She was racked with jealousy. What had happened to her resolve? She knew the answer. It had flown right out of the window, and she felt powerless to stop the urge to lunge at this girl and tell her she had no right to him, that she was an intruder and should leave him alone. But she couldn't do that. It was Josie who had no right to him, not this girl.

She wanted to get away. To walk around in the fresh air and do some thinking. She made a big show of looking at her watch, which had actually stopped because she had forgotten to wind it.

'Oh, goodness,' she said, sounding aghast. 'Is that the time? I really must be going.'

'Oh, do you have to?'

'I'm afraid so. Things to do, you know. I'll look forward to seeing you again,' she lied.

'Me too,' Sally replied.

Josie arrived home several hours later feeling no better. She had given herself a long talking to but try as she might her feelings remained unchanged. She loved Stephen as she had always loved him and the passing of time had made not the slightest difference. She knew that she would have to learn to live with these feelings unless she was to do something drastic, like move completely out of the area. But how could she? Her roots were in Leicester and so were her friends.

She let herself in through the front door of the house and was met by Sophie who had obviously been listening out for her. She followed the old lady through into her living room.

'How goes it, gel?' her landlady asked.

'Fine. Stephen's on the mend. He's looking heaps better.' She put her back to the fire and lowered her gaze. 'I met his girlfriend today.'

'And?'

Josie raised her head. 'She seems very nice.'

'Very nice? Is that all you can say? Why don't you tell the truth, Josie? Why don't you say you hate her and you want Stephen for yourself?'

'Sophie!'

'Don't Sophie me. I might be old, Josie, but I've still eyes in me 'ead. Does this lad know 'ow you feel? 'Ave you ever told 'im?'

''Course not. What d'yer want me to do, Sophie? Make a right fool of myself? Don't yer think I've done enough of that already?'

Sophie pursed her lips. 'Better to make a fool of yerself than let love pass yer by. 'E's obviously very fond of yer, gel . . .'

'Yes, as a friend,' Josie interrupted. 'That's all. Besides, he's got a girlfriend and it seems to be very serious from what I can gather from her. Now if you don't mind, I'm gonna have a bath and go to bed. I'm knackered.' Josie stopped her flow and raised her eyes to the ceiling. 'What was that noise just then?' Her eyes opened wide. 'Someone's in my flat!'

'Why don't you go and find out?' Sophie said cagily.

Josie missed the smile on her face as she raced from the door and headed up the stairs.

She entered the flat and frowned. The passage was strewn with clothes and toiletries and someone was singing loudly in the kitchen. Josie held her breath then gasped in delight.

'Sue!' she yelled at the top of her voice.

She appeared at the kitchen door, a mug of coffee in her hand. She looked tanned and fit but very tired. She grinned broadly as Josie bounded towards her and hugged her tightly, nearly sending the coffee flying.

'Oh, Sue, Sue! It's wonderful to see yer. When did you get back?'

'About an hour ago. Fine welcome, I must say. No one in and hardly any food in the larder. I'm starving.'

'How was I to know? I only had one scribbled postcard from you, and that didn't say very much.'

Sue grinned mischievously. 'I was busy. Still, I'm back now and I want to know what's been happening?'

'Well, you get the gas fire on and I'll make us some toast. There's some bread around here somewhere. We can go down the chippy later. I've lots to tell you and I've no doubt you have me. But first . . .' She stopped and rummaged around in her handbag, pulling out the postcard that had arrived several weeks before. 'What does this say?' she demanded, thrusting the card under Sue's nose.

'What does what say?'

'These French words. They're rude, I know they are. But I don't care, I want to know.'

'Oh,' Sue laughed. 'They say – "This is a French Onion Seller".'

'What! Is that all? I don't believe it.' Josie burst into laughter and embraced her friend warmly. 'Oh, I've missed you. You don't know how much.'

'Me too. It's good to be home.'

213

'Come on, let's get the fire on and this toast made and then we can get down to business.'

Sue stretched her feet out across the hearth, lounged back and rested her glass of cider on her stomach. She frowned deeply. 'Well, you've certainly been through the wars since I've been away, Josie Rawlings. But I'll tell you this,' she spoke seriously, 'just thank your lucky stars I wasn't around when that Terry showed his true colours. I'd have killed the bastard for what he did to you. I hope he gets life when they sentence him.' She raised worried eyes. 'Will you have to go to court?'

'Don't know yet. I'm just hoping our statements are enough. I honestly don't think I can face him across a courtroom.'

'I could. No problem.'

Josie shuddered. 'But you're not me. If I have to go to court, I'll be a quivering wreck.'

'Don't you want to see him get his just deserts?'

'Yes. 'Course I do.'

'Well, then, when the time comes, you'll have to face him. But don't worry, I'll be with you.' She smiled. 'And so will Stephen.'

Josie puffed out her chest at the mention of Stephen. 'Well,' she started off-handedly, 'the way the system works it could be ages yet before we know. So in the meantime, I'm not thinking about it.'

Sue took a sip of her drink. 'Will Stephen have any permanent damage?'

'The doctors don't think so. They reckon with lots of rest and care he should be back to normal pretty soon. And he's got plenty of people taking care of him.' She lowered her voice. 'Especially his girlfriend.'

Sue raised her eyebrows. 'Do I detect a hint of jealousy?'

'No,' Josie denied sharply.

'Mmm.' Sue didn't believe her but from the tone of her voice decided it was best to change the subject. 'I must say this book-shop lark sounds a good idea.'

'D'yer think so?'

'I certainly do.' She looked at Josie keenly. 'I'll give you a hand if you like?'

'What! You?'

'Yes, why not? I've got nothing else to do at the moment. It'll keep me off the streets.' She sat up and rested the glass on her knee. 'But I'm not going round door to door asking people if they want to sell their books. I draw the line at that.'

Josie smiled. 'I wouldn't dream of asking you. And if I ever do anything about it, I'll keep you in mind as my first assistant.'

'First assistant?' Sue tutted loudly. 'Surely I'd be manageress at least?'

214

Josie laughed, finished her drink and re-filled both their glasses. 'You're as bad as Stephen. It's only an idea at the moment. To hear you both talk, you'd think I'd already got the shop and all the stock in it. An idea like this needs planning, and more importantly money, to start it up with. And as the latter is out of the question, I think we should drop it for the time being, unless I win the pools or summat. Anyway, at the moment I'm too busy helping Gertie with her wedding plans to think of anything else.' She breathed deeply. 'Enough of me. I want to know what kept you in France so long. It was a bloke, wasn't it?'

Sue grinned. 'How did you guess?' She breathed deeply and stared dreamily into space. 'He was fabulous. His name was Bruce and I fell in love.'

'Love, eh?' Josie sat up in interest. 'So. What happened?'

'He went back to Australia.' Sue looked unconcerned. 'It was only a holiday romance, Josie. We both knew that. He's studying to be a doctor . . .'

'Doctor, oh. And I suppose you let him practise on you?' Josie said, laughing.

'Might have,' Sue replied, grinning wickedly. 'The rest of the crowd had to come back, but I stayed on with Bruce and we had the most wonderful time. He's promised to write but I won't hold my breath.' She rose and stretched herself, yawning loudly. 'I need an early night. Haven't had much sleep just lately. And I must go and see the folks tomorrow. Let them know the prodigal daughter has returned. With a bit of luck, Dad will give me some money until I'm earning.' She smiled and gazed across the room. 'I must admit, they were great about my exams. Far better than I dared hope.'

'They love you, that's why.'

'Yeah, I think you're right. And it's about time I did something to repay them.'

Josie raised her eyebrows in surprise. 'My, you have grown up.'

'We all have to at some stage, Josie. I just wish, though, I knew what it was I wanted to do.'

'Oh, go to bed, Sue. I'm not in the mood for any of your psychological talk tonight.'

'Suit yourself. Is there any hot water?'

'Should be.'

'Good, I'm going in the bath. It'll be the first decent one I've had for ages. If I'm not out in half an hour, give me a shout because I'll have fallen asleep.'

Josie sat back and listened to the sound of water filling the bath, Sue humming 'Waltzing Matilda' softly as she prepared herself for her much needed soak. She smiled. It was so good to have her back. The loneliness she had experienced over the last few weeks lifted. Her best friend was home.

She bent down and idly picked up one of the magazines Sue had purchased at the port in Dover, something to read on the coach home. It was ages since Josie had had time to read a magazine and she sat back hoping there were a few interesting articles and a good story inside. She curled her legs under her and flicked through the pages. She stopped as something caught her attention.

A model draped in a well-known fashion designer's latest creation gazed out at her. She stared agog for several moments. The model was her cousin Marilyn. She had changed. She was thinner, her hair had been cut short in a Mary Quant style and she was heavily made up, but it was Marilyn all right, and the other model with her was Viv Neves. The article accompanying the pictures was very complimentary to them both, but acclaimed Marilyn as the latest 'find'.

Josie studied the page for several moments and a warm feeling rushed through her. She felt proud. Proud that her cousin had achieved her aims, despite the deceit that had helped to get her there. And to be posing alongside someone as well known as Viv Neves and for a fashion designer such as this, meant she had made it against all the odds. There were hundreds of girls willing to murder to be in such a position. Even with her limited knowledge of the fashion world, Josie knew that.

Well, good luck to her, she thought sincerely. At least one member of the family has managed to achieve something. It was then that she wondered if she herself ever would. Without dwelling any further on that thought, she jumped up. She wanted to show the magazine to Sue. She had a top fashion model for a cousin. Now that was something to brag about.

Several short weeks later a small congregation stood before the vicar in St Margaret's Church and listened intently as Gertrude and Brian took their vows. Josie, dressed in a delicate pink mini dress and matching accessories, shivered violently. The centuries old church was freezing cold and she wished she had had the vicar's sense as she spied a thick pair of long johns poking out beneath his cassock and white surplice.

The service completed and the register signed, Gertie and Brian made their way back down the aisle. Gertie looked radiant. Over the last few weeks the woman had blossomed. She was in love, that love was returned, and the transformation was a pleasure to behold.

Later at the small reception in The Fish and Quart public house on Churchgate, Brian sought Josie out.

'Thanks for all your help, Josie. Me and Gertrude wouldn't have managed without you.'

She smiled warmly. 'It was my pleasure. It's great to see her looking so happy.'

'And she'll stay that way, Josie. She deserves looking after and I'm going to make sure she is.' He took her arm and guided her towards a vacant chair. 'I'm taking her to Mablethorpe for our honeymoon. She doesn't know yet, it's a surprise. It's a really nice hotel on the front, and full board.'

'Oh, Brian, that's a wonderful idea.'

'Yes. But I don't know how she'll cope with being pampered. I can just see her volunteering to help out in the kitchens.'

They both laughed at the thought and then Josie watched with concern as his face grew serious.

'Josie, I've persuaded her to sell the shop and move into my house. She needs time to herself. Time to do whatever it is you women do. She can't do that if she keeps on the shop. I can support both of us and she can do whatever she likes with any profit she makes from the sale. Mother left me a bit and I've saved from my wages over the years. We'll be well provided for.' He took her hand. 'Of course that'll mean . . . I'm sorry, Josie.'

'That's all right, Brian,' she said quickly, giving his hand a fond squeeze. 'I'll get something else. I'm just so glad for you and Gertie. Anyway,' she said with a smile in her voice, 'I'm well overdue for a change of job.'

Just then Gertie joined them.

Brian looked up at his new wife. 'I've just explained the situation to Josie, my love.'

Gertie looked relieved.

'You're not too upset, are yer? Only I wa' dreadin' telling yer. You've put your heart and soul into that shop . . .'

'Gertie, that's enough,' Josie interrupted. 'You just get on with your new life and enjoy yourself.'

Brian patted her hand. 'You'll be welcome any time, Josie. There'll always be a warm welcome for you at our fireside. That right, my love?' he addressed Gertie.

'Josie knows that,' she replied. ''Ave you got that envelope, Brian?'

'Yes.' He searched inside his jacket and pulled out a brown envelope. 'Me and Gertie want you to have this as a token of our appreciation.'

'What is it?'

'Why don't you open it and see?' Gertie beamed.

Josie did as she was told, and gasped.

'A 'undred and fifty pounds, gel. You could buy yourself a car or summat and have a good holiday and still have some change left. Anyway, you do what you like with it,' Gertie said sincerely.

Wide-eyed, Josie stared at them both. 'I can't take this.'

'You can and you will!'

Brian rose. 'Now come on, there's plenty of food, it's a shame to let it go to waste.'

Josie watched as they both departed towards their other guests. She stared down at the envelope and fought back a sob. How kind some people were. This gift was a fortune to her. She slowly lifted her eyes. She knew what she was going to do with her windfall. She was going to use it to bring her book shop to reality. Enthusiasm surged through her. Now that Gertie was well and truly settled and she herself had the necessary funding, there was nothing to stop her.

Fate certainly had a funny way of working things out. Certain events had to happen in life to steer your direction, some of them terrible. A chance encounter, an idle remark, all were relevant. Josie knew without a doubt that she was meant to have this shop. Everything that had happened was just a stepping-stone towards achieving her goal.

She smiled as she rose. She had a lot of work ahead but first she might as well relax and join in with the rest of the celebration. It could be months before she had time to enjoy herself again.

Despite that daunting thought, she couldn't wait to get started on her new venture.

Chapter Twenty-Seven

Sue trailed her hand across a shelf and eyed with distaste the thick layer of dust on her fingers. 'This place is filthy,' she grimaced.

Josie tutted loudly as she peered inside an empty cupboard. ''Course it is. It's been shut up for ages.' She closed the door and walked into the centre of the large room. 'But it's nothing that plenty of elbow grease wouldn't put right.' She placed her hands on her hips and eyed the shop thoroughly. 'Well, what d'you think?'

Sue sniffed loudly and looked around. 'It'll do, I suppose.'

'It'll do!' Josie exclaimed. 'I'll say it'll do. After all the dumps we've seen, this is a little palace in comparison. The rent's cheap and the location's not bad.'

'No, it's not,' Sue agreed. 'Plenty of people pass this way towards the bus station, and hopefully word will quickly spread.'

'Yeah, just what I was thinking. You know, this room doesn't need all that much work. Just a lick of paint to brighten it up. And I could put some shelving up against that wall, and I thought of getting a carpenter to make some trays.'

'Trays?'

'Yeah, like bread trays only much much bigger. I could stand the books in rows and people could flick through them at their leisure. 'Course, I'll have the books in different sections such as romances, novels, adventures, or books by the same writer all together. But I think the trays would be a good idea, don't you? Make it easier for the customers to select what they want.'

Sue raised her eyebrows in admiration. 'Yes, it would,' she agreed.

Josie turned around and surveyed the room once more. 'I think it's just what we need,' she said with enthusiasm. She clapped her hands together. 'Oh, I'm so excited. Fancy having my own business!' It was then she spotted the door at the back of the room. 'Oh, I wonder where that leads to?'

She walked over and pulled at the handle. 'It's locked,' she said, frowning.

Sue grinned, and joined her friend. She ran her hand over the lintel and held out a key. 'Didn't you learn anything in Wentworth Road?'

Josie snatched the key and placed it in the lock. With a lot of effort the key turned and after several tugs the door creaked open. She hesitantly peered round.

'Ugh! If you thought the front room was filthy, you should see in here.'

Sue shoved past her and walked into the smaller room and looked around.

'Looks like it was a store room to me. There's no window, so it couldn't have been used as an office or anything. And from the looks of the walls, I'd say there used to be lots of shelving in here at one time.'

'Mmm, you could be right. There's another door,' Josie said, pointing towards the back wall. 'It must lead outside. Look, there's a key in the lock.' She walked over to the door, cleared off several cobwebs and a thick layer of dust, and turned the key. Surprisingly it opened without much effort and she looked outside. 'Yeah, it leads into a small yard and there's a building at the bottom. Oh, that's what the entry is for at the side of the shop. It's for access around the back. I suppose whoever had it before had their deliveries made that way so as not to have to trail through the shop.' She pulled the door to and locked it. 'I shan't need this room. The other's big enough for my needs and I won't be keeping any stock as such. Everything we have will be out on view for sale.'

'Does the rent include the store room or can you tell the landlord you won't need it and pay less?' Sue asked.

Josie took the sheet of particulars out of her coat pocket and quickly scanned through them. 'The rent is for the whole of the ground floor,' she said, folding up the particulars and shoving them back into her pocket. 'Never mind. The room might come in handy for something later. We'll keep it locked in the meantime. No point in having to clean something we won't be using.'

'So, you've made your mind up then?'

Josie smiled. 'Yes, I think so. It's really just what I've been looking for and better than anything else we've viewed.'

As they walked back into the main part of the shop, Sue nudged Josie in the ribs. 'I've thought of a use for the store room.'

Josie turned to face her, expectantly. 'Oh?' she said with interest as she locked the door behind them and placed the key back over the lintel.

'We could hold our orgies . . .'

'Sue! I thought you were going to say something sensible.'

Sue laughed loudly and tried to open the main entrance door. She frowned. 'This door's stuck.'

Josie undid the door without any problem. 'It's just the snib on the Yale lock that's faulty. Nothing that can't be fixed.'

She pulled the door behind them and then secured both the Yale and the mortice locks. Josie linked her arm through Sue's and they crossed the road, turned and stared back at the premises.

Josie nodded. 'Yes, this will do nicely. Come on, let's get back to the agents double quick and sign the lease before someone else snaps it up.'

Several hours later they arrived back at the old Victorian house full of excitement, talking nineteen to the dozen about all the things they had to do before the shop could be opened. Josie wondered if the list would ever end. As they began to climb the stairs towards their flat, Sophie popped her head out of her door.

'Oh, 'bout time you two were 'ome. I wa' beginnin' to think you'd got lost. Come in 'ere,' she demanded. 'I've summat ter show yer.'

Josie and Sue looked at each other, turned and retraced their steps. They followed Sophie through to her living room.

The old woman stood back and let the girls pass. Josie stopped abruptly and stared in amazement at several large cardboard boxes filled to overflowing with books. She leapt forward, closely followed by Sue, and they both looked down.

'Where did you get all these?' Josie asked in awe.

'From me cronies down at the centre. They were all thrilled when I told 'em what you were up to, and as well as clearing out their own cupboards asked all their neighbours and relations too. I thought it'd give yer a start.'

'A start?' Josie shouted as she turned and hugged Sophie tightly. 'I could open up tomorrow with all this lot. Oh, Sophie, thank you. You angel.'

'My pleasure. There's a few knittin' patterns an' all. Some of 'em are fairly old but might serve a purpose and there's some other odds and ends. I don't know if they'll be any good, but I took 'em just in case.'

'Oh, Sophie, I don't know what to say.'

She grinned. 'The look on yer face sez it all, gel.'

'How much do I owe for this lot?' Josie asked.

'Nothin'. They all just wished you the best a' luck and asked about discounts if they came in to buy anythin'.' She giggled. 'Seems me years of telling 'em that we old 'uns should give you youngsters a break 'as paid off. 'Bout bloody time an' all.'

Josie giggled. 'Good job you weren't around in Emily Pankhurst's time. I can just see you chained to the railings. But I'll tell you what I'll do. Next time there's an outing, I'll put in a donation to help towards the cost.'

'No need to, but if you insist, that'd be a grand gesture, gel.'

221

Sophie folded her arms under her sagging bosom. 'Well, come on then, 'ow did you get on at the agents this time? For God's sake tell me you've found summat suitable at long last?'

A delighted Josie told the older woman her news.

'Oh, that's great, Josie love. I know the place yer on about. It used to be a sweetie shop when I were a youngster. Owned by a wida' called Fanny Small. She wa' as thin as a clothes prop and mean with it. We kids all knew she rigged her scales so they overweighed.'

'Didn't anyone say anything about it?' Sue asked, interested.

'No. We were all too scared of 'er, and so wa' the adults. She'd 'ave got the brush to us and sent us packin'. But her sweets were well worth it. Can't get home-made sweets like that these days – and 'er gob stoppers! Kept yer quiet for a week. It were a sad day when she died and the place changed hands. Can't remember what it wa' turned into after then. But I know it weren't a sweetie shop.' She stopped abruptly and burst into laughter. 'Oh, I'm sorry, me loves. I wa' fair gettin' carried away. I wa' a little girl again, praying me mam had a few coppers to spare for a treat. Which weren't very often, I can tell yer.' She rubbed her hands together. 'I'm so glad you've found a shop at last. Yer on yer way, gel, and there's no one more pleased than me. Tell yer what, I'll look out me polish and cloths, and first thing tomorrow we'll get down to some scrubbin'. By the time I've finished, that place'll look a treat. You see if it don't.'

It was three full weeks before the shop was ready; three tiring weeks filled with scrubbing, painting and polishing, carpenters hammering, tempers flaring, and books – so many books Josie thought she'd never have enough shelving and trays to hold them all.

She fretted and she worried. The shop would never be ready; she had not enough money to pay the tradesmen; she didn't want to go into business anyway, it was a silly idea. But somehow she got through it, somehow they all got through it and still remained friends.

Peter had not long returned from a visit home to Manchester. With the aid of several of his acquaintans, he set to and painted the drab outside in strong bright colours; several shades of blue, orange and green. One thing was for certain: it caught the eye and made people stop and stare. Josie hoped it was enough to entice them inside.

One damp, late-November morning in 1969 an excited Josie, not having slept a wink for several nights, opened the door of The Book Cave for business.

The first day no one ventured in, but Josie and Sue kept themselves busy re-arranging their stock, glancing nervously over at the door, visualising the hordes that would hopefully descend upon them soon. They were to be disappointed. They were greeted home that night by Sophie, given a plateful of delicious stew and dumplings, and told in no uncertain terms not to get down-hearted. Fortunes were not made overnight.

The next day two middle-aged ladies, arms laden down with carrier bags full of shopping, opened the door expecting to be served with a pot of tea and home-made cakes on red gingham table cloths by plump cheerful waitresses. Well, this was a new cafe, wasn't it? They had heard there was one opening round here somewhere. They eyed the girls then the books suspiciously and sidled out.

By the end of the week, Josie found it hard to keep smiling. She was fed up re-arranging the books, knew exactly how many stitches needed to be cast on to make a matinee jacket for a six-month-old baby, and had lost count of how many bricks it had taken to build the shops in view on the opposite side of the street.

'This was a bad idea, Sue,' she said, plonking herself down on the stool at the small table that held the till, receipt pads and a pink pot specially bought to hold pencils and pens. She sighed deeply and drained the thermos flask of the last of its coffee. 'Tell me I was a fool. What's someone like me doing trying to run a business? Well, I ask yer – it was a stupid idea, wasn't it?'

Sue put down the book she was reading and looked across at her friend. 'No, it wasn't stupid. It's a marvellous idea.' She rose and walked towards Josie, took the coffee cup out of her hand and drained the dregs. She banged down the empty thermos flask top. 'I'll make you a promise,' she said.

'Oh?'

'If we haven't had any customers by lunchtime, I'll personally stand in the street and drag them inside. Can't say fairer than that. And don't scowl. I can assure you, Josie Rawlings, I mean what I say.'

Josie opened her mouth but was stopped by the opening of the door. An elderly man hobbled through with the aid of a walking stick. He quickly glanced around, turned and shouted behind him: 'This is it, Wilfred.' He turned back and addressed Josie. 'Got any Agatha Christies, me duck?'

They sold eight books that day and bought nine, one minus its cover as Josie hadn't the heart to tell the old lady who brought it in that it was of no use to her. Slowly but surely The Book Cave began to thrive and was soon giving the local libraries and new book sellers some sleepless nights.

Running her own business suited Josie. It gave her a reason to rise in the morning and something to more than occupy her mind throughout the day. She had no time to dwell on any events from the past and at long last had managed to put Stephen, for the most part, out of her mind. She purposely avoided all contact with him and as he didn't know, as far as she was aware, the location of her shop or the exact address that she lived at now, there was little chance of their meeting.

Occasionally, as she lay in her bed after a tiring day, a vision of him would drift into her mind, but she could now smile at his memory and then tuck the vision away. The only thing she dreaded was his wedding announcement in the *Leicester Mercury*, so she now skipped the 'hatched, matched and despatched' columns, thus avoiding any further heartache.

Sue was still deciding her future and in the meantime had taken up permanent residence as assistant in The Book Cave. Luckily, with thriftiness on Josie's part, the small profits were just about supporting both of them and she felt no need to hurry her friend away. When Josie herself went out and about door-knocking in order to replenish dwindling stocks of books, Sue was left in charge. So Josie was happy, Sue was happy, and Sophie was definitely happy acting as their housekeeper, cooking them an evening meal and giving the flat a good weekly once over.

Christmas and the New Year came and went with both girls receiving lots of invitations. Josie, cajoled relentlessly by Sue, accepted dates from several very nice men, but woe betide them should they try to get close. Josie soon put them in their place. She was determined she would suffer no further heartache at the hands of a man. She was a free agent. Free to go out with whoever she chose. She was tied to no one and preferred it that way.

In early-January 1970, when the threat of snow and the icy winds had kept most people indoors, Peter paid one of his regular visits to the shop. It was just on closing time and Sue, fed up with fighting Josie for a place in front of the paraffin heater, had gone home ahead to have a bath before she went out for the night.

Peter sat down on the stool and stretched out his long legs as he warmed his hands in front of the heater.

Josie smiled down at him. He was such a nice man, always willing to lend a hand, and she liked the way he breezed in at any time for a chat or to catch up with events. He willingly helped with the shop's books, taking no payment for any of the time he spent on them. She liked Peter and hoped sincerely that he was happy. He did seem to be.

'So,' Josie said, pouring the last of the coffee from an enormous flask, 'how's things with you? Still liking your job at Chawner's?'

Peter accepted the coffee gratefully and took a sip. 'Ah, it's okay,

224

Josie. But it's about time I moved on. The firm's run by old men with old ideas.' He sighed. 'To be truthful, I think my colleagues have guessed about me being gay and they are making things very difficult for me. So you see, darling – I need something else.' He raised his eyes and looked at her for several seconds. 'That's why I'm here tonight.'

'Oh?' she said, frowning quizzically. She pulled the other stool from under the table and sat down opposite him.

He gazed around the shop. 'You've done well, Josie. You should be proud of yourself.'

'I am,' she replied. 'Though I doubt I'll ever make a fortune. There's not much money in buying and selling second hand books, but it keeps me and Sue off the streets.' She looked hard at him. 'Come on, Peter. Out with it. What's on your mind?'

'Am I that transparent?'

'To me, yes.'

He grinned. 'I'm thinking of following in your footsteps and going into business for myself. I wondered if you would rent me your room at the back, just while I get established?'

Josie clapped her hands together. 'Peter, that's the best idea you've ever come up with. 'Course you can have the room. It's only gathering more dust. And I won't take any rent, not 'til you get on your feet at least.'

'I must pay you rent, Josie. It wouldn't be fair.'

'Shut up,' she said sharply. 'Someone said to me once it's rude to reject a gift. You'll need all the coppers you can get whilst you drum up trade. I take it your business will be in the accounting line?'

'Er . . . yes,' Peter replied hurriedly.

'That's a relief. You'll still continue to do my books then? That'll be in exchange for the rent. Deal?'

Peter beamed. 'Deal.'

They shook hands on it.

'You do know there's not even a window in that room? It's pretty basic. A' you sure about this?'

'It'll do for what I need. And I wouldn't even need to disturb you. I can use the entry and the back door.'

'Yeah, you could. But it's no bother to me if you want to come through this way.'

'No. Best if we keep it separate.'

'Oh. Okay then. Move in any time you like. But you'll need to give it a bloody good clean. Maybe Sophie will give us a hand? I know Sue won't.' Josie laughed. 'D'you remember when we were doing this place up? All she did was the supervising.'

'Yeah, I do. She's good at that, is our Sue. Well, I'd better be off and let you get closed up. Don't suppose you'll see any more customers tonight. The town's pretty deserted.'

'It's been quiet all day. We'll be busy tomorrow, whatever the weather, with people coming for their weekend supply. Bit like the greengrocery trade.'

'Do you ever miss that, Josie?'

'Sometimes. I was raised in it, remember. That reminds me, I must pay a visit to Gertie. It's long overdue.'

'How is the old bird?'

'Less of the "old bird". She's only in her late-thirties.'

'To us that's old,' Peter laughed.

'Yeah, it is. Ancient,' she agreed. 'Gertie's fine, though. I've never seen such a happy couple. To see 'em together you'd think they'd been married for years. Gertie's loving every minute of it. She's joined the Women's Voluntary Service and she helps out with Meals-on-Wheels and is on about taking up ballroom dancing.'

'Ballroom dancing?' Peter scoffed. 'She's a bit hefty for that, darling, surely?'

'That was unkind, Peter.'

'Sorry.'

'I'll give her your regards when I next visit, shall I?'

'Yeah, do that.'

Josie looked at him for a moment. 'On the subject of couples, how's your romance progressing?'

Peter inhaled sharply. 'Oh, I wouldn't exactly call it a romance. I wish I could. We're still just very good friends at the moment.'

Josie grimaced. 'Seems to me you've been very good friends for a very long time. Wouldn't you be better off dropping him and finding someone else?'

'Oh, no, Josie. This man's special – very special. I'll wait. I've all the time in the world.' He rose, leaned over and kissed her lightly on the cheek. 'Now I really must be going, and Josie – thanks.'

She pushed him playfully on the shoulder. 'No need for thanks. Just you make a success of it.'

Peter laughed, kissed her on the cheek again and made his way to the door. He tried to open it without success. 'Let me out, Josie. This damned door's stuck.'

Josie rose and quickly joined him. 'You must have dropped the catch when you came in. I always leave it up 'cos it sticks.' She opened the door and allowed him to pass by. 'I must get it fixed as I'm the only one who seems able to manhandle it. Anyway, see you soon, Peter.'

'Yeah. Tarra, sweetie.'

She quickly tidied up, switched everything off and put on her thick coat and boots, wrapping a large knitted scarf several times around her neck. The thought of braving the cold was not a welcome one but she would be glad to get home to one of Sophie's dinners and the fire. She hoped it was not tripe and onions. She hated tripe, the thought of it made her feel sick, but she hadn't the heart to tell the old woman.

She locked the door, put the keys into her handbag and turned into the wind. A horn sounded and she jumped. The noise had come from her old Commer van, she'd know that sound anywhere.

'Josie! Josie!'

She slowly turned her head and looked towards the kerb. There sat the dark blue vehicle, Stephen's head poking out of the window. He beckoned her over.

She stood and looked at him. He did not seem very happy.

'Get in,' he demanded.

'Pardon?'

'Don't "pardon" me, Josie. I said, get in.'

'I can't. I'll miss my bus.'

He leaned over and opened the passenger door. 'I said, get in.'

Josie walked round the other side of the van and climbed aboard.

He stared at her, annoyed. 'What are you playing at?'

'Sorry?'

'Josie, I thought we were friends?'

She gulped. 'We are.'

'Oh. That's not what it looks like from where I'm sitting.'

'Sorry, I don't follow you?'

'Don't you?' Stephen said dryly. 'Why did you stop visiting me in the hospital? The last time we met you promised to keep me informed of your progress with the shop. Then all of a sudden, nothing. You had me worried, Josie. I thought something had happened to you. I had a hell of a job tracing you.'

She stared at him. 'I . . . I didn't think you'd be all that concerned.'

'Why? Why did you think that? We've known each other since we were nippers. I care very much what happens to you.'

'Do you?'

'Of course I do,' he said, hurt. 'When you vanished without a word, I began to think all sorts. I couldn't work out what I'd done to upset you. It was only one of Mam's regulars from the market happening to mention how well you were doing, and Mam telling me, that brought me here.' He scowled at her and wagged his finger. 'Josie, don't you ever do that again, do you hear?'

She stared at him. 'Sorry,' she whispered.

His scowl softened. 'Why didn't you tell me you weren't engaged any more and that the man who attacked you in the 'dog van was your ex-fiancé?'

She gasped. 'How did you know that?'

'Never you mind. Why didn't you trust me enough to tell me?'

She lowered her head, a red flush of embarrassment covering her neck and face. 'I couldn't, I felt so stupid,' she said slowly. 'I suppose you know he was married as well?'

'Yes. But I don't know why you're feeling stupid. It wasn't your fault.'

'Wasn't it? That's not how it felt to me.'

He shifted in his seat to face her. 'We all make mistakes, Josie.'

She nodded in agreement. She wanted to change the subject and a picture of Marilyn came to mind. Should she tell him of her cousin's good fortune? Maybe he already knew because she was posing in practically every magazine Josie picked up these days. She felt the urge to ask after his girlfriend, but fought it. She really didn't want to know.

'Can you take me home, please?' she asked instead.

Stephen opened his mouth to speak, then thought better of it and turned and started the engine.

Josie told him her address and they drove in silence. Stephen stopped the van in front of the house.

'Thanks,' she ventured.

'Don't I get asked in for a coffee?'

'Some other time. I'm tired, Stephen.'

'Okay,' he said flatly. 'But I'll be down to the shop to get some books.'

She managed a smile as she alighted from the van. 'And you'll be welcome.' She took a breath. 'Look, I'm sorry. I thought you'd enough on your plate without me hanging around.'

He frowned. 'Never, Josie.' He started the engine. 'See you soon.'

'Yeah,' she said, closing the sliding door.

She stood and watched as he drove away, her thoughts muddled. She hoped desperately his reappearance would not rewaken feelings she had struggled hard to bury. It was then she realised she had not once asked after his health or how his business was faring.

She turned and slowly walked towards the house.

Chapter Twenty-Eight

'That'll be fifteen pence, please,' Josie asked the old lady as she handed over several books wrapped in a brown paper bag. 'And I hope you enjoy them. Don't forget to bring them back when you've finished.'

The old lady smiled. 'I won't, me duck, ta.' She fumbled in her purse. 'Fifteen pence! 'Ow much is that in real money? I can't get the 'ang of this foreign money lark. Don't know why they couldn't leave well alone.'

Josie quickly did the calculation, her thoughts mirroring the old lady's. Decimalisation had caused so many problems to young and old alike. 'Er . . . Three shillings.' She looked at the handful of change the old lady was holding out and selected three five-pence pieces. She held them up. 'There, see. These three shillings make fifteen new pence.'

'Do they? Don't mek sense to me,' the customer said, frowning hard. 'S'pose I'll get it eventually. But I'm sure it's just an excuse to put everythin' up. It's us poor pensioners that suffer. Daylight robbery, if yer ask me.'

Josie watched as the old lady left the shop, then turned and summoned Sue over.

'Is Peter in this morning?'

Sue shook her head. 'Don't know. There's never any noise coming from in there at the best of times. What is he up to?'

'Well, he says he's running his own accountancy firm, but there's never anybody visiting. Mind you, not that we'd know that. He always uses the back entrance. The telephone rings often enough, though. But I can't see how he can do all his business over the telephone. Can you?'

'Not really. But then, I don't know how accountants operate. Why don't you get a telephone installed in here?'

'What for? So you can spend all day chatting to your boyfriends?' Josie laughed. 'We don't need a telephone. You use the one in Sophie's flat enough.'

'I pay my share.'

Josie blew out her cheeks. 'You mean, we both pay your share?'

229

Sue grinned mischievously. She paused thoughtfully for a moment and then raised her eyebrows. 'Why don't we take a look in Peter's office one night when he's gone home? We can see what he's up to. The key for the door is still over the lintel.'

'No,' Josie said sharply. 'That'd be invading his privacy. I wouldn't be able to look him in the face again if we snooped.'

Sue shrugged her shoulders. 'I suppose not. It was just a thought.'

Josie turned to serve a customer.

'Stephen's asked if I fancy taking a pile of books to a Sunday market. He's taking the 'dog van too. He reckons the books would go well,' she said as the customer moved away.

'As long as you don't ask me. I'm not working on a Sunday.'

'Did I mention you?'

'No.'

'Well, then.'

'Are you going to?'

'Don't know. Sounds worth a try though. But . . .'

'But what?' Sue folded her arms under her shapely bosom. 'Oh, you don't need to answer. I know. It's Stephen, isn't it? It would mean spending time with him and that thought frightens you, doesn't it, Josie Rawlings?'

Josie turned away. 'No, it doesn't. But like you, I need a rest on a Sunday. It's the only full day we're shut.'

'If you think I believe that, then you're mistaken.'

'I don't care what you think . . .'

'See, I was right,' Sue cut in. 'You're losing your temper. Just because the subject's Stephen. When will you open your eyes?'

'What d'you mean?'

'Josie, I'm not blind to your feelings. And if you think that bloke hangs around because he's just a friend, then you're a fool. I've known enough men in my life to know when one's got the hots . . .'

'Got the hots?' Josie repeated angrily. 'Shut up, Sue. The man is a friend, that's all. And I'd thank you to keep your mucky thoughts to yourself.'

Sue shrugged her shoulders nonchalantly. 'Suit yourself.'

'I will. Now if you want to keep your job, go and help that man over there. He's looking for a couple of Alistair MacLeans.'

Sue shrugged and walked away. She stopped, turned back, bent down and pulled forth with a struggle a large box that was hidden under the table.

'I forgot about this,' she said, prising open the lid.

'What is it?' Josie asked.

'A set of saucepans.'

'What's it doing here?'

'My friend got it.' She lowered her voice. 'Off the back of a lorry. It's a good set of saucepans and he wondered if we could sell it and split the profits?'

'I bet he did. Sue, we could be had up for receiving stolen property. Get it out of here, quick.'

'Ah, Josie . . .'

They both froze as the door opened and a policeman walked through. He strode up to the counter, the look of officialdom stamped upon him.

Josie gulped as she and Sue pushed the box back under the table with their feet, hoping the policeman noticed nothing amiss.

'Can I help you?' Josie asked, her heart thumping madly.

'Yes, er . . . My wife wants to know if you have any Catherine Cookson books in.'

Josie breathed a sigh of relief. 'Yes, Inspector,' she said, raising the constable's rank several grades. 'I've one or two. I'll show you.'

As she guided the constable away towards the right tray, she glanced back and eyed Sue menacingly.

'Get rid of it,' she mouthed.

She turned and smiled sweetly at the policeman as she picked up several books. 'Has your wife read these?'

Later that day Peter appeared.

'Darling, can you spare a cup of coffee?' he asked, rubbing his hands together. 'Only my kettle's broken.'

'Yeah, sure,' Josie replied. 'I think there's some left. If not, as soon as Sue comes back I'll pop up to the cafe and ask for a refill.' She shook the flask. 'Yeah, there's enough for you.'

He accepted the cup. 'Thanks, Josie.' He looked around. 'Where is Sue?'

Josie shrugged her shoulders. 'I dunno. Gone on some mystery errand . . . Ah, here she is.' Josie grimaced as Sue kicked the door open and struggled through with a small heavy box. 'What have you got now?'

Sue grinned and placed the box on the table. 'Letterheads and business cards.'

'What! What do I need those for?'

Sue scowled fiercely. 'You want to look official when you do any correspondence, don't you?' She opened the box and allowed Josie to look inside. 'I think my pal's done a good job, don't you?' she said, pleased with herself.

Josie nodded as she looked at the top sheet of paper. The Book Cave was printed in heavy inks, the colours matching the outside paintwork of the shop.

'Yes, most impressive. How much?'

'To us, nothing. It was a favour. But if we want any more we'll have to pay.' She picked up one of the small business cards. 'You should hand these out at every opportunity and leave them lying around in telephone boxes and such like.' She turned to Peter. 'You should get some letterheads and business cards printed too. I could have a word with my friend for you. Might be able to get you a good deal.'

Peter cleared his throat. 'Er . . . not just now, thanks all the same. I'll wait until business is a bit better.'

Josie looked at him in concern. 'Isn't it going well then?'

'Yes,' he replied hurriedly. 'But not enough to splash out on things like this.' He drained his cup. 'I have to go. See you both soon.'

'Oh, Peter!' Josie shouted. He stopped and turned round. 'I've got a proper cleaner coming in once a week now. Do you want her to give your place a dust and sweep? She's reasonable.'

Peter's face reddened. 'No, thanks. I manage quite well, and with only me the place doesn't get that dirty.'

'Oh, all right. But if you change your mind, just let me know.'

'Will do. Tarra.'

'Tarra,' they both said.

Josie looked at Sue. 'I thought he'd jump at it. Men don't like cleaning, do they?'

Sue pursed her lips together. 'Not most men,' she whispered.

'Oh,' Josie replied knowingly.

She turned to face the door as Nelly Preston shuffled through, carrying a baking tray covered by a tea towel. She smiled at the girls.

'I thought yer might like one of these wi' yer afternoon tea.'

Josie accepted gratefully, wishing they had the tea to go with them.

Nelly Preston was a kindly old soul who resided above the shop. The flat she occupied was ancient and needed new windows, new doors, a bathroom and a modernised kitchen. In fact, it needed gutting and refurbishing completely. The landlord didn't think it worth spending money modernising a flat to house an elderly lady from whom he would not be able to recoup his outlay by any increase in rent. He would wait until the conditions either drove her away or she died. His money would be well spent then on attracting a more suitable tenant.

But Nelly couldn't move, she had neither the means nor the know-how. She had lived in that flat since she had married. Had raised her nine children in two small bedrooms, nursed her husband through years of illness until his death, and watched her selfish brood leave home never to return, not even for a visit. She was on her own. Her only pleasure was making up excuses to visit the two nice young girls who were renting out the shop premises beneath her. They welcomed her now as they always did and it made her feel needed, which was something she hadn't felt for years.

'Mmm,' Josie said, her mouth watering as Nelly removed the tea towel. 'Scones. My favourite.' She looked at Nelly fondly. 'Won't you join us? Sue was just going up to the cafe to fill the flask.'

'Was I?' she asked in dismay.

'You were, and hurry up about it.'

She handed Sue the flask and a few coppers and watched as she stormed out of the door.

'You are a card,' Nelly giggled. 'I could easily have made yer some tea.'

'Serves her right,' Josie chuckled back. 'She's been throwing her weight around here and I'm just teaching her a lesson. Showing her who's the boss.'

Josie picked up one of the scones and bit into it, quickly catching a sliver of hot butter as it dripped down her chin.

'These are wonderful, Nelly.'

When she didn't reply, Josie looked hard at her.

'What's the matter?' she asked.

Nelly hurriedly looked up, her faded grey eyes wide. 'What, wi' me? Oh, nothing, me duck. It's me bones. They're givin' me gip today.'

'It's more than that. Come on, tell me?'

Nelly ran a gnarled hand through her snow white hair. 'It's im, that whipper snapper of a landlord. I think 'e's doin' things to get me out.'

'Doing things? What sort of things?'

Josie paused as a customer came towards the desk and handed over several books and a couple of knitting patterns.

'Don't forget to look out for that book, Josie love,' the customer said as she accepted her purchases and handed over the exact money.

'I won't. Enjoy your read, Mrs Brown.'

The woman smiled. 'I will, me duck, ta.'

Josie turned her attention back to Nelly.

'Now, what sort of things?'

Nelly made to busy herself tidying up the table top. 'Oh, don't mind me. It's just an old lady's fancies.'

'But I do mind, Nelly. Now tell me what's going on?'

Nelly stopped what she was doing and raised watery eyes. 'Well, I keep getting threatening letters and late at night people banging on me door . . .'

'These letters. Have you kept them?'

233

Nelly shook her snow white head. 'I threw 'em away. Nasty things they were.'

'You should have kept 'em, Nelly. We could have taken them to the police.'

'Oh, we can't get them involved. Me life's 'ell enough already. They wouldn't believe me anyway. Reckon I wa' senile or summat.' Nelly sank down on to a stool. 'I'm so lonely, Josie. I 'ate that flat. It used to be me sanctuary. But not now. I dread shuttin' me door at night for fear of what might 'appen.'

Josie stared down at the old lady, who was drying her eyes on the bottom of her apron, and her heart cried out for her. She suddenly felt angry. Old people shouldn't be treated like this. It wasn't fair. The beginnings of a plan began to form, but she would have to tread very carefully in order to let others think they had come up with the idea, for it to work successfully.

She placed her arm around the old lady's shoulders. 'Don't upset yerself, Nelly. Don't let that landlord think he's got the better of you. He'll soon give up, you'll see.'

Nelly smiled up at her. 'I'll try, Josie love. 'Cos there ain't much else I can do. None of me family'd 'ave me.'

Later that night Josie sat at Sophie's table tucking into egg and chips with plenty of bread and butter.

'I'll have to watch it, Sophie.'

'Watch what?' she said, placing a mug of tea in front of her.

'My weight. If I don't watch out I'll start getting fat again,' she said, tipping the bottle of tomato sauce upside down and shaking some more on to her plate.

Sophie frowned. 'You young 'uns are all the same. If yer want my opinion it ain't 'ealthy to be skinny. No fat on yer bones to ward off illness. But then who'd listen to me? I'm just a ramblin' old fogey.'

Josie nearly choked on a chip. 'An old fogey! You? Never.' She placed several chips between a slice of bread and took a big bite. 'Oh, I love chip sarnies.' She eyed Sophie thoughtfully. 'Nelly popped down again today. Made some lovely scones,' she said casually.

'Did she? I like that Nelly. She's a good ol' soul. Did you bring me one home?'

'No, sorry. I will next time.' Josie finished her sandwich and pushed away her plate. 'That was lovely, Sophie, thanks.'

'More chips?'

'Oh, no ta. But I'll have another cuppa.'

Josie poured for them both and sat back.

'I feel sorry for Nelly,' she said.

'Sorry. Why?'

'Well, she lives all on her own . . .'

'So do I,' Sophie said sharply.

'No, you don't, you've got us. And you ain't got the landlord hounding you.'

Sophie eyed her quizzically. 'What d'yer mean? What's that landlord doing to 'er?'

Josie told Sophie Nelly's tale.

'That landlord wants 'is backside tannin',' Sophie hissed. 'Nelly don't deserve that.' She sat back and sipped thoughtfully on her tea. 'What time does Nelly usually pop down?'

'Around three. Why?'

'Nothing,' Sophie said secretively. 'I just wondered.'

Josie hid a smile. Everything was going according to plan.

The next day at three o'clock, Nelly bustled through with a plate of jam tarts, piping hot from the oven. Just as she had placed them on the table, Sophie opened the door. She walked up to the table and put down her shopping bag.

'Oh, I see I'm just in time,' she said, eyeing the jam tarts. She looked across at Josie. 'Get the tea then,' she ordered. 'Me and Nelly could do wi' a cup. That right, Nelly? And I don't want none of that stuff outta the flask. I'll 'ave a fresh one from the cafe.' She shook her head. 'I don't know why you don't get yourself one of those newfangled electric kettles. It'd save you all this bother.'

Josie raised her eyebrows but said nothing. She opened the till and took out some money. 'I won't be a tick.' She beckoned Sue over. 'Make yerself scarce and let them two have a chin wag. Sophie's taken the bait,' she whispered.

Sue winked in understanding and went to assist several customers over by the book shelves.

Sophie bit into a jam tart. 'These are good, Nelly. I can't mek pastry meself. Now I'm all right wi' everything else, but me pastry you could build 'ouses wi'.'

'Oh, it ain't that 'ard. I could show yer. You just 'ave to have a light hand and plenty of air, that's the trick.'

'I'll take you up on that,' Sophie said.

They both expressed their thanks when Josie presented them with the tea she had fetched. Sophie waited until the girl was out of earshot.

'Actually, Nelly. I'm glad I've bumped into you today. There's summat I want to ask yer.'

'Oh,' Nelly said keenly.

Sophie picked a raspberry jam pip out of her dentures and wiped several crumbs from her mouth. 'D'yer know anyone that's looking fer lodgings?'

'Lodgings?' Nelly frowned.

'Yeah. On a permanent basis. I've got several rooms lying empty and it's a shame really. So I thought I'd let one of them. I've been thinking about it for a while.' Sophie leant forward and lowered her voice. 'Between you and me, Nelly, I could do wi' the money. Not that I'd charge a lot, but the extra would come in 'andy.'

'I understand,' Nelly answered sincerely.

'Only don't tell the girls 'cos they'll worry.'

'Oh, no,' Nelly said, shaking her head.

'But I don't want just anybody.'

'Oh! What sorta person then?'

Sophie scratched her chin. 'Well, somebody that'd get on wi' me for a start, and the girls. I wouldn't want anyone upsetting them. They like to play their music and they can make a lot of noise.'

'I like music and I don't mind noise,' Nelly said slowly.

'Ah, someone like you then. Someone that needs a nice room and a bit of company, 'cos they'd be welcome to sit wi' me and listen to the radio or 'ave a natter.' She eyed Nelly keenly. 'If you know of anybody, can you let me know soon before I advertise?'

'Yes, I will.'

'Good. Right then, I must be off and get the dinner prepared. Giving 'em a nice dish of tripe and onions tonight. They'll like that.'

She rose and picked up her bags. 'See yer tonight, gels, and don't be late, supper's on the table at six-thirty sharp,' she shouted across. She turned back to Nelly. 'Thanks for the tarts, Nelly. I'll be hearing from yer.'

Nelly nodded thoughtfully.

'Ere'a, Josie,' Nelly beckoned her over excitedly. 'Sophie's just told me she's thinkin' of lettin' out one of 'er rooms.'

'Is she?' Josie said in surprise.

'Yeah. What d'yer think of me applyin'?'

Josie smiled warmly. 'I think that's a great idea. It'd be an answer to your prayers and she's got lovely rooms, you know.'

Nelly clasped her hands together. 'D'yer think she'd 'ave me, Josie? D'yer think I'm the kinda person she's looking for?'

'There's only one way to find out. And I'd hurry if I were you, in case someone else gets to hear and snaps it up.'

'I will, Josie. Ta, me duck. I'll get me coat and go and see her about it now.'

Josie giggled to herself as Nelly rushed out of the shop. She picked up a jam tart and bit into it.

Sue joined her. 'I take it your plan worked?'

'Like a dream.'

'What are you laughing at?' Sue asked.

'Old ladies. I'm plagued by 'em.'

236

Chapter Twenty-Nine

Josie, humming along to music on the transistor radio, tightened the buckle on the strap of her knee-length thonged sandals, straightened up and adjusted her flowing, floral-patterned gypsy dress. 'What d'yer think?' she asked, addressing Sue.

'Fine,' Sue answered casually, her nose in a letter that had just been delivered. She looked up, eyes wide. 'I don't believe it,' she gasped.

'Don't believe what?' Josie said absently, spitting into her block of mascara. She rubbed the brush backwards and forwards and applied a layer to her lashes.

'It's from Bruce. I've got a letter from him.'

Josie finished applying her mascara and then puckered her lips and covered them with a very pale pink lipstick. She pressed her lips together and turned around.

'Bruce? What, that Aussie chap?'

'Yes.'

'He took his time about it, didn't he? It's months since you came back from France.'

'Nine months to be precise.'

'Well, nine months then. What's he got to say for himself?'

'He's given up doctoring and gone to help out on his uncle's sheep farm.'

Josie laughed. 'That's after he examined your bits! It put him off.'

Sue shifted position uncomfortably. 'He wants me to go and join him.'

Josie stared blankly as the words sank in.

'Bit of a cheek that. You're not seriously considering it, are you?' she asked in concern as she sat down at the table.

Sue joined her. 'Might be. I've nothing to lose.'

'Nothing to lose! Sue, Australia is the other side of the world, and what about your parents, me, and the shop?'

Sue shrugged her shoulders. 'What about them?'

'What about them! Is that all you can say?'

Sue tutted loudly. 'Oh, Josie. Come down off your high horse. I only said I was considering it. But you must admit it sounds

237

exciting. It's not every day a girl gets an opportunity like this. I mean, think of it. Sun, sea and plenty of fun.'

'What, on a sheep farm?'

Sue looked at her in disgust. She rose and grabbed her handbag, stuffing the letter deep inside. 'You coming?' she growled. 'Don't want to keep the customers waiting, do we?' she added sarcastically.

Later that day, Josie caught Sue reading the letter again at the side of one of the bookshelves. She hurriedly tucked it inside the envelope when she realised her friend was peering over her shoulder, looked at Josie haughtily and went over to help a customer.

Josie returned to sorting out some books, her face expressionless. Sue was taking this offer seriously and it worried Josie.

For several days the matter was not mentioned between them and Josie began to relax. It was a hare-brained idea anyway. Who in their right mind would traipse halfway across the world on the strength of a holiday romance and one letter written nine months later? Sue had more sense than that.

Josie stretched out her legs in front of the fire and yawned loudly. She felt comfortable and relaxed after an appetising meal made by Sophie, and for once felt at peace with the world.

At this moment in time everything was running smoothly. The shop was making an ever-increasing profit and it was a nice feeling to have money in the bank. Stephen had mentioned to her the possibility of expansion, but she felt it was too soon, though several ideas were playing around in her mind.

She sighed as she thought of Stephen. True to his word he paid regular visits to the shop, often not staying long, just enough to have a cup of coffee and pass the time of day. Deep down Josie wished wholeheartedly that things could be different between them. But Stephen showed not one sign of encouragement; he treated her no differently than he did Sue. With a lot of soul searching, Josie learned to accept Stephen's visits for what they were: calls between friends.

Nelly had grabbed at Sophie's offer and was now installed in the large attic room above their flat. She was happy and content for the first time in years and it showed. She was up in the morning, her old bones no longer giving her gip, and she and Sophie were often seen around the town together or down at the centre, playing whist or helping to organise coach outings for the more handicapped members of the club. It warmed Josie to see the pair together. She was glad her idea had worked.

The landlord had not even waited until Nelly's last piece of furniture had been removed before an army of workmen had descended. The hammering and banging from above the shop was annoying, but they had been assured that it would soon end. Josie just wondered who the new tenant would be.

Sue broke into her thoughts as she came through the door, wrapped in a towel, her wet hair clinging to the sides of her attractive face. She sat down in the chair opposite and looked over at her friend.

'I'm going, Josie,' she said slowly.

'Yes. I thought about coming with you,' she replied sleepily, tucking her legs underneath her. 'But this chair and a good book have won, I'm afraid.' She eyed Sue closely. 'I hope you're not going out dressed like that?' she said, laughing. 'And when you come in, don't wake me up like you did last night. I couldn't get back to sleep.'

Sue breathed deeply. 'I don't mean out. I mean to Australia.'

Josie stared at her for several moments before she pulled herself upright. 'You're joking, aren't you?'

Sue shook her head. 'No, I'm deadly serious. I've nothing to lose.'

'But you have . . .'

'What?' Sue said flatly. She breathed deeply. 'Look, Josie, I failed my exams, this flat's rented, and I work for you in your shop. I own nothing. I've nothing to give up. But I've everything to gain. And if I don't like it, I can always come back.'

Josie blinked back tears as the full impact of her friends' words struck home.

'Australia's a land of opportunity, Josie. There's loads to do and see.'

'There's loads to do and see here, Sue,' she replied, trying to dissuade her from making, as far as Josie could see, a terrible mistake. 'England's got just as much to offer as Australia has, except I suppose the sun.' She paused. 'And what about this Bruce? You ain't mentioned him once.'

Sue clasped her hands together over her knees. 'I liked him, Josie. I liked him a lot. But I don't know whether we'll still feel the same about each other until we meet up again.'

'And you're willing to travel all that way to find out?'

'Yes. You've got to take a chance in this world. I don't want to grow old wondering if I made the wrong decision by staying here.' She paused for several seconds and eyed her friend keenly. 'Josie, why don't you come with me?'

She was astonished. 'What, me?' she spluttered. 'All the way to Australia?'

'Yes, why not? We could have a whale of a time.'

'But what about the shop, Sophie, and . . . and . . .'

'And what, Josie? You can start a shop anywhere, especially now you have the experience behind you. You'd easily sell the business now that it's doing reasonably well. Sophie's busy organising her new friend Nelly. And you've no family to worry over. So what's to stop you?'

Josie held her breath. There was nothing, nothing to stop her grabbing this chance of a new life. And Australia did sound exciting. She had seen travel posters showing the beautiful countryside, the miles and miles of beaches and the famous Barrier Reef. She had watched a documentary film whilst at school in a geography lesson and could remember then thinking what a wonderful place it looked. She had even felt envious when several of her school friends had emigrated to this land of opportunity with their families.

She exhaled slowly as the truth dawned. She didn't want to go. She loved what she was doing and her surroundings, and didn't want to go off to unknown territory, however much it beckoned. Leicester was where she belonged – had always belonged.

She slowly shook her head. 'Thanks for the offer, Sue, but . . .'

'But, no?' Sue finished for her.

Josie nodded.

'You're daft,' Sue said sharply. 'Fancy giving up a chance like this.'

Josie laughed. 'Yes, I must be. But think of Bruce. If I had agreed, he wouldn't just be confronted by one mad Englishwoman but two! Poor chap. I think you'll be enough for him to contend with at the start. Anyway, I can't see me sheep shearing, can you?'

Sue tittered at the vision of Josie chasing sheep around the Australian outback, a huge pair of shears held aloft. 'Me neither,' she guffawed. 'Especially not in platform shoes and mini skirt.'

Josie exhaled deeply and leant back in her chair. She knew Sue had not thought very deeply about what she was about to undertake. She had only visualised the glamour and excitement of it. She hadn't touched on the reality. She frowned. It was no good arguing or outlining any pitfalls to her friend. Sue had made up her mind and whatever Josie said wouldn't make any difference. She would have to find out the hard truth her own way.

She leaned forward, her face serious. 'I wish you all the best, Sue. But you must promise me one thing?'

'What's that?'

'That you'll come back if things don't work out. And if you haven't the air fare, you let me know and I'll get it for you somehow.'

Sue smiled fondly. 'I'm going to miss you. Only a friend as loyal

240

as you would say something like that and, more importantly, mean it.' She sighed softly. 'We've been through a lot together, haven't we, Josephine Rawlings?'

Josie nodded. 'We certainly have. And one thing's for sure – it won't be the same without you.'

Sue stood up and secured the end of the towel under her armpit. 'I was dreading telling you . . .'

'Why is it,' Josie interrupted, 'that people always dread telling me things?'

'Because we all love you so and don't like to see you hurt.'

'Is that why? Thanks, Sue, that was nicely put.' She looked up at her friend. 'Are you still going out?'

'I'm going to break the news to my parents.'

'Oh.'

'Yes – oh.' Sue laughed. 'Mother's not going to like this one bit.'

Josie sighed deeply as she left the room. Sue's announcement posed problems; she would have to find someone else to help in the shop and get another flat mate to help towards expenses. She shook her head. She was too upset at this moment to make plans. All she could think was how much she would miss Sue and the hole that would be left in her life.

Three days before her departure Sue charged through the door of the shop and flopped down heavily upon the stool next to the desk, looking up at Josie who was opening the post.

'Well, that's everything done,' she said, patting her handbag. 'I've got my passport, visa and my flight arranged. All I've got to do now is finish my packing.'

Josie slid her finger nail along the top of a long brown envelope and looked at Sue out of the corner of her eye. 'Isn't there something you've forgotten?'

Sue frowned quizzically. 'No, I don't think so.'

Josie put down the envelope and folded her arms. 'The party. I haven't once heard you mention one and it's not like you to miss an opportunity like this.'

'No, you're right there. That's why I've booked a room at The Fish and Quart for tomorrow evening. I've invited everyone. If I'd left it to you, I'd have been winging my way across the ocean without a by-your-leave.'

Josie giggled and picked up the envelope, extracting the contents.

'You will manage without me, won't you?' Sue asked tentatively.

Josie looked down at her. 'I'll have to, won't I? I've got Sophie and Nelly poised at the ready, and your mother has also offered if I'm really stuck, which I thought was nice of her.'

'Has she? I didn't know that.'

'Well, you wouldn't, been too busy making your own arrange-ments.' Her face softened. 'You'll be a hard act to follow, Sue, but I'll manage. I just hope things work out for you, I really do. If not, you'll be back in this shop and making my life hell again before I know it.'

She turned her attention to the sheet of paper she held in her hand, trying to push Sue's impending departure to the back of her mind. She frowned hard. 'What's this?' she asked.

'What's what?' said Sue, rising to join her and peering over her shoulder.

'It's a final demand.'

'Demand for what?'

'It doesn't say. Just for goods to the value of over eight hundred pounds. But we haven't had any goods on credit and certainly not to that value.'

'Eight hundred pounds?' Sue spluttered.

'That's what it says.'

'Well, it's a mistake. I'd ignore it if I were you.'

'It's a mistake all right. But how come it's addressed to me? Look, it's even got my name as a reference on the top.'

'Search me,' Sue replied, shrugging her shoulders.

Josie swiftly opened the rest of the post. It was all junk mail. She picked up the final demand again and studied it.

'This is silly,' she cried. 'How come I'm getting demands for goods I haven't had?'

Just then Stephen breezed through the door.

'What's the long face for?' he asked, eyeing them both.

Josie threw the letter towards him across the table.

'What d'you make of this?' she asked. 'And don't for God's sake say demands for goods, because I know that. But I can assure you I haven't had the goods, whatever they are.'

Stephen raised his eyebrows as he scanned the correspondence. 'It's a mistake then, it has to be.'

'That's what I said,' Sue replied tartly. 'Throw it away and let's talk about this party.'

'What party?' Stephen said, sliding the paper back towards Josie.

'My leaving party. It's tomorrow night. Can you manage it?'

'Oh, Stephen doesn't want . . .' Josie began.

'I'd have loved to have come,' he cut in, 'but I can't, more's the pity,' he said, his eyes fixed upon Josie. He turned his gaze back to Sue. 'I've a venue and it's too short notice too get someone reliable to take over for me. If I don't see you again, Sue, all the best.'

She grinned. 'Thanks.'

When he had left, Josie turned to Sue.

'Did you have to invite him? You embarrassed him. You could see he didn't want to come.'

'Didn't he?' Sue said tartly. 'I think you're wrong.'

Three days later a small gathering stood on the London Road railway station. Josie waved heartily long after the train with her friend aboard had disappeared from view. She turned to Mrs Shaw with tears in her eyes.

'D'you think I'll ever see her again?' she asked soulfully.

Mrs Shaw smiled as she tried to hide her own tears. 'I damned well hope so, my dear.' She placed her arm affectionately around Josie's shoulders. 'You should know by now that my daughter is full of great ideas but never quite manages to carry them through. I wouldn't put it past her to get to Heathrow, meet someone who catches her eye, spend a few days in London and come back full of the joys of spring.'

Josie looked at her hopefully. 'D'you think so?'

'As I said, nothing would surprise me.' She gave Josie a hug. 'Now if I can manage to survive, then so can you. You've a lot going for you, my dear. A book shop that's doing very nicely, and somewhere to live. All you need is to fall in love with a nice young man. And I bet before you settle down, Sue will be back so she can be your bridesmaid.'

Josie laughed. 'Falling in love's no problem, it's the aftermath I can't cope with, when things don't turn out as you expect.'

'Oh, we all have disappointments and get hurt, dear. Nothing in life is ever won easily. You'll probably suffer a few more upsets and broken hearts before you meet Mr Right.'

'If I ever do,' Josie said lightly.

'You will, dear,' Mrs Shaw said with conviction. 'Anyway, take a tip from me. Have fun looking.' She leaned over and whispered in Josie's ear, 'Remember, I never got the chance.'

Josie smiled and dug her hands into her coat pockets as a stiff wind whipped along the platform. She looked over at Sue's father as he stood talking to Sophie, Nelly and Gertie – several of Sue's friends having already left to return to their work places. He was still a very handsome man and loved his wife and daughter dearly, and Mrs Shaw, she knew without a doubt, returned those feelings. But she knew what the older woman was getting at and agreed with her wholeheartedly. Not that she ever intended getting married. That was something that never entered her head these days.

She entered the empty flat later that day determined not to let Sue's departure get her down. She would pretend Sue had just

243

gone away for several weeks. That way it wouldn't seem permanent.

As the days passed by, coping with the loss of her friend proved more difficult than she'd envisaged. The evenings were the worst. Those were the times when the pair, if not out enjoying themselves, would have sat and talked long into the night about all sorts of things that young women in their early-twenties discuss and argue over. The flat felt so empty without her. Before long, though, Josie made a decision. She would not get a replacement for Sue. No matter how hard she looked or how many times she tried, it would be an impossibility. Whoever she chose would always be suffering from unfair comparisons and that wasn't right. Sue was unique, their friendship was special, and besides, the book shop was making enough to cover her expenses. It was about time Josie started doing things by herself. And, of course, she would need to keep the room free, just in case her friend returned.

Chapter Thirty

The shop door banged loudly and Josie's head jerked up. She saw a strange man standing just inside the threshold. He had a cashmere coat draped over his immaculate suit and puffed nonchalantly on a large cigar. His small grey eyes travelled around the empty shop, coming to rest upon her sitting at the table. He took the cigar out of his mouth.

'Can I help you?' she asked falteringly, wondering what on earth someone looking remarkably like Al Capone was doing in a second hand book shop.

'I sincerely hope so,' he said gruffly as he walked casually towards her. He placed the fat cigar back into his mouth, delved into the inside pocket of his coat and held out a piece of paper. 'I've come to collect personally as you don't seem willing to pay by the normal methods.'

Josie frowned. 'Pay? Pay for what?'

A length of ash fell from the cigar and drifted to the floor as the man narrowed his eyes. 'You should go on the stage, my dear. That was good, but it didn't fool me. You didn't really expect my client to let you have his goods for free, did you? He wants his money and he wants it now.' He thumped a fat fist hard on the table, leaned over and stared straight at her. 'My client doesn't like being taken for a mug. And I'd suggest you honour your commitment if you don't want to land yourself in a whole heap of trouble.'

Josie shrank back and shook her head, bewildered. 'What commitment?'

The man straightened up and breathed deeply. 'You are J Rawlings and this is The Book Cave?'

'Yes.'

'Right – at least we've got that clear,' he said patronisingly. 'Now, you ordered goods on your own letterheaded paper from my client and he wants paying. Which I don't think unreasonable, do you? He's been very patient, but his patience has finally run out. I'm your final warning.' He grinned at her through clenched teeth as he blew a cloud of foul-smelling smoke out of the side of his mouth. 'Get the picture, lady?'

Josie nodded, her face wearing a worried frown. 'But I haven't ordered any goods. Why should I pay for things I haven't had?'

'Look, lady,' the man said, his tone low and menacing, 'you either pay up like a good little girl or . . .'

'Or what?' a voice said from the doorway.

Josie looked up to see that a woman had entered. She looked vaguely familiar but Josie couldn't for the life of her think who she was. The man swung round.

'And who the hell are you?' he growled.

'Me? It's *you* who needs to answer that question,' the women said, taking several steps forward on her high platform shoes, her expensive calf-length pale blue suede coat flapping open to reveal a short navy dress, edged in white. 'I seem to be witnessing a demand for money with menaces. Is that correct?'

The man scowled. 'Put it any way you like, lady. This money should have been paid long ago. I'm not leaving without payment.'

Josie jumped up. 'I keep trying to tell you,' she shouted angrily, 'I haven't had any goods. The first I knew of all this was when I received the final demand through the post. I couldn't do anything about it 'cos there was no telephone number or proper address for me to contact. It's all a mistake.'

The man swung round. 'Don't bother playing that game with me. Do you know the number of times I've heard that one? Now pay up or else.'

'Oh, yes?' the woman spoke again. 'Or else what? Going to break some knee caps, are we? Well, let's just see what the police have to say about that. Because if she says she hasn't had the goods, then she hasn't, got that?' She turned and headed for the door.

Just then, as if summoned by magic, two beat bobbies strolled by. The man gulped, rushed towards the door and pushed himself between it and the women. 'You haven't heard the last of this,' he spat as he opened the door and hurriedly left.

Josie exhaled slowly and turned her attention to the woman. 'I don't know who you are, but thanks.'

The woman raised her eyebrows. 'Don't you, Josie? Take a closer look.'

Josie frowned and stared hard. Her mouth dropped open. 'My God, Marilyn? It's you, isn't it? I don't believe it.'

Marilyn took several steps forward, flipped back the side of her long suede coat and placed an immaculately manicured hand on her hip. 'Yes, I look great, don't I?' she said smugly. 'I told you I'd be a success. I slayed them down in London.' She eyed Josie critically. 'I see you've lost some weight. It suits you, you should try and lose some more. I've lots of old clothes that I could send up for you.' The side of her mouth twitched. 'But you're still letting people walk all over you, aren't you, Josie? Who was that man?'

Josie's back stiffened. 'I don't know,' she said quickly as she gathered a pile of books together and picked them up. 'I'll get it sorted out. But thanks for your help.'

'My pleasure.' She turned from Josie and took a long look around the shop. 'So, this is all yours, is it?'

Josie nodded proudly.

'Mmm. Ma Simpson told me you had a shop when I went to look for you this morning. I thought she meant a proper book shop.'

'This is a proper book shop,' Josie snapped.

Marilyn looked at her and smiled sweetly. 'Yes, of course. It would be to you, wouldn't it?'

Josie put down the books and folded her arms. 'Is this a social visit, Marilyn, or have you just come to gloat?'

Marilyn stared at her. 'My, we are touchy. I came to see you. And a good job I did, considering the situation I found you in.'

'I said thanks, Marilyn, and I meant it. Now what can I do for you?'

She breathed deeply. 'Fine way to treat your cousin, I must say. I came to Leicester 'specially to see everyone and this is how I'm greeted.'

'You took your time about it,' Josie said flatly. 'How long has it been, Marilyn? Two – three years?'

She flicked back her hair. 'I've been busy,' she said defensively. 'Modelling is a tough job, Josie. You don't get much time to yourself, especially when you're in such great demand and get jetted off at a moment's notice all over the world to exotic locations. This is the first chance I've had. I thought you'd be pleased to see me.'

Josie pursed her lips. 'I am, Marilyn. But you can stop showing off. You're not with your London lot now.'

'Showing off! Josie really, I am not.'

'Yes, you are. And you can cut it out.'

Marilyn held up her hand. 'Okay, okay. Let's call a truce. I'm only up here for the day. Deal?'

Josie relented. 'Deal.' She pulled out a stool. 'Why don't you sit down?' She noticed Marilyn eye the stool critically. 'Sorry, I haven't got a chair. You'll have to make do with this.'

'Oh! Er . . . can't you shut the shop up so we can go somewhere more comfortable? I have a room at The Grand Hotel. I was thinking . . .'

'No,' Josie cut in, shaking her head. 'I can't go shutting my shop up willy-nilly. I've customers to think about. Oh, sit down, Marilyn. You've sat in worse places in your time. It's a lot more comfortable than the orange boxes we used to sit on at the back of the stall.'

Marilyn smiled in recollection. 'Yes, it is.'

She flicked back her coat and sat sedately down, crossing her shapely legs. She looked fondly at her cousin. 'It is good to see you, Josie,' she said sincerely.

'Is it?' Josie replied.

'Oh, yes. I've missed everyone. How's Gran?'

Josie stared at her in horror. 'You don't know?'

'Know? Know what? I only arrived late last night and first thing this morning I went round the market. I thought I'd surprise you on the stall. It was me who got the surprise. All Ma Simpson said was that you had a shop. She was quite shirty about it as well.' Marilyn pouted. 'She never even asked how I was getting on.' She looked at Josie quizzically. 'So what's happened, Josie? Gran finally get too much for you or what?'

Josie rested her eyes on the pile of books on the desk. 'Gran's dead,' she said softly.

Marilyn's face fell. 'Dead! Oh, Josie, I thought the old bugger would live for ever.' She clasped her hands together in remorse. 'I know I didn't show it much, but I was fond of her.' Her face brightened. 'Ah well, she was getting on, wasn't she? What did she die of, old age?'

Josie tightened her lips. 'Yes, something like that.'

'So you got the house, and what did you do with the stall? Sell it? I can't say as I blame you. It was no fun standing out in all weathers just to earn a tuppenny ha'penny living.'

Josie froze. Marilyn was speaking as though the stall had meant nothing. To her it might not have but to Josie it had been her whole way of life. She raised angry eyes. 'No, I never sold the stall and I never got the house. Your father saw to that,' she blurted out.

'My father?' Marilyn frowned. 'Why, what did he do?'

'Claimed the house and the stall and chucked me out on the streets without a penny. That's what your father did.'

Marilyn stared. 'He did what? The bastard!' She went to lean back then realised she was sitting on a stool. 'He hated Gran, and as far as I know Gran hated him. Though God knows why. She would turn in her grave if she knew what he'd done.' She grimaced. 'I'm not surprised though, Josie. My father is capable of anything. I've no illusions about him.'

'You don't like him then?'

'Like him? I detested the man and still do. He treated my mother like dirt. He never acknowledged I existed until I was about fifteen. Then, for some unknown reason, he decided he wanted to be a father to me. Well, I was having none of that.' She stared out across the shop. 'There's something about my father, Josie, that I could never put my finger on . . .'

248

'What d'you mean?'

'I don't know. Just something. Something weird.' She paused for a moment. 'What about my mother? Is she still with him?'

'Don't you know?'

'No. I daren't write in case he charged down to London and spoiled everything for me. You know how forceful he can be.'

Josie nodded in agreement and proceeded to tell Marilyn about her mother.

'Good for her,' she said with conviction when Josie had finished. 'I'm glad she's got away from him. I shall make a point of writing when I get back to London and maybe visit when I can fit it in.' She laughed ruefully. 'I know people down the smoke that'd make my father look like a saint. It's a pity I can't introduce them to him!'

Josie was shocked by the savage tone of her voice.

'Well, it's too late now, Marilyn. What's done's done. To be honest it's been the making of me, although at the time I thought it was the end of the world. But I ain't done so badly.'

'No, you haven't, considering,' Marilyn said sincerely, much to Josie's surprise.

'So,' Marilyn smiled, 'tell me what happened after my father chucked you out? You must have had a tough time of it.'

'Oh, not so tough. I met some wonderful people. Without them it would have been hell, though.'

Josie told Marilyn her tale, even about Stephen and the accident.

'How is he now, Josie?' she asked.

'Stephen? Fine. His business is doing well. He's a lovely man, Marilyn.'

'Yes. I can see you still think very highly of him.'

'We're just friends, the same as we've always been. As far as I know he has a very nice girlfriend and it's pretty serious between them.'

'Girlfriend, eh? Mmm.'

As if on cue the door opened and Stephen walked through, his arms laden with books. Both women watched him closely as he strode to the table and put them down. He smiled warmly at Josie.

'A few books for you, Josie. My mother asked me to drop them in. She says you can sort out the money later.'

'Thanks,' she said.

'Hello, Stephen,' Marilyn whispered seductively.

He turned his head and stared at her blankly.

'It's me, Marilyn.' She rose and moved round the table, gazing up into his eyes provocatively.

'So it is,' he said, eyes wide with shock. 'How are you?'

'Me? I'm fine. Couldn't be better, thanks,' she said, trailing her fingers through her blonde hair.

Josie watched them both with a sinking heart. Although dressed fashionably, she suddenly felt very dowdy and insignificant against her glamorous cousin. Her shoulders sagged as she watched Stephen's eyes travel over Marilyn and come to rest upon her face.

He cleared his throat. 'You look great,' he said. 'I heard of your success. Congratulations.'

So he knew. He'd known all along how her cousin was. He must have been following her progress. Did he still love her? thought Josie with a touch of jealousy. She lowered her gaze as Marilyn placed her hand on his arm.

'How about a bite of lunch, for old times' sake?' she asked, batting her heavily mascaraed eyelashes. 'We've a lot to catch up on.'

Stephen coughed again and glanced at his watch. 'No can do, I'm afraid. Too busy.'

Marilyn pouted. 'Oh, surely not too busy to have lunch with me?' she said.

'Yes, Marilyn, I am. You should have let us know you were coming. I might have been able to juggle my appointments around to fit you in for an hour or so.' He half turned towards Josie and gave her an unexpected wink, then back to face Marilyn. 'Sorry, have to dash.' He held out his hand and shook hers. 'Nice to have seen you again.' He made to walk away, stopped and turned. 'Oh, Josie. Any developments on that demand you got? Did you manage to sort the mistake out?'

Josie gulped as she suppressed a smile. If Stephen was taking out time to deliver her books then obviously he wasn't busy at all. She didn't know what he was playing at but she would go along with it.

'Er . . . no, I haven't. I've had a visitor, though. A right nasty piece of work he was.' She smiled at her cousin. 'Marilyn got rid of him but I'm sure he'll be back.'

Stephen's lip curled. 'Not lost your touch, I see, Marilyn?' He turned back to Josie. 'I had a feeling something like that would happen.'

'Did you?' she asked.

'Mmm, I did. You'll have to get the matter sorted.'

'I know,' she agreed. 'But how?'

'Look, I haven't the time to discuss it now. Would you like me to come round so we can put our heads together, see what we can do to put a stop to this nonsense?'

'Oh, yes, please. I'd really appreciate that. That's if you can spare the time?'

Stephen smiled at her. 'I've always time for you, Josie.' He started walking towards the door, stopped and turned. 'I'll be in touch.' He inclined his head to Marilyn and walked away.

250

Marilyn raised her head haughtily as she stared after him.

'Huh!' she fumed. 'You'd have thought he could have spared the time for a spot of lunch. It's not every day a famous model drops into town. You'd have thought he'd have been honoured to have been seen out with me. Still, not to worry. Small fry like Stephen don't figure much in my life these days.' She smiled broadly at Josie. 'What about you? We could have some food sent up to my room at The Grand. I don't suppose there's anywhere else decent to eat in this pokey hole of a town.'

Josie did not appreciate being second choice. She knew without a doubt that had Stephen accepted she would not have been invited to join them. She began to gather together the books that he had dropped off and pile them alongside the others on the table. 'Thanks for the offer, Marilyn, but as I said before, I can't shut the shop.'

'Oh, well, suit yourself,' she said flatly. She inched up the sleeve of her suede coat and made a great display of looking at her gold bracelet-styled watch, making sure Josie saw how expensive it was. 'Oh, I must be off myself soon. I've a train to catch. I've an assignment for *Vogue* magazine tomorrow and I have to get my beauty sleep.'

'Oh, that's a shame,' Josie said, trying to sound disappointed. 'I was going to ask you back to my flat tonight. I could have cooked you something.'

'Some other time, perhaps. I want to catch the shops before they close and my train leaves at six.'

'Shops?' Josie said, raising her eyebrows. 'I wouldn't have thought ours stocked your kind of goods,' she said.

'What d'you mean by that remark!'

'I was only stating a fact, Marilyn. We haven't got a Harrod's in Leicester.'

Marilyn narrowed her eyes. 'Well, poor ole me will have to make do, won't I? Besides, it'll be a treat as I don't get much time to shop for myself. I usually have to get other people to do it for me.' She tossed her head. 'I'm in such demand, you know. Lesley and I were only saying the other day what a bind it is not to be able to walk the streets without being besieged by fans.'

Josie pressed her lips together. 'Lesley?'

Marilyn eyed Josie with a superior air. 'Of course, you'd know her as Twiggy. But she's Lesley – Lesley Hornby, to her friends. She changed her name to stand out from the others. I didn't have to do that. My name says it all, don't you think?'

'Does it?' Josie asked.

'Of course it does,' she snapped. 'It's provocative. After all, I was named after Marilyn Monroe.'

'Oh, I see.'

251

'Even pop stars do it.'

'Do they?' Josie asked tonelessly, knowing very well everything that pop and film stars got up to.

'Oh, Josie,' Marilyn sighed, taking the bait. 'You don't really think that Screaming Lord Sutch was christened that, do you? Flavell's real name is Jeremy Biggles, but he knew no one would take him seriously with a name like that so he changed it to Flavell Farnsworth. Much more dramatic, don't you think?'

Josie slowly nodded.

'Flavell is marvellous,' she continued. 'He introduced me to so many influential people, and of course they soon realised I had talent. Lots of talent. Before I knew it, I was being photographed by the likes of David Bailey. He's just the best, Josie. You're a nobody until you've posed for Bailey. You have heard of him up here, haven't you?'

Josie sighed. Marilyn was beginning to get on her nerves with her blatant bragging. Her cousin had long outstayed her welcome. She feared she wouldn't be able to stay in control of her tongue for much longer.

She watched as Marilyn glided across to a bookshelf, selected a book and idly flicked over the pages. She put it back.

'You should come down to London sometime, Josie. It'd open your eyes to the real world. It'd show you just what a backwater Leicester is.'

'Backwater?' Josie said sharply. 'Leicester's no backwater, Marilyn, and you know it. Who d'you think makes most of the clothes you parade round in? The folks of Leicester, that's who. And most of the shoes and accessories.' She paused to control her rising temper. 'For your information, I have been to London. I'm not completely in the dark about our wondrous capital city. Personally, I thought it was a mucky hole,' she lied, having been captivated by it at the time. 'For all I care, you can keep the place.'

'You came to London? When?'

'Last year. As a matter of fact, I saw you.'

'You did? Where?'

'In Soho. You were with a group of people coming out of a club.' She paused. 'I thought at the time you were a call girl or summat. Well, you did have rather an expensive fur coat on and I couldn't work out how you could have afforded it.'

Marilyn laughed loudly. 'You'd be surprised what I can afford now, Josie. And as for being in Soho, I expect I'd gone with friends for a night out. We were probably slumming it, then went on to the theatre afterwards.'

'Oh, very nice,' Josie said tonelessly. 'Is that what you're doing now, Marilyn – slumming it?'

She ignored Josie's remark. 'Actually, I was with Flavell. I could have introduced you.'

'Oh, I wouldn't have wanted to embarrass you, Marilyn. Me being a country cousin from a little backwater up north. How would you have explained me away?'

'Yes, you're right. That would have been rather difficult. Still, I suppose we all have our crosses to bear. Oh, that reminds me,' she said, opening her leather handbag. 'I've just remembered the real reason for my visit back home.'

'Oh?'

'To give you this,' she said, holding out a bulky envelope.

'What is it?' Josie asked, accepting the envelope.

'The money I borrowed. I said I'd pay it back.'

Josie pulled out the wad of notes and flicked her thumb through them. She put them back into the package and held it out. 'You've no need to repay it. It was Grandma's money and I can't exactly give it back to her can I?'

'She would have left it all to you. So just take it.'

'I can't,' Josie said sharply, feeling strongly it was her grandmother's blood money and she wanted no part of it.

'Oh, for God's sake, just take it, Josie. By the looks of things you could do with it. Use it to smarten up this shop, it might bring in more customers, or treat yourself to some decent clothes, or have a holiday. Yes, that's a good idea, the break might do you good. I told you at the time it was only a loan. And it's all there, every penny, you needn't bother counting it. Now I must be off.' Marilyn paused and eyed her cousin. 'It was nice seeing you, Josie, and I mean that. And if ever you're in London, look me up.'

She leaned forward and kissed Josie lightly on the cheek, turned and headed for the door. As she reached it, it opened and Sophie shuffled through. The older woman eyed Marilyn for a second then looked across at Josie, her eyebrows raised.

'Who was that?' she asked, closing the door after Marilyn had left.

'My cousin,' Josie replied flatly.

'Oh? The little madam you told me about. Bit posh for round 'ere, ain't she?' Her lined face creased into a smile. 'Now I'm just off up the butcher's. Nelly's in the baker's getting a nice crusty loaf. So I thought I'd pop in and ask what yer fancy for yer dinner?'

Sophie dealt with and sent happily on her way, Josie set about putting away her new stock. She smiled to herself. Marilyn hadn't changed one little bit. Underneath the fine clothes she was still the same sarcastic little know-all she'd always been. Josie could imagine how she had used her wits relentlessly to claw her way to the top, and for a moment pitied the people she had used and hurt in the process.

But it was Stephen's attitude that had surprised her. She had thought he would be delighted to see his longlost love, but he hadn't been. He'd been just the opposite in fact. He had verbally given her a slap in the face. Serves her right, she thought wickedly, but wondered if Stephen now regretted his actions? After all, he had loved Marilyn very much, and as Josie knew to her cost you could carry a secret longing for years.

Still, one good thing had come of Marilyn's visit. The money was the answer to something that had been worrying her for a while and with it she could put a stop to that worry once and for all.

A vision of her visit from Al Capone sprang to mind and her heart started to pound with worry. She would have to get the matter sorted out, and quickly. It obviously wasn't going to go away. She knew she would have to accept Stephen's offer of help, and the sooner the better.

She raised her head and smiled as two young women walked through the door and made their way over to the book trays. She pushed the events of the day to the back of her mind and went over to offer her help.

Josie rose promptly the next morning. She had an important errand to do before she opened the shop.

Hiding behind a factory wall, she peered around. The house she was surveying across the road still had its curtains drawn. She glanced up and down the street. Several people were scurrying about and she hoped she didn't appear suspicious.

She pondered for a moment as to the best course of action to take. It was then that she spotted the paper boy making his deliveries. She called him over.

'Yes, Missis?' the boy said cockily. 'If it's about yer paper, I shoved it through the letterbox. 'Tain't my fault if it got ripped or the dog chewed it up.'

Josie quickly put the boy's mind at rest, asked him to perform a task for her and held out a fifty pence piece.

He grabbed at it. 'I'll deliver a package to Timbuktu for ten bob, lady. That 'ouse over there yer say?'

Josie nodded. 'And make sure you give it personally to the woman and say you know nothing about it. Okay?'

'Okay, Missis.'

The lad cycled over, threw down his bike and banged loudly on the door of number seven Briton Street. Josie watched from her vantage point. It was several moments before the door was tentatively opened.

From where she stood Josie could hear the baby crying and was shocked at Gilly's uncared for appearance. She saw the lad thrust the parcel at her, pick up his bike and cycle off.

Gilly stared down at the parcel for several moments. She looked up and down the street, turned back into the house and shut the door.

Josie sighed with relief. Her mission had been accomplished. Gilly would now be able to support her children for some time to come and it would surely ease at least her financial burdens.

She pulled up her coat collar and walked hurriedly down the street. Her actions, she felt, didn't compensate for the fact that she had unwittingly planned to marry Gilly's husband or that she had slept with him, but she would rest easier at night, knowing they were financially taken care of. And she hoped wholeheartedly that Gilly used her unexpected wealth to make a new life for herself away from Terry and all he stood for.

Chapter Thirty-One

Stephen, elbows on knees, chin in hands, stared unblinkingly into the flames of the gas fire. Josie, perched on the edge of the chair opposite, watching intently as his face grew grimmer. She chewed her bottom lip anxiously as she awaited his verdict. Regardless of the grim situation, she could not help but feel warmed by his presence, especially now that she had learned to cope with her feelings for him. He was a friend, a good friend, and one who had dropped everything in order to help her, just as a special friend would do. Stephen had always had a way of making her feel special, even when she had been fat and awkward, and that characteristic of his had never changed in the slightest.

After long deliberation he eased his long body further back in the armchair and eyed her thoroughly.

'I can't fathom it out, Josie. A company doesn't just demand money for no reason.' He picked up the final demand notice and studied it again. 'It's a pity it doesn't say what kind of goods were ordered. These reference numbers don't mean anything to me. But the quantities of whatever they refer to are huge. Three hundred of one, six and four hundred of another.' He shook his head. 'It doesn't make sense. Who on earth are the Brown Paper Packaging Company anyway? I've never heard of them.'

'Me neither, 'til now,' she ventured.

'It's a pity there's no telephone number or proper address printed on this demand,' Stephen continued. 'We could have contacted them and asked them to explain.' He pursed his lips. 'Fishy that, a company having a post office box number as an address.' He shook his head. 'I don't like this at all.' He watched the worried frown on her face deepen. 'Is there something you're not telling me?'

She quickly raised her eyes. 'No, nothing. I've told you. I haven't ordered any goods, especially not to that value. The whole lot comes to over eight hundred pounds. What the hell would I order for that amount? I sell second hand books and the odd knitting pattern. I'd have to order a warehouse full to warrant that amount. Anyway, as far as I know, you can't buy second hand books that way, only new ones.'

'Well, someone must have ordered something.'

'What d'you mean?'

He sighed in exasperation. 'Josie, you don't think that someone methodically goes through the telephone book, picks a company at random and sends them a bill, do you?'

'No,' Josie replied defensively. ''Course not. Besides, I haven't got a telephone in the shop.'

Stephen laughed wryly. 'So someone must have ordered these things, using your official paper.'

Josie reluctantly nodded in agreement. 'But who? It certainly wasn't me.' Her eyes flashed. 'Marilyn? You don't think she could have something to do with it, d'you? It's just the kind of stunt she would pull and it was funny the way she turned up like that after all this time.' She stopped abruptly and shook her head. 'It couldn't be her. She'd have needed access to the shop to get at the letterheads.'

'So who else is there?'

'Only me and Sue, Sophie and Nelly. You're not implying it's one of them, are you? They wouldn't, they're my friends.'

'But somebody did, Josie. What about Sue?'

'Sue! Never. I'd trust that girl with my life. I'd have known if she was up to something like that. And Sophie and Nelly ... well, they're two old ladies, what would they know about ordering goods?'

Stephen exhaled loudly. 'Well, I don't bloody know then!' he said, exasperated. 'Could any of the customers get hold of the letterheads?'

Josie shook her head. 'No, we keep them in the cupboard at the back. Besides, the shop is never empty. There's always one of us present. I always make sure of that.'

He leant forward and eyed Josie keenly. He saw her mouth drop open as a thought struck her. 'What is it? he asked.

'What?' she said, eyeing him blankly. 'Oh, er ... nothing.'

'It must have been something to make you look like that. Come on, out with it.'

She raised her head. 'Well, it's Peter.'

'Peter? What about him?'

'Well, he rents the store room at the back and he's always in and out of my shop.'

'Would he do something like this? You know him pretty well.'

'No, he wouldn't. Anyway, he runs an accountancy business. Apart from the obvious stationery and his accounts books, what else would he need?'

'Do you know that for a fact?'

'Know what?'

'That he runs an accountancy business?'

'Yes, 'course I do.'

'How?'

'He told me.'

'Have you ever checked?'

'I didn't need to. He just uses my back room, that's all. I'm not his landlord. Well, not officially.'

'He seems to have a pretty free rein . . .'

'Stop it,' Josie said sharply. 'You'll have me thinking soon that all my friends are at it.'

'Well, someone is, Josie. You have to explore every possibility.' He leant forward and eyed her fondly. 'You've always been a trusting person, Josie. Sometimes maybe too trusting. I think you should check Peter out. To my mind he's the number one suspect at the moment.'

'You sound like Hercule Poirot.'

'Who?'

'Never mind. But do you think it's necessary? I'd feel awful giving him the third degree without any real evidence.'

'Josie, are you going to hand over this money and forget all about it?'

'I can't,' she said, eyes wide with alarm. 'I ain't got it.'

'Well, then, we start with Peter. And the sooner the better. These people aren't going to sit back and wait until you're good and ready to hand over the money. Sooner or later they're going to come and get it. They've already made their first move.'

Josie shuddered as she remembered the savage beating Stephen took simply in order to make a living selling hot-dogs. He'd upset some big noise in the game and that big noise had made sure Stephen knew about it so he would back off. But Stephen hadn't heeded the warning. He was still doing the rounds and she hoped with all her heart there wouldn't be a repetition of that awful night because of his stupid pride.

She breathed deeply. 'What d'you suggest we do?' she whispered.

He shrugged his shoulders. 'We could go round and see him. Ask him nicely if he knows anything about this matter, or . . .'

'Or?'

'Have a nose around this store-room-cum-accountancy business.'

'Oh, God! she exclaimed. 'I don't like the sound of either.'

'It's up to you, Josie. You've got to start somewhere.'

She raised worried eyes. 'You'll help me?'

Stephen smiled. 'Yes. Of course I will.'

She sat back and thought deeply. Finally she spoke. 'I don't like the sound of tackling him face to face. I'd sooner have a look round his room first. After all, I've a right, haven't I? It's me who pays the rent.'

Stephen nodded.

'We can get into the room, no problem. We'll use the connecting door. I have a key,' she said.

'Does Peter know you have one?'

Josie nodded, bemused. 'Yes. 'Course he does.'

'I see,' Stephen said slowly.

'You see what?'

'Oh, it's just a thought. But Peter could easily have got hold of that key and copied it.'

'Why would he want to do that? If he'd asked, I'd have given it to him.'

'Oh, Josie,' Stephen chided. 'If he had asked you for it, he would have had to give a reason, wouldn't he?'

She jumped up. 'I hate thinking like this. I feel disloyal. Let's see if we find out anything first before we come to conclusions.'

'Okay,' Stephen rose to join her. 'You ready then?'

'What . . . now?'

'When do you propose to start – next week?'

Josie eyed him hesitantly. 'Haven't you got other things to do? Arrangements for tonight or anything?'

'Nothing that a quick telephone call won't sort out. And I wasn't planning to take the van out. Now stop stalling, Josie. Just get your coat. You've a perfect right to be in your own shop. You're doing nothing illegal.'

Josie stared at him for a moment. 'No. No, I'm not, am I?' she said softly.

Stephen frowned and caught hold of her arm. 'There's something we haven't thought about.'

'What?'

'These goods. If you haven't seen hide nor hair of them, where were they delivered and what's happened to them since?'

'Oh, God!' Josie cried. 'This gets worse.'

She raced into the hall and grabbed her coat and the pair hurried out into the cold November night.

Stephen drew the van to a halt outside the shop and switched off the engine. Josie stared out of the window. The shop looked eerie – empty and forbidding in the deserted lamplit street – and she shuddered as she alighted. She walked across, inserted the mortice key and turned; she then did the same with the Yale key, flicking up the faulty catch out of habit and entering, Stephen following close behind.

'Leave the main shop lights off, Josie,' he commanded. 'Don't want to attract unnecessary attention from anyone passing.'

She did as she was ordered and made her way across the darkened room. She felt above the lintel, found the key and unlocked

259

the connecting door. She reluctantly turned to Stephen, unable to see his features in the darkness, but instinctively knowing he was watching her movements intently. She suddenly felt like a criminal but she had come this far and pride would not let her back down now. As Stephen had forcefully pointed out, her business was at stake, maybe her life if Al Capone was to be taken seriously. This problem had to be sorted out one way or another.

'Here goes,' she said softly.

They entered the room and she felt for the light. Brightness flooded the tiny space and she blinked several times to accustom her eyes.

They both stared around in amazement. Apart from an old desk that held several drawers, a black telephone sitting on top, and a swivel chair to the side, with some coffee making equipment on a tray on the floor, the room was empty.

She turned to Stephen standing next to her.

He shook his head. 'It doesn't look a very productive office to me.'

'Me neither,' she agreed, scratching her head.

She walked further in and had a proper look round.

'There's not even a filing cabinet. I don't understand it. I don't understand it at all. It doesn't look to me as if he does anything in here, except make coffee.'

'Does the telephone ring much?' Stephen asked.

Josie shrugged her shoulders. 'Sometimes I hear it. To be honest, I'm too busy to take much notice.'

Stephen walked to the back of the desk and stared down at it, puzzled. He tried the drawers. They were all locked.

'Damn!' he said. Suddenly his eyes lit up and Josie watched as he ran his fingers along the underside of the desk. He shook his head. 'Nothing doing.' He looked around. 'Now where would he hide a key?'

'Maybe he's taken it with him?'

'Could have. But let's make sure. The desk must hold something, or why lock it?'

They both searched every nook and cranny but found nothing. Josie straightened up and brushed down the dust that had gathered on her knees as she had knelt to feel along the skirting boards. She grimaced at the ladder in her tights that was running down her leg.

'Everything all right, Miss Rawlings?' a deep voice asked.

Josie swung round in fright to find a policeman standing in the doorway.

'Oh, Constable Wrigley,' she breathed. 'What a scare you gave me.'

'Sorry. I just saw a chink of light shining from under this door through the window during my rounds and thought you had trouble.'

'Oh, no trouble,' she said quickly. She sought for something to say. 'I . . . er . . . just forgot to take something home with me and came back to fetch it.' She turned to Stephen. 'My friend came to keep me company. Just in case, you know.'

'Very wise. Can't be too careful these days.'

'Actually, I was just about to make a coffee. Fancy one?'

'Er . . . no ta. But thanks for the offer.' He turned and began to walk away. 'Now don't forget to lock up tight after you leave,' he called back.

Josie smiled. 'I won't, Constable, thanks. Oh, Constable . . .' she said, running after him. 'There is something you could help us with.'

He stopped and turned round. 'Yes?'

'The drawers to my desk are locked and I've left the key at home. I don't really want to break it open. Is there any other way of getting in without damaging the wood?' she asked politely, noticing out of the corner of her eye a look of horror flash across Stephen's face.

Constable Wrigley frowned as his size 12 boots plodded back towards her. He bent to ease his six foot three frame through the doorway. 'Well . . .' he began. 'You shouldn't really be asking a copper for advice like this.' His severe expression broke into a grin. 'Being's it's you, Miss Rawlings, I'll have it open for you in a tick. Providing, of course, you don't mention a word to anyone about it?'

'I wouldn't dream of it,' Josie said sincerely. 'But you're doing me a great favour.'

She heard Stephen's intake of breath and quickly glanced at him to see him about to explode into laughter. She eyed him menacingly. If he did that he would give the game away and they would both be in trouble. Luckily he managed to control himself.

Josie held her breath. She couldn't see what the Constable was doing clearly but in no time she heard a click. 'There you go, Miss Rawlings, it'll lock automatically once you've shut them up again.'

She breathed freely. 'Thank you. You've saved me a trip home.'

Constable Wrigley inclined his head and once more headed for the door.

'If you want to drop by tomorrow at any time, I'll look out some books that your wife might like,' she volunteered.

'Thanks, I will,' he shouted as he left the shop.

Josie sank back against the desk and exhaled loudly.

'That was a close one,' Stephen said, then unable to control himself, burst into laughter. 'You should have gone on the stage, Josie Rawlings, you've missed your vocation.'

She eyed him sharply. 'Let's just get on with it, Stephen. I want

261

to get out of here before anyone else catches us.'

She made a dive for the desk and opened the top drawer. It was empty except for a couple of biros and a half used note pad; the used pages were absent.

Careful not to shut the drawer in case they all locked, she opened the next. Stephen moved to join her, watching the proceedings closely.

The second drawer was more fruitful. The pages from the note book, stapled together, were hidden at the back under a pile of large plain brown envelopes. She pulled out the pages and quickly flicked through them. They were filled with names and addresses from all manner of locations in the British Isles.

'That's funny,' she frowned. 'All the names are mostly Mr Smith or Mr Jones, and all but the last few are ticked in red ink at the side.'

A bemused expression settled on Stephen's face as Josie, leaving the stapled pages on the desk top, continued to search the drawer. It held nothing more revealing so she pulled open the last one which was much deeper than the other two.

Delving underneath yet another pile of thick brown envelopes, she reddened deeply as she pulled forth several pornographic-type magazines. She tried to avert her eyes from the naked women posing on the covers.

Stephen took them from her. 'Not the type of thing I would have thought Peter would have subscribed to,' he said flatly.

'What d'you mean?'

Stephen raised his eyebrows knowingly. 'Josie, any man in his right mind would know what Peter was about. Now this isn't his kind of stuff, so what's it doing in his drawer?'

She shrugged her shoulders. 'Dunno. Maybe he's converted or something.'

Stephen put one of the magazines into the inside pocket of his jacket and handed the others back to Josie.

'You're not taking one, are you? What if he misses it?'

'Tough if he does.'

Josie eyed him in disgust. 'You men are all the same!'

'No, no, Josie. You've got it wrong. I'm only taking it because it might hold a clue.'

'Pull the other one,' she muttered as she shoved the other magazines back. 'Well, that was a wasted exercise. Apart from the fact that you have your bedtime reading. What do we do now?'

Stephen raised his eyebrow at her then scratched his head. 'Put the rest of the stuff back, I suppose, and go home. The only other option is to tackle Peter face to face and see his reactions. We'll soon know if he's involved or not.'

Silently Josie picked up the pad ready to return it to the middle

262

drawer. A piece of paper fluttered to the floor and she bent to pick it up. She quickly scanned over it. Peter had obviously used this as his doodling page and instead of throwing it away it had somehow been caught up with the rest of the pages. Several words caught her attention and she gave a small cry as their meaning registered. Slowly she slid down on to the swivel chair.

'What is it, Josie?' Stephen demanded, noticing her frozen expression and the beads of perspiration forming on her brow.

She raised her eyes. 'Peter . . . he's . . . he's definitely involved in all this. Look, he's doodled the name of the Brown Paper Packaging company on this sheet of paper.'

'Oh, that's it then. I was right!' Stephen cried.

'But that's not all,' she whispered, distraught.

'What! What else does it say?'

She held out the piece of paper. Stephen took it, studied it intently, then lowered troubled eyes.

'Oh, my God,' he uttered as he placed it back on the desk in front of her.

Josie slowly lowered her head and looked down at it.

In bright red ink, in the centre of a crudely drawn heart, was the name 'Stanley Rawlings'.

Chapter Thirty-Two

Josie sat rigidly in the chair, her hands clasped firmly in her lap. She couldn't remember the journey back to her flat, in fact she didn't even know what the time was, her mind was too full of confused thoughts; thoughts so terrible she felt that she must be in the middle of a nightmare. But it wasn't a nightmare, she had seen the evidence with her own eyes. Not only was her friend Peter behind this matter but somehow so was her uncle and with this knowledge she dreaded to think to what extent his involvement went. Finding his name like that was too much of a coincidence and one which she couldn't ignore.

She looked across to see Stephen watching her from the chair opposite.

'You don't think . . . you don't think it could be another Stanley Rawlings, do you? she asked falteringly.

Stephen breathed deeply and put down his empty coffee mug on to the hearth. He shrugged his shoulders. 'Could be, I suppose,' he said, trying to soften the terrible blow she had just suffered. 'The name isn't unusual by any means.'

She shuddered as an icy cold sensation of doom settled over her. 'But I know it's him. I just know it,' she said, her voice rising. 'He threatened me once and I know that he's somehow keeping that promise. Even Marilyn said there was something weird about him. And if his own daughter can say that . . .' She turned her gaze towards the gas fire and stared blindly into it. 'Oh, Stephen, it's the one name that strikes the fear of God into me. I only have to look at that man and he reduces me to a quivering wreck. What the hell am I going to do?'

'Hold on, Josie. We don't even know yet whether he is involved.'

'Well, how come Peter has drawn his name inside a heart? That means something, surely?'

'Yes, it does,' he agreed. 'And I know what's going through your head, Josie Rawlings. You think your uncle is queer like Peter. But that's a hell of an accusation to make.'

'I know. I know. But you can't blame me for thinking that, can you?'

'No, I can't. But let's wait and see what we uncover first before we make assumptions. Your uncle could be perfectly innocent of all this. Peter could have met him purely by accident and taken a fancy to him. Hence the doodled heart.'

'Yes, that could be the answer. But somehow I don't think so.'

Stephen paused for a moment and eyed her closely. 'Let's face it, Josie. Any of us could have an ardent admirer and know nothing about it.'

'Fat chance of that happening to me,' she replied flatly. 'But I still have a dreadful feeling about all this and I can't shift it.'

He cleared his throat. 'That's understandable, considering the way your uncle treated you. But you told me off several hours ago for jumping to conclusions. Let's see what facts we can find out first, before you start worrying needlessly.'

'Okay. But I hope to God it's like you say.' She relaxed back into her chair and squared her shoulders. 'All right, what do we do next?'

'That's what I've been trying to work out.'

'And?' she asked hopefully.

'We should follow him. Peter, I mean.'

'What, like private detectives?'

'Yes. He doesn't do much in that office, so he must be doing whatever it is somewhere else. It'd be a start at any rate.'

'Yeah. But what if he sees us?'

'That's a chance we'll have to take.' Stephen laughed. 'But if the episode with the constable this evening was anything to go by, you'll have no problem making excuses.'

She giggled. 'You don't know what a shock I got when I saw him standing there. I said the first thing that came into my head.'

'Yes, I could see that. I thought I'd explode when you asked him to have a cup of coffee. Then when you asked him to open the desk – well, I couldn't believe my own ears.'

They both laughed together for several moments until Josie's face grew serious.

'You don't mind helping me out? I mean, you have your business to run and . . . friends you have arrangements with.'

'Nothing that can't be put on hold while we sort this out. I'll stick with it to the bitter end, Josie. It'd be my pleasure. Besides, this matter intrigues me and I'm itching to find out what's going on.'

She smiled warmly. 'Thanks, I do appreciate it.'

'Can you get someone to watch the shop?'

'Oh, yeah. No problem. Sophie and Nelly will jump at the chance. Those two are in their element in the shop. The trouble will come when I go back and take over. I'll have to take a crowbar to prise them out.'

'Good. At least your mind'll be at rest on that score. Now I suggest we take it in turns. I've one or two things to do in the morning. You'll have to get up early and follow him from Wentworth Road. See where he goes and so forth. We'll compare notes tomorrow night.'

'Oh, it all sounds rather exciting. But I'm not happy about spying on one of my friends.'

'Josie, friends don't steal stationery to order stuff and land others with the bill. And until we find out otherwise, that appears to be what Peter has done. So I would stop thinking of him as a friend if I were you. It could hamper our investigations.'

'You're right,' she agreed, and started to laugh. 'Oh, but you do sound like a proper detective.'

'More like Inspector Clouseau,' Stephen chuckled. He looked at his watch. 'I must be going.'

'Oh!' Josie said in dismay. 'I've kept you. I am sorry.'

'That's all right. It's just that I have someone to see and if I hurry, I might just make it.'

'Oh, of course,' she said lightly.

After Josie had seen him to the door she returned and sat by the fire, staring long and hard into the flames. Stephen had obviously hurried off to meet Sally; after all, who else could it be? Josie felt tears prick the back of her eyes. If she was truly honest with herself, she would have given anything for him to stay. She could have cooked him a meal, she would have enjoyed that. She clasped her hands together in her lap, raised her eyes and gazed round the empty flat. A feeling of loneliness crept up and settled over her like a lead weight. Slowly she rose and made her way to bed.

Chapter Thirty-Three

Josie shivered violently as the early morning mist swirled around her. It seeped relentlessly through her clothes; she felt damp, extremely cold, and miserable. At this moment in time she could have cheerfully given up the whole idea and let the Brown Paper Packaging Company either beat or sue her for the money if she could only go home and plant her backside right up against the gas fire. She conjured up a vision of the hot flames heating her frozen skin, a pile of hot buttered toast and a pot of scalding tea sitting invitingly upon the hearth.

She scowled deeply and forced the picture from her mind. If Stephen hadn't been her ally she would have found it very easy to have given up, but as he was, thoughts of him spurred her on. If he was willing to put time and effort into sorting out her problem, then so could she. Once again she parted the thick shrubbery that edged the park railings opposite number two Wentworth Road and continued her stake-out.

Unfortunately for her, Peter's room was at the back of the old house and she had no idea whether he was in or not, still asleep or up getting ready for work. So she had to wait. Finally he emerged, hurriedly buttoning up his thick camel coat, and walked swiftly down the street, disappearing around the corner of Fosse Road.

Josie, with the aid of Sophie's old trunk in the attic, was dressed in a long brown macintosh, a bright floral headscarf knotted tightly under her chin and a pair of Sue's old black-rimmed sunglasses clamped right up against her eyes. She inched her way along the shrubbery and sneaked out of the gates. A woman with a pushchair eyed her suspiciously. Josie did not notice. She was too concerned about losing sight of Peter.

She quickly crossed the road and turned the corner. Peter was waiting at the bus stop, the first in a long queue of people. That posed a problem. He would surely see her if she caught the bus. But if she didn't she would lose him, and the pneumonia she had risked would have been in vain. As she spotted the bus in the distance she quickly made a decision. She would have to chance it.

The bus came and Peter climbed aboard. It was packed and

Josie, standing in line behind a very large lady, worried for a moment that she wouldn't be allowed on. Luckily the conductor took pity on her.

Peter did nothing more exciting than arrive at the shop, saunter down the entry and let himself into his office, with Josie at a very safe distance watching his every move.

She hesitated at the entry and exhaled loudly. This detective work sounded good, but was pretty boring when put into operation, not to mention the extreme cold and the hunger pangs that were causing her stomach to rumble loudly since she had had nothing to eat since the night before. The sandwich bar across the road proved too much of a temptation and she hurried across and bought herself a cheese and beetroot cob and a sausage roll, oblivious to the peculiar looks she was receiving.

The only place to observe Peter and not be observed herself was the large outbuilding in the yard at the back of the premises. She stole down the yard, careful to avoid the metal rubbish bins and odds and ends left lying around by previous tenants, and settled herself on a large wooden crate inside. A hole where some of the bricks had fallen out provided a good spy hole directly on to the old store room door.

As she sat and hungrily munched on her food she looked around. The outbuilding was filthy. Cobwebs hung from every corner; insects of every description scurried across rotten woodwork, and the wind that had now risen sharply whistled through all the cracks and blasted through the opening where the broken door hung from its buckled hinges.

Several hours passed. Josie, now frozen to the marrow, shifted uncomfortably on the crate and as she did so it overbalanced and she tumbled off, falling heavily upon the dusty stone floor.

Before she could gather her wits Peter was upon her, pulling her up.

'Are you all right?' he asked, deeply concerned.

'Yeah, I think so,' she said, brushing the dust and dirt off her mac as she fought frantically for a plausible explanation for her predicament.

He ran his eyes over her in astonishment and placed his hand upon his cheek. 'Darling!' he exclaimed. 'What on earth are you dressed like that for? And for that matter, what are you doing out here? You must be frozen.'

Josie shivered. 'I am.'

'Well?'

'Well, what?'

'Why are you out here, dressed like that?'

'Oh – like this! Er . . . well . . . macs are coming into fashion, you know, and I scrounged this from Sophie. It belonged to one of her old tenants. It's a real antique.'

'I can see that. But are you sure about the fashion bit? I've never seen anyone else in a macintosh, especially not one that's at least three sizes too big. An old army great coat, yes, but not one of those.'

'Macs are gonna be all the rage,' Josie said with conviction. 'And you know me, Peter. I don't like to be behind in the fashion stakes.' She paused for a moment, her mind rapidly working overtime. She placed her gloved hands on her hips and stared slowly round. 'Well, what do you think?' she said matter-of-factly.

'Think? Think of what?'

'This place. I've been wondering what I could use it for. After all, I do pay rent for it.'

He frowned quizzically. 'Josie, the only thing you could do with this place is knock it down before it falls down.'

'Mmm. I suppose you're right. Well, that's that.'

Peter stared at her, bemused. 'Are you sure you're all right?'

'Yes. Couldn't be better, thank you.'

'Shouldn't you be in the shop?'

'No, I've got Sophie and Nelly looking after it for a couple of days.'

'Why?'

'Why? Oh, I'm having a break.'

'I see. Well, I'll leave you to it then, my old love. I have to go out.'

'Out!' Josie exclaimed, catching hold of his arm. 'Where to?' she asked before she could stop herself. She quickly realised she was clutching his arm, let go and stuffed her hands down inside her pockets.

'Just out, Josie. Now if you don't mind, I'll have to go.'

'I don't mind. You go,' she said hurriedly, desperately worried in case he twigged something was amiss.

He stared bewilderedly at her for several seconds, before he slowly shook his head, turned and walked back into his office.

She gulped. That had been a close call. She hoped Peter hadn't any suspicions as to her real motives.

From her new hiding place across the street she watched him emerge from the entry about half an hour later. She stealthily followed as he weaved his way down several side streets. For several moments he disappeared from sight and she quickened her pace, worried in case she lost him. Suddenly the houses stopped. A large flattened area stretched before her, in the centre of which stood a snack bar; a converted van similar to the one Stephen owned. Several people were milling about.

Peter was standing just to the side of the van, drinking from a large white mug. She hid inside an alley and flattened herself against the wall as she watched him. After several minutes a man approached carrying a large bulky brown carrier bag. Peter put his mug back on the van counter, extracted something from his pocket and gave it to the man. In turn the man handed over the carrier bag. This done, both went their separate ways.

Peter returned straight to the office.

Stephen found her just after one o'clock, huddled back inside the shop doorway.

'Josie,' he said in concern. 'I thought you were going to hide in the building in the yard? I nearly missed you.'

'Bad idea, I thought he might spot me,' was all she replied, not wanting to explain the events of the morning.

'Anything to report?' he asked expectantly.

Josie related her journey.

'Very suspicious,' Stephen mused. 'Any idea what was in the carrier bag?'

She shook her head.

'Oh, well, let's see what our friend gets up to this afternoon. When I know he's safely in bed for the night, I'll come around to your flat.' He patted his pocket. 'I have some sandwiches and two pairs of socks on, so I'll be all right.'

'But what if something happens and you need me?'

'Josie, if I need you, don't worry, you'll know. Believe me.'

'Okay. But the slightest thing. Promise?'

'Promise.'

She left him on guard whilst she went home to a welcoming gas fire.

At seven-thirty that night, a knock sounded on the flat door. She opened it to find Peter standing on the landing.

He quickly noticed her alarmed expression. 'Anything wrong, darling?' he asked.

'No. Er . . . I was just expecting someone else, that's all,' she said, peering down the stairs. Stephen was nowhere in sight and she wondered where he was hiding. 'Come in,' she said, leaving the door wide open, hoping Stephen was around so he could hear their conversation.

'Thanks, sweetie. It's just a quick visit. Just something I need to tell you.'

'Oh?' she said, stopping in the middle of the passage and turning to face him.

'Just to let you know I'll be giving up the office. I thought you might like plenty of warning so you can consider letting it out on a proper basis.'

'Oh! Are you moving to bigger premises then?'

'Er . . . no, Josie. I'm giving up the business altogether.'

'Why? I thought you were doing okay?' she pressed, continuing on into the living room and standing before the fire.

'No, not really,' he said flatly. 'I don't have the right connections and the few clients I do have won't in the long run pay all my bills. So I'm getting out while I can.'

'Oh, that's a shame,' she said, trying to sound sincere. 'When were you thinking of vacating the premises, and what will you do?'

'Well, I'm just tying up all the loose ends. I should be out by the end of next week.'

'So soon?'

'No point in hanging around now my mind's made up. I suppose I'll look for a job with more forward-thinking accountants. Preferably back home in Manchester. But I'll let you know.'

'Manchester? But I thought you liked living here?' She paused for a moment and took a breath. 'What about your boyfriend?'

She saw the way his eyes narrowed. Then he smiled. 'What about him?'

'Well,' Josie began, 'you have been seeing him for rather a long time. Won't he be upset if you pack up and go home?'

Peter laughed, showing small even white teeth. He walked towards her and placed his long manicured hands on her arms. 'I'll let you into a secret, Josie. He's coming with me. In fact it was his idea in the first place. Manchester is a large city with so much more potential for business opportunities.'

'What kind of business opportunities?'

'Oh – this and that,' he answered cagily. 'Something he started off here and feels could be much more lucrative elsewhere.' A look of blissful happiness crossed his face. 'He's a very clever man is . . . is . . . my "friend". I admire him so much.'

Josie swallowed hard. 'You really do like him, don't you?'

'Yes. So much I'd do anything for him,' he said dreamily. He breathed deeply and smiled down at her. 'I'm glad you understand, Josie. Not many people do. I hate all this having to hide and being made to feel ashamed of how I feel. But I can't help the way I was born and I'm not on my own. There's thousands of us. It just annoys me so much that in this age of sexual freedom, people like me still have to pretend. It isn't fair, Josie. Is it?'

'No,' she agreed softly, shaking her head.

'Well, I for one will be glad when attitudes change and they let us live like normal human beings,' he said aggressively. Unexpectedly his anger subsided and he bent to kiss her on the cheek. 'Oh, I do love you, Josie. If you were a man I'd make advances towards you.' He glanced over at the clock. 'Well, I'd better go

271

before your mystery visitor arrives. Don't want to cramp your style.'

'He's no mystery,' she stuttered.

The tone of her voice made Peter stare at her quizzically.

'Josie, you've been acting very strangely today. Are you sure nothing is wrong?'

'Sure, I'm sure. I'd tell you if there was.'

'Okay,' he replied. He turned and headed out of the room and down the passage. 'You left the door open,' he exclaimed. 'Silly girl. Your gas bill will be enormous.' He turned and waved. 'See you soon.'

Josie gave a half-hearted wave back and closed the door behind him.

Half an hour later Stephen joined her.

'You heard all that?' she asked.

'Certainly did. Quick thinking that, leaving the door open. I had to run down the stairs quick though when I realised he was on his way out. But there's one thing he's right on,' he said with a shudder.

'What's that?'

'Well, I for one don't understand how one man can love another. It gives me the creeps just thinking about it. Still, it takes all sorts, I suppose.' He lowered his long body into an armchair. 'The rest was interesting listening.'

Josie nodded. 'It definitely was. They're on the move.'

'Yes.'

She sat down in the chair opposite and tucked her legs beneath her. 'I just wish I knew if this "friend" of Peter's is my uncle.'

'At the moment, Josie, that's neither here nor there. What does concern me is that whatever Peter's doing, I don't think he's doing it in the knowledge that it will affect you in any way.'

Josie frowned. 'What makes you say that?'

'Just the way he spoke. He thinks very highly of you. I don't think he'd deliberately do anything to cause you grief in any way.'

Josie thought deeply for a moment. 'This convinces me even more that Stanley is behind it. Maybe somehow he's tricked Peter?'

'Yes, but into what? We must find out.'

'Did anything happen this afternoon?'

'No. Peter left the office at five, went straight home then came round to see you. I made sure he was in for the night before I returned.'

Josie groaned. 'So we have to go through the same thing tomorrow?'

'Afraid so, and carry on until we find out once and for all.' Stephen leaned over and patted her knee. 'I'll do the early watch in the morning, so you can have a lie in.'

Josie smiled. 'Thanks,' she said gratefully.

He looked hard at her. 'What else are you worried about?'

'Eh! Oh, I was just hoping that I don't receive another visit from Al Capone, not whilst Sophie and Nelly are in the shop. They wouldn't be able to stand up to him. They're only old ladies.'

'Al Capone? Oh, I see who you mean. I shouldn't worry too much on that score. They'll leave it at least a week. Make sure they've lulled you into a false sense of security before they pounce again.'

Josie shuddered. 'I hope you're right. I don't fancy walking in and finding Sophie and Nelly . . . Oh, it doesn't bear thinking about.' She stood up. 'Er . . .' she hesitated. 'Do you want something to eat or do you have to get home?'

Stephen smiled. 'I wouldn't say no if you're making something for yourself, but I can't be long. I've a couple of things to do before I get to bed tonight.'

'OK, I'll be quick. Egg and chips?' she said lightly as she headed for the kitchen.

'Egg and chips sounds fine,' he answered.

The next two days revealed nothing of interest. Peter went about his business, followed closely by either Josie or Stephen, and did not do the slightest thing out of the ordinary.

On the evening of day five, after another uneventful day, Josie climbed exhaustedly into bed and snuggled under the covers, clutching her hot water bottle to her chest. She was so tired and dispirited that she wanted to abandon the whole idea. Let them have the shop and everything else for that matter, she thought defeatedly. Why go to all this bother anyway? If they ever did manage to find anything out, she would still end up having to pay that demand. Her weary mind could not fathom any other alternative.

She decided there and then to approach Stephen about it. If truth be told he was probably as fed up as she was. Not that he'd ever hinted as much. He appeared to be as keen as ever on wanting to solve the mystery. But she had made her decision and would make sure he saw things her way.

She turned over and closed her eyes, but it was a long time before she finally fell asleep.

Chapter Thirty-Four

Friday morning dawned. A heavy, dark grey sky hung over the city, and as promised by the weather forecasters the heavens opened. Like a tap turned to its fullest, water poured down in torrents for the rest of the day.

Soaked to the skin, Josie continued her surveillance. She was relieved when Stephen arrived just after five to take over.

'Anything?' he asked, rubbing his gloved hands together.

'No,' she replied, shaking her head. 'He's not long returned home and he has a bulky carrier bag with him, but I don't know what's in it.' She looked at him through tired eyes. 'Should we really continue with this? I've had enough, Stephen. I'm cold, hungry and fed up. Even my knickers are wet through.'

He eyed her thoughtfully. 'Do I detect defeatism, Josie Rawlings? Are you really serious about giving up?'

She took a deep breath. 'Yes, I am. I've got to the stage where I can't see the point. Five days we've been trailing him and nothing's really happened.' She lowered her head. 'I don't think I can go on any longer.'

'Well, okay, Josie. You give up if you like. But I'm not. I'm going to stick with this 'til the bitter end.'

Josie stared up at him. 'But why?'

Stephen placed his arm around her wet shoulders and gave her a friendly hug. 'Because I don't like to see any friend of mine made a fool of, and if we give up and let them get away with it, then they'll have made a fool of you and I personally don't like it.'

A slow smile spread across her face. 'When you put it like that, neither do I. All right, if you can stick it, so can I.'

Stephen grinned. 'That's my girl. Now get home and dry off. I'll report in later.'

She nodded and departed.

Once home, she gratefully stripped off her wet clothes and laid them to dry over the clothes horse. Gripping a mug of piping hot tomato soup, she sank down into the armchair and promptly fell asleep.

She woke with a start, still clutching the now stone cold mug of

274

soup, and marvelled that not one drop had been spilt. She looked up at the clock. It read eight-thirty-five. Obviously Stephen was still keeping watch or he would have called in by now. She sniffed loudly and her nose started to run. She had the beginnings of a cold which wasn't surprising in the least.

She felt much better after her sleep, though, and a renewed determination to clear up the matter rose inside her. She decided to dress and go and find Stephen. After her bout of moaning earlier she felt it the least she could do. At least her appearance would reaffirm her commitment to the cause.

As she reached the bottom of the stairs, Sophie charged through her door. She jumped as she collided with Josie.

'Oh!' she exclaimed, stepping backwards. 'What a fright yer gave me.' She eyed Josie, dressed in her outdoor clothes. 'Where you off too?'

'I've just got to pop out. Just a quick errand.'

'What, at this time a' night? It's pouring wi' rain.'

'I know that, Sophie,' she said sharply. 'I shan't be long.'

'You'll catch yer death, yer know. And by the looks on yer, you've already got a cold comin'. Now come on, leave what you've got to do 'til tomorrow and I'll make you a nice hot barley with some Beecham's Powders. That'll soon put yer right.'

'I'm all right, honestly, Sophie. I can't put it off 'til tomorrow. I said I shan't be long.'

'Huh!' Sophie fumed, annoyed. 'You young 'uns always seem to know best. Well, don't blame me if you go down wi' the flu.' She narrowed her eyes and puffed out her chest. 'Now before you scoot off, I wanna know what's goin' on. And you ain't leavin' 'til yer tell me. I was just on me way up to ask yer.'

Josie frowned. 'What d'yer mean?'

'What do a' mean? What do a' mean?' Sophie grumbled. 'You know what a' mean, gel. Now tell me?'

Josie took a breath. 'Nothing's going on,' she said innocently, thinking that the less Sophie knew the better.

'Pull the other one, Josie Rawlings. I weren't born yesterday. I saw yer.'

'Saw me?'

'With Major Thompson's old mac on, the one you said you were borrowing for a fancy dress do. You looked mighty suspicious if yer ask me, standing in Bluett's doorway. Now what were yer doing?' she demanded, folding her arms under her chest, her face set firmly.

Josie groaned. 'Look, Sophie. I can't tell you.'

'Can't or won't?'

'Neither. Both. Oh, stop it, Sophie, please. Yes, I admit, there's something going on, but I can't tell you about it. Not just now,' she said, her voice rising. 'I don't want to get you involved.' She dug her hands deep inside her pockets, lowered her head and made to walk away.

'That's all right you saying that, me duck, but it don't stop me worryin' about yer. Nor does it explain the visit we had this mornin'.'

Josie stopped abruptly and swung round. 'Visit?'

'Yeah. From two men who looked just like they'd stepped out of a gangster movie.'

'Oh, Sophie, what did they say?'

'Not much. I didn't like the look of 'em. Especially the fat one, blowin' his cigar smoke in me face. So when they asked for yer, I told 'em yer'd gone away fer a week or so. Said yer'd had a bereavement. They mumbled between themselves. I couldn't 'ear what they were sayin', neither could Nelly. Anyway, they said to tell yer they'd be back and it were no use you trying to avoid them. Be back for what, Josie?' she asked in concern. 'Look, a' you in some kind of trouble or summat?'

Josie froze. 'Yes, I am. But not of my own doing. And that's what I'm trying to sort out.' She sighed deeply. 'I'm sorry you've been dragged into this, Sophie,' she said apologetically. Then she frowned as a thought struck. 'They didn't threaten you or anything, did they?'

'No. I can tek care of meself. It's you I'm concerned for. You're like the daughter I never 'ad, Josie. I love yer.'

She sniffed hard. 'Oh, Sophie,' she said, stepping forward and grabbing the old woman, hugging her tight. 'I promise I'll tell you everything as soon as I can. In the meantime it might be best if we shut the shop in case those men come back again.'

'Shut the shop!' Sophie exclaimed. 'And turn away paying customers? Not on your life. Now you look 'ere, Josie Rawlings. I ain't afraid a' no jumped up Sonny Jim and his crony. They didn't scare me or Nelly. Tomorrow, I'm tekin' me rolling pin. Let 'em dare come back and start 'ote. They'll get a taste of it, I can assure yer.'

Josie stared at her in awe, then giggled. 'Oh, Sophie. You are a gem. Thanks. Thanks so much. Now I must be off.' She bent forward and kissed Sophie fondly on the cheek. 'I love you too,' she said, before she turned and darted out of the house.

She found Stephen, soaked through, hiding in their usual place in the shrubbery. He jumped as she approached.

'Anything?' she whispered, noticing the rain dripping off the ends of his hair.

He shook his head.

'Hadn't you better call it a day?' she said. 'It's well after nine.'

'Yes, I was just thinking that myself.' He straightened up and stretched. 'Nobody in their right mind would venture out in this weather tonight. So I think we're safe.'

Josie looked at him hard. 'Sophie had a visit today from that man, and he had another bloke with him.'

Stephen's face hardened. 'Oh! They're moving quicker than I thought they would.' He ran his wet gloves over his even wetter chin. 'I think we're going to have to re-think our strategy,' he said flatly. 'Maybe we're following the wrong person.'

'What. Follow my uncle, you mean?'

'Well, this is getting us nowhere fast, Josie.'

Just then they heard a door slam shut in the distance and simultaneously both stooped down and parted the bushes.

Peter, standing just inside the entrance, was trying to put up his umbrella. He succeeded, pulled up the collar of his coat, picked up the carrier bag he had brought home earlier and hurried down the path, along the street and round the corner.

'Quick, after him,' Stephen cried. 'This looks promising, Josie. Let's hope the bugger's finally made a move.'

Keeping as safe a distance as was possible, Josie and Stephen followed their prey down King Richard's Road towards the town.

'I wonder where he's going?' Josie whispered.

'We'll soon find out.'

They both stopped abruptly and dived into a shop doorway as Peter dropped the carrier bag and stooped to pick it up.

Inside the doorway, Stephen took hold of Josie's arm. 'I really think you should go home. This isn't suitable for a woman. I'll soon let you know what's going on.'

Josie grimaced. 'You won't need to do that,' she snapped, 'because I ain't going home.'

Stephen glowered at her. 'I don't think you're taking this very seriously, Josie. This could be dangerous. Look what happened to me . . .'

'I am taking this seriously,' she cut in. 'And I'm trying very hard not to think of the danger. Anyway, what can happen to us just following someone down the road . . .' She stopped talking. 'Look,' she pointed with her finger, 'he's on the move again.'

Before Stephen could protest she had stepped out into the pouring rain and was walking casually after Peter as though she was out on a summer's evening stroll. Stephen caught up with her.

'What am I going to do with you, Josie Rawlings?' he breathed, annoyed. 'What if this turns nasty?'

She turned her head and smiled at him. 'When this is all over, you can buy me a drink, that's what you can do. As for the rest, I'll take my chances. It's just a pity I didn't think to bring Sophie's rolling pin!'

Stephen shook his head, laughing. 'Josie, when this is all over . . .' He stopped abruptly. 'Oh, look, he's heading towards the railway arches on Great Central Street.' He turned to face her, his eyes wide with excitement. 'This does look promising. Most of those arches have been converted into small workshops.'

They dived quickly into the shadows as they saw Peter pause before an archway. He turned and looked around before he opened a small door and entered.

'What do we do now?' she asked.

'We wait, that's what.'

Their wait lasted for over an hour before Peter emerged, carefully looking up and down the street before he closed the door and walked away. He passed right by their hiding place. They both held their breath. To be discovered now would be a catastrophe.

'You follow him, Josie.'

'And what about you?'

'I'm staying here for a bit to see if anyone else comes out.'

'So will I.'

He turned abruptly to face her. 'Josie . . .' he began, but the look on her face told him that to argue would be pointless. They both settled back inside the dark recess of an arch and waited again.

Their wait was worthwhile. After another half hour several people emerged through the small doorway, laughing and joking as though finishing a shift at the local factory.

When the last person had disappeared down the road, Josie made to walk out of their hiding place. Stephen caught her arm.

'Where d'you think you're going?'

She looked at him. 'To see if by chance they've forgotten to lock the door. Maybe we can get a look inside?'

'All in good time, Josie. Let's just hang on and make sure everyone has definitely gone.'

'But we saw them,' she said.

'We saw people leaving but we don't know how many were in there in the first place. Now just do as you're told and be patient.' He held out his hand. 'At least this damned rain has stopped.'

Josie sniffed and settled back into the shadows. Several moments later she jumped in alarm. From further down the street, by the last archway that hadn't yet been converted into a lock up, she saw movement. She grabbed hold of Stephen's arm.

'What was that?'

'What was what?'

'Down there,' she pointed. 'I can just see several people going into that archway.'

Stephen smiled. 'Oh, it's just tramps, Josie. It's well known they all hang out here.'

She sighed in relief. 'Oh, of course,' she said, remembering the night so long ago when she had been accosted by a vagrant and offered shelter.

Once again they settled down to wait.

Twenty minutes later the figure of a man appeared in the doorway. He closed the door behind him and secured it tightly with a large padlock and chain, turned and started to walk towards them. They both pressed themselves up against the wall as the man passed by, his head held high, a smug smile of satisfaction upon his face.

When he was well out of sight, Josie exhaled loudly.

'You saw him?' she uttered.

Stephen nodded. 'I saw him, Josie.'

'Oh, God,' she groaned. 'I was so hoping he wasn't involved.'

Stephen turned to face her, unable to find any words of comfort. He put his arm around her shoulders.

'Come on,' he said firmly. 'We've work to do.'

Chapter Thirty-Five

They stood before the huge arched wooden door and Stephen tugged on the padlock securing the smaller door cut inside it.

'This lot is locked up tighter than Fort Knox,' he fumed. 'He's got to be hiding something important. He's just got to be.'

Josie shrugged her shoulders. 'What do we do now?'

Stephen ran his fingers through his wet hair in frustration. 'I don't know. Let me think.'

He paced backwards and forwards, Josie looking on, biting her bottom lip helplessly. Finally he stopped.

'We'll have to break in,' he announced.

'Break in! Oh, God. How?'

'Scout round, Josie. See if any of the other tenants using the arches have left behind anything strong enough to break a padlock.'

'Are you sure . . .'

'Just do it, please, Josie. We can't exactly call the police, can we? And we haven't got the time to sit around any longer. There's nothing else for it. We need to see what's inside here, and breaking in is the only answer.'

'But what about those tramps? What if they see us?'

'They won't be bothered about us. Probably all high on meths now anyway and sleeping it off. It's a chance we'll have to take. Now come on, we'd better get cracking.'

Josie froze in horror. The thought of breaking into anyone else's property was against her upbringing. Then she visualised Stanley Rawlings, a smug grin of satisfaction spread across his face, arms swinging loosely by the sides of his immaculate dark grey top coat as he had walked jauntily past them several minutes previously. Then she pictured Sophie and Nelly being confronted by those two awful men, saw herself being declared bankrupt or even worse beaten to a pulp – and all because of an enormous bill that was none of her doing. She raised her head and took a breath.

'Yeah, let's get to it,' she said with relish.

Luck was on their side. After scouring the area, Josie triumphantly lifted up a large pair of bolt cutters some kind soul had left at the side of a vehicle near an automobile repair shop further down the arches.

Stephen beamed. 'Just the job,' he said. 'Remind me to thank the chap who forgot to put them away.' After several moments, the padlock gave way. 'Now for the door,' said Stephen, discarding the chain and broken padlock on the ground. 'We could do with your constable to give us a hand with this one.'

Josie suppressed a giggle. 'I'll go and find him, shall I?' she asked matter-of-factly.

He narrowed his eyes at her then stroked his chin thoughtfully as he slowly shook his head. 'It's a mortice lock, Josie. We'd need a stick of gelignite to blast this open.'

Josie frowned, placed her hand on the door knob and turned. Stephen's jaw dropped open as the door swung open. He turned to her.

'What made you do that?'

She shrugged her shoulders. 'I don't know,' she said, as surprised as he was. She made to step over the threshold. He caught her arm.

'You stay here,' he ordered. 'We don't know what we'll find in there.'

She tugged her arm free. 'And let you take all the glory?'

He sighed loudly as she climbed through the doorway.

The place was in total darkness. Stephen closed the door behind them. 'Try to find the light switch, Josie,' he whispered.

They both felt along the walls, bumping into several obstacles en route. Josie caught her leg several times on hard objects but managed to suffer the pain in silence. Finally Stephen found the light switch and turned it on.

The covered-in cavity was much larger than either had expected and Josie shivered as she lifted her eyes upwards. The arched ceiling loomed eerily above them and she wouldn't have been surprised in the least to have seen bodies suspended from chains bolted into the walls. The whole place reminded her of a medieval dungeon and she desperately wanted to get on with the job in hand and leave as quickly as possible. This mirrored Stephen's thoughts exactly and without a word they proceeded across the dirty concrete floor.

A space at the far end held several work tables, and against the walls Dexian shelving had been erected. This held a variety of objects which Stephen went over to investigate whilst Josie inspected the work tables.

They held an assortment of packaging materials, large white labels, thick black felt pens and sticking tape. Stacked under one of the tables was a pile of oddly shaped parcels. She bent down to examine them. Each one was individually addressed ready for delivery. She straightened up, deep in thought.

281

'You'd better come here,' she heard Stephen say.

She turned and joined him over by the shelving. Silently he nodded towards the variety of objects on the shelves.

Her eyes opened wide as she picked up a can of film and scrutinised it. 'Are they all like this one?'

Stephen nodded. 'And look at this,' he said, pointing further along the shelves.

Josie gazed. 'It's all pornographic, Stephen,' she gasped. 'It's disgusting!'

'Certainly is,' he agreed, running his eyes along a row of sexual implements. 'Looks to me like your uncle is catering for every taste, however depraved.'

Josie turned and leaned heavily against the shelving. 'This is the stuff I'm being chased for payment on from the Brown Paper Packaging Company – the name is just a cover up – isn't it? Why? Why is he doing this?'

'Money, what else? There's big money to be made in this sort of game as long as the police don't catch you at it. But it takes a warped mind to dabble in this kind of material.'

'It takes an even more warped mind to buy the damn stuff,' she fumed.

She noticed Stephen looking intently towards the far end of the workshop.

'What are you looking at?' she asked.

'There's a small recess. Let's take a look.'

They both stood at the entrance and stared inside. Another table stacked with a pile of printed paper; large brown envelopes, the same as they had found in Peter's desk; and an old manual typewriter.

Stephen picked up a printed sheet, turned it towards the light and quickly scanned it. He frowned deeply. He picked up one of the addressed envelopes and tore it open, pulling out the contents. He threw these down and, with Josie looking on bemused, rushed over to the table beneath which sat the pile of parcels. He grabbed at a parcel, again ripping it open. Quickly he studied the contents and nodded in satisfaction.

'So that's his game,' he said.

'What? What's his game?'

'Let's get out of here, Josie. I'll tell you when we get back to your place.'

'No. Tell me now,' she cried exasperatedly.

'I said out – now,' he hissed.

Josie froze, fear overwhelming her. She quickly gathered her wits and did as she was told.

Stephen hurriedly gathered up both the envelope and the parcel

282

he had just opened, extinguished the lights, and once outside put the chain back through the metal loops embedded in the door and balanced the broken padlock. To a distant observer all would look intact. The break-in would hopefully not be discovered until someone arrived to open up the next day.

They hurried home in silence. Once inside her flat, Josie turned on him, her patience finally snapping.

'Tell me now,' she commanded, stooping to light the gas fire.

Throwing the parcel and the envelope on the coffee table, Stephen lowered himself into the armchair.

'From the beginning?' he asked.

'Yes, yes,' she cried. 'Just tell me, Stephen.'

'Right. The way I see it is . . .' He took a deep breath. 'Your uncle's in the mail order business.'

Josie stared at him quizzically. 'What, like the Kay's catalogue?'

'Similar, yes. But he's definitely not selling clothes or furniture. You saw first hand what he's selling.' He leant forward and looked at her keenly. 'I wish I had read that magazine I picked up in Peter's office.'

'Didn't you?' Josie asked, reddening deeply.

'No, I didn't. It's under my bed. I hope my mother doesn't find it. But I've no doubt there's an advertisement in there somewhere.'

'Saying what?'

'Giving a very sketchy outline of the kind of items they sell, enough to whet appetites, and telling people if interested to write in for a catalogue. That's what those printed sheets were, Josie. A list of things they can order.'

'Oh, I'm beginning to see,' she said slowly. 'You could sell that kind of stuff at any price you wanted to name. People would pay, wouldn't they?'

Stephen nodded. 'Yes, without a doubt. It's not as though you can go to Woolworth's and purchase dirty films. Did you notice he had a whole range of items from leather wear right down to the projector to show the films on? I've realised tonight what a devious bastard your uncle really is. He's thought this scam out right down to the last detail. I bet nothing has his name on it. Not one little thing will come down to him. Not even the rental of the lock up.'

'But how . . .' Josie began. 'But surely . . .' She shook her head in frustration. 'Look, going by the parcels we saw, he is sending stuff out. So how is he making money over and above the normal profit?'

'Just bear with me, Josie. All will be clear after I've explained. Now, we've already established that people write in for a catalogue. I bet that was what was in that bulky carrier bag Peter collected the other day. They're paying someone to be a mail drop. Peter then takes the letters back to his office and makes a note of the names

283

and addresses catalogues have been sent to. I think what we found was an old check list, though, because in my view they've moved the whole operation into the arches. Probably because it soon became clear that it was going to prove more lucrative than even they'd imagined.'

'Yeah,' Josie said thoughtfully. 'But if it's so lucrative, why are they moving to Manchester?'

'Could be for several reasons,' Stephen replied. 'The main one is possibly that too many people know them in Leicester, and Manchester is a bigger place to get lost in. I guess they decided on Manchester because of Peter's connection.'

Josie sighed deeply. 'So after they receive the catalogue, people make their order?'

'Yes, and send in the required remittance by postal order. If you look at the bottom of the catalogue I brought home in that envelope, it does stipulate payment will only be accepted by that method. Again, very clever. Anyone can cash a postal order. They probably use many different post offices. But the really good part is . . .'

'Yes?' Josie breathed.

'Well, when the order is received, only the cheapest item is actually mailed out to keep the customer quiet. In that parcel I ripped open there was a note explaining that the other items ordered were out of stock due to huge demand and the residue would be despatched within a certain period of time. It also said that if they want their money back for the items not sent, they can have it. Just to write in and ask.'

'Oh! What's the point of that?'

'They never get their money back, Josie. It's just a delaying tactic. It's all done by post and you know what the post is like. It takes ages. Enough time for your uncle to make a lot of money and then disappear, leaving thousands of dirty old men grossly out of pocket waiting for goods or money they are never going to receive. And who's going to inform the police? No one. They'd be too afraid of the backlash. Their little habits would be made public.'

Josie sat back, circled her arms around her knees and stared into the gas fire. After several moments she turned her attention back to Stephen.

'What are we going to do?'

'Tell the police, Josie.'

'Oh, but . . .'

'No buts, Josie. We have to. Even if it's only to report the fact that your letterheads have been used to order goods without your knowledge. That in itself is illegal. And we must tell them what else we've found out. Innocent people – and I say that lightly, considering the nature of the material that's involved – are being taken for a ride.'

284

'But we can be done for breaking and entering, surely?'

'Yes, we can. But maybe the police will treat us favourably, Josie. Let's hope so.'

She groaned loudly. 'I wish to God I'd never opened that shop. But most of all, I wish to God I'd never had an uncle.' She looked at him hopefully. 'You don't think there's a chance we could be mistaken?'

Stephen shook his head. 'Not a hope. We saw it with our own eyes. It just makes me wonder what he's been up to in the past. I don't think, somehow, this is his first crooked deal.'

Josie grimly shook her head. 'No, I don't think it is either.'

'So we're agreed then? First thing tomorrow morning we'll visit the police station and see what they have to say about all this.'

'Yeah. Then afterwards I'm going to pay a visit to Big Jack.'

'Why?'

Josie breathed deeply. ''Cos I'm sure he knows what happened between my grandmother and my uncle years ago, and once and for all I want to find out about it, for my own satisfaction. I'm gonna make him tell me.'

'Oh, right,' Stephen said, raising his eyebrows in surprise. 'I should be prepared for anything, if I were you.'

'After this, Stephen, I wouldn't be surprised by anything my uncle had done.'

He stood up and stretched himself. 'I'm going to get off, it's after one. You try and get some sleep.'

Josie stood up to join him. 'You could stay here if you wanted? You could use Sue's old room,' she said softly.

Stephen smiled gratefully. 'That offer sounds very inviting. But if I don't go home, my mother, bless her, will have the cops on to me and I'll never hear the last of it.'

Josie smiled to hide her disappointment. 'Okay. I'll see you tomorrow then.'

'Yeah, and put them away safely,' he said, pointing to the parcel and envelope. 'That's our evidence.'

Josie saw him to the door and after a hurried wash climbed gratefully into bed. She somehow managed to put all worrying thoughts to the back of her mind and within moments was fast asleep.

She woke with a start. Someone was banging on the flat door. Bleary-eyed, she fought to read the time on her alarm clock. It read two-thirty. The banging continued and reluctantly she rose, pulled on her dressing gown and plodded towards the door.

She found Sophie, minus her false teeth, her hair flattened beneath a blue hairnet, her faded beige quilted dressing gown pulled tightly around her, standing shivering on the landing.

'What's up, Sophie?' she asked, confused.

'The police. I've 'ad a telephone call. Someone's broke into the shop and they want yer down there.'

Josie groaned loudly. 'Oh, God, no. Have they taken much? Is there much damage?'

Sophie shrugged her shoulders. 'Didn't say. Inspector . . . er . . . I can't remember 'is name, just said you were to go down now and 'e'd be waitin' for yer.'

Josie placed her hand on the old woman's shoulder. 'Okay, thanks, Sophie. I'll get dressed and go down now.'

'I'll come wi' yer.'

'No, no. You go back to bed. I'll be all right.'

'A' yer sure, me duck?'

'I'm sure, Sophie. And thanks.'

Josie shut the door and hurriedly pulled on a pair of slacks and a jumper plus her warm coat. Within ten minutes she was hurrying down the street wishing with all her heart she had transport; even a push bike at this moment would have been a luxury.

The remains of the day's deluge still lingered heavily on the pavements and before long her shoes and the bottom of her trousers were soaking wet. She was extremely agitated and very cold by the time she arrived at The Book Cave. She hesitated in surprise as she took the keys from her pocket. She had expected to see the shop ablaze with light, several policemen wandering around and at the least broken glass scattered across the area. Instead the shop was in darkness, the windows appeared intact and nothing seemed amiss. She frowned deeply.

Cautiously she tried the door. It was unlocked and very slowly she entered, trying to accustom her eyes to the darkness. She wished now she hadn't decided to put bookshelves up against the windows which blocked the light from the lamp outside in the street.

'Inspector,' she called. 'Hello . . . Is anyone there?'

She stopped in the centre of the shop and listened. A sound from behind startled her and she swung round. She heard the click of the shop door as it shut and the snap of the catch being pressed down.

'Who's there?' she uttered, suddenly afraid – very afraid.

She heard the slow plod of footsteps as they advanced towards her and the outline of a figure emerged from the shadows. She placed her hand to her mouth but no scream came forth. She knew the figure, she would know it anywhere and the sight of it standing before her paralysed her with fright. He'd found out. Somehow he had found out that she had discovered his plan. But how?

'Hello, Josie,' Stanley Rawlings said mockingly. 'How nice to see you again.'

She gulped for air, still frozen with shock, her eyes fixed upon

Stanley as he walked past her and opened the connecting door into Peter's office. He held out his hand.

'Come through,' he requested firmly.

Josie unwittingly obeyed him. Without her eyes leaving his face she entered the smaller room, Stanley Rawlings following close behind. He closed the door and stood, legs astride, staring at her.

'Sit down,' he commanded. 'And you can give me those,' he said, reaching forward and snatching the shop keys out of her hand.

Shaking in fear, Josie looked around for the chair to sit upon. It was then she noticed Peter cowering on a stool by the desk; one of hers taken from the other room.

'Peter,' she said, noticing his expression. 'What . . .'

'Sit down and shut up,' Stanley spat. 'I'll do the talking.' He waited while Josie sat down upon the swivel chair next to Peter. 'Now isn't this cosy?' he said sarcastically, his eyes wandering from one to the other. They settled upon Josie and he smiled coldly. 'Couldn't leave well alone, could you, Josephine? You had to poke and pry. Well, my dear, this time it's got you into a whole heap of trouble.' His eyes widened in anger. 'And there's no way you're going to get out of this one,' he spat, banging his fist heavily upon the desk top.

She shivered violently at his savage tone and glanced sideways at Peter. He sat with his head hanging low, hands clasped firmly in his lap. She sensed he knew she was looking at him but he moved not one muscle to acknowledge the fact. It was then that she realised that Peter, like she, was terrified of Stanley Rawlings. They were frightened to such an extent they were both letting the man make utter fools of them.

She suddenly saw Stanley Rawlings for what he was, a paltry bully whose joy in life was seeing other people grovelling to his command. Well, she for one was not going to comply any more. She suddenly didn't care that he knew she had uncovered his secret, or how he knew for that matter. She was tired and wanted to get home. Besides, she wasn't the soft-natured, easily put upon, overweight teenager of several years past, the one who had been overawed by his presence. She was Josie Rawlings, businesswoman, someone of purpose; someone who hadn't the time to sit here and listen to his threats.

She took a deep breath and rose. 'Excuse me,' she said flatly, 'but I haven't the time to sit here and be threatened by you.'

She made to leave the room, but Stanley was upon her and thrusting her forcibly back on to the chair.

'Oh, these are not threats, Josephine. Far from it,' he said icily. He turned to Peter. 'You tell her, Peter. I mean business, don't I?'

Josie cast her eyes in Peter's direction and watched him slowly

287

nod his head, his eyes not leaving the floor.

'You've gone too far this time, my dear,' said Stanley patronisingly. 'No one crosses Stanley Rawlings twice and gets away with it. And don't say I didn't warn you.' He held his hands out in front of him and pressed his fingertips together. 'You've been a very silly girl. You should have given me my mother's book when I asked for it instead of playing grown-up games. You have brought this all on yourself. You've only yourself to blame.'

'And what do you propose to do with me?' she uttered.

Stanley stared at her, his eyebrows raised in surprise. 'Do! Do? Why my dear, get rid of you, of course. I would have thought you would have worked that out by now. After all, I can't risk you going to the police, can I?'

'Stop it!' she cried. 'I've had enough of this. You need help,' she said, waving her hand towards Stanley. She rose and grabbed Peter's arm. 'Come on, we're getting out of here.'

As quick as lightning Stanley screwed his fist into a ball, swung back his arm and punched her on the jaw. She fell back on to the chair, her eyes glazed with shock, the pain of the blow stunning her for several seconds. She felt the stickiness of blood.

'Now, tell her, Peter,' he growled. 'Tell her I mean business.'

'He does, Josie. He does,' Peter whimpered.

Stanley strode back across the room, placed his hands on the door, took several deep breaths, turned and smiled at them, his cold grey eyes unblinking.

'Now, as I was saying,' he continued tonelessly, eyeing the pair in satisfaction as they sat shaking in their seats, Josie gently rubbing the colourful bruise that was beginning to form on her chin, 'that was a lucky stroke, my returning to the arches like that. It was pure chance. But I suddenly remembered I hadn't locked the door properly. Too much on my mind, you see, and it was a careless mistake, anyone could have broken in. And they did, didn't they? I returned to find two thieves had broken into my premises.' He clicked his tongue several times. 'I can't have that, can I? Thieves must be punished.' He walked slowly towards the back of the room and then turned. 'We're going to have a nice little fire. And when the fire is out, what shall we find but two dead bodies?'

Peter jumped up in alarm. 'You're going to kill us!' he cried.

Stanley turned on him. 'Well, what did you think I was going to do? Throw you a party?' he said icily, his eyes narrowing in disgust. 'Ah, for God's sake, you whimpering little queer. I don't need you any more. Like her,' he said, thrusting a finger towards Josie, 'you've served your purpose. I only needed you to get to her. I couldn't believe my luck when you told me she was rooming in the same house as you.' He smirked wickedly. 'And you thought I wanted you for yourself? Ugh, you make me sick.'

Peter let out a sob of anguish. 'But I love you,' he wailed.

'Love! What a fool,' Stanley laughed. 'Can't you get it through your thick head that I used you. You were my passport to her and you came up trumps.' He turned to Josie. 'I knew practically every move you made, my dear. Who do you think it was who suggested Peter use your back room? It certainly wasn't him. He hasn't the brains.' He gave a bellowing laugh, 'The poor soul didn't even know we were related.'

Josie turned to Peter.

He looked at her through tear-filled eyes. 'I'm sorry, Josie,' he whispered. 'I didn't know. I swear I didn't.'

'Was it you who stole my headed paper and ordered that stuff?' she asked him.

'What?' Peter replied, bewildered.

'Oh, no, Josephine. I did that. It was so easy. Peter willingly showed me around his friend's book shop late one night. I must say I was very impressed. Not bad for a little upstart who murdered her grandmother.'

Josie's breath caught in her throat. 'You know that's not true,' she gasped.

'Do I?' His eyes narrowed in malice. 'Well, I can promise you, your death won't be put down to natural causes.' He looked at Peter, sobbing quietly into a large white handkerchief. 'And as for you, you snivelling little toe rag! Just wait 'til you find out what I have in store for you!' He placed his hand inside his jacket pocket and pulled out a hand gun. From his other pocket he took a silencer and screwed it firmly in place. He raised the gun and pointed it at Peter.

'Get up,' he commanded. When Peter didn't move, he repeated his request savagely. 'I said, get up.'

Peter struggled up, his sobs rising hysterically.

'Through here,' said Stanley, opening the door into the main shop.

Peter stumbled blindly past him and into the darkened room.

Stanley turned to Josie. 'Move and I shoot him. And you needn't bother trying the back door, it's locked and I have the key.'

She sat rigidly on the chair, her mind seeking frantically for a way out of this mess. She had no doubt that her uncle intended to kill them both. And there would be no one racing to their rescue. Apart from Sophie, tucked safely in bed, no one knew where she was.

She heard a slosh of petrol and pungent fumes rose. She choked as they caught the back of her throat and froze in horror. He really was going ahead with this. He really was going to set light to her beautiful book shop and leave them both to die. Her eyes darted around the room, but she knew it was useless. The only way out was through The Book Cave.

She heard the sound of the petrol can being thrown to the floor and the next moment Peter was being thrust forcibly back into the room. He fell against the desk, pleading with Stanley to spare his life. Stanley stared coldly at him, raised his gun and fired. Josie jumped up and screamed as Peter clutched his hand to his chest and fell backwards.

Stanley raised his head, pulled out a large cloth from his pocket, and wiped the gun. 'Here, catch,' he shouted suddenly, throwing the gun at Josie.

Instinctively she caught the weapon and stared down at it. She raised her eyes to Stanley who was smiling mockingly at her.

'If by chance you're rescued from the flames, which I doubt very much, it's your fingerprints on the gun. Explain that away, my dear.'

With that he turned and walked through the door, closing it behind him.

Hysteria rose rapidly within her. The gun slipped from her fingers on to the floor and she stared blindly at it. An overwhelming desire to live overtook her fear and somehow she found the use of her legs and made a dive for the door. She inched it open. Her uncle was standing in the centre of the room, a spool of paper in his hand. She saw him reach into his pocket and pull out a box of matches. He lit one, ignited the paper and stared at it for several seconds as it roared into life. He threw the burning paper on to a pile of petrol-soaked rags by the far bookcase. With a whoosh, it caught fire.

Josie squeezed her eyes tightly shut, pulled the door to and sank down on to her knees, awash with grief and anguish for the shop and the situation she found herself in. Her eyes fell upon Peter, sprawled upon the floor, bright red blood seeping through his yellow jumper.

On hands and knees, she crawled towards him and lifted his head.

'Peter, Peter,' she coaxed. 'Speak to me.'

He slowly opened his eyes. 'He shot me,' he whispered in disbelief, staring at his bloodstained hand.

'Never mind that now, we have to get out of here. Have you another key to the back door? Peter, Peter. Answer me. Have you another key?'

He blinked his eyes slowly. 'No,' he mouthed. 'Stanley took it from me.'

Suddenly a loud wail of protest rent the air and Josie's head jerked up. It had come from the other room. She gently lowered

Peter's head and moved towards the door. She placed her ear against it. She could hear the crackle and hiss of flames and the door was already warm.

She gulped several times and, holding her breath, made a grab for the door handle. She inched the door open and peered through the crack.

The trays loaded with books by the side wall and the two book-shelves by the right front window were ablaze, flames already licking across the ceiling. Thick black smoke swirled around and she shut the door quickly and gasped for breath. The shouts of protest came again, followed by several obscenities. She knew they could only have come from Stanley. He was in serious trouble and suddenly she knew why. He could not open the faulty snib on the door. He was as trapped as they were.

She inched open the door again and through the swirl of smoke saw him struggling with the catch. He jumped back and kicked his foot against the toughened glass panel in temper, looking around for something to throw to break the glass. But there was nothing. The stools he could have used he had moved into the back room for them to sit on earlier.

Without warning there was a loud explosion and the bookshelf nearest the wall, complete with burning books, crashed down. Stanley leapt backwards in shock and as he did so lost his balance. Desperately trying to keep his stance, his shoulder caught the corner of the other burning bookshelf and the movement made it overbalance. It disintegrated, sending down a cascade of flaming timber and paper on top of him. He hadn't a chance. His clothes ignited in a ball of flames, his screams of anguish and excruciating pain filling the air.

Josie's stomach heaved and she quickly shut the door and placed her back against it, shuddering violently as she fought for breath, her mind racing frantically for a solution. She had just witnessed the most horrific scene and if she didn't do something, and quick, the same thing would happen to her and Peter. They were not going to be miraculously saved at the very last moment. That only happened in fairy stories and she couldn't die such a horrible death without putting up a fight.

Smoke was already pouring under the door and she knew time was running out. Her eyes alighted on the kettle in the corner and an idea formed. She prayed it just might work.

Pulling off her coat, she grabbed at the kettle and emptied the water over the material, plus a half empty pint of milk. She held it over her head and, taking several deep breaths, opened the connecting door. She pressed herself through it, closed the door shut behind her and threw herself down on the floor, conscious of the shower of burning splinters of wood and debris that was falling around her. Her heart thumped painfully and the thick smoke made her eyes smart.

Slowly, skirting around to the left where the fire was just taking hold, she crawled along the floor towards the front door. If she could just manage to reach it she could summon help for them both. The smoke thickened and the heat of the flames scorched her skin but the desperate longing for survival and the need to save Peter kept her moving forward.

Her progress was slow, hampered by the acrid smoke and the heat which was becoming unbearable; her nose was pressed right against the floor in the hope of catching any air that had been forced down there. She knew that shortly the ceiling would surely collapse on top of her, it couldn't hold out forever.

Suddenly her fingertips felt hot glass. She had reached the door and renewed hope for their safety overwhelmed her. With rasping short breaths, her smoke-filled lungs about to burst, she clawed her way upright and felt for the snib. Under an expert twist of her fingers the hot metal gave way and the door burst open. With all the energy she could muster she threw herself out into the street just as the cold blast of air fuelled the flames to fresh intensity and the ceiling collapsed with a crash.

Prostrate, in the middle of the road, she struggled to raise her head. Hazily she saw figures clad in nightclothes rushing towards her, inaudible shouts of anguish and distress filling the air. Unseen hands grabbed at her and she was forcibly dragged further across the gravelled surface of the road. She felt her skin tear as the tiny stones found their mark. From a distance the sound of loud sirens reached her ears. She struggled to rise.

'Peter, Peter,' she rasped, looking pleadingly into unknown eyes. 'He's . . . he's still . . . in the back. Please, please . . . get him out,' she begged.

Her head swam and her legs buckled beneath her as she fell in a heap to the ground.

Chapter Thirty-Six

Doctor Samuel Boothby scanned quickly over the clipboard he was holding then rested his kindly eyes upon his patient.

'You've been very lucky, my dear,' he addressed her. 'Your chin is just badly bruised. You'll have a few scars on your legs to tell the tale, and of course a very sore throat for a day or so, but apart from that you should make a full recovery. We'll keep you in for a few days for observation.'

Josie painfully nodded her head, a smell of singed hair wafting to her nostrils. 'Peter?' she rasped hesitantly with pleading eyes.

Doctor Boothby sighed softly as he shook his head and perched on the edge of her bed. 'He's in a bad way, my dear. But be assured, we're doing our best.' He placed a hand gently on her arm. 'He lost a lot of blood from the bullet wound and unfortunately by the time the fire brigade got to him, the smoke had done its worst.' He smiled wanly. 'He has talked to the police, though God knows how.'

'He has?' Josie whispered, trying to raise her head.

The doctor nodded. 'Yes, he's managed to explain what happened. You're in the clear, my dear. I've no doubt they'll want to talk to you later. But I won't allow that until you've had a good rest.'

Josie sank back against the pillows. If the doctor had let the police talk to Peter, then . . . then . . . She turned her eyes towards him.

'You don't expect him to live, do you?' she asked feebly.

The doctor shook his head. 'No. No, we don't. It's no good saying otherwise.'

'Can I see him?'

'It's not wise, my dear. Not just at the moment. He's in a very bad way and you're still in shock yourself.'

'Please, doctor. Please let me see him,' she croaked. 'If . . . if he dies, I might not get a chance to make my peace with him.'

The doctor stared at her thoughtfully. 'All right. But just for a moment.' He rose and replaced the clipboard on the end of her bed and left the room. Several moments later he was back with a nurse pushing a wheelchair.

Slowly they helped Josie lower her pain-racked body into the chair and covered her up with a blanket.

'All right, my love?' the nurse asked kindly.

Josie nodded and they pushed her carefully out of the room.

Josie was not prepared for the sight that met her eyes. Peter, his chest encased in thick bandages, drips and tubes protruding from his arms, several monitors bleeping from the side of his bed, lay almost lifeless upon the snow white pillows, his face ashen and drawn. He looked far older than his twenty-five years and she choked back a cry of anguish. Her uncle had done this to him. He was solely to blame for this state of affairs and for the first time she was glad he was dead. Uncharacteristically, she prayed he was trapped in hell, suffering eternally for the pain and suffering he had caused because of his greed and total indifference to anyone other than himself.

The policeman sitting by Peter's side smiled briefly at her as she was pushed forward.

She stared at her friend for several moments before she took a painful breath. 'Peter,' she murmured hoarsely. 'Peter, it's me, Josie.'

Slowly he opened pain-filled eyes and settled them upon her. The shame written across his face spoke volumes. 'Josie . . . I'm . . . so sorry,' he gasped breathlessly, his eyes pleading for forgiveness.

'Don't, don't,' she whispered sadly. 'It wasn't your fault. I don't blame you. Please, just get better. Please, Peter,' she said with deep emotion.

She watched as his eyes slowly closed, and her body sagged. She raised her face to the doctor who motioned to the nurse and she was wheeled away.

Back in her own bed, the nurse handed Josie two yellow tablets and a glass of water which she accepted without a murmur.

'They'll give you a good sleep,' the nurse said firmly as she tucked the blankets around the cage that covered her legs. 'Try to lie still, now. Give your burns a chance to heal,' she said soothingly.

Josie lay back against the pillows, waiting for the tablets to take effect. She didn't care whether she ever woke again. At this moment she felt she had nothing to live for.

But she did wake, twelve hours later, to find Sophie sitting by her bed.

The old lady sighed with relief as she watched Josie slowly open her eyes. 'How yer feelin', me duck?' she asked with deep concern.

Josie focused her eyes. She felt stiff, the burns on her legs smarted painfully, and her throat was very sore. It felt as though all the skin had been ripped from it, leaving the red raw remains underneath. For several seconds she wondered where she was and what Sophie was doing sitting by her bed. Then memories flooded back and she closed her swollen eyes.

'Oh, you didn't 'alf give us a scare,' Sophie said in a worried voice. 'I'll never forgive meself for not goin' with yer. I should have insisted. I know I should 'ave,' she blurted as she awkwardly rose and poured a glass of water. 'Stephen's beside 'imself, poor lad. He can't understand why you never fetched 'im neither, considerin' what was goin' on.'

She held the glass to Josie's lips and watched intently as she took several sips.

'Stephen – he knows what's happened?' Josie rasped.

'Yes, I went round and told 'im, and right upset 'e is too. 'E's bin sittin' wi' me by yer bed for 'alf the night, but I made 'im go 'ome to get a bit of sleep. 'E should be back shortly.' She sighed deeply. 'Oh, Josie love, I blame meself. I should 'ave come with yer.'

Exhausted, Josie sagged back against the pillows. She managed to raise her arm and placed her hand on the other woman's. 'It's all right, Sophie,' she wheezed as she broke into a painful coughing fit. 'Sense should have told me not to go. But I never gave it a thought. I was just too annoyed at the thought that someone had broken into my shop.'

Sophie sniffed loudly and lowered herself on to the chair by the bed. 'When they let you out, me and Nelly are gonna make sure you have plenty of rest. I've made meself a bed up in me living room and you're havin' me bedroom where I can keep an eye on yer.'

Josie slowly shook her head. 'There's no need for that. At the moment, Sophie, I just want to be by myself. But I do appreciate the offer.'

Before Sophie could respond, Stephen walked through the door. He stared at Josie, relief appearing on his face when he saw she was awake. He put down a bunch of flowers on the cabinet and smiled fondly. 'You look awful,' he said, laughter in his voice.

Josie swallowed. 'Thanks,' she croaked.

'How do you feel?' he asked, concerned.

'Just like I look,' she replied flatly. She looked hesitantly at them both. 'Peter,' she whispered. 'Any news . . .'

Sophie and Stephen glanced at each other.

Sophie grasped her hand. 'He died, Josie love,' she said gravely, Stephen looking on helplessly. 'Early this mornin', while you were still sleepin'.'

Tears welled up and flooded over. 'Oh, no, no,' she wailed. 'Poor Peter. Poor, poor Peter.'

She closed her eyes tightly, trying to shut out the vision of Peter's happy smiling face swimming before her. She couldn't believe he was dead; that she would never again listen in fascination as he played his guitar or hear his high-pitched voice call her 'darling'. He would no longer simply be there as a dear friend.

Uncontrollable grief overtook her.

Two days later she had a visitor. She heard Gwen Bates' high heels tapping across the floor long before the woman thrust open the door of the small room Josie occupied at the end of the ward. Gwen stared at Josie in horror before she threw herself upon her and planted a kiss on her sore cheek, leaving the stain of bright red lipstick.

'My God,' she exclaimed sharply, laying a large bunch of flowers on the cabinet. 'But you do look a sight, me duck!' She shook her head grimly as she pulled off her gloves and sat on the chair next to the bed. 'Thank God that bastard perished in the fire or he'd have suffered a worse fate from our Jack.' She eyed Josie warmly. 'Now, is there 'ote you need, gel?'

Josie shook her head. 'No thanks, Gwen. But it's nice to see you.'

She smiled. 'I wanted to come as soon as I heard, but the 'ospital said not to, that you needed your rest. Jack sends 'is apologies. 'E couldn't leave the garage. Anyway, we 'ad a talk. Me and Jack, that is. And we want you to come and spend some time with us, 'til yer better like.' She raised her hand. 'Now, no buts, it's all settled. Jack'll fetch yer in the car as soon as they say you can come 'ome.'

Josie smiled at her fondly. 'Gwen, I appreciate your offer, but I can't. I've already turned down Sophie's. If I accept yours, I'll upset her. To be honest, I just want to be by myself for a while.'

Gwen sniffed. 'Oh, well, suit yerself. But the offer still stands should yer change yer mind.' She stared around the room in admiration. 'Not bad in 'ere, is it? Bit like a private room. Does it 'ave tea makin' facilities?'

Josie tried not to laugh for fear of cracking open the sores on her lips. 'The trolley'll be around soon. I'll see if I can scrounge you a cup.'

'Good. I could do with one. And I'll have a couple of those nice chocolate digestives on yer locker to go with it.' She loosened her best brown woollen coat, smoothing flat its broad dark mink collar. 'We're all sorry about yer shop, Josie,' she said sincerely. She shook her head sadly. 'It's a tragedy, it really is, 'specially after all the 'ard work you put into it. We couldn't believe it when we 'eard.' She pursed her lips together. 'But as for that Stanley . . . well . . . I knew 'e were capable of doin' some rotten things, but to shoot the poor young man in cold blood then set fire to yer shop!' She shook her head savagely. 'It defies belief, it really does. You're in the clear though, ain't yer, Josie?'

Josie nodded. 'I spoke to the police at length this morning.

They're quite happy I'm not implicated in any way.' She stifled a sob. 'It was Peter's doing. Despite his injuries, he managed to tell the police the whole story.'

Gwen folded her arms under her ample bosom. 'I should bloody think so,' she said grimly. 'I'm not sayin' 'e deserved to get killed for what 'e did. But after all, 'e was as much to blame for what 'appened, weren't 'e?'

'No, no. That's where you're wrong, Gwen,' Josie said sharply. 'Peter had no idea that Stanley was my uncle, or that he used my letterheads to order the stuff and leave me with the bill. As far as Peter was concerned, he was only using my back room free of rent.'

'Oh, come off it, Josie. I weren't born yesterday. That lad must 'ave known what Stanley was doin'. From what I can gather, 'e 'elped tek the orders and send 'em out. All that stuff wa' pornographic. A' yer tryin' to tell me the lad wore a blindfold all the time 'e was 'andling the goods?'

Josie looked hard at her. Gwen was right. In a way Peter was as guilty as Stanley, but in another respect he was as innocent as she was. She grabbed a glass of water and gulped it down. All this talking wasn't doing her throat any good at all, and besides, she could spend hours trying to make Gwen see her side of the story and the woman wouldn't be convinced. Her mind was set. Peter was guilty as charged and that was that.

Gwen noticed with concern that Josie had grown quiet and wondered if she had gone too far.

'Look, I'm sorry, Josie love,' she said softly. 'Peter was a friend of yours and it must 'ave been a shock to find out all this was goin' on behind yer back. But at least 'e managed to clear yer name and we must be thankful for that.' She sighed deeply. 'I'm just glad yer gran's not around to witness this. If she 'adn't been dead already, this latest episode would surely 'ave killed 'er.'

Josie eyed Gwen quizzically and decided to seize her chance. 'Latest episode?' she repeated. 'D'you mean Stanley's done this kind of thing before?'

Gwen inhaled sharply. 'Did I say 'e 'ad?' she blurted.

'No. Not in so many words. But that's what you implied.' Josie swallowed hard. 'Gwen,' she said hoarsely, 'please tell me about my grandmother and Stanley? What did go off between them? I know you know all about it.'

'I know nothing, Josie. What yer askin' me for?' Gwen's eyes darted wildly around the room. 'Can yer smoke in 'ere?' she blustered, diving in her handbag and pulling out a packet of Park Drive. She lit one and drew on it hungrily. 'Are they feedin' yer all right?' she asked lightly. 'By the looks on yer, gel, you could do with a few good dinners inside yer.'

'The food's not bad,' Josie replied. 'But stop avoiding my

question, Gwen. I know something awful happened and I need to know what. Please, please tell me.'

Gwen sniffed loudly, lowered her eyes and stared hard at the floor. 'I can't, me duck. Our Jack'd kill me. 'E idolised yer grandmother.'

'I won't breathe a word, Gwen. Honest, I promise.'

Gwen drew hard on her cigarette, threw the stub on the floor and ground it out with her stiletto heel. She picked up the remains and put them in a paper rubbish bag hanging from Josie's locker. She raised her eyes.

'If I tell yer, Josie, d'yer swear you'll never repeat what I say? It's yer gran's memory I'm thinking of,' she said, then scowled deeply. 'Plus the fact that Jack would strangle me if 'e found out I'd blabbed.'

'I swear,' Josie said with conviction.

'Okay. I can see you'll not rest until I do and you've a right to know, me duck. Although I don't think you're goin' to like what I 'ave to say.' She lit another cigarette and blew a long plume of smoke across the room. She settled her gaze on Josie's bruised chin. She took a deep breath. 'Yer Uncle Stanley was always a little bleeder,' she began. 'I should know, I was at school wi' 'im and 'e terrorised the life out of the other kids. Usually ones younger than 'imself.'

'Doing what?'

'Demandin' money with threats, that sort a' thing. Your gran was always bein' summoned up the school. Nobody was surprised when 'e got expelled.' She sighed loudly. 'It broke yer gran's 'eart. She 'ad 'igh 'opes of 'er son.'

'What about me grandad? Could he not have knocked some sense into him?'

'No one could handle Stanley. Least of all yer grandad. Besides, 'e 'ated the sight of 'im. Did so right from the moment 'e wa' born.'

'Why?' Josie asked, horrified.

Gwen shrugged her shoulders. 'Don't know, me duck. Just summat about the lad, I suppose. 'E wa' a good-lookin' little boy but . . .'

'But what?'

''E 'ad . . . er . . . a kinda . . . arrogance, yes, that's the word, arrogance about 'im. And, boy, could 'e throw a tantrum if 'e didn't get 'is own way.' She stubbed out her cigarette the same as before and looked towards the door. 'Is that tea ever goin' to come?' She turned back to Josie. 'Shall I go and 'ave a look down the corridor?'

'She'll be here shortly, it's not quite time yet.' Josie inched herself gingerly up against her pillows. 'What happened after he left school?'

298

'Hmm. Well, for a couple of years 'e 'elped out on the stall and 'e seemed to settle down. That's when yer gran decided to start up the van sales to give 'im more responsibility. Your grandad was right poorly around this time and Lily, bless her, was up to 'er eyes in it. Maize – yer mother – took complete charge of the stall, with you in tow.' Gwen laughed. 'Oh, you were a sweet little thing, Josie Rawlings. We women all used to beg yer mam to let us tek yer for a walk.' She laughed again at Josie's red face. 'Anyway,' she continued, 'with the stall taken care of, and Stanley doin' the van sales, yer gran wa' free to concentrate on your grandad and she spent most of her time up the 'ospital. She also, for the time bein', entrusted Stanley with collecting her dues from 'er clients.' She leaned back in her chair. 'And everything was hunky dory, or so everyone thought.' She paused. 'Until . . .'

'Until what?'

Gwen ran her hand over her chin. 'A little birdie whispered a warnin' in yer gran's ear. Seems young Stanley was doin' a first class job sellin' the fruit and veggies, but as a sideline, 'e was also supplying cut price booze and fags, all dropped off the back of a lorry, of course. Nice little earner 'e 'ad goin'. And that's not all.'

'Not all!' Josie exclaimed.

'No, far from it. The bugger 'ad only raised the interest rates on the loans. Told everyone it was on instructions from yer gran. Only a copper or two, but it wa' enough to line 'is pockets. You sure 'ad 'is card marked when you guessed, and rightly so, what 'e would 'ave done if 'e'd got 'old of yer gran's notebook.'

'I knew it. I just knew that's what he'd do. I'm glad I put a stop to him.'

'You and everyone else concerned,' Gwen said gravely. 'Anyway, yer gran wa' fumin' when she found out. She went chargin' back to the 'ouse, ready to give 'im a pastin'. She wa' gonna knock 'im to kingdom come.'

'And that's when they stopped speakin', was it? I can't say as I blame 'er.'

Gwen shook her head and eyed Josie worriedly. 'Oh, no, Josie. I ain't finished yet.'

Just then the door shot open and the tea lady bustled through.

Gwen pounced on the rosy-cheeked, jolly woman and seconds later they sat nursing cups of tea and chunks of Madeira slab cake, plus Gwen had two of the chocolate digestives. Josie hadn't the stomach for hers and pushed it upon her visitor who accepted readily.

'Sure you don't want it?' she asked with her mouth full.

'No, thanks. Can you just get on with the rest of the story?'

'Okay, okay,' Gwen said defensively. She put down her plate and continued. 'When she reached 'ome, she knew Stanley wa' in 'cos the van wa' parked outside. So she crept in to catch 'im on the 'op.' She stopped abruptly. 'I ain't 'appy about tellin' yer the rest, Josie. It ain't for the likes of your young ears.'

'You can't stop now, Gwen,' Josie erupted.

Gwen pursed her lips. 'Well, don't say I didn't warn yer.' She clasped her hands together. 'It were yer gran who got the shock, Josie. When she charged into the livin' room . . .'

'Yes?'

Gwen swallowed hard and took a deep breath. 'Two young boys were rolling around the floor. They were naked, Josie. Fornicatin', they were.'

Josie held her breath, stunned, even though she had been expecting something of this nature, considering Stanley's association with Peter.

'So my gran caught Stanley having sex with another male?' she uttered.

Gwen shook her head. 'No, Josie.'

She frowned. 'No!'

'Stanley . . . well, 'e wa' watchin', Josie. 'E'd paid those two young boys to perform for 'im. And apparently it wasn't the first time. Sometimes, 'e'd 'ave two girls or a boy and a girl. It didn't seem to matter to 'im. Stanley didn't like sex, full stop, Josie. 'E got 'is kicks from watchin' other people doin' it.'

Josie paled in shock. 'Oh, my poor grandmother,' she gasped. She looked at Gwen, eyes wide in horror. 'He was a pervert, wasn't he, Gwen? Just a rotten, dirty pervert.'

'Of the 'ighest order, Josie love, and that's when yer gran chucked 'im out and told 'im never to darken 'er door again. 'Course, she never told your grandad or your mother the full story. She couldn't, could she? She unburdened 'erself to me and Jack. She trusted us, you see, Josie, and we swore never to tell a livin' soul.' She raised her eyes, ashamed. 'I've broke me promise to yer gran, Josie.'

'Under pressure from me, Gwen, and I'm sure Gran would have understood,' she whispered reassuringly. 'I needed to know the whole truth to make sense of what he did to me.' She sighed deeply and ran her hand slowly through her ruined hair. 'But I can't understand why he married Hilda. It doesn't make sense.'

'To put up a front, Josie. That was all 'e married poor timid little Hilda for. And it worked. There was never any rumours going round about Stanley.' She shook her head savagely. ''E ruined that poor woman's life, and young Marilyn's into the bargain,' she said harshly. 'I ain't surprised she turned out the way she did. 'Aving 'im for a father.'

Josie eyed Gwen thoughtfully. 'Stanley was her father then? I'm only querying it in the light of what you told me about him.'

'Oh, yes.' Gwen spoke firmly. 'Hilda wa' as pure as the driven snow on 'er weddin' night, I can vouch for that. No other man 'ad ever before looked at 'er twice. That's why she wa' so keen to marry 'im. She couldn't believe her luck. After all, 'e wa' a good-looking man, Josie, and Hilda, like most other people, hadn't a clue about his true nature, although I tried me best to warn 'er.'

'Wouldn't she listen?'

Gwen shook her head. 'No. She was besotted. Stanley 'ad well and truly pulled the wool over 'er eyes. It probably near killed him to touch 'er. But once 'e'd done 'is duty and got 'er pregnant, nobody could question 'is sexual 'abits, could they? And 'e black-mailed yer gran for years. Either she paid up or 'e'd spill the beans and bring the whole family into disgrace. Said 'e couldn't give a monkey's what people knew about 'im and 'e were serious, yer gran wa' in no doubt about that. So she paid up for yours and Maisie's sake, just like 'e knew she would. She couldn't bear the thought of any stigma attached to your names.'

Gwen cleared her throat, reached for a tissue and blew her nose. She raised her eyes. 'Now you know it all, Josie, and you must keep yer promise.'

'Don't worry, Gwen.' She spoke quietly. 'I wouldn't tell a living soul any of this. But I thank you for being honest with me. I know it must have been hard, considering your promise to Gran.'

Gwen leant over and patted her arm. 'It was, me duck. I can't say as I enjoyed it, and I don't expect for one minute you did either. No one likes 'earing tales about members of their family.' She smiled warmly. 'But you just be thankful, my girl, that you ain't got one ounce of 'im in yer. You're a good 'un, Josie. One of the best. Yer mother and grandmother were proud of yer, and would be even more so if they were both still alive. You've come up trumps despite all that's 'appened.'

Josie reddened. 'Thanks, Gwen,' she said.

Gwen rose and gathered her belongings. 'Now I'd better go before that sister chucks me out. I'm sure she's been trained by the Gestapo.'

'What, Sister Chidicks?' Josie tutted loudly. 'She's a softie, she is. Can't do enough for me.'

'Ah, well, you're a patient. We visitors are intruders, Josie. Anyway, I'm goin' before I get it in the neck. Now don't forget me offer. It still stands should you get fed up wi' Sophie's fussin'.' She leaned over and kissed Josie on the cheek, straightened up and tapped the side of her nose. 'Now don't ever forget. Mum's the word.'

'I won't, Gwen. See you soon, and thanks for coming.'

Long after Gwen had departed, Josie mulled over the tale. If it had come from anyone but Gwen she would have had a job to believe it. Finally everything slotted into place in her mind and she was more than ever glad Stanley was dead. She was grateful for the fact he was no longer around to ruin any more lives. He had been an evil man, and evil men didn't deserve any compassion, she thought with conviction. Her grief was for Peter; for the friend she had lost and for the fact he had lost his life so young and so tragically, and all because he had fallen in love. She would miss him dreadfully.

Her thoughts were disturbed by Sister Chidicks as she bustled through the door and began to straighten her covers.

'Doctor's orders,' she said sharply, with a twinkle in her eyes. 'You're to eat all your dinner tonight, my girl. Cauliflower cheese. Now how does that sound?'

Scrumptious, Josie thought disgustedly. What she would give for a plate of Sophie's steak and chips.

Chapter Thirty-Seven

Two weeks later, Josie sat at the table, an unopened packet of biscuits and a jam swiss roll on a plate next to a pot of tea. She smoothed out the letter she had received that morning and re-read it for the third time.

Sue was having a wonderful time. She and Bruce were made for each other and emigrating to Australia was the best decision she had ever made. The sheep farm was massive, so massive that she still hadn't seen all over it. She had learned to ride a horse and was becoming accustomed to the heat and flies. The food wasn't up to much and she sorely missed English fish and chips and the mounds of bubble and squeak they used to cook in her old frying pan. Otherwise the life suited her and she had no intention of ever leaving. But most of all, she wrote with feeling, she missed Josie.

Josie re-read again the paragraph that followed. She leaned back in her chair and absent-mindedly reached for the jam swiss roll. She ripped open the cellophane and cut a large slice.

Sue wanted her to come to Australia. She more than wanted, she was begging. There was a job waiting. A roof over her head and plenty of freedom and sunshine. How could she refuse? Sue begged her to come to a new life which she'd be a fool not to accept.

It sounded so inviting. After all, what had she left here? Her friends were scattered around the globe. There was nothing left of her shop but ashes and she rattled around the flat aimlessly, wondering what to do to fill her day. The thought of getting a job didn't excite her in the least. At the moment it was a miracle that she actually rose each morning. And as for Stephen, she knew he only visited because he felt sorry for her, and that once she was fully recovered his visits would cease.

Sighing, she folded up the letter and put it back in the envelope. She got up and went and stood before the bathroom mirror. She looked a mess. Her skin looked grey and taut, her hair needed washing and her clothes a good press. She was letting herself go and she knew it. But she hadn't enough enthusiasm to do anything about it.

Her face had just about returned to normal. The blackened

bruise, having turned purple then yellow, had now receded and only a faint outline remained. In several days it would be gone. Not so the red weals on her legs where the burning timbers had rained down, nor her nightmares.

They were still very vivid and would take many months to fade, as the doctor had gently pointed out. She doubted whether they would ever go. How could she forget the sight of her shop ablaze or the screams of her uncle as he met his horrific end?

She shuddered and retraced her steps. If she didn't do something soon she would go mad. She needed something to occupy her mind. Maybe Sue was right, she thought. Maybe Australia was the answer. Maybe she did need to get away from her past and begin a new life.

Just then Sophie bustled through the door.

'Stephen's 'ere,' she said, smiling fondly. ''E's just 'aving a natter with Nelly. That's the third time this week 'e's come round.'

Josie sighed. 'It's just a friendly gesture, Sophie. 'Til I'm on my feet properly. D'you want some tea?'

'No, ta, love. I'm up to 'ere wi' tea,' she replied, thrusting her hand under her chin. 'Nelly's not 'appy unless the kettle's permanently on. Ah, 'ere 'e is. Come on in, Stephen,' she shouted.

He strode through and smiled at the two women. 'Nelly says to tell you the tea's mashed.'

Sophie grimaced. 'I'm sure she wants to drown me,' she muttered as she departed.

Stephen sat down in the armchair by the fire. 'How are you today?' he asked.

'Fine,' Josie said curtly. She sat down opposite him. 'Look, Stephen, you don't have to keep coming round, you know. I'm all right now. Really I am.'

'It's no trouble to me,' he replied lightly. 'Besides I have come round for a reason. There's something I want to ask you.'

'Oh?'

He cleared his throat. 'Is that tea?' he asked, eyeing the teapot. 'And I wouldn't mind a piece of that cake.'

Josie stood up and reluctantly poured him a cup, and cut a thick slice of the jam roll. She passed them to him and returned to her seat.

'What was it you wanted to ask me?'

Stephen took a bite of the cake and a gulp of his tea. 'That's better,' he said. 'I came straight round after parking my van. I've not done badly today. If it carries on like this, I'll soon get my restaurant.'

'Stephen,' Josie cut in impatiently.

He placed his mug on the hearth and stared into the fire. He turned his gaze to meet hers.

'I want your advice.'

'Oh?'

He eyed her for a moment before he spoke. 'I'm thinking of getting married,' he said slowly. 'And I want to ask you how I should go about it? I don't want to make a hash of it, you see.'

An icy lump settled in the pit of her stomach. 'Why me?' she asked abruptly.

'Well, you're a woman. If you were getting a proposal, would you want it to be a romantic one or doesn't it matter?'

Oh, God, she groaned inwardly. Of all the questions to be asking her. The man facing her had no idea that she loved him with all her being, that she worshipped the ground he walked on and had done so since childhood. A surge of anger mounted. She wanted to scream at him for the further hurt he was causing her. How dare he ask her this question, and in aid of another woman? She fought the tears of frustration that threatened. After all she had gone through, she now had to face seeing the man she adored walking down the aisle with someone else. Well, that was something she couldn't and wouldn't face. She would make sure she was gone long before this happy event took place. She rose abruptly and stood with her back to the fire.

'It doesn't matter, Stephen,' she said coldly.

'What doesn't matter?'

'How you propose. If she loves you enough, it won't matter how you do it.'

He stood up to face her. 'Thanks, Josie. You've told me exactly what I wanted to know.' He placed his hands on her arms. 'And she does love me. Nearly, I'd say, as much as I love her.'

He turned and walked away and left her staring after him.

She grabbed a pad of writing paper from the sideboard and sat down at the table.

Dear Sue,
    Thanks for your offer, I accept . . .

Later that night, Josie sat dozing in the chair. The letter to Sue lay on the table ready to be posted. Sunday Night at the London Palladium flickered from the black and white television screen; Shirley Bassey was strutting her stuff in a near non-existent dress, singing, 'I Who Have Nothing'.

Josie stared blankly. The magnetic star could have been singing about her. That was exactly what she felt like. Like the words of the song, she had nothing and no one to call her own.

She sighed, got up and switched off the set. In all her twenty-three years, with all she had gone through – the loss of her mother and grandmother, losing her home and her job, the business with

Terry, and the fire and all it entailed – she had never quite felt like this, so desolate and so alone. The thought of Stephen's forthcoming marriage was more than she could bear. While he had remained single, she still had hope. Maybe she had tried to push it from her mind and deny her true feelings, but the hope had been there nevertheless. Well, now even that had been taken from her. The prospect of a new life suddenly held appeal. She didn't care what faced her out there. It couldn't be any worse than what she was facing now.

She jumped as the door opened and Stephen strode in.

She stared at him, bewildered.

'You left the door off the latch,' he said, smiling. 'Get your coat,' he commanded.

'What . . .'

'Josie, just do as you're told. I want to show you something.'

Her shoulders sagged. She wanted him to go. She didn't want to be part of all this. She didn't want to be presented to his future wife and have to make polite conversation.

'I'm not going anywhere,' she said tonelessly. 'Except to bed.'

Stephen turned and walked through to the passage, returning with her coat. 'Put it on.'

'But I look a mess . . .'

'You look perfectly all right to me. Now hurry up.'

Moments later she was seated in his old van. 'Where are we going?' she asked.

'Just wait and see,' he said, turning the vehicle into the traffic.

They drove through the streets in silence. Finally, they arrived before a row of shops on Cheapside, next to the market square. He switched off the engine, alighted from the van, ran round and slid open the passenger door.

'Would Madam care to get out?' he said, his eyes twinkling.

Josie climbed out of her seat and stared around.

She waited while he ran across the pavement, took a bunch of keys out of his pocket and opened a shop door. He stood aside.

'Pray enter,' he requested.

Frowning, Josie walked across the threshold and blinked rapidly as he pressed a switch and the place was flooded with light.

He beamed at her. 'Well, what do you think?'

'What do I think?' she asked, frowning.

'Yes. What do you think?'

Bemused, she slowly walked around the spacious room. She nodded. 'It's great,' she said with forced enthusiasm. 'What do you propose to do with it?'

'Me?' Stephen said, shaking his head. 'I don't propose to do anything.'

'Well, who . . .'

'You, Josie, that's who.'

'Me?' she gasped.

He walked towards her and placed the bunch of keys in her palm. 'It's all yours, Josie.'

'Mine!'

Stephen nodded. 'The rent's paid for a year and I've spoken to a joiner about doing you a good deal on shelving, etcetera. You could re-launch your old business or do something different. It's up to you.'

She stared at him. 'You did this for me?'

'Yes.'

'Stephen, I don't know what to say. This is such a shock.'

'You are pleased though?' he asked in concern.

'Pleased? Yes, of course I am,' she lied, thoughts of her future plans coming to mind; plans that did not include starting up a new business in Leicester. How would she tell him without hurting his feelings? She felt his hand on her arm.

'I've something else to show you. Come through here,' he beckoned.

He guided her towards the back of the shop and opened a door.

He fumbled in his pocket, pulled out a box of matches and lit two candles that sat in the centre of a table. The candles flickered into life and cast a soft glow over the room.

Josie stepped forward and stared down at the table. The crisp white tablecloth was set for two. On a hot tray sat several covered dishes, and on a smaller table at the side an ice bucket held a chilled bottle of champagne, beads of cold water running down the sides.

Stephen hurriedly pulled out a chair. 'Would you care to sit down?' he said, walking round and taking off her coat.

She looked up at him in bewilderment. She put her hand to her chest. 'Me? You want me to sit down?'

Stephen, unable to control himself any longer, grabbed hold of her hands. 'I love you, Josie Rawlings,' he blurted before his nerve left him. 'Will you marry me? Please?'

He held his breath and waited.

Stunned, she stared up at him. 'You love me?' she whispered in disbelief.

'Yes, I do,' he replied with emotion. 'I've loved you for a long time, Josephine Rawlings.' He dropped her hands and gathered her in his arms. 'I realised for the first time the morning after we made love.'

She pulled away from him. 'You remembered?' she cried.

He smiled down at her. 'Oh, yes, Josie. And I won't apologise for my actions, however much you might feel I took advantage of you.

It was through getting senselessly drunk that night that the truth started to surface. I will apologise, though, for rushing out without eating that wonderful breakfast you cooked for me. I'm ashamed to admit it wasn't until I got halfway down the street that what had happened between us did start to come back.' He paused, looking longingly at her. 'It was then that things began to strike home and I saw . . .'

'Saw? Saw what?'

'You, Josie. I felt I'd seen you – the real you – for the very first time and I realised just what an idiot I'd been.' He took a deep breath. 'Marilyn was a good-looking girl, but always shallow, self-centred and incapable of having feelings for anyone but herself. I'm just mad about the time I wasted with her. I never really loved her, Josie. Just the superficial image of her. You can't build a life with a woman like that. But you can with a woman like you. A real woman.'

Josie stared silently.

'I've had the devil's own job trying to tell you my feelings,' he continued. 'I could never quite manage to get the right moment. And, of course, there was also the added worry that you might not feel the same way about me.' He let her go and took several steps across the room. 'I knew you thought I still carried a torch for Marilyn and whatever I said you wouldn't be convinced. So I decided to wait a while. Then your grandmother died and all that happened with your uncle and we lost touch for a bit. When we did meet up again, you were going with Graham – Terry – whatever he called himself.' He turned and looked at her, love shining from his eyes. 'You can't imagine how I felt when you told me you were marrying the man.'

Josie ran her hand through her hair. 'I never dreamt you felt like this. If only you had managed to tell me!'

'I had planned to say something the night you helped me out on the 'dog stall.' He laughed. 'I'd even rehearsed my speech word for word so as not to get anything wrong. But those thugs put paid to that.'

'Oh, Stephen,' she sighed, then stopped as a thought struck. 'But what about the girl I met at the hospital – Sally? She told me you two were very close. I thought . . .' She gulped. 'I thought it was her you were going to ask to marry you. I was so angry.'

'Were you?' he said with a smile.

'Yes, I was. I was incensed that you had the nerve to ask me how to go about making a proposal to another girl, when all the time I wanted so much for it to be me.'

Stephen smiled wickedly. 'Well, you got your wish, didn't you?'

She eyed him sharply. 'You . . . You did that on purpose! You beast!'

Stephen laughed. 'Guilty, I'm afraid. I wanted to see your reaction and it was just what I'd hoped for. You practically threw me out of the flat, you were so angry.'

Josie lowered her head. 'I didn't think it showed.' She raised her eyes. 'What happened to Sally?'

'You don't have to worry about her, Josie. She's going strong with another man. In fact, I introduced them.'

'You did? Well, I'm pleased for her,' she said sincerely. Her eyes suddenly flashed. 'I never knew that you weren't seeing her any more. You never said a word.'

He grinned. 'Didn't I? Well, you can talk. You're not averse to spinning a few yarns. You told me you and Graham were in the process of buying a house, when all the time you had finished with him.'

Josie bit her bottom lip, ashamed. 'Who told you?'

'Nobody told me. I found out. But you still lied about it. I was hurt, Josie. You didn't trust me enough to tell me.'

'I couldn't,' she said softly. 'Because . . .'

Stephen strode towards her and placed his hands upon her arms. 'Because of what, Josie?'

She raised her eyes to meet his. 'Because of how I felt about you. I tried to put a wall up and disguise my true feelings.' She grimaced. 'Not that it worked,' she said tartly. 'Nothing I did worked. Every time I saw you it cut me to the quick.' Her eyes flashed in anger. 'Stephen Kingsman, you don't know what you've put me through. All the time I thought you just wanted me for a friend, when really . . .'

'When really all I wanted was to make mad passionate love to you and let everyone know you were mine,' he finished for her.

She blushed scarlet, wondering whether she was dreaming all of this. She took a deep breath.

'Did you really, Stephen?' she asked to clarify his feelings once again and make sure she wasn't imagining it. 'Did you really want me as badly as I wanted you?'

'Probably more so. If truth be known, I loved you for years, even when I was seeing Marilyn.'

She frowned. 'But how could you? I was so fat and . . .'

'Not to me,' he cut in. 'I love you for being you, Josie. You look great to me, fat or thin. If you put on ten stones it wouldn't change my feelings towards you. I'm just mad I never managed to get the chance to speak up before. I feel we wasted so much time.'

'So do I,' she breathed happily, all thoughts of her new life in Australia flying from her mind.

He studied her face. 'So will you marry me then?'

'Yes. Oh, yes. I'd be delighted.'

Stephen bent his head and sought her lips. He kissed her long and hard. She closed her eyes and melted against his body. How long she had wanted this to happen. How long she had thought it never would.

She drew back and stared up at him. 'Oh, I do love you,' she said with feeling.

'And me you,' he responded. He studied her for a moment. 'I can't wait to tell my mother the news.'

'D'you think she'll be pleased?'

'Pleased? She'll be over the moon. She'll have the church booked and my father's suit ordered before the night's out.'

Josie laughed with happiness. 'I don't care, Stephen. I'll be happy to go along with whatever your mother wishes as long as at the end of it I've got you.'

'You'll have me for always, Josie,' he said tenderly.

He kissed her again with all the passion he had kept pent up for so long and she willingly responded. Finally he drew back from her and eyed her lovingly.

'Now, Madam,' he said, his eyes twinkling merrily, 'are you going to sit down and eat this food? I've slaved over a hot stove preparing it all.'

Josie scanned the table. 'It looks lovely,' she said sincerely. 'I'm so sorry, Stephen. I know you've gone to a lot of trouble but I couldn't eat anything at the moment. My stomach's turning somersaults.' She paused and her eyes lit up. 'But I know some people who'd be glad of it.'

'Oh?'

'Those tramps who hang out near the arches on Central Street.'

Stephen laughed. 'Josie, Josie. There you go. Always thinking of others. That's one of the many things I love about you.' He raised his arms in mock surrender. 'Okay, the tramps win. We'll take the food down now before it spoils. But then, Josie, we concentrate on us and all the plans we have to make for our future. Deal?'

'Deal,' she agreed ecstatically.